JONATHAN GASH

A Rag, a Bone and a Hank of Hair

The Twenty-first Lovejoy Novel

PAN BOOKS

First published 1999 by Macmillan

This edition published 2000 by Pan Books
an imprint of Macmillan Publishers Ltd
25 Eccleston Place, London SW1W 9NF
Basingstoke and Oxford
Associated companies throughout the world
www.macmillan.co.uk

ISBN 0 330 37377 3

9 8 7 6 5 4 3 2 1

A CIP catalogue record for this book is available from
the British Library.

Phototypeset by Intype London Ltd
Printed and bound in Great Britain by
Mackays of Chatham plc, Chatham, Kent

A fool there was and he made his prayer
(Even as you and I)
To a rag and a bone and a hank of hair
(We called her the woman who did not care)
But the fool he called her his lady fair –
(Even as you and I!)

Rudyard Kipling, 'The Vampire'

'What is aught, but as 'tis valued?'

William Shakespeare, *Troilus and Cressida*

1

LONDON'S TRAFFIC ROARED past as I prepared to attack.

'Don't, Lovejoy.' Shar was beautiful and furious. But she's a lawyer. They always say don't. 'You'll get arrested.'

People on passing buses stared. Old crones called things like, 'Riff-raff!' It gets me narked. This was *me* out in the rain, fighting for *them*. We could all sit in warm buses and do nothing while the world dies.

Nothing for it. I went to the middle of the road with my placard and howled at Holloway University, 'You swine stole my Old Masters! You thieving—'

Two weary bobbies arrested me.

Shar was still arguing two nights later in bed. Do lawyers ever give up? I honestly think they're abnormal.

'This behaviour must stop.' Shar was giving it me – aggro, I mean.

'I'm not the criminal,' I shot back, indignant. '*They* are!'

'The law clearly states—'

'The law is a—'

'Say that once more and you're out of this bed this instant!' She was blazing.

I was amazed. 'Tell me just one thing I've done wrong.'

She glared along the pillow. Nice hair, lovely eyes, but a lawyer's a lawyer for a' that.

'You bawled abuse at Holloway University.' Even in bed lawyers sound extra-terrestrial. 'Despite,' she said bitterly, 'your lawyer's advice. The magistrates show forbearance—'

Oh, aye, like slamming me in the pokey.

'Thieving swine sold my paintings.' My hand had accidentally fallen on her bare thigh, but she shoved it off.

'They aren't your Old Masters, Lovejoy. And stop that.'

Her breast had accidentally come into my palm, but whose fault was that? Typical woman, drags me naked into bed, wreaks her savage lust on my defenceless body, then tells me to lie still. Is that fair?

She sighed. 'Lovejoy. I'm utterly tired of this. The Cottesloe Report says the University couldn't sell the objects *unless authorized* by the Courts or Charity Commissioners or the Minister of Education—'

'Fraudsters,' I muttered. 'They flogged my paintings.' To flog is to sell.

Shar cuffed me as my face reached her belly. '*You* got arrested. *They* are in the right.'

It was time to make smiles again so I pretended to give in. I'd not got long.

'You're right, dwoorlink.' I put a smile on. 'Thanks for keeping a clear head.'

'Promise you'll remember the law, Lovejoy?'

'Very well, dwoorlink.'

It worked, thank heavens. Shar was mollified. We slept afterwards, had another breakfast, though she'd run out of bacon, which really narked me because what is breakfast for? We parted with endearments.

'Be good, darling. Remember you're bound over to keep the peace.'

Pure love shone from my eyes. 'I shall, luv. Back in an hour.' Another promise, but promises aren't the trouble, I find.

As I waved up at her window from the street below I tried to remember her surname. Maybe I'd still got her trade card somewhere.

Then I went to Bermondsey, where Floggell lives. He'd know how to burgle a university better than anybody. 'Not my paintings' indeed. Universities always say they've a right to steal. Once, only banks and politicians made that excuse. Now, theft's called progress. Remember that detail, or you'll get lost in the murk of this story.

But cheer up. One dauntless warrior is still in the arena fighting for honesty and justice against the forces of evil, greed, and law.

It's me, Lovejoy, honest antique dealer. It's blinking lonely, especially when they slam you in the dock as soon as you want them to play fair. Unfortunately, I'm on my tod. So far, nobody had lifted a finger to help.

I'd come to London's street markets to find who the heck was flooding the antiques world with dud padparadshas (lovely gemstones; tell you about these in a minute). I'd been hired by Dosh Callaghan for the purpose against my will. I'd been feeling sorry for myself after a really bad day.

I'd backed an illegal Carlton Ware forger's pottery with a load of IOUs. Staffordshire's maniacal Trading Standards Officers raided it, in Longton, Stoke-on-Trent. Can you imagine anything so unfair? I was seething with self-pity and poverty. They weren't even fakes of antiques, because the Carlton factory only closed in 1989. A so-say 1957 vintage Guinness toucan lamp, for God's sake? I honestly think morality's gone to the dogs. If you can't make pots in the Potteries, where is truth? Needless to say, dealers all across East Anglia jeered at me.

Me and a lass called Iana had made a go of total permanent unending eternal love for a couple of days once, but she proved unreliable. She had a rotten temper, accused me of infidelity just because I'd stayed with Jessica at Goldhanger when trying to buy Jessica's Regency cabinet. For all that, our valencies always linked whenever she zoomed in. And she tended to broker antique sales. Iana had promised me a genuine Holbein miniature painting, owned by a hunchbacked Romford dealer called Syme.

'Genuine Holbein!' Syme protested as I gave it back across the tap-room bar.

'No, Syme. Hans Holbein was lefthanded.'

'So?' Syme asked, puzzled.

'Miniaturists paint their portraits with northern light on their left. Righthanded, they sit facing east, see? Holbein's subjects have the light coming the other way.'

Syme's pal had done the commonest forger trick of all. In any book on miniatures, the photographs are reproduced actual size. So forgers simply trace them in reverse, to look like different versions of some famous portrait – like Syme's, of Lady Catherine Howard, date about 1540.

'Also, Syme,' I added sadly, 'it's on Ivorine. Holbein painted his miniatures on vellum stuck to card.' I could have gone on about the brilliant art of 'limning' – painting miniature scenes and portraits. It's a miraculous art-form. I love it. But like I say I was down in the dumps, instinctively feeling that worse was on the way.

Dealers like Syme get taken in by the old forger's trick, to do quite a good fake using the wrong materials. Ivorine is a synthetic modern plastic. Good stuff, though, you can cut with scissors. Respectable miniaturists use it all the time. But no way is it ivory. Nor is it real vellum – that stretched skin of aborted veal calves. I could have sworn Syme's miniature painting was done over acrylic 'carnation', as ancient limners used to call their ground. And acrylics, like Ivorine, are modern.

'No good, Lovejoy?' Iana had asked. I sat with her.

'Bad, love. The original belongs to the Duke of Buccleugh.'

While we were talking Fakes I Have Known, that saga of antique dealers everywhere, Dosh Callaghan hove in and told me to go to London.

Dosh saw nothing unreasonable in forcing me into slavery while he took gorgeous women out to belly-rumbling restaurants.

'Why, Doshie?' I pleaded. 'I hate London.'

He's one of these criminals who wears alpaca coats down to the heels, has gold teeth and a gunslinger hat. He has two goons, to enforce whatever rules he dreams up for us on the spot. The charm of a boil, and lies like a gasmeter. In spite of this, I like Dosh. His party trick is to find obscure relatives, claim close kinship, and do them out of every penny. He owns a propeller plane at Earls Colne airfield, says an auntie left it to him.

He beamed, flashed his rings about the tavern. We were in the Welcome Sailor at East Gates, that being where our town's antique dealers congregate to enter terminal decline.

Think of a dodo graveyard but where all extinct species are still pretending they know life.

'You *used* to love London, Lovejoy,' Iana said. This is her way, prettily taking me over every time she returns from Cyprus.

'Me? I've always hated London, ever since—'

Some things you can't tell. I'd known a London lass who got me to do two forgeries. I faked a Monet – his now-lost-for-ever painting of the bridges of Venice on that tatty little rio – and a Boudin watercolour. The latter's one of the hardest painters to forge, incidentally, though they're appearing now in numbers at the New Caledonian street market. Go and see for yourself. (Last-but-one barrow, farthest from St Mary Magdalene church.)

'Ever since who, Lovejoy?' Iana purred prettily.

'Ever since you wuz knocking that tart, Lovejoy!' Dosh burst out laughing. Everyone within earshot laughed along, being scared of him.

'Who was she?' Iana demanded, her frown suddenly less pretty.

'Doshie,' I begged. 'Can't you send somebody else? I've this sick uncle. And my motor's laid up.'

'You won't need wheels, Lovejoy. Buses and the Tube'll do fine. And your uncle's playing bowls for Manchester.'

People roared at Doshie's cleverness. Oh, it was such a merry scene.

'Find out who duffed my padpas, Lovejoy. I bought a job lot last week, and they're fake.'

He said this in high indignation, though he sells more frauds, fakes, and forgeries than any other antique dealer in the Eastern Hundreds, including me. Then he dropped two small green brilliant-cut gemstones on the bar. Maybe half a carat each. I love jewellery, even gems hatefully called 'semi-precious', and couldn't help snatching them up for a look with a x10 loupe.

'These aren't padpas, Doshie,' I said. 'They're tsavorite.' A tsavorite is properly green grossular, a sort of garnet discovered some seventy years ago near Kenya's National Park at Tsavo. Its lovely green lies between deep Sri Lankan emeralds and a peridot. (Tip: Don't buy a tsavorite unless it's above one carat in size.) 'Measure its single refraction, Doshie, to prove it isn't green tourmaline or green zircon. Save me a trip to London. Also, I know nothing about precious stones.'

Dosh grinned. 'Lovejoy. A few of these came in antique settings. You're a divvy and you can tell an antique by *feel*. So go.'

'Advance me a week's salary?' I asked, hoping he'd say no.

'Okay, Lovejoy,' Doshie amazed me by saying. He's started smoking these thick cheroots. He stuck one in his mouth, graciously tilted his head so that his shelt wouldn't have too far to reach with the lighter, puffed smoke to share his carcinogens, and left saying, 'Pay the lazy sod seven days.'

And that was that. I'd be able to buy Iana's Minton cup. I'd square my conscience later. I always invent excellent reasons for surrender. I bought the Minton cup from Iana, endured her tearful farewell, and left on the London train after an equally tearful farewell from Cathy to whom I sold the Minton cup for twice what I'd paid Iana. I also was in tears, because the Minton is the most exquisite early pottery you'll ever see. Tip: if you find a piece that seems *greyish instead of pure white*, and is troubled by little black flecks, then you've got in your hand one of the most important pieces in the history of the world. Phone any Minton collector, and he'll run up panting, bulging wallet at the ready.

Having to sell it broke my heart, but I exacted a promise from Cathy that she'd give me first refusal. I made her swear on everything she held dear, and I didn't believe a word. I'd have sealed it with loving smiles, but her bloke was in. He's a mechanic hooked on axles and carburettors. Cars that actually go, he thinks a waste of time.

It was on that fatal train that I read – the lady opposite had a newspaper – of Holloway University's criminal sale of their vast heritage of Old Masters. I went berserk. The lady was called Shar, a lawyer, astonished at my anger. I said I'd hire her to sue Holloway University. Which is how I got arrested, bound over to keep the peace, three days late for my doomed encounter in the antique street markets.

These markets look the soul of innocence, street barrows lined up under merry bunting. In fact they can be scary, while seeming the friendliest places on earth. You've been warned. Much good warnings ever do, though. When greed and antiques meet everybody ignores warnings. Like me, like you. Into antiques, in Olde London Toon.

2

SOMETIMES, EVERYTHING SEEMS the opposite of what we're told. That Benedictine monk Dom Perignon, experimenting with double fermentation, is supposed to have sipped his prototype champagne and yelled out, 'Come here! I'm tasting the stars!' Did he really? What are the odds he actually called out, 'This batch is no good, lads! Another failure!' then sat there alone in his cellar cackling his head off and wickedly swilling it all back himself? You can't help thinking.

Free of Shar, I inhaled the London antique market's perfumed air. Pure nectar, aroma of the gods. Paradise, but where you can lose your shirt. You might be in raptures thinking you've finally collared that missing Da Vinci and made zillions, when in fact you've just mortgaged your whole future and put your children into penury.

It's still life's most glorious arena.

Across the Bermondsey greensward, by St Mary Magdalene church, with twittering birds pecking among the tombstones, you see warehouses, antique shops. But the main feature delighting your eye is shoals – no other word – of stalls, stalls as far as vision allows. Among them drift two or three thousand hopefuls. You hear every language under the sun – Greek, Italian, French, Chinese. The globe flocks.

To find it, go to Tower Bridge. Walk south down Tower Bridge Road. Takes you fifteen minutes. I'd advise you to take sandwiches, because you may never leave. There's tales of folk who've turned up with an hour to kill before zooming home to Rotterdam, wherever, and simply stayed. Everyone's dazzled by the antiques, forgeries, collectibles, the sheer exhilaration of hundreds of stalls bulging with antiques. It is concentrated wonderment.

The good cheer is ineffable, if that's the right word. Euphoria rules. Stallholders joke, laugh, arguing good-naturedly about everything on earth from corruption to cricket. Here, an old lady wears a tall Ascot topper with serene aplomb. Over there's a delectable lady in enticing attire, and everywhere's noise and pandemonium with – I assure you – some utterly genuine antiques among the dross.

Lesson for today: Go to Bermondsey at six a.m. Fridays. It dwindles about noon. Other days, you've to roam in warrens of converted warehouses and godowns near the green. Oddly, the indoor stallholders are less jovial than the open-air barrow folk. Is it the gypsy element, some thrill of travelling as opposed to the lurk? Dunno. But go there, best entertainment on this planet. Not only that, but you might finish up with a priceless silver salver or that porcelain Worcester jug you just *know* is waiting. (Sorry. I've just realized this reads like an advertisement. Won't let it happen again.)

I made for a bloke who might help me. Crooks first, saints second. A warning, though: never in the field of human nonsense is so much gunge being sold as antique. Even in a posh listed auction, only 3 per cent will be genuine. The rest will be bodge-ups, twinners, or downright fakes. Never, never ever, is more than one in ten genuine.

Sir Ponsonby P. Ponsonby, Bart. – no prize for guessing that middle initial – was there, bold as brass. He's a florid bloke of forty, has a stall on the Corner Green, a little triangular plot beyond the main market. You go up three steps to it. Make sure you don't fall off the raised little plateau, where eager tourists sometimes come a cropper. Kindly souls rush to help you up, meanwhile nicking your purse, wallet, and every credit card and groat you possess. Subtlemongers, our ubiquitous pickpockets, are about, so beware.

'Wotcher, Sir Ponsonby.'

'Lovejoy, old sport! What brings you to this urban decay?'

He seemed delighted to see me. Sir Ponsonby was once headmaster of an imposing public school – which every other country calls private – and was deposed for embezzling funds. He's never looked back. He dresses flamboyantly – deerstalker hat, Sherlock Holmes cape of expensive Harris tweed, plus-fours and spats. He sports a monocle, muttonchop whiskers, knows Ancient Greek, Latin. He's one of the few stallholders in this most fabled antiques market to sport his own sign above his barrow. The rest go anonymous into the good fight, or have discreet cards.

One reservation: Sir P wears wren's feathers in his hat. It's a hideous country custom. St Stephen's Day, village lads beat the hedgerows, chanting a gleeful ancient rhyme – I'll not give it, not wanting to encourage grue. They kill wrens. The tiny corpses are plucked, and the feathers worn as adornments until next year, when they do it again. Wren feathers in your titfer, bad mark from me.

'Sent,' I said. 'Somebody duffed a spark.' Translation: faked a gem. Heaven knows why we don't just use English, a language for which there's been a transient vogue, but antiques has its own lingo. What with that and Cockney rhyming slang, it's a wonder London is able to communicate at all.

'Oh, dear!' he boomed. Sir Ponsonby's notion of subtlety is to bellow as if addressing an Eton prize day. 'Allow me to present my new apprentice, Miss Moiya December.'

'Er, wotcher, miss.'

A beautiful lass was coiled on a stool beside Ponsonby's barrow. She was gloriously blonde. Everything about her shone, teeth, lips, eyes, tan leather coat. In bed you could have used her as a nightlight. I'm ever in hope. Religion did wrong, making sex a sin. We'd all be holy, if Moiya took the evensong collection of a Sunday.

'Is this he?' she asked Sir Ponsonby, as if I'd been expected.

'Yeah verily, I be he,' I said. Which raised the question, who she?

Ponsonby leant to confide some secret, and thundered, 'Moiya's learning the trade, Lovejoy!' He swelled like Mister Toad. I recognized a gay quip on its way, and stepped back a yard. 'Isn't the trade lucky?' And he guffawed.

This is not your average splutter. Harness its latent energy, we'd not need fossil fuel. Nearby stallholders laughed along with him.

'Hey, Sir Pons!' a silver vendor called when the decibels finally lessened. 'My trouble in Aldgate says keep the racket down!' Trouble and strife, wife, the Cockney rhyming slang I was just moaning about. 'Is that you, Lovejoy? Where y'been, mate?'

'Wotcher, Sturffie. I'll look over your clag in a sec.'

That set nearby traders roaring, giving me chance to tell Sir Ponsonby I was anxious to find the source of padpa fakes. I phrased it with care, not wanting my investigation broadcast by Radio Ponsonby.

'See you when you get a minute, Sir Ponsonby?'

'Oh, secrecy, is it, Lovejoy?' he roared. 'Right! By the tuck shop, ten minutes, hey?'

He meant the nosh vans, of which Bermondsey antiques market has half a dozen. I made a cursory inspection of Sir P's stall – one enormous chipped Satsuma vase among old cameras, militaria, bayonets, photos of pale youths in uniform staring beyond life, and some decent Victorian watercolours of cottages with village women in aprons, with a few fruitwood boxes and other treen. Politely I lied how marvellous his antiques were, then went to Sturffie.

'How'd yer know Lord Haw-Haw, Lovejoy?'

The best about London marketeers is you can take up where you left off. Even after a lapse of years, bump into them and they'll say, 'Wotcher, mate. Come and look at this. Picked it up on Portobello Road. And how yer keeping?' No hard feelings because you didn't keep in touch.

'Eh? Oh, met him years since. You've a good piece there, Sturffie.'

'Me?' He was amazed, stared at his goods as if they'd just swanned in from outer space. 'You having a pig, Lovejoy?' Pig in a poke, joke.

'Straight up, Sturffie.'

The market was now crowded. I was being jostled by dealers and tourists shoving down the narrow barrow lanes. Itinerant dealers carry carpet bags, or canvas-lined holdalls. One per dealer, never two. Some of the lads claim to be able to recognize nationalities. I don't think it's true. I suspect it's just clothes, maybe having glimpsed individual dealers the week before, that sort of thing. However, stall and barrow traders are a canny lot. Some work a sort of illegal ring deal if opportunity strikes and other hawkers don't notice. And even if they do.

'Which is it, mate?' Sturffie grinned through clenched teeth.

He was once a lowlife, got done for knifing somebody outside an East End pub. I like Sturffie, though. A hard nut, he once did me a favour. It was inexplicable, really, because before the incident he hadn't known I was a divvy or that I was anything to do with antiques at all. I must be the only bloke on earth saved by genuine charity.

It had been near the famous Prospect of Whitby tavern in the East End. In the gloaming I'd accidentally stumbled on cobbles, and bumped against a motor. A long natty bloke had angrily uncoiled from within, and belted me so I fell against the kerb. He'd been just about to punt me into the Thames when this little whippet of a man said, 'Here, knock it orff. He did nuffink,' meaning me.

'Who sez?' asked the natty thug.

'Me.' Sturffie, only I didn't know him then, had walked over and helped me up. My head was ringing, me legs wobbling.

The tall yobbo looked the sort who'd normally tackle anything, on principle, but Sturffie's eyes never wavered. The motorist finally shrugged, abandoned his rage, and strolled into the tavern.

'You okay, mate?' my saviour had asked.

'Aye, ta. Good of you.'

'Think nuffin of it. Me old man wuz a bad drinker too. Looked arter him times out of number.'

He'd thought I'd been drinking. I hadn't. I'd just spent forty hours driving a massive pantechnicon of antiques from

Carlisle to the loading bays for Poppy West and her cousin Walshie. I was naturally bogeyed. Sturffie and his mate strolled away.

I'd called after him for his name. 'Here, mate. Got a moniker?'

'Ferget it, mate.' He was already off down the alley, as if rescuing me was nothing.

'He's called Sturffie.' His pal gave a cackle. 'Nasty piece of work.'

'Ta, then.' I knew better than use his name without his sayso.

Later, I'd bumped into him, him surprised when he'd realized I too was in antiques. Cockneys can be gents, despite rough edges, and he never asked. I was pleased to get a definite bonging vibration from his barrow.

'How much?' I picked up the tea caddy. It was solid fruitwood, shaped like a pear but the size of a large coconut.

'Forty quid,' he said, looking at me.

Its lid opened, genuine lovely interior, lovely handmade hinge as genuine as the day it was made two centuries before. The best tea caddies were made of fruitwood, shaping the final container to match the fruit. If you're lucky, you get apple-shaped tea caddies of applewood, pear-shaped ones of pearwood, and so on. Lovely big ones are rare, rare. The last one I'd seen was found in an old rector's study. He'd used it as a tobacco jar. It sold straight off for three thousand quid, no haggling. Tea was anciently regarded as a most important herb, full of magic potency for health, sexual power, heaven knows what and consequently went for unbelievable sums. I passed a surreptitious hand, palm down, over Sturffie's tea caddy. He saw my gesture, the dealer's universal sign to keep it back for a fortune.

If Sturffie hadn't been a pal, I would have bought. As it was, leaving it there broke my heart.

'Ta, Lovejoy. Can't afford it, eh?' he said, jocular, because the woman on the next barrow might have caught my sign. He put it in his capacious pocket, which was even more of a giveaway, but that was his business.

We talked of this and that, me telling him I was up in London to buy gems and I'd see him later. Then I went to the nosh van to meet Sir Ponsonby. I noticed the exquisite Moiya December (Miss) on guard at his barrow.

Going through the market is always hard. I took my time, not wanting folk jumping to the conclusion that I'd come specifically to see Sir P. Traders who knew I was a divvy were keen for me to prove their wares 100 per cent genuine and therefore highly valuable, while buyers wanted me to pretend that the antiques they wanted to buy were worthless, to lower the price. The best, and riskiest, game on earth.

Sir Ponsonby was sitting on a low wall eating bacon and eggs from a silver tray. He brings his own cutlery, cup and saucer, milk jug. Tourists photograph him in mid-nosh. His white napkins are monogrammed with his crest, and he affects a George III table screen of walnut, date about 1815, a lovely piece worth more than the entire nosh van.

'Here, Sir Ponsonby,' I asked, wondering. 'Why is it, keen antiques trader that you are, you don't sell that table screen?'

Georgian ladies used them to protect their lovely pale complexions – sign of high breeding, before leathery tans became fashionable. They wrote letters in a sunlit arbour, by firelight or candlelight. There's a daft belief among antique dealers that protecting fair cheeks is the pole screen's only value. Wrong. Why, I can remember my old dad reading by firelight. He'd sit by the hob, one hand holding his book, the other shielding his eyes from the embers. I do it myself when Electricity Board fascists cut the power.

'Sprat to catch a mackerel, old boy,' he boomed. 'They trek me to my barrow, object of all their desires!'

Sir Ponsonby embarrasses me. The lads say glitterati, slitterati. Me, I'm not even sure if he really is who he says, or if he's one gigantic fraud. A cynic would ring the public school, ask outright, but I haven't the heart. Whose business is it but his own? All about, the market milled as only Bermondsey Antiques Market can. I noticed an old lady, struggling to hump boxes of porcelain from a handcart. You see these desperate folk about – past it, hoping to keep Time at bay by reliving a successful youth. I looked away, ashamed for her, for all the greedy lot of us.

Meanwhile, Sir Ponsonby noshed on. I stood awkwardly making conversation while he finished his repast. Seeing I wasn't gainfully employed for the moment here's details of the padparadsha: Deep in Sri Lanka's fruitful mountains, gemstone orchard to the world, an occasional enticing precious stone is mined. The 'padpa', as dealers call them, is of all things a true sapphire. But no plain old sapphire, this miracle. It's a luscious transparent orangey-pink! These lovely wonders aren't common. So, naturally, greedsters thought of manufacturing synthetic padpas. Lo and behold, now they're everywhere. Fashions worry me. I keep warning myself of my homemade law: Fashion today, fool tomorrow. Like, an entrancing orange skirt of last year today looks ridiculous, but who resists fashion?

Nobody, because fraud raises its ugly head. Synthetic padpas (they're actually corundum, if you're hooked on taxonomy) soon became cheap, while genuine gemstones stayed costly. Which is why, back in rural East Anglia, Dosh Callaghan decided to buy some genuine padpas, have them made into ornate 'early Victorian' jewellery. He'd mount a score of synthetics in similar settings – rings, necklaces, earrings, suites of ladies' jewellery. I guessed he'd got the whole scam planned, fake settings, forged certificates. He'd already had me paint an early portrait of Lady Howarth wearing the settings he was having made. The cost to Doshie would be about eight thousand. Profit? Half a million, played right.

Except the original 'genuine padparadsha gems' he'd bought turned out to be cheapo tsavorites. I was here to suss out who'd done Dosh down. Once I'd fingered the miscreant, he would wreak vengeance. I was unhappy, but beggars can't, can we?

With a genteel dabbing of linen at his lips, Sir Ponsonby concluded his nosh, handed his tray to the noshbar proprietor, and strolled with me into the churchyard among the winos.

'You see the problem, Sir Ponsonby,' I said sadly. 'Dosh Callaghan is well narked. You met him when he collected a thick-skirted late card table, supposedly Hepplewhite only the drop wasn't shallow enough, remember? He's paid me to discover who swapped his genuine padpas for tsavorite.'

'Didn't you ask him?'

'Dosh said they were delivered by a wonker called Chev, who's somewhere in Edinburgh.' A wonker is a driver who ships small antiques, up to about chair size, anywhere in the kingdom, door to door. Very reliable, wonkers are, because they lose their livelihood – maybe their legs – if they default. 'Chev' after his huge American car. Dosh had given me registration, phone numbers, address.

'Can't you contact him?'

'Tried that. Chev's due back Thursday. Something going down.' Meaning a clandestine robbery, when a trusty wonker is worth his weight in gold.

Sir Ponsonby gazed at me. My scalp prickled, because he wasn't your actual warm-hearted instant mourner. 'Sure you want to know, Lovejoy? Sturffie recently sold some genuine padparadsha gemstones.'

'Sturffie?' Sir Ponsonby grasped my arm in a grip of steel as I turned away towards the teeming market. 'Think, Lovejoy. Sturffie boxed them up last Friday.'

I said, 'Thanks, Sir Ponsonby.' My pal Sturffie? Who'd once saved me a clobbering, if not worse?

'Sorry, Lovejoy.' He knew the consequences for Sturffie. 'Look,' he said kindly. 'Come round for supper, what say? Moiya cooks fairly well for an idiot.'

'Thank you, Sir Ponsonby.' I'd intended to catch the train with my bad news, but suddenly wanted to remain safe in London's mayhem. 'You still live in Dulwich?'

'St James's now, Lovejoy. Give me a bell.'

He palmed me his card. I trudged off, feet heavy.

What the hell had Sturffie been thinking of? Surely to God he'd have known his trick would have been rumbled, and that retribution would follow? When in doubt, go for a nosh, listen to the gossip, feel for a way out. I followed the aroma.

3

IMI WELKINSHAW WAS at her dad's van, thank goodness. I needed her help. She waved hello with a forged tribal mask, all ebony and exotic feathers, grinning. I signalled yes, I'd buy it. She rolled in the aisles at that, and chucked it into her van among the other dross. It gave me a wry smile.

Antiques foster mysteries. We even encourage them. Look at the Great Dogon Mask mystery, for instance. A queer business, it still drives antique dealers daft.

It began once upon a time when two French anthropologists went a-wandering in Africa. They took recorders, cameras, gadgetry to get the story right. They studied the Dogon, a tribe who did a complicated dance every sixty years. For this, tribal priests stole away to secret caves where they unearthed sacred masks. These masks are megagalactic rarities, and contained information about heavenly bodies – stars, not people – in the night skies. So far so good?

It was interesting – tribal priests, a sacred cult, every sixty years a dancing jubilee. Our own folk do this sort of thing at Stonehenge. The Chinese climb mountains on special days. My own home town trudges up a hill called

Sixty-three Steps on Good Friday, for no reason. It's simply what folk do, no harm done.

But these French anthropologists learned that the dance concerned two stars. One was Sirius the Dog Star, famously the brightest. The other star, so necessary to the ancient cult dance of the Dogon tribe was nearby – well, near as stars go. It was called Sirius B.

Bad news for logicians, for Sirius B is all but invisible.

You can see it if you've a modern telescope. But this tribe's been dancing their ritual dance for century upon century upon . . . See the problem? Ancient African tribe, keeping records on cult masks in concealed caves *about an unseen star*. The Dogon priests admitted sure, they knew all about the good old invisible star, so what? They danced to a star they could never have seen.

Astronomers take beautiful photos of this star, so we know it's really there. Mystique mongers had a field day, proving the Dogon came from Outer Space, all that. The real impact, though, was on antique dealers who sulked, because they wanted those sacred – *priceless*! – masks. They couldn't get them by fair means. This meant forging them, making them up. Never mind that none of us has the slightest clue what a Dogon mask looks like. Antique dealers everywhere, especially in Belgium, bought common old (read new) masks from anywhere, decorated them with weird symbols, oven-dried them, then sold them – furtively and with grave warnings to keep them secret – to anybody daft enough to buy.

See what I mean? The Great Mask Mystery is alive and flourishing. Where two or more antique dealers are gathered together in greed's name, there'll be a Dogon Mask among them. Where was I?

In Bermondsey, alone and palely loitering, wondering

how the heck I could warn Sturffie off and still keep my skin. Make no mistake. If it came to Sturffie or me, it'd be goodnight Sturffie, no question. Okay, so he'd saved me that time. But fair's fair. I'm a survivor.

Thumping music started up. Dealers yelled. I couldn't help grinning as Mimi started her famous striptease. She plays a scratchy old gramophone, with her van doors wide open like a stage. (Dance in your vehicle, the law can't stop you. Obstruct London's streets by dancing, you're for it.) Dealers and tourists immediately gathered. Cameras clicked. Admiring laughter rose in the jostling crowd. There was a lot to admire because Mimi is bulbous and you get a lot for your money. Some dealers were narked, wishing that they too had some pulchritude to entice unwary spenders. Mimi has a sweet nature, is quiet and pure. Because of her show, though, ribald gossip stories abound. Vice escapes gossip, where virtue never does. I loved her dance and hummed along. You can't help worshipping women, big or small, whether full of youth's honey promises or faded crone's loving experience. I love them all, because they're the only source of delight. It gave me an idea. The most magic words ever spoken are the pure and simple 'Listen and save' of the immortal Milton. They were the only words the River Severn's exquisite goddess Sabrina heeded. She did listen, and did the job.

All I needed was a goddess who would listen and save! I watched Mimi buh-buh-buh-booooom. The crowd thickened in more ways than two. She was down to knickers and bolero as the record gave its final ta-rrrrah! whereupon she slammed the van doors amid yells for an encore. I applauded. I love art.

*

In nearby converted warehouses there's an occasional nosh bar. Some are elegant with flowers and trellises, where you could safely take your grandma. Others are wobbly trestles and a steaming urn spewing tenpenny grot. I prefer the grime, because Billia is usually there.

'Why Billia, Billia?' I asked, paying for a gill of outfall and a cheese wedge. I was relieved she hadn't gone walk-about with some rambo. She's prone to it.

Actually she made her name up. Pretty slim and shapely with flowing blonde locks and the most amazing mouth. It's never still. She doesn't use much makeup, which is a shame, but always wears bright colours. Today's theme was every shade of reds, scarlets, rose. She was sitting smoking a fag. Fire is not her only hazard.

'Thought you'd be along, Lovejoy, soon as I heard.'

'I'm that famous, eh?'

She glanced around. The nosh place was in an arched doorway leading to a hall crammed with antique stalls. By the wide wooden stairs a couple or three dealers had managed to slot in archaic church furnishings, glass trinket-filled cabinets, display boards festooned with jewellery. Throngs of tourists mingled. Like dining on a shrinking ice floe.

'You, down-hearted?' I stared, partly because I can't help it, but mostly in disbelief. 'You're beautiful, got your own shop. God's sake, your car goes!' I couldn't imagine greater wealth.

She smiled a bitter smile, her mouth fluttering. It tor-tured me just looking. Yet anguish communicates, doesn't it? I felt the same shame as I had moments ago watching that struggling crone. Reminded me of someone, dunno who.

'Typical, Lovejoy. But bless you for coming.' She stubbed

out her fag end, the symbolism momentarily stopping my synapses. 'I began to wonder if you'd got my message.'

Had I? I'm not good with messages. 'What's the problem, love?' A little hope crept into me, because a dazzling beauty's gratitude might mean that ecstasy followed close behind.

'Dang took a drop last week. I wanted you to prevent it.' She touched my hand in tearful forgiveness. 'I'm not blaming you, Lovejoy. I know you'd have come earlier if you'd been able.'

'Better late than never, eh?' I thought, what the hell? I'd come to her for help, and she thought I was her rescuer.

Dang I vaguely knew. He lived over her antique shop in Islington. I'd met this muscle mountain when I'd delivered a rare 1786 vase-shaped mustard pot there. He'd dismissed me with a terse ta-goodnight, which could only mean heavenly choirs as soon as the riff-raff, namely moi, departed. He'd grabbed the mustard pot so hard I'd told him to be careful. Billia had emerged. I explained to him that 'wet' mustard pots came after Queen Anne. Until about 1730 or so, diners mixed mustard powder as they dined along. He'd just gaped at me with complete incomprehension. Bodybuilder, boxer, Dang and Billia later did an antiques stall in St Edmundsbury market, him toting her barge and lifting her bales with massive dedication.

'I'm scared, Lovejoy.'

Glam, rich, delectable, all these are superlatives. But scared was a definite grounder. It was also impossible. Women, having it all, cannot possibly have any reason to be scared. Lovejoy logic was called.

'You can't be, love. You've got everything.'

'You're just thick, Lovejoy.' She said it listlessly.

Folk bullied into the hall clamouring arguments about

clock hands they'd failed to re-blue properly. If I'd not been mesmerized by Billia's kaleidoscope mouth I'd have gone after them to explain. The temptation is to do it on a naked flame, but that's wrong. You do it in a crucible of brass filings, on a gas ring. It calls for split-second timing. Watch for the colour change from a grubby brown to deep slate, then soon as you see a pretty steely blue whip the hands into an oil bath. Leave them to cool. The blue's exactly that on flintlock gun barrels. Incidentally, take care not to set your place on fire.

Had she just said hospital? 'Hospital?'

'You're not listening, are you?' Bitterness reigned. 'I saw you lusting after that fat cow Mimi. And that dim whore Moiya. You're just weak, Lovejoy.'

I said indignantly, 'I heard every word.'

'Dang's so gullible, Lovejoy.'

'He didn't look it to me.' Hospital, though?

'Far too trusting. Now it's too late.'

I cleared my throat. 'Who's in hospital?'

'The other boxer. They hurt him badly because he didn't lie down in the sixth round.'

Took a drop, she'd said. She meant throwing a fight.

'You know who did it?'

'The money men sent their friends.'

'Lovejoy? Suss these, wack. Brilliant, eh?' I stared at the stack of greeting cards plonked in front of me. Ballcock's a shifty madman who travels on a bicycle. It has butcher-boy paniers, so he can carry his fakes.

I riffled through them. 'They all Father's Day, Ballcock?'

'All dated, 1868 to 1903, genuine Victoria.' He was so proud.

'Great, Ballcock.'

Sometimes I don't have the heart. Everybody from

Camden Passage to Petticoat Lane knows that Ballcock fakes and decorates these greeting cards himself. He went into it four years ago to meet alimony payments. Mrs John Bruce Dodd of Spokane, Washington, USA, would have been surprised, for it was that sentimental lady who in 1910 (note that) petitioned the US president Mr Woodrow Wilson to designate a special day for remembering dads. Her own widower father raised his six children unassisted, did a grand job. June's third Sunday got elected as the modern Father's Day, joy of retailers everywhere. Now here came Ballcock with cards dated 1868. And he'd sell most by dusk. I just said, 'Great, Ballcock,' and he departed rejoicing. *Caveat emptor.*

That little incident made me notice how other dealers were behaving. Usually, antique dealers are one big bustle, yapping worse than any wine party. They shout, catcall about deals gone wrong, Leonardo paintings missed by a whisker, amazing antiques found in some old lady's cupboard. Fables, lies, and crises are the soul of the antiques game. Yet since I'd joined Billia – usually as popular as fish and chips – not a soul had said a word to me, except for Ballcock, a known crazo. Something was wrong. To test, I deliberately grinned as Legs Leslie clumped past – he lost both feet in a motor race years agone. I got cut dead. Legs pretended not to see me. This, note, from a bloke who I'd got a job for at Pasty's oil-fired pottery kiln in Long Melford.

They were shunning me because I sat with Billia. Whose bloke Dang had thrown a fight. Oh, dear. One plus one equalled exit.

I went ahem, ahem. 'Look, love. I can't do much for you just now. I've got this sick dog that's dying of . . .' What do dogs die of, for God's sake? ' . . . er, viruses. And I've to fly to Chicago. A sick uncle . . .'

Her eyes filled. 'You too, Lovejoy?'

'No, love,' I said earnestly. 'I'll help, sincerely.'

'You will?' Her magic mouth moved, opened, closed on her tongue.

I demanded, hoarse, 'Tell me what you want.'

'See me later? The Nell of Old Drury?'

'Up the West End? Why there?'

'I want you to meet someone.' It was her turn to look furtive.

I couldn't imagine anybody on earth big enough to put the frighteners on Dang. I smiled reassuringly, with no intention of meeting her.

'About seven do, love?' I rose, poised for flight.

'Seven o'clock,' her delicious mouth said. 'I'll do whatever you want, Lovejoy, if you'll help.'

Life's a swine. I dithered. 'I promised, didn't I?'

'Remember that mustard pot, Lovejoy? I've got the original. It's yours, if you'll stand by me.'

I bussed her cheek, and took off. Until she said that, betrayal seemed easy. After all, promises are made to be broken. And me protecting Man Mountain Dang from a lorry load of rabid East Enders was ludicrous. But temptation's never done me much good. Within a couple of minutes I'd worked it out. By seven I'd want a drink, and where better than one of London's most famous taverns?

I emerged into the open market, intent on sizing up Moiya December, and came upon Fawnance Duleppo, who I'd been avoiding ever since I could remember. What with Sir Ponsonby, Miss December, and the woebegone Billia, names weren't my thing today. With a name like mine I should talk.

4

THERE ARE PUBLIC gardens where Tower Bridge Road crosses Abbey Street near St Mary Magdalene. Facing the New Caledonian Market proper, Fawnance Duleppo sits. He plays a tuba – only oompah, oompah – in memory of a great-great-grandpa who, he says, in 1853 led the first ever national Brass Band Champions, that started the Victorians' brass-band fever.

Seeing this grubby musician in his tattered trenchcoat, crutches temporarily laid aside, you can easily forget what brass bands meant. Passions seethed. Everything was choirs, silver bands, marching concertina teams. Millmasters vied with each other to bribe away rival factories' best trombonists. There was a corrupt transfer system because rival mine owners hated the thought of some other coal mine seizing the glory at Manchester's famed championships. Judges were seduced, threatened, even waylaid. Nowadays, it's still a musical tradition in the north, but the fervour is no more. We're down to Fawnance playing oompah, his cloth cap out for coins. He wears a medal, *Mossley Temperance Band, Winners, First Brass Band Champions 1853*. Don't laugh. On that brilliant day there were 16,000 competitors, outdoing our drug-riddled, bribe-skewed so-called Olympics. When the Bess O'T'Barn Brass Band visited Australia in the early 1900s all Melbourne thronged to a standstill. Like I say, though, progress has reduced yet another art-form to a toothless beggar in a cloth cap. I think his medal's home-made, though.

'Wotcher, Fawnance. Nice tune.' It wasn't a tune at all, just parps.

He paused, took a breath. 'It's me teeth, Lovejoy,' he said. 'You're never the same when your lips melt. Mine went both together, lips and teeth.'

'Still, you play pretty well.' I dropped coppers in his hat.

'Ta, wack. Having a bad day? I heard Dosh sent you here.'

'Aye. Don't know where to start.'

'Do Sturffie a favour, Lovejoy. Whatever you do, do it fast. I seen that Doshie here with Chev a week back. Looked a nail job to me.'

'Cash and dash? Ta, Fawnance.' I hesitated, wanting to repay him for vital information. 'Look. They sell a brass renaissance trumpet kit up in Bradford, Manningham Lane I think. It's in the modern D major, which is a pig of a key, but they do a brass crook to get it to D, low pitch. It's got no ornamentation. Get Jerry Sorebones to engrave it. You know him, in Farnworth? Tell him I said not to do modern soldering, okay? Aged right, you'd sell it easy as an antique. Don't for heaven's sake get one of them modern angel faces to decorate the trumpet bell. It's a dead giveaway.'

'Ta. You're a pal, Lovejoy.'

Aye, I thought morosely, to everybody else. Never to me. I drifted into the market, listening, watching, getting shoved.

You can't help loving words. Words were everywhere, this particular Friday. If it wasn't Gock from Pontipool shouting about some duff bureau that was supposed to be priceless Ince and Mayhew but wasn't, it was flirtatious little Samanta Sellers working hard – she alone knew how hard – to sell her dud gemstone inlays to fund her next face-lift. God knows why Samanta resorts to surgery. She's a lovely smooth (not to say surgically whittled) lass of twenty-three. Her loving sister once told her she'd got an odd face and she's been paranoid ever since. Women. Forlorn, I sat on the wall swinging my legs, absorbing the balderdash. The stallholders' patter was so daft I wonder if antiques cause brain damage.

I'm not big on words. You may have noticed. They're strange. For instance, we have a useful word to utter false-hood – to lie – but none for speaking the truth. Is it because words can be lethal? Once you've spoken a word, it becomes a terrible deed. Words can mean that murder is on the way. Look at Rache, who moved in with me. I hardly knew who she was at first. Ten times a second Rache told me that she was hooked on holidays. Four days later she suddenly blazed away at me for 'not communicating!' and swept out in rage. I'd thought I was doing her a favour by keeping quiet. See the problem? Words.

And take Stan, the Treble Tile's barman. Well, Stan set his sights on this lovely bird called Angharad. Her husband's an amateur cyclist forever pedalling up and down the Pennines. Handsome Stan really campaigned for Angharad. He did everything a wooer could – gifts, flowers. He even dashed her his priceless antique watch. The whole tavern was agog. We were worn out.

The luscious Angharad took his largesse with disdain.

Quietly observing this sorry pantomime most nights, was Percy. Percy was a mediocre market gardener. The business was actually run by his go-for-gold missus while Percy imbibed. One night at closing time, this conversation, I swear, occurred:

Percy: Don't blame Stan, Angharad. You're gorgeous.

Angharad (*amused*): Not you too, Percy?

He (*smiling*): I know I've no hope. Only, I'd woo you different.

She (*amused by this pot-bellied oaf*): How?

He: I'd say: Angharad, I'm desperate for you. Give me thirty minutes in the car park, and you can have any Mediterranean holiday. With anybody you like. One condition.

She (*eyeing the daft old git*): Oh? What condition?

He: Book the holiday through Cumbersedge and Darff Travel Agent. I own a third, see.

She (*laughing*): Oh you do, do you?

He (*smiling along*): Expenses-paid Med holiday, for half an hour with you in the car park.

She (*cool*): Come on, then. Night, Stan.

(*Exeunt, the world aghast.*)

I heard every word.

See? Once words are out, the deed is all but done. I'm sure Shakespeare's said it better because he always has, but it's true. Rache had simply planned whisking me on holiday. And make no mistake, I truly loved her. Reflecting on this, I saw again that old lass tottering under a stack of obsolescent black LP gramophone records. Soon after Rache left, I took up with an older grand dame of ancient lineage, who owned a Chelsea antiques firm. Now, why did I think of that?

Highborn or lowly, women trust words. I don't. Words, dear friends, are scary.

Here endeth today's gospel. Except for that tip about holidays. Bribe a woman, you may get nowhere. Bribe her with a holiday, you're into yippee land. Where was I? Forlorn, in Bermondsey.

Mimi was tacking up fraudulent ethnic falsities outside her dad's van – authenticity nil, ethnicity nil, colour ten out of ten – and being chatted up by passing marauders of impressive dubiety. Sir Ponsonby was milking the lovely Moiya December as an enticing advert for all he was worth, making her ascend his stall, the better to make dealers gape. She lounged, sprawled, innocent of the impression she was creating. It's lucky women don't know the effect they have.

'You sap, Lovejoy.' Alice plopped down beside me. 'That Moiya knows what she's doing, the bitch.'

Palace Alice is a pleasant Northamptonshire lass, brings her own caravan every market day. She has a little lad in Daventry, and does all the London street markets. Her two brothers and her bloke Kayzo are in clink for general naughtiness, namely inflicting harm on a traffic warden while in execution of a robbery. They run fake auctions, but a fake auction is a long time for antique dealers to stay lucky.

'Does she?' I was surprised.

'Why d'you think she shows herself off? Posing, so hundreds can ignore her? Men are stupid.'

I went for it. 'Gemstones, love. Who?'

She eyed me. 'Dosh Callaghan, wasn't it, got gold-bricked? It couldn't happen to an uglier bloke. Ask Gluck.'

'Who's Gluck?'

Alice smiled. 'You ought to drop by more often, Lovejoy. Dieter Gluck's one of the new wave. Has a placer in Chelsea. Deals in Camden Passage, Islington, Portobello Road, Cutler Street by Petticoat Lane.'

'He a gemstone man?'

'He's everything.' She spoke with envy. 'Wish I'd half

his clout. Pal of Sir Ponsonby. You know his Chelsea shop, Lovejoy.'

Know as in knew? They've lately discovered a new physics particle. It's one of those quark things, and exists for a billion-trillionth of a second, give or take a yard. For a brief moment I knew how it felt, one flash and goodnight Vienna. To an outside observer, the antiques game might seem pretty static, but from within it's zoom city.

'Is Gluck here?' I looked about.

'Him, in a market? Too grand. Took over that pal of yours in Chelsea. The lads still mutter about it.' That pal of mine? I was worn out.

'Padpas, Alice. I need an answer. Dosh is a sod.'

She stood. 'Thought you'd never ask. Come into my parlour, Lovejoy.'

Her van was just by the church, being watched over by a couple of graveyard winos. She pays them in scotch. I didn't really want to, because divvying gives me hell of a headache in daytime. It's easier in the lantern hours but I don't know why.

'Look, Alice. I'll come later. What time will you leave?'

'About two, Lovejoy.'

Applause rang out for Mimi Welkinshaw's next striptease. I promised to call on Alice, and eeled into the maelstrom. Things had got on top of me. I wandered, listening and looking. I don't know about you, but when despond takes hold I seek the familiar. Nostalgia soothes. I looked for Doctor Coffin, who used to lie down in a gilded coffin, and bought any antiques to do with death. The Victorians were great celebrants of mortality, so he did a roaring trade. He dressed as an undertaker, black everything, went for the cadaverous effect. He even had ghoul-riddled patter. Other dealers fed him comic lines: 'You'll be the death of me,

Doc!' and he'd say, grinning, 'Promise?' to great hilarity. He's not been seen for donkey's years.

And there used to be a middle ager dressed up as a Navaho squaw. Probably got every detail and feather wrong, but she ran a neat Regency porcelain stall. Puntasia, she called herself. Always had one dazzler, a genuine antique – whoops! *There she was*! I stopped, joyous.

'Wotcher, Puntasia. How's it doing?'

'Better than you, Lovejoy!' She offered me her peace pipe. It's phoney, smokes like a burned barn and stinks worse. You have to accept it or she does a tomahawk war dance. 'Chatting up Alice? She knows zilch about your gemstone problem.'

Rumour is slow in some places. In Bermondsey it's quarky, if there's such a word. I choked on her pipe's carcinogenic filth.

'And you do?' What had Alice said about Chelsea? I guessed, fishing, 'My pal lost everything to somebody called Dieter Gluck, I hear.'

Puntasia took her peace pipe back and adjusted her feathered head-dress. 'Colette was doomed, Lovejoy. Ever heard of a younger bloke staying with an ageing tart? Always ends in tears. Don't go down Chelsea. It'll break your heart.'

The bobby dazzler on her barrow shone like the sun. A few dealers stopped to eye it with lust. I said nothing, just felt its warm clamour shudder through me. I've always been interested in pot pourris.

Back in older days, homes stank. Coaches, towns, rivers, alleyways, churches, schools, elegant ladies and their beaus ponged to high heaven. Factories were stews from hell. Miracle of miracles, mankind bravely held on in the filth. In spite of all, civilization advanced by creating wonders. One genius was young Josiah Spode who, about 1762, managed the Turner and Banks pottery in Stoke-on-Trent in the English Midlands. Risking his all on a dicey mortgage he bought the joint, and began experimenting. His talent made him a front runner, like Wedgwood. Under-glaze transfer printing, 'Staffordshire Blue', white pearl ware, his own blinding Spode blue, and his precise (*never smudg*y the way forgeries and fakes are) designs, made him a legend. His firm was always honest, even after he died in 1797. This is why antique dealers love Spode, because Spode marks are simple and never cunningly frilled to pretend they were the marks of other manufacturers. He had a Josiah Spode II and Josiah Spode III, and they copied Meissen, Chelsea, and others superbly. The plain fact is that old Spode spells money.

The pot pourri evolved in the smelly past. It's a container to hold mixtures of scented flowers and herbs. These mixtures were kept dry in England, but were wet on the Continent. It's still popular. Find one like Puntasia had on her stall, and you can sleep in next Monday morning. The most sought ones have two lids. One lid is fenestrated – has pierced holes so the lovely aroma will make your room fragrant. It is bigger than the solid inner lid, which is merely to keep the petals' perfume in. When a lady's gentleman was about to call, maidservants would rush about the house removing the *inner* lids and leaving the *outer* lids on the pot pourri vessels. The rooms would become scented, allowing romantic thoughts to bloom.

With a mute appeal to Puntasia – her name's a mixture of Fantasia and Pocahontas because she's daft on cartoon films – I removed the lids. Inverting the container I groaned. William Copeland joined Josiah Spode II as the eighteenth century turned. The indented Spode mark changed to a painted Spode and Copeland, which met my eyes. You can't match the feeling. Just think of the romantic trysts this lovely porcelain had witnessed! Reverently I returned it, my vision misty.

'Genuine, Lovejoy?' Puntasia asked, real pity in her voice.

'Perfect, love. Give me first offer?'

'Can't, Lovejoy. You only pay in IOUs. How much should I ask?'

'As much as you like, love. That's Spode blue. Buy the market.'

'Good luck in Chelsea, Lovejoy.'

'Chelsea? Who said anything about going to Chelsea?'

Quickly I walked down Tower Bridge Road, crossed by the Old Kent Road, and eventually survived the maddening traffic at the Elephant and Castle, to catch the Tube.

If I'd the sense I was born with, I'd have raced to find Colette earlier. That doddering scrumper lady in the market had reminded me of her, yet I hadn't taken my mind's hint. Colette, my 'old pal', was the rich owner I once made smiles with. When in trouble, reach for money.

The journey took minutes, just long enough to think of Colette.

5

THE STEAM HAD left me. I felt lost, my head 'filled with jolly robins' as Gran used to say. She stored up various proofs of this, like proving the same theorem over and over. I didn't mind. She knew where she stood. 'Vague, do what's necessary,' she used to say, moving about our one room. 'Idle, get on with it.'

London's traffic gets worse. I stood at Tottenham Court Road, where William Blake walked and wrote his poems about Innocence and Experience, meaning, I think, their opposites. A street lady slid past. 'Want business, dear?' I walked into a Charing Cross Road bookshop pretending to hunt some title. Chinese furniture? I looked, and thought of Wrinkle. Now, Wrinkle owed me serious money, had for a twelvemonth. And here was me short of brass. A hint!

The crossroads is properly called St Giles Circus. It was here that the carts carrying condemned prisoners halted on the way to Tyburn's gallows for their last drink. People still joke, when summoned to see their grim boss, 'Better have a St Giles bowl, eh?' Except it feels ghostly. Take away the swirling buses, the chugging taxis, hurrying people, and all that's left is the silent church with its silent churchyard. The eerie rumbling of tumbrils and the victims' pale faces are too recent for comfort. It was here too that child pick-pockets – think Dickens – teemed. They even had schools for subtlemongers to teach the trade, infants grubbing for crusts in these very alleys.

For a while I watched the traffic. Make yourself forget the spirits, you instantly see that modern life is beautiful. That's why America must be pure heaven. A country that has everything, free of all these phantoms and dark histories. I got quite a lump in my throat. Good old Yanks, getting it together. No wonder they're all millionaires.

Yes, time to be decisive. I shook myself free of vagueness, and caught the Tube for Whitechapel.

Wrinkle's lock-up garage where he does his forgeries abuts on a furniture retailer's in Spitalfields. I crossed Commercial Street. Jack the Ripper's first victim Martha Turner was found nearby, but who believes in spooks? Anyway, it was daylight.

Shinning up the corrugated tin roof, I peered through a grimy window, and there he was. The god of fakery was with me. Watching a craftsman is one of life's pleasures.

He was carving a chair arm. Chinese, from the curvature. That too warmed me, because he fakes nothing but Ching Dynasty and earlier. Standards lived in Spitalfields! The radio was playing, some lass crooning of inadequacy. Wrinkle said something, testy and sharp. I sympathized. Being interrupted at vital creativity's a nuisance. A lady moved into frame. She wasn't young, but so? She danced to the music, writhing, enticing. I blinked, a bit embarrassed, but couldn't resist spying.

Years ago me and a bird were walking past an alley on our way to the pictures. Lamplight revealed a couple snogging against the wall. The bloke was, as it were, entering oblivion, the lass clinging for dear life. I stared. My lass hissed, 'Lovejoy! Don't look! It's *mean*!' So I stared straight ahead. And glimpsed, from the corner of my eye, my bird having a right old butcher's, gaping at them. See what I mean? We all want to be thought proper, but deep down we're rotters.

Wrinkle's called Wrinkle because he's got the smoothest face on earth. Cheeks, brow, smooth as a babby's bum. He looks about fourteen. I only know two things about Wrinkle besides his forgeries. One is, he owes me for a fake Angelica Kauffmann painting. I did him a beauty on genuine panel like she did for the Adam brothers. Wrinkle never paid me. Kauffmann was a Swiss bird who came to London, helped to found the Royal Academy, being a friend ('nuff said) of the great Reynolds. Wrinkle wanted me to copy some fake antiques of her lovely Georgian porcelains but I wouldn't because they're ten a penny, and faking signed Angelica Kauffmann porcelain plates is really naff. They're dead obvious. Shepherdesses in their nighties, colours marvellous, playing musical instruments in idyllic groves, they look the business, the sort of decorative porcelain plate you'd show to your friends. Except Angelica never signed her name, and never really did paint on porcelain. You can see the tiny dots where the colours were printed on – and the skill of printing pictures on porcelain wasn't invented until she'd long passed on. I'd slaved over my panel. In fact, I remember making my own Naples Yellow, hell of a risk—

The woman started to dance voluptuously.

Wrinkle tried to keep working but his strokes, like my concentration, weakened. His interest in the sinuous lady became what I can only call unconcealed.

The woman shed some clothes.

Wrinkle weakened, angry, complaining.

The woman shed all her clothes.

'Look!' Wrinkle yelled, frantically trying to keep going, his former chisel shaking, his mallet definitely on the wobble. 'I'm finishing this frigging—'

The naked woman wrapped herself round him, smiling. I sprawled flatter. I heard Wrinkle moan as he dropped his chisel – and it takes a lot to make a craftsman surrender his tool.

Some things I'm not proud of. There was I, mesmerized on his roof while she and he went at it on his workbench. She didn't complain about the wood shavings. And Wrinkle no longer objected about interruptions. It was a beautiful scene. Okay, I ought to have gone about my business. But love is filled with enchantment. And what's wrong with it? I felt honoured, really privileged.

At the finish, waves and heavenly violins and smiles made, she lay among the wood fragments, replete, and looked up. *And smiled at me.* While Wrinkle was pulling himself together she even gave me a little wave, rippling her fingers. I almost waved back, caught myself in time.

Sliding quietly off the roof, I went for a walk, gave them ten minutes, then came up shouting, 'Wrinkle? It's me, Lovejoy.'

The only other thing I know about Wrinkle is his scam. It's called the lone bone. Before I go on, I suppose I'm making us antique dealers out to be all crooks, on some nefarious con trick. I want to be frank. We're no better or worse than other folk. It's just that antiques are high profile. Money's where it's at, so can we be blamed? Take ten thousand antique dealers, a thousand will make some sort of precarious living. Of those, a hundred will be doing well. Of those, nine will have decent holidays and a good motor. If you harbour a lifelong ache to be an antique dealer in a 'nice little antique shop', remember Lovejoy's Law of Dealers: of every ten thousand wannabe antique dealers, nine – repeat *nine* – are affluent. The rest give up, go broke, lose heart, scrape by.

Where was I? The lone bone scam is survival, Wrinkle style. It's unpleasantly easy.

He replies to lonely hearts adverts, pretends he's middle-aged gentry. Ex-officer, own car, loves theatre, Rome holidays, adores animals. He sends photos of handsome minor actors, even using their name. When the lady replies – he accepts them up to seventy, give or take an hour – he visits, gets to know, etc. She's impressed, if a bit puzzled. He's so much younger! But true love finds a way, and he milks her of whatever goods and chattels she feels inclined to offer. This is Method A. Alternatively, in Method B he arranges to meet her, usually after several confiding phone chats, at some station or theatre. By then he's got her address, of course, for haven't they exchanged letters? While she's on her way to Mayfair for that ground-breaking hand-holding lunch, all eager, Wrinkle the swine turns up at her house and steals whatever antiques he can cram into his Ford van. The lone bone.

Meanwhile, he creates his fakes in London's Spitalfields.

'Is that you, Lovejoy?' He looked bleary.

'I bawled my name, Wrinkle. It was a clue.'

'Look.' He tried to block my way. 'I'm a bit pushed.'

'That what they call it?'

I shoved in anyway, and immediately halted at the most glorious sight. Not the middle-aged lady in her nip, but a magnificent array of furniture. I went giddy as vibes shook me. For one second I thought he'd discovered some way to fake genuine antiques. Then I saw three pieces of ancient furniture against the side wall. They were his models, and genuine. My shivering knees almost let me down. I sat on a stool.

The workshop was no bigger than the ground-floor area of your house, say. The centre held the workbench where I'd seen Wrinkle, er, hard at it. On the left wall furniture was stacked. It looked desiccated, practically ready to fall to powder.

Don't know if you're into Chinese antiques, but it's certainly where money is, these switchback days. Before communism fragged, all interest was in porcelains. After the 1980s, though, Chinese furniture – pottery too – soared. Dealers everywhere spoke about Ching Dynasty (1644 to 1912 – think from our Great Civil War to King Edward VII) and Ming (preceding, to 1368). In the USA, it was Ching time in the Rockies. Dealers went doolally for Chinese furniture and porcelain. Europe bulged with artefacts robbed from Chinese tombs. Folk say China has eight million burial sites, 'of which 99.5 per cent remain unlooted', archaeologists licking their lips like it's their duty to ruin ruins. The figure's important, since in 1974 a serf blundered into the Terracotta Army of over seven thousand massive figures in a huge underground City of Burials. That peasant was honest – I'm not kidding, there is such a thing – and told his guv'nors. Wholesale looting began.

China was displeased. Beheadings followed. So stern did China become about this, that if some kulak was found homeward plodding his weary way with a Warrior's terracotta head in his knapsack he himself would suffer the same gruesome penalty. Did the looting of tombs and archaeological sites halt? Certainly not. Peasants simply got the message: If authorities executed a starving villein simply for stealing an earthenware figure, it meant something earth-shaking. It meant the figure was valuable. Lovejoy's formula: hunger + treasure = loot.

Loot exports boomed. Hong Kong was doing its stuff. Exports hurtled merrily to dealers everywhere. Then the oddest thing happened.

During the 1980s and 1990s Chinese unglazed earthenware tomb figures became common. They were in every dealer's window, on every collector's shelf. Their value tumbled. Small figures costing the price of a good new car in 1980 wouldn't buy a respray by 1995. But furniture? Furniture soared, and soared. *And kept on.*

A hardwood yokeback armchair in pretty good nick would have cost you the price of a mere week's holiday twenty years before the millennium. And they were common. You simply phoned Hong Kong, paid your four hundred dollars, and took delivery. Then China realized. Simultaneously, Hong Kong's lease ebbed. And the price of that hardwood curved-spine squarish chair? It rose hundredfold. If rare, like your folding swing-pin hardwood sitter that museums fight tooth and nail for, you're into half a million US zlotniks, and pay your own security guards. The prices, and the scarcity, have got worse.

Enter Wrinkle. I honestly don't know where he gets his woods from, but they're good. The usual ones are what we call huang-hua-lee (dunno what it means). There's some called zee-tan – ditto – and of course a whole variety of Indonesian and illicit Burmese redwoods and mahoganies. One piece already finished took my breath away.

'Here, Wrinkle,' I gasped. 'That's zylopia wood!'

Zylopia's curiously coloured, hard and tough. I went closer and peered. Its grain is tight, close, and very straight.

You can get it fairly easily from importers. Except it comes from Africa, and is often a curious grey. Using zylopia was a stroke of genius, saving the need for dehydrating and staining all in one go.

He reddened, shrugged. 'I'm in a hurry, Lovejoy. A friend's lending me the gelt. Make hay while the sun shines, eh?'

'Doesn't it pick up when you're working it?' I was fascinated.

Picking up is horrible. It means the wood tends to break away where the grain interlocks or crosses. A forger's nightmare, and a real giveaway.

'Terrible, Lovejoy. You have to be so careful.'

Wrinkle's lifetime ambition, I might add, is to fake all the main variants of furniture design of the Ming and Ching periods. One example of each, in the right woods. He'd done about twenty-six when he'd defaulted on paying for the Angelica Kauffmann panel I'd done.

'How many so far, Wrinkle?'

'Thirty-seven, Lovejoy. Nine to go.'

Full of admiration, I whistled. A true craftsman, he uses original methods, tries to make the right glues. He even makes his own tools.

'Got my money, Wrinkle?'

His innocent eyes blinked. 'Money, Lovejoy?'

I grabbed him by the throat. A woman's voice said drowsily, 'What's the matter?'

In the corner was a vast four-poster bed, four blunt-S shaped legs, carved low railings top and bottom. It was beautiful (I mean the bed). The lady stirred. Now, this was a forgery (the bed) but wondrously done. It was a year's job, piercing and slaving (t.b.). I walked over. The surface could have been ancient, powdery in places just like the real thing.

The joints had come away from contracture and shrink-age. The surface edges looked genuine. Only the absence of my bells told it was a fake.

Wrinkle had discovered his own ageing process. I had tears in my eyes. 'Beautiful, mate.'

'Why, thank you kind sir,' she fluttered.

'Not you, you silly cow,' I said. 'The wood.'

She sat up and glared. I touched the genuine three pieces against the opposite wall. I knew where he'd got those. They were from a colonel's elderly widow in Norfolk. He'd met her through his lonely hearts ploy, got them as a gift. The curvature of Chinese arms is just that little bit odder than on our furniture. I came to.

'Can't you hang on a month, Lovejoy? You'll get your money.'

'How do you shrink this wood, Wrinkle?'

There's a rough rule that wood cut in the long axis of its grain shrinks only one per cent. Wood cut radially, 2 to 7 per cent. Cut it tangential, it can shrivel up to 15 per cent. This is why old oak pews hurt your bottom when the sermon drones on – the dowel pegs poke up after a century by as much as an eighth of an inch. This is why church seats ladder ladies' stockings and scag your trousers.

'Got a good Far East supplier.'

'Excuse me!' This harridan stormed up. 'I've spoken to you three times and you've ignored me!'

It was Wrinkle's woman, presumably the one 'helping' him with gelt. Close to she was even bonnier.

'It's only Lovejoy, Honor,' Wrinkle said, fumblingly brought out a note. 'Here. On account.'

'I need it all, Wrinkle. I'm skint.'

Honor was wrapped in a large towel, furious. 'I'll pay you, Lovejoy. Then you get right out of here!'

She wrote a cheque. I demanded she write her address on the back, said so-long, wished Wrinkle luck, caught the bus to Liverpool Street station.

Where the bank politely informed me that there was no such account. The cheque was phoney. They politely asked me to wait while the police arrived. I politely said I'd just go to the loo, and eeled out into the street. Infallible at antiques, excellent at forgeries, useless with money.

And with people? Dud, dud.

6

ODD HOW RELIEVED I was to catch the Tube away from the street-barrow life I love. Old enemies, old friends, make me tick. Yet here I was, jostled by commuters and tourists, heading out of my natural grotty world into the sleek wonderland of Chelsea's glamorous King's Road.

The King's Road, Chelsea, starts at Sloane Square and heads south-west, towards Parsons Green. Oddly, road maps number its upper stretch A3217 and its lower the A308, but this is only cartographers having us on. They make changes in case we cotton on that they've no real job. Incidentally, note that definite article – *The* King's Road, like there's no other. It's deserved, for the King's Road, Chelsea, has its own peculiar message. That message has only one word in it, but is utterly vital: *Money*. Nowhere else in the antiques world does money bend behaviour more than in pricy, spicy, decidedly dicey Chelsea, where Cheyne Walk runs from Cremorne Gardens along Old Father Thames to the suave Embankment. If ever you stroll this way, keep your hand on your ha'penny, as folk say, because every single thing is expensive, from the stones beneath your feet to the windows gazing haughtily down onto thronged serfs hoofing glumly below. Money rules.

In spite of all, it's gorgeous in ways that other streets aren't. Chelsea's antiques shops, their facades announce snootily to us hoi polloi, not only have made it but also have it made. Provincials like me snort derision at some signs. I mean, The Original Chelsea Antiques Market (EST. 1967), for God's sake? A grocer in our local East Anglian town says how badly his business fared during the war. 'Yes, sir, 1648 was a bad year,' he'll sigh with regret, 'on account of disturbances concerning the late King . . .' and so forth. You are expected to understand that Mr Gunton of course means the Great Civil War, and the late King Charles I. So Chelsea's antiques mart hardly dates from the Dark Ages. But it's a commercial law that touristy venues must claim themselves ancient, even if they're not.

Outside on the pavement, I felt the peals. Because of worries collected in Bermondsey I stoically walked on past 'London's Oldest Antiques Market', as it advertises, Mon–Sat, etc, thinking aye, make that claim among the traders of Camden Passage or Whitechapel and you'd be for it.

One place I'd not visited for a while was The Furniture Cave. The ruinous music that dins you is enough to drive you to drink, but its antiques are reward enough – if you have money. Another of my laws is: Fakes recede in gelt's gleam (meaning the more affluent the antiques shop, the less likely you are to happen on a fake). I honestly mean it. You can lay odds that in the King's Road forgeries are less common than in grotty flea markets.

But I'd a job to do. I had to find Colette, and quickly get some sanity into my troublesome little jaunt. London's antiques venues are droolsome, sure, but the prices I saw coded everywhere were giving me a headache. I even managed to march, eyes averted, past 'Antiquarius', where they cram their stands too densely with antiques. Life's a pig. I was heartbroken, feeling the bonging of antiques as I forced on past.

And came at last to Lovely Colette Antiques, Ltd. My spirits rose. The sign was now silver on sap green, where it used to be scarlet, but that only made me smile. Colette was a traditionalist. I pinged the door and entered smiling, knowing she'd be delighted to see me. Once a duckegg, always. It's another of my laws, but like a fool I forgot it.

'Hello?' I called, quite at home. 'Colette? Arthur?'

No answer. The place was tastefully done out, fresh flowers, a load of antiques that literally set my teeth watering. I forced myself to ignore them and walked into the office, beaming at the enthusiastic welcome I knew was coming. Things had changed – a computer, swirling multi-coloured coils craving commands. A filing system in red tin drawers made me chuckle. I'd pull Colette's leg over this. She always said she'd never have computers or filing systems in the interests of sanity.

'Hello?' I called blithely. 'Come out wherever you are, or I'll start nicking your forgeries!'

Not a sound. Now, this is odd even for the King's Road, because so much stuff is whipped nowadays that even rich ladies like my – well, Arthur's – elegant Colette Goldhorn have to pay heed to locks and chains.

Still, I felt at home. I settled myself at her desk and pulled out the books. Colette normally keeps one set for the Customs and Excise. Her husband Arthur always has them up to date, Colette being above all this sordid lucre business. She's lust, joy, and antiques, more or less in that order. I used to know her once, in a way I'd best not reveal. I saw that Arthur had taken to smoking cheroots. I was tempted, but smoke has harmed even more antiques than looters, so resisted.

A snuff box on the desk made me wince. Bountyana, they call it now, is a collector's nightmare. This was mounted on a transparent resin plinth and labelled, 'Copper Snuff Box made from HMS sloop-of-war *Bounty*, Pitcairn Islands, 1789'. I touched it, didn't feel a thing. Modern fake. The faker had got the name and the 'sloop-of-war' right, but seeing the mutineers didn't reach Pitcairn until 15 January, 1790, where they burned HMS *Bounty* to the waterline on the 23rd, that 1789 date was a sloppy mistake. Also, the museum at Greenwich has several items made from the ship's copper bottom, and this copper snuff box was too thin. The engraved lettering was worn, but I could see the regular miniature nicks along each letter's edge. Somebody had used a modern engraving tool, and hamfistedly at that. Laughing, I decided I'd give Arthur a giggle and wrote a note on a card's reverse:

Dear Arthur and Colette,

This fake snuff box would be worth a mint, but lacks chimes. Check (a) the correct copper thickness of HMS *Bounty*, and (b) that your engraver Sorbo isn't on the vodka again. This is stagnacious junk.

A. Friend.

Stagnacious means so neffie and horrible you can't get rid of it.

Chuckling, I slipped the card under the snuff box. Then I noticed this stranger standing in the doorway.

Not sparse exactly, more of a slender athlete. Dark hair, bushy eyebrows, a bristly chin, he looked every inch the socialite eager to dash the hopes of rivals. His clothes shouted money. He held a tennis racket, obviously fresh from Wimbledon.

'Got you,' he said, smiling in a punitive way I didn't like.

'Wotcher.' I came round the desk. 'Colette about?'

He swung the racket so the edge hit his other hand, smack.

'Arthur, then?' I asked, uneasy.

'Bern,' he shouted, hard eyes on me. 'Get the police.'

Strange accent, not quite guttural. Somebody moved in the shop behind him.

'No, mate,' I explained. 'You've got it wrong. I'm a pal of Colette's.'

He swung the racket so fast. It thumped me on the temple. I fell heavily against the filing cabinet, almost pulling the flaming thing down on me. I struggled to get up, but he rained blows on me with a kind of metronomic regularity, like how mothers tell children off. 'I – thought – I – told – you—' I tried to shield myself, catch the racket, crawl away, anything, but the swine tripped lightly about swinging at me.

Hopeless to evade. I tried to make a rush past him. He easily kneed me to the carpet. I heard him laugh, a deep bray I thought only hunters used.

'Right,' he said, to somebody's muted remark. 'Now we wait.'

Thank Christ he wasn't carrying a knobkerrie, or I'd have been done for. Where the hell were Colette and Arthur?

Blood stained the carpet near my face, I noticed in a mist. This geezer must be some security nerk. He'd catch it when Colette found out this was how he behaved. I asked could I get up, only to earn more blows, after which even I had the sense to shut up and cringe in the foetal position.

He moved to the desk. I noticed his brogues, the white socks. He lit a cheroot.

'Ya, Dieter, police come.' Dieter, as in Gluck?

Another pair of shoes entered, thick soles and scuffed. Bern the serf, talking foreign. Bern's heavy heel ground my hand. They laughed, chatted. I swear I almost nodded off, partly ache and partly contusion I suppose.

Then voices, a door slamming, questions, dour mutters. Somebody hauled me up, and I was stared into by a face that could only belong to the plod, straight from Bramshill. Bramshill's the police staff college in Hampshire where they're supposed to train, haha. Even the police call it the Palace of Varieties, after the olde tyme music hall. We whose taxes pay for it are expected to praise their humour and efficiency, as now.

'This the thief? What did he steal?'

'A valuable snuff box, Mr Saintly. Made of *Bounty* copper sheath, cast iron provenance.' That was Dieter. I saw the liar's hand scoop the copper box off the desk. My card flipped to the floor. A bobby picked it up. Mr Saintly took it.

'He resisted?'

Mr Saintly? In other circumstances a joke about his name would have bubbled to the surface, but I was out of froth. His eyes bored into me. I felt relieved. This was a pro ploddite, cold and cynical. At least I'd escape from the hooligans. Two uniformed ploddites stood about doing sod all, boredom their only art-form.

'He tried to run. Bern caught him.'

'Don't I know you?' Saintly said to me.

'Me? No, guv.' I lapsed into vernacular. 'I phoned the owner, Arthur Goldhorn. He told me to wait inside.'

'Wrong. Arthur Goldhorn is dead.' Mr Saintly was still looking hard. 'Sure I don't know you?'

'Dead?' I went wobbly. A bobby held me up until the room straightened.

'Mr Gluck has been the new owner for months.'

A terrible suspicion gripped me. Arthur and Colette would never have gone, unless—

'Where's Colette?' I asked. Sudden realization made me grovel into my trusty whine. 'Er, sorry if I come in when I shouldn't, guv'nor. I didn't nick anything, honest.'

'Pressing charges, Mr Gluck?' Saintly asked, reading my card note.

'Not really. We got him before he managed to escape.' Gluck sounded smug.

Saintly turned, paused. 'Name and address?'

'James Churchill,' I said. 'No relation. Of 4, Hyde Park Gate, Sandy, Bedfordshire.' The best I could do, seeing my giddiness was back. I clung on the desk.

'Who really told you to come in here?'

'Bloke I asked for a humping job, shifting furniture. I'm a vannie, guv.'

'All right.' Saintly's eyes were everywhere. For some reason he seemed reluctant to go, but finally gestured me to leave first. On the pavement I reeled a bit. Dieter Gluck's henchman Bern had disappeared. 'Off, lad,' Saintly said. 'Behave yourself.'

'Yes, guv. Ta.'

The pavement went up and down like those trick footways on fairgrounds. I swayed along, shoving my feet out ahead of me with a thump. I wasn't even sure which way I was heading, wanting only to put some distance between me and the shop I'd thought the abode of friends. I glimpsed Bern on the opposite pavement. Scared, I flagged a taxi. The cabbie said, 'What the friggin' 'ell 'appened to you?'

'I lost. Liverpool Street Station, please.'

Nightfall, I was back in my cottage. I washed in well water, cold because the gas and electric were off again. I tried to phone my latest, Camilla, but the phone was off. I lit a candle stump to inspect myself in a piece of mirror I was re-silvering. I looked like nothing on earth, but my face was spared. Clever old Dieter Gluck. My shoulders ached, my spine throbbed. My upper arms, legs, chest were black and blue. Moving made me yelp. I had no aspirin. I would have been hungry as hell if I'd had any food to be hungry for. I creaked into my divan bed. I couldn't even reach the candle to blow it out.

Geologists say you can find the street level of Roman Londinium best by standing three men, average height, atop one another. The top man's hair would touch the Roman streets' paving. Modern London has sunk nearly eighteen feet, six yards.

I thought, thank you, London, fare thee well. The way I felt, London could go on sinking forever.

7

NIGHT DOZING IS the best I can do at sleeping. I realized that my trouble was antiques. To me, they're more real than people. I knew this when a lad. Ever since, my life's been lived in a mental world of distortion. Except for antiques. They alone are as they seem. It follows – ugly thought – that people are peril.

Antiques alone have the power to eliminate, to change. I once knew this woman Eth, lovely, determined politician. She'd have been in the Cabinet now, except for an antique. I met her at some village thing. She gave me a lift, talked politics all the way. At Braiswick, I asked her to drop me off at Alfredo's junk shop. It masquerades as a jeweller's. Posh exterior, grot within. She said that she'd hand in her earring. It needed a new clasp.

Alfredo showed me this chalice thing. It was blotchy, parts gilt, parts gold leaf, other bits looking like dirty ivory. Eth laughed as I took a shufti.

'Lovejoy, even I can tell that's not genuine!'

'Sorry, love,' I told the chalice. 'She's ignorant.' I sat down, smiling, and held it so it would know some of us humans were as human as any antique.

'*What* did you say?' Eth turned puce. She'd given her wonky earring to Alfredo.

'There's a tree grows in Malaysia, missus,' I told her. 'They called it *Isonandra gutta* in the mid-nineteenth century. It secretes a gum, gutta percha. This clayey stuff is it. Can I turn you over, love?' I asked the chalice, and examined its base.

No marker's mark, yet the pale grey gives itself away. Try to ping it with a finger nail, it tries desperately to sound like metal, yet fails. You only ever get a dullish ponk, like a really resonant heartwood. This doesn't mean it's worthless, as the lady assumed. It's tough, firm, so the item – chalice, bowl, figurine – seems, and nearly is, hard as ivory, and is nearly as whitish, too. The heyday was the mid-1860s, following the Great Exhibition. Tip: don't ignore gutta percha artefacts.

'Of all the insolence!' she was going. Alfredo was trying not to grin.

'Don't run it down,' I said sternly. 'This is worth ten times your ugly earring.'

Which cured her scorn. She came over, curious.

'Label it as exhibited at the Great Exhibition, Alf,' I told him.

'Ta, Lovejoy,' he said, relieved. 'What, a thousand?'

'More from a collector.' I hesitated, not wanting to offend an influential politician. Who does? 'If you've the money to get some raw gutta – they fly it in from Kuala Lumpur, on order – I'll do you a few fakes.'

'Ta, Lovejoy.' He was thrilled. His daughter was getting married, and Alfredo'd never been well off. 'I'll phone you, eh?'

'Er, the phone's off.' I invented, 'The storm brought

down the power lines last night. Drop it off when you're passing.'

'There was no storm last night,' Eth said in her motor as we resumed the journey.

'There was in our village,' I shot back, narked.

When will women ever learn to accept an honest lie? They rile me sometimes.

'Lovejoy,' she said after a mile or so. 'That old cup thing. Was it really what you said?'

'Aye.'

'Worth so much? And so easily faked?' She pulled into a layby, and said, eyes gleaming, 'You mean to say . . .?'

Join those dots, you get the rest. She resigned from politics and entered the sordid world of commerce. She now owns an antiques firm in Wolverhampton and an auctioneer's in Lancaster. I saw her again at the West London antiques fair. I said hello. She stared right through me, and said, 'Who *is* that?' and had me slung out. Sic transit whatever. The message? True greed conquers all, in antiques. Still, look on the bright side. I'd rescued the world from yet another politician. Do I deserve a medal, or what?

Dozing makes thoughts. It's unfair, because sometimes thoughts ought to leave you alone at night. Nights, I find, are to wear you out, and days exist to be worn out in. I'd taken up with Colette some time back.

The day I first met the Goldhorns, it was Dinty Carmichael sent me to Lovely Colette Antiques. He'd added money for the train fare. 'It's in the King's Road, Chelsea. Hand it only to Arthur, okay?'

The trick in the antiques game is to combine several jobs, so I did several antique shops along the North Circular

Road. I'd borrowed Dolly's old Morris motor, and saved the train money for grub. Life was good. Later that day it got even better.

Carrying my valuable parcel, I'd knocked. Vannies are trained never to intrude unless invited because they've a dodgy reputation for lifting things. A lady came to the glass door and did magic things with chains. I stepped in.

'Name and where from?' she asked, suspicious.

'Lovejoy. East Anglia.'

'Code?'

Like those blinking KGB spy stories. 'Buttercup?' I said hopefully. 'Er, antirrhinum?' Dinty Carmichael's girls grow flowers.

Suspicion became hate. 'Arthur!'

A portly gent with a beer belly stepped from the office, slippers, cardigan, specs, smoking a pipe. He didn't look menacing, but the lady clearly expected him to bayonet me at the very least.

'Afternoon,' he said mildly.

'Afternoon. Sorry, I forgot Dinty's code.'

Dinty Carmichael's mad on security. His place is like the Tower of London, everything but the Beefeaters. His wife once had to go to a hotel because she couldn't work his electronic bleepers out. Daft, but there's plenty like him.

'He's one of them, Arthur,' the lady said.

'Who?' I asked, blank. 'Can't you just phone Dinty?'

'We've been robbed before. Don't think you'll get away with it!'

Late forties, hair dyed blonde, her silk dress a mass of coloured rectangles, gold bracelets, thick caked cosmetics, she looked simply beautiful.

'Got you. You bastard.' She locked the door.

Arthur had been inspecting me. 'Colette, you've got this one wrong.'

'Shut it, Arthur. Phone Demure-Secure.' She seized the parcel, and placed it on a marble Victorian wash stand, inspected the seals. She tore it open, brought out a small sauceboat and crowed in fury. 'See? It's a fake! You guttersnipe!'

'It's genuine, missus,' I told her, walking to the door.

'Colette, dear,' Arthur sighed, evidently used to her tantrums.

'Genuine?' She pointed to the seals – Dinty's parcels are all seals, with his own insignia. 'Are these seals Dinty Carmichael's, Arthur?'

I'd had enough of this, and said so. 'Dinty never lets anybody else wrap his antiques. He never tells smurfs what they're carrying.'

She weighed me up. 'Then how did you know it was genuine?'

'Look at it for God's sake.' I was losing my rag. 'Original Worcester is painted in enamels that sink into the glaze, see? Even in a little sauceboat like that. Samson copies were enamelled thinly on transfers printed on. There'd be a giveaway black outline to the enamels.' I asked its pardon, and held it, smiling at its beauty. 'In torchlight, it will be translucent and slightly greeny. Samson of Paris did them in opaque earthenware, so you'd get no light through at all. And this gilding's golden. Samson's gilding is an ugly brassy yellow . . . What?'

The man Arthur was shaking his head. Colette was silent. I put the sauceboat down.

'I'm going, love. Keep me here against my will, Dinty Carmichael'll be cross.' The understatement of the year. I

was to divvy some Regency silver for him the following day.
He's wild about money, not an all-time first.

'Colette,' Arthur said. 'I rather think we have a divvy
here. He'd not seen the object before. Yet he knew.'

'Divvy?' She walked round me, looking up and down. I
felt on sale, bargain basement. 'There's no such thing.'

'I'm not a thing, missus. Nor is this antique.'

'Then what's this?'

She pointed to an early sofa table, genuine old wood
with lovely patina. I felt its embarrassment. I tried to smile
at it, cheer it up, but couldn't speak without sorrow.

A sofa table is a lovely light thing, two drawers facing
you and a small flap each side. Its bifid legs join by a single
stretcher. The genuine article's lovely.

'You poor thing,' I told it. 'Who did it to you?' I rounded
on the woman. 'Was it you, you rotten cow?'

'What?' She recoiled, looking to her husband for protec-
tion. I'm a fiend, frighten small women any time.

'You took the legs from a cheval mirror, and a plain old
Victorian dressing table's body. You ignorant bitch. You
chucked away the dressing table's legs, rims and back. Then
added the flaps from a genuine old Pembroke table. And
finish up with a bastard hybrid instead of three respectable
honest pieces. Just for money? Missus, may you rot in hell.'

'Of all the . . .' She petered out, aghast.

I crouched down, spoke quietly to the fraudulent sofa
table. 'Look, mate. I'm sorry for these oafs. I'll rustle up
the money and come back for you. Try to hang on.' I peered
at the price tag. It was in the old SUTHERLAND code,
one letter for each number. The Goldhorns had stupidly
put the GOLDSCHMIT code on the ticket as well, like
the Swiss in Geneva secretly use. A kid could read it. I
almost fainted at the price, but I'd promised now. 'Keep it

for me, please,' I told the Goldhorns. 'Have you still got the pieces of wood you stole?'

'Stole?' Colette Goldhorn cried.

'Lady,' I said harshly. 'You stole the cheval mirror's main frame. You butchered back, sides, and legs of the Victorian dressing table. And you thieved the rest of the Pembroke table. You're a frigging air raid, you horrible bitch.'

Arthur came forward, puffing benignly. 'All right, son. Yes, we did it. We still have the pieces. Pay the market price, we'll sell you the lot.'

'Deal.'

Ten days later, Colette silently arrived at my cottage with the forged sofa table and the remaining pieces of wood. She handed them over, on condition that I divvied some rubbish mock pewter she'd just bought. It was a pretence, though like an ape I worried my way through the pewter, giving myself a terrible headache.

Arthur, it seemed, had gone to the Continent to do some auction buying and Colette was on her own for the next five days. I said she'd have to go to a hotel because I was broke.

'I'll stay, pay, make hay, Lovejoy,' she said. I can see her now, standing there in my candlelight. Odd how women glow in the dusk.

'I've only one bed.' I remember clearing my throat.

'Then we'll share.' She locked the door. A great one for doors. 'I'm older but bolder.'

'Your pewter's junk.'

She started to undress. 'Lovejoy,' she said with a sigh. 'Just shut up. There are other things in life than antiques.'

Clearly a nutter. That was how Colette, er, came into my life. Arthur never suspected, or he pretended. Are they the same thing? Me and Colette even went to Holland together once, and Norway. She was jealous and hated other women sight unseen, but a model of propriety when Arthur was around. I liked them both. Colette was my friend for obvious reasons, mostly the overwhelming gratitude a man feels when a classy lady gives him herself. Arthur was my friend because he was always a gentleman.

Now he was dead, and Colette was vanished.

Before the dawn I was up making tea. I drew some well water into a jerry can, dug a small hole in the garden, put old rags in it. I chucked a drop of petrol on, lit it and stood back. I found two old dried-out used tea bags in the waste. No milk, so I crushed garden cob nuts to a paste, and used that the old way. Sitting naked in the garden, I spooned in my last bit of honey. Nectar.

The birds start chirping about five o'clock, and came on the scrounge as usual. Crispin my hedgehog – the dirty little sod lives in the compost heap – ignored me when I explained I'd have some grub for him tomorrow. I thought of Colette.

She had belonged to a minor showbusiness family. But Arthur was a Suffolk scion whose folk owned his land for centuries. It adjoined a vineyard a score miles away. I could do it today, lay Arthur's ghost, and try and help.

Time I did. She'd been good to me, until the Great Farewell. Maybe I'll tell you about that. I creaked upright, washed and dressed, and hit the road to the auction before the village woke.

8

THIS PARTICULAR AUCTION I'd last visited when my don't-get-tricked-in-antiques book came out. I'd gone because of a spate of stolen antiques. Grudgerham and Daughter Auctions Ltd wasn't long established, as auctioneers go, which in East Anglia means this side of Queen Vic. Local dealers joke that Grudgerham is simply the original founder, recycled. He looks it, mistrustful old devil. His daughter Shirley's a different matter. She knows a few antiques especially, rumour has it, those stolen in the Home Counties.

Some twenty dealers and casuals drifted among the furniture and assorted junk. The former always try to look disinterested. The latter – called 'women' in the antiques trade, irrespective of actual gender – always reveal their fascination. It's only when they find what they're hoping for that they pull themselves up, look guiltily around like they've been caught out. *Then* only do they pretend casual, dart into a corner and make surreptitious notes. People are lovely. You have to smile.

Heaven knows why, but every drossy auction rooms has a tatty notice board with clippings tacked there to brown and curl with age. Today, I stood reading them trying to keep a straight face. 'Up To Ten Thousand Reward', was blazoned in massive type. Beneath was a line of minuscule print saying *subject to the usual conditions*. This is the ultimate con trick, because what exactly *are* 'usual' conditions? Who defines them? Answer: the advertiser, that's who. He can invent any old conditions he likes. Think of the small print in insurance policies – then distrust 'usual' conditions a little bit more.

Equally wounding was a display from some trade paper: STOLEN from a residential property in St Edmundsbury were a large number of fine antique propelling pencils in gold, silver, porcupine, with various writing ancillaries. These are now highly sought by collectors. Everybody has an old fountain pen they don't want, because maybe it doesn't fill properly or the nib's no good. Take a minute to look it up in the public library, and you might be the proud owner of a Dunhill-Namiki floral-lacquered fountain pen worth at least two months' holiday in posh European hotels. Called 'scribiana' or 'postiana' by those strange folk called collectors, it's anything to do with writing, desks, ink, even postal weighing scales.

'Seeing if your own ill-gotten goods are posted yet, Lovejoy?'

'Wotcher, Shirley.' I turned smiling. Everybody likes her.

Shirley actually runs the auction. The lads take the mickey, of course, as a means of concealing their inveterate lust while she gavels away on the rostrum. She takes no nonsense. I wish she would. She dresses old-tyme, pinafore dress, high neck, starched white apron, stiff samite cuffs, with a lace bertha and a maid's mob cap. It brings publicity. She's always in the local papers demonstrating treasures. Oddly, she has a degree in economics, and jokes that she's now going straight, har har.

'These aren't the ones nicked from Archway, then?' I asked casually.

'Who knows, Lovejoy?' she said demurely. She meant who cares. 'I hear you're doing Dosh a favour. How come?'

'Poverty, love.' I glanced around at the trestle tables. She had a hundred pieces of furniture in, two dozen paintings, and some ten score 'handies'. These last are antiques you can hold in a palm, anything from a small carriage clock to a channel-mounted ruby nipple ring, an amber brooch or a necklet.

She smiled. Only women can do this amused I-know-you expression. It's why they're always one up even when they aren't, if you follow.

'Yet you're here to buy, Lovejoy?' She increased the watts in her smile. 'Such trust!'

I nodded at the adverts. 'Chartered Loss Adjusters. Good title.'

This is the other side of the coin. If you get burgled and want your antiques back, swarms of Chartered, Affiliated or Certified teams will leech onto you. Of course they'll say it's to 'mobilise resources in your interests'. My advice? Tell them to get lost. If your special treasure was a two-handled Sunderland loving cup of 1825 left you by your Auntie Faith and it got stolen in some smash-and-grab, the chances are it'll have been sold three times before tomorrow midnight. So what chance have you? None.

And if it's a collection of antiques – lead soldiery, models, porcelain dolls, jewellery, scent bottles – the whole lot will have been 'sold on' only once, but to a specialist 'wallet', the person who commissioned the robbery. Crooks who fund burglaries of collectors' homes pay a tenth of the burglar's fee up front, and the rest on safe delivery of the stolen goods. Such bludges, as they're termed, are arranged in every tavern in East Anglia. They're talked of loudly in every tap room, no secrecy worth mentioning. It's a horrible world.

'You're just cynical, Lovejoy.'

She interrupted herself to answer a few questions from Vern Cappuchin, a rogue from Stowmarket who sells antiques he sees in Sotheby's auction catalogues. He's utterly fraudulent, never been prosecuted.

'Wotcher, Lovejoy,' he said. 'Got enough to buy a 1780 teapoy?'

'Ta, Vern.' I wasn't having any. 'Nice picture, is it?'

He's always got some moan, which is a nerve, since he doesn't own the things he sells. Just picks up an auctioneer's catalogue, does a reverse print of any photograph and alters the colours by hand from a paintbox. Then he shows his photo around, hoping to take a deposit. It's astonishing how many people get taken in. I've seen Vern accept money deposits from as many as three customers in one afternoon in the same auction crowd, all for a photographed antique that some famous London auction house hadn't even auctioned off yet. It's as if folk are simply desperate to get tricked.

'No, Lovejoy. It's rubbish.' He showed me a picture, a lovely genuine teapoy. 'I'm honestly wondering whether to write and complain to Christie's. Their colours are simply wrong. It's just not good enough.'

See what I mean? Yet he drives a Jaguar, holidays in the USA, has a yacht on the Deben, golfs at Lytham St Anne's. I'm going wrong somewhere.

'No box, though,' he grumbled.

'They didn't have, at first, Vern,' I told him, from kindness. 'It's only in modern times that hostesses served tea from one table. In the late eighteenth century, each visitor was provided with her own separate small table. Like that one.' I nodded at his – well, Christie's – teapoy photo. 'Lift it with one finger, it's so light. Simple pillar-with-claw construction, two feet six inches tall, the surface's width only half that.' I admired the titchy table's elegance.

Now, though, dealers alter these rarities into a plant stand or a larger table. They do it because they're mesmerized by dimensions. The early, and rare, teapoy table – so light, so plain – is worth a fortune. Cackhanded forgers routinely mangle them into some different monstrosity. The teapoy – originally *tipai*, 'three legs' from Hindi and Persian – is among the most common of murdered antiques. Like the pole screen, like the old plain stool. I honestly don't know why the teapoy doesn't make a comeback. They're such lovely pieces. Interestingly, elderly ladies who lived out east in the Raj still provide you with your own little table with everything on it for teatime, but the gracious habit is dying out. Now, all meals are plop, slop and hop.

Vern glumly wended his way. Shirley grimaced.

'Wish I'd one of those to auction, Lovejoy.'

'Want one?' I asked, serious. 'Take me a fortnight, if you'll buy the heartwood.'

'Deal,' she said. 'On commission, or buy outright?'

'Buy.' We shook hands. 'Catalogue it as you want. I'll see it's aged right.' I smiled. 'You know what they say about a fake antique. First auction, it's a forgery. Second time, doubtful. Third time round it's genuine.'

Shirley didn't even blush. She's famous for carouselling antiques, changing their fictional history. This way, nobody's ever quite sure if the 'antique' they're inspecting is the one they saw last week or something completely different. Her catalogues are balderdash, of course.

'I was surprised you're doing Dosh's job, Lovejoy.'

One of her whifflers was signalling, should he ring the bell to start. She gave him the nod.

'How is Dosh, Shirley?' I asked, seeing every dealer in the place was drifting our way, wondering what we'd just agreed. She'd been Dosh's lass for about a year, swapped herself over from a wild Welsh cabinet maker from Carmarthen who got gaoled for hijacking antiques vans on trunk roads.

'Just the same,' she said. A trace of bitterness in there? This was the reason I'd stopped by.

'No legal trouble, Shirley.' I pretended relief. 'I'm glad.'

She gestured swiftly to the whiffler stop bothering her. Some of the dealers were catcalling, whistling the old refrain *Why are we waiting?*

'He's had some lawsuit, Lovejoy.' The acidity became anger. 'If he's . . .' She gave up, shoulders drooping, and gave me a wry smile. 'Don't get your fingers burnt, Lovejoy, will you?'

'Me?' I went all innocent. 'Look, love. If I do you a set of ancient casts of rare golds, Romans, Greek, some medals, would you caravan them for me? Half and half?'

Her I-know-you look is a better smile than the wounded sort. To caravan is to move antiques in one lot and sell to a different part of the country via some friend. Shirley has plenty of crook auctioneer pals, being a crook herself.

'You're a chiseller, Lovejoy. You know that?'

'Yes,' I said seriously.

She laughed and went to the rostrum shaking her head at the wicked ways of the world. The antiques trade is full of friendships sealed with love and wine. We forget love doesn't last. And wine evaporates, not like blood.

So I went to see Harry Bateman, who lives on North Hill with, but more often without, his wife Jenny.

Here's one of the quickest ways to fake antiques which are really worth selling. Only one, mind. There are a dozen others you can do in an afternoon, but a good forgery deserves technique.

Harry Bateman had been holding some antique coins and medals, including ancient Roman and Greek, for a solicitor in town, supposedly to make a valuation for probate. The solicitor, rapacious for his fee, had had each one photographed and weighed, so Harry couldn't get up to no good.

Who was aggrieved, and welcomed me with surliness.

'Bloody lawyers, won't trust me an inch,' he grumbled.

'Jenny in, Harry?' I asked, to be safe.

Jenny, his missus, adores a bloke called Klayson who hates women. She devotes her all – and a good chunk of Harry's all – to serve him, and pay for his every whim. Harry can't understand it. Nor I, in fact, because Klayson treats Jenny like dirt. She just goes on worshipping, in spite. 'Nowt as queer as folk,' my Gran would say, adding after a wry pause, 'And women are worse.'

'No.' Harry spoke with resignation. 'She's at that queer's place doing his washing. You know, Lovejoy, he beats her?'

'Oh, er . . .' I'd been about to say a routine, 'Good, fine,' but words are no help. 'Help me, Harry.'

I held up a piece of isinglass, a few pence from the chemist's on Head Street. It's gruesome stuff, being sturgeon gelatin.

'You making copies? You'll get me hung, Lovejoy.'

Morosely he went to his safe and opened it up. 'Don't never say I don't never help you nothing.'

'Eh? Ta, Harry.' I was relieved. If he'd not been feeling especially down he might have refused. 'I owe you.'

'Promise me you won't nick any?'

Narked, I went into his kitchen while he settled down to watch the football match on telly. Everything on the North Hill slopes, including churches, houses, lintels, the lot. The houses and shops have a zero mortgage rating, can you believe, when they've been there nigh nine hundred years. Banks trust modern builders, but won't trust those of the thirteenth century whose edifices are proudly still here, if slightly on the wonk. Barmy.

Here's how you make a decent forgery, costing only a few moments of your time and virtually no money. (Honest readers please skip this bit.) Cut up isinglass into rainwater in a warmed pan. Bring slowly to the boil. Stir. Scum away the surface dross – I use a washed stick of firewood. Keep it heated, de-scumming as you go. Remove it from the stove, and let cool.

Meanwhile, I'd laid out the coins and medals on the kitchen table, touching them only with my hankie. I had to use Jenny's best pouring pans. I added a little powdered ochre to some of the goo, and poured it onto – not over – the coin to a thickness of an eighth of an inch. (Metric loons may convert, if they want.) Cool. Let it dry slowly. It comes away of its own accord, and there you have it. A genuine impression – neater than any modern setting epoxy resin can manage – of an ancient coin.

The point? Whole collections of these impressions were once made as collector's items by gentlemen on the Grand Tour two centuries ago. So finely is the surface imprinted into the isinglass, that they were posted home. They were sold in cabinets. If I'd had the money, I'd have got some expensive colours, but had to make do with what Harry had on his shelves, malachite green, some naffie Prussian Blue (I *hate* Prussian blinking Blue), ochre, scarlet lake, the usuals that antique dealers, ever hopeful, always have but never use.

In three hours I had a collection of Roman staters, a few Greek, and one real treasure. It was a James I gold rose rial, which is a thirty-shilling piece. My wretched honesty almost made me weep. If I hadn't promised Harry, I could have nicked the gorgeous thing. And a five-guinea gold piece of William and Mary, 1694. All in all, thirty-nine impressions. I was worn out.

Harry was asleep in the front room, so I forgot the mess – well, what else is a kitchen for, but to leave in a mess? And Harry had nothing else to do except clean up. The medals and coins I replaced in the safe. I made a telephone call, brewed up, watched some game show where you had to guess whose face was behind a coloured disc. While I was waiting for Topsy to arrive I ate Harry's biscuits. He snored on.

She beeped her car horn. I let myself out and handed the impressions through the motor window.

'Ta for coming, love,' I told her. 'Careful. They're only wrapped in Harry's tea towels. Shirley'll caravan them.'

Topsy's a dancing teacher from the Institute, trains infants to prance and whatnot. Reputedly forty, is fifty. I like her friendliness. We once made smiles, and I'm grateful. Her husband Ben designs windows, which must be the neffiest job I've ever heard of. She's a mean forger of boxes and velvet. No better person to dress up a collector's box of precious hard-won coin impressions taken by some Regency traveller on the Grand Tour.

'Any writings to go with them, Lovejoy?'

That was a thought. 'Aye. Get Fonk – you know him? – to do me letters to somebody in, say, Yorkshire. Hint at a literary connection, but no Brontës. Everybody's had them up to here.'

'Right. How much can Fonk charge?'

'You second it, love.' That meant she'd pay him out of the price she'd charge me.

'Will do. I take it you're in a scramble?'

'Well spotted.' I'd have bussed her, but North Hill has a constant stream of traffic. 'Toodle-oo.'

'Come round, Lovejoy. You can stay overnight. Ben's working away. Pity Sturffie's involved.'

'You come round to me, eh?'

I watched her drive off, thinking, does everybody know everything I do, or is it simply me?

9

WALKING IN THE country quickens you, but towns are more pleasant. I got a lift from a commuter who wanted to tell me about falling – rising? – bank rates. I made the right noises. He asked after my job. I told him. He was eager about that, too, and said he'd bring an antique for me to see, left him by some uncle. I said fine, and alighted at a housing estate, all the roads named for roses. Pretentious, though Daniel Defoe did say that the town was famed for 'beautiful roses, ugly women'. He'd got it wrong. All roses are beautiful, aye, but so are all women. Nil points, Dan, good luck with *Robinson Crusoe*.

When I knocked, she thought I was the blinking milkman, called out of the bedroom window, 'Two pints of skimmed, please.'

'Can I interest you in some solid protein, missus?'

'Who . . .?' She peered, withdrew.

Chains eventually rattled. The door opened. (Sorry about all this pedantry, but Lydia enforces it on everyone with whom she comes into contact. See? Even *that* little sentence.) Lydia looked through a crack. I could see that she wore a nightdress, a thick woollen dressing gown, tufted pink slippers.

'Good morning, Lovejoy. It's only fourteen minutes to six.'

And nine seconds, I daresay. 'Could I enlist your assistance, please, dwoorlink?' I always feel in school with Lydia. She's my apprentice. Don't laugh. 'Will you travel with me to Saffron Fields?'

The door didn't waver. Lydia affects a stern, unrelentingly prim mode dinned into her by convent school. I'd finally discerned the passion beneath, but have to pay by watching everything I do and say. Morality rules, except when she permits otherwise in seclusion, meaning my cottage when I get round to mending the locks. Lydia's morality is hard-as-nails puritan.

'Hadn't you better ask Rosanne for assistance?'

This is women all over, the innocence of a toxin.

'Look, love,' I said indignantly. 'I had to butter Rosanne up. She had a collection of Victorian witches' balls I wanted.'

A witch's ball is a glass sphere, sometimes with a slender glass rope (sic) attached. Witches tether one to their belts and peer into it for arcane assistance. The glass is too densely coloured to see through, or even into, unless you're a witch I suppose. They date from about 1865, are usually ultramarine or that disturbing dark green. I've even seen a red one, which put the fear of God in me. They sell for about three hundred quid, going to press. Rosanne runs an infant crèche in Nine Ash Green. Hate to think what she teaches the babbies.

The door didn't move. 'You failed. Rosanne declined to sell.'

'I wasn't trying to buy them for profit. It was for,' I invented in a burst of genius, 'her babies' school. They need, er, bottles and things.'

The door instantly swung open and there stood Lydia. 'And the horrid woman wouldn't sell her antiques to help the babies?' she cried, furious. 'There! I warned you she was positively wretched!'

'You were right, dwoorlink.' I allowed myself to be coaxed inside, very contrite. 'I should have listened.'

She slammed the door seething with outrage. She's good at seething. 'Indeed you should, Lovejoy!'

'This journey to Saffron Fields is for the same reason,' I extemporized. Never change a winning team. 'The babies need desks.'

One thing about Lydia is that she's always voluptuous. Dishevelled from sleep, tousled from dusty auctions, glammed up for glitzy occasions, Lydia dims all other women. She'd look good in rags or nothing. I tried not to reach for her.

'Desks?' She paused, suddenly cold. 'Another of your tales, Lovejoy?'

Didn't infants need desks, for Christ's sake, lazy little sods? I'd had a desk at school. 'Er, she's planning. But,' I added solemnly, 'is she the right sort of person, I ask myself.'

She quivered with vehemence. 'I also have doubts!' she cried.

'We must help, Lydia.' I went all noble. 'If we don't, who will?'

'Lovejoy.' She misted up. 'Sometimes, you have a heart of gold. Up so early, just thinking of those little ones . . .'

I felt myself fill up too, because it truly was a beautiful effort on my part. I reached to embrace her. She stepped back.

'Have you had breakfast, Lovejoy? I'll have a bath and dress, then make you something before we leave.'

'Maybe I could wait upstairs with you, talk over plans?'

'Certainly not! Please wait downstairs.'

Deprived, I foraged, made a ton of toast and marmalade, brewed up, tried to boil three eggs but they always come out runny and I can't stand that gooey white so I fried some cheese and tomatoes and had that with a mound of bread. Lydia never has sliced bread. She makes her own loaves that you've to cut yourself, though my slices always go thick at one edge and dwindle to infinity on the other. She writes angrily to Ministers of the Crown about the quality of shop bread.

In the living room – the house is semi-detached – I found a small mystery. On the mantelpiece was a nickel-plated gadget I'd seen before. There's a well known device for automatically making tea by your bedside when you wake, called a 'Teasmade'. Rotten name, still on sale. This was the earliest version, patented by the gunsmith Frank Clarke of Snow Hill in Birmingham in 1903. I could actually remember telling Lydia, on her second day as my apprentice, to bid for this very instrument at Gimbert's auction. I even recognized the faint scratches on the spirit burner. She'd gone into the auction trembling, white as death, though I'd told her not to worry. Lydia had come in a fraction too soon, and stimulated the bidding beyond her 'add one' limit.

(Just a small point. Remember that, if you get somebody to bid for you at an auction, custom allows your bidder to go one bid higher if she thinks she can swing it. And you *must* pay up no matter how high that one extra bid takes you.)

I smiled. I'd forgotten all about the incident until now. This was typical Lydia, to let that early mistake rankle. She must have hunted the item down, then saved up and bought it – four thousand zlotniks at current prices, note. Sentiment? Or her famous rage at not having done something exactly right? The nickel surface shone. This silly little instrument appeared cared for, loved even, on its wooden plinth with its spirit burner, spring-worked match striker, original matches, automatic tilting kettle, its alarm clock actually working. She'd had it lovingly restored.

'I see you had breakfast, Lovejoy,' Lydia said behind me. 'If we—'

She halted, noticing me and the tea maker. I looked. She was just as beautiful, but now dressed to kill. Matching accessories, gloves in the strap of her handbag, hair perfect in her inevitable bun. Good enough to eat.

'Well done,' I said. 'To find it, I mean.'

She blushed. 'I just came across it. It seemed so neglected. No particular reason, Lovejoy.'

'Of course not.' Awkward of a sudden, I waited. 'The Automatic Water Boiler Company of Birmingham made them, I think?'

'That is so,' she said primly.

We stood like lemons. She finally said she'd make some fresh tea and have a slice of toast, then we could be on our way. I said fine, fine. I honestly don't know what we're playing at half the time.

'Oh, Lovejoy,' she said in the kitchen, safe from past reminders, 'there is good news. Tinker comes out of rehabilitation today. I have ordered a motor car to transport him.'

The Lydias of this world can't say words like gaol.

'Thanks, love.' Good fortune at last. I'd have the world back on its axis in a trice, the three of us together.

'One question puzzles me, Lovejoy,' she said, dabbing her mouth with a napkin. It had been ironed into folds. I remembered the old trick challenge: How many times can you fold a standard piece of foolscap writing paper of average thickness? Answer: Eight. No more, not even if you're Morgyn the Mighty. I'd bet Lydia could iron a napkin into a million folds without effort. I ate her toast because she was slow.

'Yes, dwoorlink?'

'Who injured you, and why?'

She'd spotted my wince and my limp. Sometimes she's a right pest. 'Oh,' I said heartily, 'good heavens! I stumbled off the kerb.'

She rose, cleared things away.

'Please do not dissemble,' she said. 'You may enlighten me should you feel so inclined. Come now. We have a journey.'

Which is how, at a breathtaking nineteen miles an hour, bumping onto every gutter grid for mile after mile, we reached the ancient manor of Saffron Fields Hall.

Where at last we found Arthur Goldhorn, but not his missing lady.

We alighted at the ornate gate. I was all but asleep from Lydia's reckless driving. With her, you've time for a coffee at every crossroads. In Lavenham we'd been overtaken by an invalid chair.

'Why not drive up to the house?' I suggested. The drive is five furlongs long. 'Seeing it's our destination?'

'Certainly not, Lovejoy!' she said, scandalized. 'Didn't you tell me that Mr Goldhorn is possibly deceased? The present incumbent might not wish it.'

Give me strength. 'Good point,' I said.

Saffron Fields Hall is imposing. Queen Anne style, twelve windows across, four storeys high, red brick covered in that green creeper thing, set in immaculate grounds. Once, the lawns hadn't been quite so stencilled. Several gardeners slogged away. I called out to one I recognized but he ignored me. They had orders.

'How rude!' Lydia exclaimed, preparing for war. 'Not even to answer when . . .' et Lydia cetera.

'We'll visit a friendly neighbour instead, and find out.'

We stuttered along the rough track that led beside the Saffron Fields estate. It was three furlongs off, took us a couple of aeons.

'Where are we, Lovejoy?'

'This friend's nice. You'll like her. She grows grapes,' I quipped, now troubled by my investigation's tardiness. With Lydia's help I'd be even slower. Dosh Callaghan would come along any minute, wanting answers about his gems.

The vineyard is one of those places in East Anglia where the Romans supposedly grew their grapes. I actually believe it of Carting's Vineyard. It's set back from the main road, a mere twenty acres, with two large ponds trying to be lakes in truly rural surroundings, woods, a bridge over a freshet, thickets. Countryside gets me down.

Two wooden buildings stood adjacent to a reeling farmhouse. Nothing stirred. Lydia exclaimed at its prettiness.

'Oh, look!' she cried. 'A kingfisher!'

Something red and blue zoomed over the water, vanished among trees. I winced. Great to be reminded that Nature was carnage, just when I wanted to find out if my old pal Arthur really had died.

'It caught a little fish, Lovejoy!' she carolled. 'How sweet!'

'Not for the fish.'

'That you?' a voice exclaimed to my relief.

'Wotcher, Dottie.'

There she stood, pleasantly plump, garbed to battle agriculture in wellingtons, a shift thing smocked at collar and hem, with frayed brown cuffs and an amorphous canvas hat garlanded with hedgerow flowers.

Dottie Kelvedon was born and raised on Carting's Farm, back when it had been a smallholding with cows and pigs and a dog called Goon. Dottie had evaded the various forms of penury planned by successive governments. She'd turned it into a vineyard, bottling her own red and white wines – Cymbeline Red and suchlike. I'd sold a stock of antique farm implements for her. She'd paid me in kindness.

'Who's the grumble?' Dottie speaks like a rough soldier sometimes. Comes from delivering calves, foals, and rearing chickens for unspeakable purposes. Grumble and grunt is Cockney slang for a female.

'Dottie Kelvedon,' I said with gallantry, 'may I introduce my apprentice Lydia?' I sounded like Beau Brummel.

They wittered a bit, those irrelevant non sequiturs with which women fence on meeting. Lydia decided she liked Dottie. I was surprised. Dottie insisted on showing us round the barn where she organizes wine tastings and supper evenings. She has a lover called Tory, dunno why.

'We've done the fish pond since you were here last, Lovejoy.' Dottie walked us over the little bridge. 'Koi carp cost a fortune. Don't worry,' she said with a laugh I remembered, 'we only sell them for decoration, not eating. Lovejoy is squeamish,' she added for Lydia's benefit, leading the way to her bottling plant. It's in a shed. 'I once saw him rescue a fledgling in a thunderstorm. It had fallen from its nest. It died, of course, but only after Lovejoy'd tried to feed it with milk for two days. He's barmy.'

We stared at her bottling machines. 'Great, Dottie,' I said.

'You'll want to see this next bit, Lovejoy.'

We went along a narrow path, trekked down an over-grown path into thick trees. The ground sloped up. I realized we were on one of those ancient Celtic ramparts, probably no more than mere cattle compounds but which are now invested with folklore tales of primitive battle-ments. You get a lot hereabouts.

'Here,' Dottie said.

It was a glade some fifty feet across. Wild flowers were everywhere. An astonished fallow deer peered at us, sprang and vanished.

'What?' I said.

'Arthur Goldhorn.' Dottie looked sadly at me. 'I trust it wasn't for the pleasure of my company that you called, Lovejoy.'

'Arthur?' I said stupidly. There was nobody but us.

Lydia said quietly, 'The stone, Lovejoy.'

The headstone wasn't quite in the centre of the clearing. It was knee high, not as tall as they stand in our churchyard, faced with slate incised with bold letters done in brass. It announced that Arthur H. Goldhorn lay here. H for what? No epitaph, no sentimental Hoping On The Resurrection and all that. Nor was there any Beloved Husband Of and suchlike. Just *Requiescat in pace*, and that was that.

Dottie didn't speak. I read the inscription over and over.

Weeds had flourished since the burial. The earth mound was overgrown. Greenery stood taller even than the head-stone itself. I stared, kept on staring, couldn't take my eyes away. The lettering was a professional job. I cleared my throat to say something, couldn't.

The women were talking quietly. I couldn't catch what they said, didn't try. A small bunch of wild flowers had been laid by the headstone. Who by? They were faded, petals fraying.

This was Arthur. It signified his arrival, birth, life, death. It was all he was or ever had been. No more.

'Look,' I said after a bit. 'See you back at the barn, okay?'

'Yes, Lovejoy.'

'One thing, Dottie.' It took me time to get the words out. 'Whose land is this?'

She didn't reply for a few pulses. 'It's mine, Lovejoy. Those two hornbeams. See them? Six, seven perches off? That's my boundary.'

'Oh, aye.' I couldn't recognize a hornbeam tree if I fell over it. 'Whose land comes next, then?' I already knew.

A longer pause this time. 'Saffron Fields, Arthur's own land until lately.'

'Just making sure.'

'It belongs to Dieter Gluck now. Colette works for him in the London antiques markets. A bag lady, people say.' I actually heard Dottie shrug, all that heavy rural garb susurrussing on her. 'She can't keep away. Like you, Lovejoy. A street lover, Arthur used to say.'

Nothing more. Arthur Goldhorn, ancient owner of an ancient manorial estate, had finished up a piece of discarded rubbish. Only the kindness of a neighbour had given him rest.

Eventually I heard them both go off down the footpath, weeds squelching underfoot. Dottie does this to keep paths free, but it never works. Come back a day or two later, every track is almost completely overgrown like nobody had ever passed that way. Very like Arthur. Or you.

I sat on the ground by the grave, wondering who it was standing watching among the trees.

10

ME AND ARTHUR in the glade. One thinking about death, the other knowing all there was to know about it, thank you very much.

He was buried in a remote wood.

Now, the law about burials in silent, leafy old East Anglia is exactly that for the rest of Great Britain, give or take a patch or two. People don't know this, but you can have yourself buried anywhere, as long as you stick to certain rules. Report the death to the Registrar General. Get the death certificated. Find a place, and that's it.

You don't have to hire a church and a priest, have grand motorcades. You can devise your own funeral service, sing whatever hymns you like, compose them yourself if you've a mind. Or stay silent. No need for posh coffins made of valuable hardwood, expensive mourners. It can be a Do It Yourself job, start to finish. In fact, it can be a festive frolic with friends. Not long since, a colonel-in-chief of the Sealed Knot – they re-enact Great Civil War battles – had his remains fired from a seventeenth-century cannon. Quite legal.

Arthur used to go scathingly on about council cemeteries, headstones on parade. It made me queasy, but he just laughed. 'Bury me under a tree on my own land,' he told me once. 'That giant mulberry, full of silk moths.'

Times out of number I'd joked back, 'It's a deal.'

Not your own land now, Arthur. Dieter Gluck now owned it. He also owned Arthur's antique dealership. And Colette too. Maybe if Arthur stood tall, he might just glimpse Saffron Fields manor where his ancestors had lived for a thousand years, maybe even see his precious mulberry tree. I couldn't recognize a mulberry either.

Nothing wears you out like sorrow. I rose, stood like a lemon doing nothing. A few birds hopped about. A robin came, looked hard at me.

'You sod off,' I told it. 'I can't do more than I do.'

It said nothing, flirted its wings and was gone. I told Arthur so-long, and left along the same path.

The glade behind me was silent as the grave – sorry, I meant pretty quiet. I stepped where Dottie and Lydia had walked.

I wondered who the bloke was who'd watched me. He'd kept still as a hunting heron.

That's countryside for you. Rotten, being in it. Anything can happen, and nobody'd be any the wiser. I felt my back prickle. I'd said the right thing to the robin, made it loud enough for a stray hunter to hear.

Glad to be back at Dottie's safe little vineyard, though. We had a glass of her Cymbeline Red, and sipped her Augustus White. English wines couldn't give you a headache if they tried, thank goodness. We said goodbye to Dottie and finally drove off towards St Edmundsbury. We were overtaken by a large limousine, which signalled us to stop on the road's hard shoulder.

Tinker got out, coughing enough to pollute the coast. He looked really smart, which for him means shaven. Lydia alighted and angrily assailed the driver.

'You drove in a dangerous manner!' she blazed. 'Overtaking at speed on a blind bend.'

'The road's straight, miss.' He was unperturbed. 'You were doing fifteen miles an hour.'

'That's no excuse for . . .' etc., etc.

'Wotcher, Lovejoy.' Tinker grinned foolishly. He carried a roll of blanket under his arm. Other than that and the shave, he looked normal: soiled ex-Army greatcoat patched to extinction, battered boots, greasy mittens, beret, teeth down to corrugated brown stubs, frayed trousers that hadn't been washed for a generation. 'You all right, son?'

'Aye, Tinker. You?' I was wondering how he'd found us here.

'Oh, not so bad.' He looked askance. 'Ta for sending the motor.'

'Lydia arranged it,' I said. 'Who's this us?'

He peered into the car. 'Lovejoy says it's okay, Trout.'

And out stepped this apparition. I gaped. Even Lydia shut up.

Trout was small, yet wore a full-size shirt. He carried a rolled-up furry garment of yellow and black stripes. He wore furry slippers, and carried a plastic inflatable club of the kind you see in Christmas pantomimes. I know you're not supposed to say words like dwarf and midget in case it's fascist, but 'little' seems too limited when the bloke you're describing doesn't come up to your waist.

'Wotcher, Trout,' I said warily. 'You a pal of Tinker's?'

'Are you?' His suspicion made me smile. I felt I needed a grin. His voice was gravelly, like a heavy smoker's.

'We were in nick together,' Tinker explained. 'Trout is a Tarzan-O-Gram. It's a joke, see? Him not being big. Get it? They give him that shirt at the nick. Couldn't send him out in his Tarzan clobber. He got done for burglary dressed like an Ape Man.'

'I heard,' I said politely. 'Saltbridge Manor, that Cotman painting?'

Trout scuffed the ground. 'I'd have got away but for a gamekeeper.'

'Only bad luck,' Tinker said eagerly. 'I thought Trout could come with us, until he finds his feet. He's tough, can do all sorts.'

'Look.' I wanted to say no. It's fashionable to be kind to ex-cons, suss out their innermost problems and prove that nothing's their fault. But a titch like Trout, even not dressed as Tarzan, would stand out like a searchlight in a pit. Besides, Trout was famous for doing Olivers. An Oliver is a method of burglary named after Oliver Twist. You prise open a fanlight and let in some child who unlocks the door for your team of burglars to nip in and strip the place of antiques. It's made a recent return to the crime scene, on account of hidden electronics spoiling things. Trout was ideal for Olivers.

The trouble was, Trout was ultra-famous. Magistrates everywhere had felt pity and let the little chap off with cautions. The whole trade knew about the scam in London's Ealing, where he'd knifed some dealer who'd cheated him out of a half share in that theft from a Düsseldorf museum. The victim hadn't lived to tell the tale, dying in the ambulance. So was it wise taking on somebody who might gut me for being slow with the wages?

Lydia solved my dilemma. 'Oh, certainly, Tinker! Lovejoy will be positively delighted! Mr Trout's expertise will be most welcome!'

Thank you, Lydia.

So it was that, grieving for Arthur, worried sick about Colette, frantic to solve Dosh Callaghan's gem mystery, I now had a dwarf Tarzan, a beautiful lady apprentice hooked on transparent honesty, and my trusted barker who could be relied upon to be at least as corrupt as me. Guess who was going to be any help.

We stopped at a child's outfitters north of Long Melford, and kitted Trout out on Lydia's charge card. She was thrilled, cooing about textures and insisting on two new sets of everything, seeing if this colour went with the universe. I grumbled we'd be here all frigging day. She got mad and scolded me outside.

Fuming on the pavement outside a bakery – they sold me some flour cakes, keep the wolf from the door – I saw a partial answer. The old flintstone church dwarfed (sorry) the village. I beckoned Tinker. We crossed and knocked at the presbytery door. Vicars are always in, having no job.

'Good day, reverend,' I said, gulping the last of my grub. Tinker had already engulfed his. 'My name is Lovejoy. Might I ask about burials, please?'

'Do come in.' He was an elderly, grave man with wisps of silvery hair fungating from everywhere. Nostrils, ears, collar rim, cuffs, he looked bulging with minute tendrils spreading beyond his confines. 'A close relative, was it?'

'Yes,' I said sadly, pointing to Tinker. 'It's my, er, uncle, Mr Dill. He wants a rural burial. Is that allowed?'

Everything's allowed these days, so they can only say yes.

'Yes!' he cried, all keen. 'Do sit down.' His housekeeper made us tea. She looked askance at Tinker.

'Uncle doesn't speak much,' I told Reverend Watkinson, giving Tinker the bent eye. 'He's always seemed eccentric. He is a poet,' I invented, the only occupation Tinker could respectably have with his rubbishy appearance. 'Lives in Bercolta.'

'Very good.' The cleric rubbed his hands. 'No possibility of an early demise, I trust?'

'No,' I said. The vicar had the grace to look disappointed. 'But you can't plan too soon, can you? Uncle wants to be buried in a woodland glade.' I waited. Reverend Watkinson wasn't surprised, just nodded and sipped his tea. 'He'd heard of one such interment locally, you see.'

'Well, it's becoming quite a fashion. I deplore it. There seems to be a definite trend away from the church funeral nowadays. Several organizations exist to promote burials in forests, beside rivers and coastal estuaries, on farms. The Natural Death Centre in London issues an information pack, I do believe.' His eyes twinkled at Tinker. 'A poet such as yourself, Mr Dill, will perhaps want to consult Green Undertakings of Watchet in Somerset, since that village is such a famous poetic landmark!' He huffled with amusement. I smiled along. Maybe I should have given Tinker a different trade. Somerset's poetic landmarks?

The vicar stared reflectively at the ceiling. 'There are wildlife trusts, as in Harrogate, that can find you a woodland. And artists who manufacture biodegradable coffins, societies that will plant certain trees the deceased admired. There's even a superstore in Walthamstow. And a West Country females-only funeral business called *Martha's Funerals*.'

'Didn't you officiate at one locally?' I prompted. This solemn old rector was a super salesman.

'Yes. A Mr Arthur Goldhorn. Buried in woodland, poor

chap. Lord of the Manor, Saffron Fields. He and his wife went into a scandalous antiques business, in Chelsea. Lost everything to a foreign gentleman, most uncooperative.' He sighed, wagged his head. 'Refused to allow the burial on the manor. Only four attended. I thought it degrading. No hymns, except one sung by a callow youth. I feel that Mr Goldhorn deserved a church funeral.'

'Was it legal?'

'Of course! Our own GP certified death. No undertakers.' Reverend Watkinson polished his spectacles. 'You see, in church funerals there is propriety, Lovejoy. Casual services go against the grain.'

We left assuring him of our future custom, he assuring us of his willingness to do his stuff when the time came. Trout and Lydia emerged from the outfitter's. Tinker helped them into the motor with the boxes.

'You look dynamite, Trout,' I said. 'Smart.'

'Here,' Tinker said as Lydia rocketed us off at a giddy ten mph. 'Know what? Lovejoy's just fixed to have me buried in some forest.'

Lydia's eyes got me in the rear-view mirror.

'Just a joke,' I said. 'Look. Who knows a bloke called Dieter Gluck?'

'Me,' Trout said unexpectedly, with venom. 'He got my pal Failsafe done for loitering outside that shop Gluck pinched in Chelsea.'

Well, that was hardly evil. I knew Failsafe, a meek bloke who functions as a racing tipster (Saturdays) and antiques thief (Sundays). He has bad feet, pays chiropodists a fortune, gets no better. His trick is to suss out places to rob.

'Anything really bad?'

'Isn't that enough?' Trout's gravelly bass boomed

indignantly. 'You should have seen Failsafe's feet when he come out! Like two plates of warts.'

I said queasily, 'I mean something truly rotten.'

'No,' Trout said.

Tinker and Lydia also said no. Then Trout did it again. 'Except he kills people.'

We clung on in silence while Lydia regained control of the motor. I eventually managed, 'Erm, kills, Trout?'

'As in dead.' Trout was preening his jacket. 'Miss Lydia, would a salmon scarf go with this?'

We eventually reached town in safety, saying nothing further except some colours don't go with blue and suchlike. I suggested we catch the train to London, where I had an old friend to find, meaning Colette.

In the station buffet I finally remembered to ask Tinker how come he'd happened along those narrow Suffolk lanes and found us.

'I phoned Lydia. Her answer-phone said you'd gone to Carting's Farm.'

Thank you yet again, Lydia. Now the entire world knew my secret movements. I watched her bring three teas on a tray, Tinker's drink a pint of ale. Before the train came in, he'd conned Lydia into buying him two more jars by spectacular fits of coughing.

'Ta, Miss Lydia,' he said soulfully wiping spittle. 'It keeps my tubes clear.'

'Not at all, Tinker.' She gave me a scathing glance. 'We must care for our gallant old soldiers.'

That was because I kept telling her not to buy him more beer, since it was a clear con. She meant I was heartless.

The London express came screeching in. We boarded. People looked at Trout, but he was happy in his new clobber and didn't mind. I kept cursing myself for not actually realizing that the oldish woman ferreting among the dross in the New Caledonian antiques market must actually have been Colette Goldhorn herself, not merely somebody who'd reminded me of her.

Odd thing, but none of us asked Trout about who killed whom, or why, or where. It was as if we knew.

11

WE LURKED AT Tower Bridge, if it's possible to do such a thing. Hordes of pedestrians gaped at us. They should have watched the sword swallower performing nearby. An escape artist was wriggling in chains while a drum beat and the crowds cheered. This is one remarkable thing about our creaking old kingdom – you can be stuck miles out in the bundu among rivers and forests, and ninety minutes later among the Tower's tourist crowds.

'Why *are* we here, Lovejoy?' Lydia asked. She looked so lovely I was ashamed of me. The throng's glances were full of mystification, Beauty with three Beasts. I pretended we weren't a menagerie. I didn't dare explain about the trouble I was in with Holloway University.

'Because we need to find out three things, love. One is a man called Floggell, whose help I need to, er, find a painting. Tinker, Floggell's down to you.'

'No, Lovejoy,' Lydia persisted. 'I mean we could have gone an extra Tube stop, and saved fare.'

'The antiques dealers would have seen us arrive together, Lydia,' I said, striving for sanity.

Trout's laconic gaze fixed me, clearly thinking we'd do

better without Lydia's painful morality. Tinker began coughing, suffering from beer ache.

'I *see*!' she trilled, delighted. 'Deception! So as not to be noticed!'

'That's it, Lydia,' I said with gravity.

'What do I do, Lovejoy?' Trout asked. 'That pig Gluck knows me.'

'Padpas, Trout. Remember I said Dosh Callaghan got zuzzed when somebody sold him some tsavorites?'

'Right, Lovejoy.'

'Lydia, love, go down the King's Road, Chelsea. The Lovely Colette. Find out what antiques they're buying or selling.'

'Lovely Colette Antiques (Chelsea)?' She has several grimaces, all of them enticing. We watched, lusting in our various ways, as her expression cleared. 'Clocks, Lovejoy. They bid for clocks, plus early scientific instruments. Shall I ask them for a list?'

'No, love,' I said, broken. 'Try subterfuge. Pretend. Surreptitiously.' I couldn't think of any other synonym except disguise, and her wondrous figure made that a clear impossibility.

'Isn't that rather *underhanded*, Lovejoy?'

'Yes, I'm afraid it is, Lydia.' I avoided Trout's eyes. 'But we owe it to Arthur. He was a friend.'

She was doubtful. 'I shall have to find a way without lying.'

'Right, everybody. Meet tomorrow teatime, Portobello Road antiques market at the Duke of Wellington pub, or the Earl of Lonsdale near the beer garden.'

Tinker coughed explosively. Even the Tower Hill traffic faltered as his rumbling roar quivered through the ancient streets. I sighed. I'd mentioned booze.

'I'll need to clear me bronchials before then, Lovejoy.'

'Oh, do let me!' Lydia rummaged in her handbag. He osmosed the notes without moving a muscle. 'One thing, Lovejoy. Do you mean actually *inside* a common tavern?'

'No, love,' I said politely. 'I'll meet you at the Corner Market. There's a line of street stalls. One specializes in dolls, a silver stall, then one selling oriental porcelains.'

I warned them all not to get lost. Portobello Road can be a right maelstrom.

'Lovejoy. Where,' Lydia asked daintily, 'shall you sleep tonight? Time is getting on. Bermondsey market will already be closed.'

'I'll work through the night. Trout has friends. And Tinker knows a pal who keeps a fish and chip shop.'

They knew better than contradict my lies.

'But what if we miss each other tomorrow?'

'Then meet in Camden Passage the day following, same time.'

Camden Passage's unbelievable surge is a stunning antiques success story. It's now the front runner, having outstripped the East End, Portobello, Bermondsey.

Mechanically I leant to buss her cheek as usual but she swiftly gave my hand a solemn shake instead.

'Very well, Lovejoy. Tomorrow, the corner hostelry in Portobello Road. Good afternoon.'

We chorused awkward goodbyes and watched her walk off up Trinity Square towards the Tube station. Trout cleared his throat. I waited. I wasn't going to have any criticism.

'Lovejoy,' he said after a bit. 'Is she real?'

'What's it to you, Trout?' I said evenly.

'Not knocking her, honest. Lovely gal. I mean it, straight up, mate. Only, will she be all right on her own?'

'She's clever and resolute.' We all listened to what I would say. I went for it. 'She's my apprentice. She's down to me.'

'Good she knowed about them clocks, eh?' Tinker said to break the ice, spitting phlegm into the gutter. 'Time for a jar, lads.'

The money was burning his pocket, and pubs abound along the Thames. I left them to it. I wanted results.

Clocks, though? I started south across Tower Bridge. Everybody in the country has an old clock that doesn't go, kept because great-grandad liked it. Or some old watch forgotten in a drawer that the Swiss museums would give an absolute fortune for – meaning like a hundred thousand American zlotniks, sight unseen if only somebody would take it to be auctioned. I crossed over to see my favourite view, the Pool of London, Wapping Old Stairs facing Cherry Garden Pier.

The trouble with antique clocks is that fakers love them for two cogent reasons: their complexity, and the ignorance of the buying public. Timepieces, clocks, watches, the lot, are a paradise for forgers. I'd have to see what Lydia came up with. I found something in my pocket as I reached the start of Tower Bridge Road. It was a card. *Sharon J. Butts, attorney at law*, of Lincoln's Inn. Good old Shar, who'd sprung me from that eternity of suffering I'd undergone in that infernal dungeon! Well, one night in the cell. The plod had given me tomato soup, slices of bread, and egg and chips.

My spirits rose. It was six o'clock. I went on, a spring in my step.

*

Shar was at home. I was warily relieved. After all, she might have had some bloke on her rope. I looked penitent. She wasn't glad to see me, but let me in.

'I'm going out soon, Lovejoy.' She was dressed to the nines, that shop-ready look women achieve before the off. 'I expected you in chambers.'

Had she? 'Sorry. I had to see a friend.'

She hesitated. I stood like a spare tool.

'Can't it wait until tomorrow, Lovejoy?'

'Just one thing, love. Is there any way I can find out if some bloke's been in trouble with the law recently? It's rather important.'

That caused her some doubt, but nothing must be allowed to impede a woman on a date. She made all sorts of promises to find out. Then it was goodnight, Lovejoy, don't call me, I'll call you. I left, obviously supplanted by some rich Lothario, but not before the oddest thing happened.

'The name, Lovejoy?' she asked. 'You haven't told me who.'

'Dieter Gluck.' I gave her the address. And just for an instant she paused, but took it down calmly enough. I didn't know how to spell Dieter, but she did. We parted amicably.

I didn't hang around, zoomed into Piccadilly's crowds as I headed towards Shaftesbury Avenue and the office where Caprice Rhodes would be slogging producing stage shows. Can you believe that people do it for a living?

'Caprice told me to stop by,' I told the girl on the desk. 'The show, see?'

'Right, Lovejoy.' I'd given her my name. She nodded as if she really knew me. It always works. Everybody in theatre is scared stiff of everybody finding out that they don't know everybody else. 'Caprice is on the phone. Take a seat.'

They're always on the phone. I sat and read the posters of past shows. Amazing what some folk do. Phones rang. People with torticollis rushed about the warren of rooms, talking into phones on their shoulders. I can't understand why they do it.

'Lovejoy?' Caprice stood there, smiling.

'Sorry about the time, love.' I followed. She started on the phone while I waited some more.

Caprice is married to a bloke she possibly never sees. Thirtyish, bonny, always looking sort of smooth and dolled up. She has – honest, I'm not making it up – a woman who comes into the office every single day to do her toe nails. I thought queasily of Trout's pal Failsafe's feet, 'two plates of warts'. Maybe Caprice could slip Failsafe in for a free go?

'Look, daaaaahling,' Caprice was ending into the receiver. 'Your poor cow might have got a fortune in Plymouth's pantomime, but that doesn't mean we all must join her parade.' She listened, sighed. 'You piss me off. So your poor cow dated His Royal Highness *once*, Mori, then got the shunt. Am I expected to pay her a fortune to forget her fucking lines? She's dead in the water.'

She clicked the phone, came and sat on my lap. A secretary dashed in with faxes. Caprice riffled through them, discarded all but one. The lass dashed out.

'Can't you give the actress a job, love?' I asked. 'She might be great.'

'She can't walk, talk, sing, dance, move, or open her mouth except for two functions, Lovejoy.' She ruffled my thatch. 'Even for an actress this is somewhat limited. What're you after, scrounger?'

I was chastened. 'Sorry. Remember when we met?'

She carolled a pretty laugh. 'Their faces! Better than a play!'

It had been in the most august London auction. A mad variety of Russian art was being sold. They'd imported a galaxy – their description – of paintings, sculptures. In true auctioneering style, meaning cavalier but mentally dim, they'd forgotten one small fact. Russian art ranged across a century, but hereabouts feminism had raised its head. Quick as a flash pickets gathered in Bond Street chanting slogans about sisterhood subjection and degradation of women. Some artists had painted nudes, you see, and such images were imperialist, whatever.

'You stopped me, you bastard!' She laughed, remembering. 'Trying to stab the painting!'

'Maybe I shouldn't have,' I mused. 'Serov's underpainting is duff. Green's essential—'

Caprice shouted for coffee, still falling about on my lap, not without hazards of various kinds. 'You knocked me senseless, you bastard.'

'Well, I couldn't see the point.' I still couldn't. Stabbing a painting is like burning books, always criminal. I hadn't liked the Vladimir Serov painting, a crowned nude, but who am I?

'Thank Christ for that, Lovejoy. It proves you're sane.' She lit a fag. I stared. She didn't use to smoke. Smoking had been a wicked male stratagem promoting women's serfdom. The coffee came. I got a theatrical special, so thick it wouldn't swallow. Caprice drank hers with a flourish, still on my lap. We talked of changing times.

Fashion alters art. It also does something scary – it changes prices. This is good news and bad news. Before the millennium, 'political correctness' became a stigmatizing accusation shrieked by anyone who wanted media time to air their prejudices, whether barmy or not. The world became miserable. Doomsters were everywhere on radio, telly, the good old tabloids. And the value – the money you actually hand over – of antiques changed. It took a year to happen. (I'm telling you this because it can happen again any time, but the mechanism's the same.)

The bad news? Quite drossy paintings shot up in price. Okay, they weren't artistically up to much – say, some poor quality Ukrainian cottage – but they were the sort of oldie that dealers tend to buy to 'body out', as dealers call it, their shops or next phoney Antiquarian Road Show Travelling Auction. Paintings of some lovely nude plummeted. It became politically incorrect to like some portrait of a crusty old cleric or kindly father. Even yet these are badly under-sold. Thousands of portraits – regimental officers, colonial stalwarts, doddering priests, millmasters – have been cleaned off so the canvas can be used by fakers. Forgers call it 'emptying' an ancient canvas. And the fakers use those genuinely old canvases to paint 'Victorian' scenes that *are* politically correct – ladies reading, children at the seashore, or boring old golf. Forgeries, in brief, where nobody has a job.

I call it sinner's stiffness, this move to make everybody glare accusingly at history through modern eyes. It's evil because it kills antiques. Because it burns books. And because it's phoney. Sorry to go on. I once came across a forged painting on an old canvas. I recognized the canvas from the marks a dealer called Tollbooth had made on its reverse (dealers often do this in pencil, so a pal in their auction ring will know how much to bid). He uses the code CRAFTY, the letters' meaning being 1 to 6, because Tollbooth never bids over 666 for anything.

The painting had come from Armenia, and was of an

elderly woman coming from a tin bath. It was obvious the artist had seen Rembrandt's painting. It was condemned by political rectitude, and went for a song. Cleaned off, the canvas was used by some forger who daubed on it a golf house in mid-Edwardian style. It went for a relative fortune. See? Fashion slaughters art, and substitutes gunge. Collectors out there, please note: if you want regimental histories, religious allegories, nudes, anything condemned in the great hogwash period of the 1990s, get out there and buy, because they'll never be as cheap again once the world recovers its senses.

'As long as there's a few like you left, Lovejoy, we can identify the norm,' Caprice was saying.

Eh? Whatever it was, I agreed. 'Look, love, I wonder—'

'Get on with it, Lovejoy,' she said. 'We've three shows, all doing bad business. The boss is near bankruptcy, driving us mad. He's got some new tart. I've to find a West End play she can star in. She has the thespian skills of *Amoeba proteus* and the dress sense of Mrs Gamp.' She sighed. 'God knows what she does in bed, but it must be brilliant.'

She waited. She ahemed. 'Come in, Planet Lovejoy.'

'Oh, sorry.' I'd got distracted by the thought. 'Er, a gun, love.'

That shook her so much she ground out her fag. I watched it die. 'You *what*, Lovejoy? I never thought I'd hear—'

Caprice Rhodes married this landowner near Grime's Graves. They own heathlands, fields, valleys, there to breed pheasants, quail, and other innocent birds, all the better to slaughter them by twelve-bore shotguns. Saves the old legs, don't ya ken, killing the birds all in one spot.

'There's eleven thousand country guns available, Lovejoy. Why mine?'

A 'gun', incidentally, isn't your actual tubes. The term actually means a place at a shoot. People pay – no joke – up to two and a half thousand zlotniks of the realm *a day* for the privilege of going out for a quick massacre. Huntin' and shootin' meets are where cabinet ministers of any political stripe are made, they say. Other, even more passionate, relationships are also fostered.

'It's near somewhere I'm investigating.'

She pondered, posing, chin on her finger. Pretty. I began to wish she'd get off my lap, or sit closer still.

'The Goldhorns?' she guessed, quick. 'They were the only people of our . . .' *of our class who would bother with a lowlife like you, Lovejoy* were the words she wanted. She finished, 'district who knew you. Is it them?'

'Yes.'

'Arthur died, didn't he? Broken heart, after some sod took your place when you left Colette.' She nodded. 'Well, since you ask, Lovejoy, I'll get you a gun.'

'Now?'

That gave her a laugh. She shook her hair like they do, as if trying to throw it away over her shoulder. 'Phone this number early tomorrow. Lovejoy?' She looked as I bussed her goodbye. 'You won't disgrace me, will you? I mean, Clovis is a stickler for behaviour.'

Well, so am I. I was just scared I'd shoot so badly I might actually hit one of the creatures. I mean the pheasants.

'I'll behave, love. And thanks.'

'You'll enjoy the dinner, Lovejoy. Tit for tat.'

'Eh?' She'd not said anything about a dinner. I saw her glint.

'The awards night. You're taking me. It's soon. I'll send the invitation.'

'Ta, love. Tarra.' I'd joined the county set.

12

Evening in London, coming on to rain. Bee the lovely Aldwych flower seller was there as usual. India House looked glamorous floodlit. Theatres were agog, last minute ladies rushing in, skirts lifted, squealing. The butty bars were giving place to pubs. Covent Garden was thronged – when is it not? Crowds, traffic, the Thames doing its swarky stuff waiting for yet another poet to rubbish it from Westminster Bridge. I love the place. And I was determined to find out what the hell, wasn't I.

So, the light of eagles in my eye, I slouched into the Nell of Old Drury tavern for some swill and a wad. It was crowded by theatricals and street lads off the barrows. Antique dealers were making last minute trade-offs – why *do* they always glance round furtively before showing their dud little silver salt cellar to a no-hope buyer? Is it to aggrandize a threepenny transaction, make it look like they're Springheel Jack? Thinking about it, I do the same. Pathetic. One was Flymo from Romford. He's expert at the old assume trick, always with a little lawn mower. He knocks on your door, puffs in carrying a mower saying, 'Where do you want it, missus?' while you express astonishment and deny all. During the baffling explanations, Flymo susses your locks, whether you live alone or not, if you've got much worth nicking. Then he'll creep back at night and burgle your house.

No good asking these dealers about Colette, though. A titled lady, wealthy, owner of vintage cars maintained by uniformed serfs, she was in another league. I sat and dreamed in the warm fug.

You send somebody out on a quest for one reason only – to bring something back. Hence Sir Galahad, the Holy Grail, Go ye hence, brave knights. The point is, you're desperate for your hunter to find whatever it is, or you wouldn't bother sending out your expedition in the first place.

Unless?

This 'unless' was troubling me. Unless you deliberately want to send out a nerk. Like, I realized, spirits plunging, me. Dosh could have made a few calls and sorted it out from home. Instead he sends me, specifically to Bermondsey, precisely where the gem courier Chev wouldn't be back for some time.

Why?

Missing padpas, said Dosh. He'd paid for them, and instead received tsavorites. Simple. Find the genuine ones, hand them to Dosh, easy. Unless?

I sipped my ale in the crowd.

Once upon a time there'd been this bloke, Pope Sylvestrus II. He quested cleverly, and found his Grail. Except it turned out a poisoned chalice. It happened like this:

Anciently, all Rome speculated about a statue in the Campus Martius. It stood there, its arm pointing. The words *Percute Hic* were on the base – means strike out, pierce, shoot, bore down. It also means dig. Over centuries, lots of Romans had a go, measuring the arm's trajectory, even burgling nearby buildings. No luck. Then Pope Sylvestrus II worked it out: the statue's finger's shadow alighted at one exact spot at noon. In the dark hours the pope and his chamberlain stole back and dug. They fell into an ancient vault, where an ancient king and queen, court and all, were mummified amid their treasures, brilliantly illumined by an eerie light from a giant ruby. The chamberlain joyously grabbed for the gold. A mummified cupid, bow and arrow ready, moved. His bow twanged, the arrow shattering the ruby into a ghastly darkness. The dead figures rose up, rustling in the subterranean blackness. Pope Sylvestrus legged it. He escaped yards ahead of his servant. Which is why some make pope and others stay mere chamberlains, I suppose.

See? Give a quest a bit of thinko, you get it right, but watch out.

Sometimes you can have the answer – treasure, wealth, antiques – in the palm of your hand, and still make a mess of things. I've done that. Like, our Ministry of Defence alone has thousands of antiques, and still creates a shambles. Last count, it had lost 205 valuable pictures. The entire Government does it too, managing to evaporate 427 pictures, nearly 700 if you take into account other bureaus. These are *our* precious paintings. The Civil Service simply lends them to itself, and forgets where. But they don't lose them all in one fell swoop. They're vanished over a long time, loss not by gush but by drip. They all ought to have stayed, of course, in the terribly secret guarded place nobody knows about (it's in Wardour Street, Soho, London). Authority is good at making barmy laws for the rest of us, useless with responsibility.

Our government could easily notify the Art Loss Register, but that would announce how cackhanded they actually were. Mind you, other folk lose things they shouldn't. In July, 1996, the famous missing pages of George Washington's inaugural address turned up – under a couch in somebody's parlour in Aldeburgh, here in Suffolk – and got auctioned off for a mint. Gormlessness rules.

For me, I wonder at hunters. They often go on hopeless quests, when the whereabouts of giant wealth are known. Along the jungles of the Shangani River, in January, 1894, the great Matabele king Lobengula passed away. By tradition his grave was secret, same as his father's, M'Silikatze. Over the years, Lobengula had received an annual gift – a piece of gold, a diamond – from each of the thousands of his warriors who downed spears and went to work in the South African mines. King Lobengula's treasure was buried with him. I'm not advocating grave robbing, just wondering why robbers don't rob where common sense dictates.

Other times, though, hunting is money for jam. Borrow a metal detector. Go to any village in East Anglia. Troll your detector along the soil near any old garden wall. You'll find old zinc alloy labels from espalier fruit trees, which came into fashion in pre-Victorian days. They're very collectible. Two dozen will net you a posh Continental holiday. Tip: Don't polish them. Just rinse them lightly in baby soap, then drip purest grade Italian olive oil over the surface, and the Indian Ink writing will come up beautifully, legible as the day some hoary old gardener wrote it. Course, there are fakes—

'Lovejoy?'

'Wotcher, Flymo.'

'Seen you down Bermondsey. Business bad out in the sticks, is it?' He chuckled harshly.

'No. Here for the padpas.'

'Dosh should never have bought them in the first place. We all knowed they was substituted.'

Did you now, I thought. I chanced it. 'I've been looking for Colette Goldhorn, but can't see hide nor hair. Times change, eh, Flymo?'

He sighed. I bought him a pint so he could sigh without spraying me with his spittle aerosol.

'I'm thinking of giving up the con game, Lovejoy. I'm too frigging old. Know what happened?' He waxed indignant. 'Three days since, I do me knock, and this bird opens the door. I race my lawn mower in, saying my, "Here's your lawn mower, love, where should I put it?", all according to plan.'

'So? Con as usual.'

'Not frigging likely.' He tapped my chest in outrage. 'Know what? She simpers, "Just leave it there in the hall. Come through. We can have a nice cosy chat." She was after a bit of the other, Lovejoy! From me! When I'd got work to do!'

I almost choked laughing. 'Behold your sins will find you out, Flymo.'

He was narked. 'It's all very well for you, Lovejoy. Shagging's your thing. But me? It takes me all my time to get round a single street these days. Mind you, Colette's been a godsend.'

'Colette? You sell to Colette Goldhorn?'

This is like hearing that a duchess does a bit of cleaning for pin money. Colette, buying nicked dross from the likes of Flymo?

'One of my few outlets these days,' he said mournfully. 'You wouldn't be interested in a little Chinese bowl?'

With Fagin-like glances about the crowded bar, he

fetched out a small lavishly decorated K'ien Lung Cantonese bowl. It felt genuine enough to warm me, and looked absolutely perfect. I waited for a lull in the chatter, though, and held it to my ear just as a precaution. You *must* do this simple test on any porcelain, because light can trick your eyes. I tapped it with my knuckle and listened. Sure enough, the clear distant 'pong' wasn't distinct. It went buzzzzzz. It's horrible. It means you mustn't buy, not even if the dealer offers you 90 per cent discount, because the bowl's side is fractured. Never mind that you can't see any crack, or that you can't feel one with your finger nail. If the faint 'pong' isn't clear as a bell, if it goes buzzzzzz, you're holding a poor wreck of a thing. And please ignore the dealer's prattle. He'll be frantic, saying how he's had the antique bowl authenticated by the British Museum, offering certificates from Sotheby's and all.

'It's got a mended crack, Flymo.'

'Thought you'd spot it,' he said gloomily. 'You wouldn't take it off me for a third third, would you, Lovejoy?'

Antique dealers work in thirds, never wanting to buy any antique at more than a third of its value, and always wanting to sell at full price. Flymo was offering me this at a third of what he might have paid, if his purchase had been legit instead of stolen. A third of a third is one-ninth.

'Thought you were going to sell to Colette?' Clever old me.

'Not tonight, Lovejoy. She's in that Soho churchyard. Winos give me the frigging creeps.'

Tut tut, those terrible drinkers hard at it. I bought him another pint, took the Cantonese bowl off him for one-ninth of its market value, and had the precise night location of Colette Goldhorn, Lady of Saffron Fields Manor. I would use the antique bowl as an excuse to talk to Colette. See how cunning I am? A little thinko, you get there. And now Flymo owed me. I was pleased with myself, forgetting that confidence is just another name for stupidity.

13

G O UP SHAFTESBURY Avenue from
Piccadilly Circus, the fire station's on
your right nearing Cambridge Circus.
Left, you pass Soho's old church of St Anne's. Facing it,
quite a narrow street, you see a minute churchyard. Couple
of benches, not much greenery, overlooked by nearby theatres and back office windows, it's one of those tiny refuges
with which London abounds.

It's also a place where deadlegs kip of a night. Nothing
against them – I've been one, done it – but it's no place to
meet your Gran in the lamp hours.

Seven or eight folks were distributed about. One or two
drank from bottles concealed in brown paper bags. Others
eyed them with envy. Others kipped, supine. There's
enough light from the streets to see. One thing, London's
always crowded, folk moving past with laughter, shouts
from taverns, still one amazing fruit barrow busily trading.
Incidentally, if you don't know the places I'm telling of, the
distances are mere paces. I'm not talking miles. London's a
place for walking, not taking taxis.

Gingerly, I went from figure to figure in steady drizzle.
The dossers were under plastic, wrapped in newspapers
beneath. One glistened in black dustbin liners. I excluded

the alert drinkers, which left five. One was a man, from his massive wellington boots. Two separate plastic-sheeted figures emanated giddy smoke. Surely Colette couldn't be a druggo as well, for Christ's sake? That left two. One was snoring, choking on every inhalation. Colette snored but kind of forgetfully, not serious.

One left.

The figure was huddled in a corner. It had a cushion, and sat lopsidedly on the end of a stone step. A black cloth bag bulged nearby.

The drinkers on the benches were watching. I cleared my throat. Ready, steady.

'Stay, pay, and make hay?' I asked it. I knew better than use her name.

No response. I tugged its bag string. The figure exploded, unravelled, came alert spitting, then froze.

'Smear me into a grease blob. Wasn't that what you said?'

The apparition was like nothing on earth. She sat there looking seventy years old, hair matted. I realized I'd recoiled, tried to apologize with a pace forward. She wore thick dungarees now, stuffed into old boots.

'Oh, Lovejoy,' she said. 'You came.'

'Think I wouldn't? I'd have come sooner.'

'Too late.' It was only half-nine, but she didn't mean o'clock.

'So come along all the quicker.'

She simply rose and walked with me, not even looking towards the other dossers. Her bag dangled. She used to take two hours to get ready, even for an auction. Things change, or have I said that?

We went to a sandwich nook near Old Compton Street, still jumping – well, hopping a bit. I had a good gape at her in the light, ignoring the askance looks the counter girls gave Colette. I ordered a reasonable amount of nosh, mainly butties, soup, bakewells, a battenburg for her because she likes, liked, sweet victuals.

She ate in a desultory way, me keeping up from politeness.

'Going to tell me, then?' I said after a while, narked. 'I found Arthur.'

'You can't say grave, Lovejoy?' she said quietly. 'You never could look things straight in the eye. Get me a pole screen, William IV, rose finial, tricorn base, rococo shield design. It would save my life.' There's an old Lancashire proverb – women, priests and poultry never have enough – but here was a titled lady who'd given everything away. I lose faith in proverbs.

'Not asking much,' I groused. 'Crowned heads of Europe queue for those.'

'He'll sack me otherwise.'

'This Dieter git?' I judged her. Her features were lined. She looked pavement tribe, unwashed, lines down her cheeks in that most telling of grooves from eye to upper lip that is the nightmare of the Sloane Square sheilas. 'Let him sack you. I'll give you a job.'

Thus spake Lovejoy the indigent pauper, on his welts and having to scrounge off his apprentice to keep going. Me, get her a job? Maybe it would be as good as mine.

'I mean I'd try, love.' I might con a dealer as a favour.

'It's no good, Lovejoy. I'm like you, a street lover. I can't do without antiques. I'd die if Dieter sacked me. I mean it.'

She'd got it bad. I noshed mechanically. I've never known dedication except for two reasons. One, sex. Two, antiques. Dunno which order, probably joint winners. She didn't look as if she'd got two Chippendales to rub together, so I reckoned that she and this Dieter Gluck . . .

'Silly cow,' I said, in a caring, compassionate way. 'You've no longer got an antiques business. You've nowhere to kip, no clothes. You look like you've not eaten for a fortnight. You're ferreting in dross with the lowlifes. Haven't you taken a look at yourself?' This was a once-stunning woman I used to make exuberant smiles with.

'I must stay with my antiques trade.' She said it flatly, like her soul had been starched rigid in emotion.

'Are you and Gluck, y'know?'

'Were.' She smiled bitterly. 'Until he'd got Saffron Fields and our firm.'

'I know. I went. The vicar told me about the funeral.'

'I've been stupid, Lovejoy.' She spoke on quickly as I drew breath. 'But I must stay here, and work for Dieter.'

'Street grubbing isn't working. It's dying.' I thought a bit. 'What are you protecting, love?'

Her smile went bitter. 'You suspicious sod, Lovejoy.'

I gave her the Cantonese bowl. It looked even tinier in the sandwich bar's glarey lighting. 'Got it from Flymo. He was too spooked to find you in the churchyard. Didn't,' I said pointedly, 'want to sink so low in society.'

'Oh, Lovejoy.' Her eyes filled. 'I've made such a mess of things. It's no good. There's no way out. I was dreading you coming to interfere. I pinned my faith on Tinker being in gaol.'

True. With Tinker banged up, I wondered how many more tragedies I'd not heard of lately.

'There's always a way out, love.'

'Arthur used to say that. I've learned different.'

'It's Dieter Gluck, isn't it?'

'I trusted him. Arthur didn't, of course. But then,' she

said sadly, 'Arthur also had your number. From the start, he knew about you and me. Never said a single word. A gentleman.'

Her eyes went past me, widened in alarm. I heard the door go with that sucking swish they make. A hand grabbed my neck and lifted me bodily from the chair. The other customers stared. Colette's expression became fright.

In the reflection of the chrome coffee urn – the girls ducked behind it, sensing trouble – I saw that Bern bloke, carrying me to the door like a rabbit.

'*Komm!*' he barked to Colette. Obediently she shuffled after, bag a-dangle.

Out in the narrow street he shook me, saying loudly, 'Thief! Not steal from old lady, ya?'

I managed, 'I were just trying to flog the old biddy an antique—'

Across the thoroughfare I glimpsed Gluck's face. He was smiling from the window of an enormous Bentley, a pretty blonde beside him also enjoying the show. Moiya December, also not rushing to my aid. Bern flung me off the pavement bellowing guttural accusations of thievery. I scrabbled upright. A passing gent and his missus tutted. Bouncers from a night club hovered angrily.

'Should be flogged,' said the gent. 'Get a job like any decent—' etc.

'Thief!' Bern boomed. 'Stop thief!'

Is anything more of a stimulus, to an innocent? I eeled off down Peter Street, dodged into Ingestre Place, back down Lexington Street like a whippet, and in seconds was strolling, oh so casual, into the bright illumination of Regent Street, struggling to make my gasps look normal breathing. I went south, behind the Royal Academy.

Plenty of evening crowds still about, taxis, buses,

youngsters lounging round Eros, gay old London Toon on the go. I was still hurting from my first encounter with Dieter and Bern. Sulks were coming on, really sorry for myself. No doubt about it, I was in a worse state than China – or are you not allowed to think that any more? I went into a tavern and sat. Flymo, rotten swine, must have bubbled me to Dieter Gluck. I owed Flymo for that.

Who, I wondered, in her right mind exchanges wealth, antiques business, her home, her possessions, in order to become a London dosser? I had no doubts any longer. She was the scavenger I'd seen humping stacks of old vinyl records in Bermondsey. Everybody else must have known it was Colette except me.

Some lads sat nearby, joking, smoking their heads off, eyeing the girls on the bar stools. From their chat they were theatre scene shifters. I used to do that in the Albury.

'It's too frigging little,' one was saying. 'Like a sewing box, innit?'

His mate argued. 'It's only bones and ash.'

'Rotten sodding play,' another groused. 'Here, is this best bitter or what?'

Bones and ash? They were talking of a reliquary. I said, 'Bones and ash?'

'Eh? Yeh, mate. No wonder the takings are down. They've this little tin box—'

They argued on, not really caring either way. I left then, walked down through Pall Mall and Trafalgar Square to Charing Cross, and sat on the Embankment looking across the Thames. The drizzle had mercifully stopped. I needed Tinker to get going, but he'd be beavering away, bar to taproom, indefatigably doing my bidding looking for Floggell.

Reliquary? Somewhere was reviving *Murder in the Cathedral*, trying to cash in on the publicity about Thomas à

Becket. I could feel the fibrillation of the Tube trains under my feet. Well, I'd cash in on publicity too if I owned a theatre.

Which made me strive to remember.

Thomas à Becket was an unpleasant man. Fraud, traitor, greedy moneygrabber, friend to embezzlers, he gets my vote for being eminently non-holy, though I should talk. He was the Archbishop of Canterbury, slaughtered in his own cathedral by four knights soon after Christmas in 1170.

When he'd, er, died, Thomas's relics were put into what's properly called a chasse. This is sort of a fancy little chest, with embossed figures in gold relief, the richly coloured enamels pointing up the importance of the relics therein. Was all this decoration, back in the Middle Ages, a waste of time and money? Not on your life, because saintly relics were highly marketable. People scrapped, bribed, forged, all in the name of holiness, filthy lucre being behind it all. I often joke that filthy lucre isn't as filthy as all that, but it definitely rules. The tourist trade – back then called pilgrimage – depended on your monastery having more saintly relics than rival abbeys in the next county. Shops, inns, roads, merchants, cities, whole towns even, all thrived where holy saints led.

I'm not being cynical, just wondering if I'd found the answer to Gluck.

The St Thomas chasse was thought to have been commissioned originally – I'm talking centuries – for Peterborough Abbey. It wandered hither and yon, then surfaced in St Neots. Finally the 1980s dawned and the British Railway Pension group collared it. It wasn't holiness that switched ownership. It was money. Genuine saints in superb genuine twelfth-century caskets don't come cheap. They change hands for millions. The thought of selling some saint's bones is sordid, gruesome and horrid. But it's what we do, because we're rotten.

Cut to now. The chasse notched over four million at auction. Hypocrisy instantly hit the fan. People who'd never been to church for yonks went ape. Politicians pontificated about heritage. Patriotism was invoked. Newspapers hinted darkly at subversion. The kindly Canadian who'd successfully bid at Sotheby's graciously withdrew, and the National Heritage Memorial Fund smoothly snaffled the copper-and-gilt chasse with St Thomas à Becket inside, so that it could be ignored for ever in the Victoria and Albert museum. No, honest, I'm truly not a cynic. *But where are the other forty-one chasses?* For, in those darksome troubled days eight centuries agone, forty-two such chasses were made. So let me ask this: Did you see one last Sunday at Evensong? Think hard, like they did in Hereford Cathedral – where they found a similar chasse in their crypt. Can Hereford be blamed, if their thoughts lightly turn to 4,180,000 zlotniks, as they seal their new discovery in their Mappa Mundi museum? Politics, as ever, comes to the rescue for as long as it suits. Then people eventually forget, and think oh well, what the hell, sell it and who cares anyway.

Rumour claimed there were nine similar St Thomas reliquaries elsewhere on our unholy old island.

Now, nine's a lot.

I remembered what I'd written on the card in Colette's – okay, Dieter's – office at Lovely Colette Antiques. Some quip about Sorbo being back on the vodka. Sorbo is Arthur Goldhorn's engraver, lives in Streatham Hill. I had the fare. The 159 bus goes right by his door. It was getting late, but I'd come this far with only slight injuries. I had to have something to tell my team when we assembled tomorrow. I was sure they'd turn up with scores of solutions. If they didn't, I would.

14

SORBO'S HOUSE FACED a school in a leafy lane three furlongs from Streatham Hill station. The area was quiet, apart from restaurants resounding to competing Elvis impersonators, traffic sedately trundling goodnight London.

Steps ran up between huge pot plants that ought to have lived honest lives in Kew Gardens. Lights were on. I knocked, and here came Sorbo, sloshed as a newt. He's like Tinker, never drunk, never sober.

'Jesus H,' he said, swaying in the paltry light. 'Or is it Lovejoy?'

He cackled, heaving his immense girth up and down, a Mr Bumble in an old bottle green frock coat straight from Dickens. I've known Sorbo years – well, five – since he engraved some Victorian drinking glasses for me with tendrils and grapey things, converting them from the tenpenny cheapos (incidentally, never pay more than one zlotnik per dozen) to a week's wage each. Sorbo's old-fashioned, meaning skilled. He's also dishonest, also meaning skilled.

'Of the two, it's probably me,' I said, causing him further mirth. 'Still got your Samuel Nock?'

'I have. And I'm keeping it, Lovejoy.'

He's been bragging about this delectable double-barrelled flintlock pistol for years. He knows I'd kill for it, given a chance. Browned under-and-over barrels, worth a king's ransom, truly beautiful. I could feel it in the room, in an old leather bag by the window. It has its tiny powder flask, flints, and two spherical lead bullets. He's a selfish blighter, doesn't deserve an antique of such beauty.

Sorbo's like many bachelors. He exists downstairs in one crammed room. He also cooks there – one gas ring – washes in a tin bath, dines there (folding stool for a table), has a small sink, and kips on a truckle bed. This, note, in a four-bedroomed house a family could romp through. I don't understand it. His room is also his factory, with a pride-of-place bench, racks of miniature tools, a kiln, easels that drop from the ceiling on pulleys. For a moment I wondered uneasily if it was *Jane Eyre* all over again, some lunatic wife up there in her nightie with candles, itching for arson. I shook myself and sat on some reference tomes stacked at bum height.

'You took your time coming, Lovejoy.' It was blame. He sat in a wicker chair, and swilled from a Rodney flask. 'For a friend.'

'I didn't know about Arthur, Sorbo.' I eyed the flask. A Rodney always looks as though it started out a proper bulbous shape but began to melt. Its base is massively flat. Admiral Rodney got it right, because no storm at sea would ever cause it to spill. But it was too light. 'Soda glass?'

'Polystyrene sheet. I found a way to mould it. Only good for distant views of multiple fakes. Still, it has possibilities.'

One thing about Sorbo, he's active, questing. He's called Sorbo because he once bet that any antique on earth could be faked from sorbo, a rubbery synthetic. He's almost right, any antique can be faked from anything.

'Dieter Gluck, Sorbo. I found Colette among the bagsters, St Anne's in Soho, but got dusted by that Bern.'

He swigged, didn't offer me any. My Gran had an earthenware bottle behind her speer. She called it her 'bronchial beverage'. We children hadn't to touch it, on pain of a sip bringing instant death and a coffin on a handcart. I mention this not because it has to do with the story, just to show how envious I am of people with stern principles. I'll invent my own soon, and be the envy of the world.

He sighed. 'Bad news, Lovejoy. It was soon after you and Colette.' He shrugged, an immense business that took time. I noticed a good long case clock, silent, standing against the wall behind him. The room wasn't well lit, just one old oil lamp burning.

'Where'd Gluck come from, Sorbo? A dealer?'

'Selling various old instruments, clockworks, automata, navigational brasses. Colette was flattered, him randy as a duck. They did it even in the shop. I seed them at it.' He shook his head, baffled at the ways of people. 'Arthur was a proper gent. Said nothing.'

'Hard to believe, Sorbo.'

His rheumy eyes fixed me. 'Why? He did the same over you and Colette. Gentleman is as gentleman does. You can't call a gent a lowlife just because *you're* dross, Lovejoy.'

Ouch. I sat, vision hard to come by. It cleared, me blinking like in a gale. Okay, so Colette was enamoured by this new handsome dealer, so clever at mechanical antiques. My question was, what happened to Arthur's feudal lordship of Saffron Fields? How come Dieter Gluck owned everything, so tightly that poor Arthur couldn't even be buried under his own mulberry tree? I asked it.

'The old ploy, Lovejoy. Gold bricking, the Yanks called it in my day.'

I was astonished. 'Arthur would never fall for a con trick!'

'He didn't. But Colette did. Hook, line and sinker.' He examined the Rodney flask in the lantern light, swigged from it with abandon.

'What was the brick?'

The gold brick con trick got its name from the time of the USA gold strikes. You're on a train, puffing across the prairies. Along comes a suave bloke, very Mississippi, waistcoat, cigar. Gets talking. He's made a fantastic gold strike, and look! Here are the very deeds to his claim! And assayer's reports, the gold yield a ton an ounce. All he needs is investors. Fancy an investment, stranger? If you look especially gullible, he'd even show you a gold brick, nugget, powdered ore, take you to his mine, where you'll discover, surprise, real gold nuggets buried in the scree.

Nowadays the bait is more likely to be one genuine antique Russian ikon, plus the promise of thousands more. Or one genuine Impressionist painting plus promise of a hundred. Or a four-carat diamond plus the promise of et enticing cetera. The gold brick con trick is *always one tempter plus a promise*. Remember to say no. It's still done on stock exchanges the world over and works like a dream. I've seen the Gold Brick work brilliantly well even when executed by duds. Because of something truly terrible called greed. Sorry if it sounds like an accusation. I'm in there too.

Once, I knew a woman, very cool professional lady, who advised banks on investments. Cynicism on shapely legs, Maisie was. Maisie was good. She could swap outdated yen into extinct lire and back into dollars without changing wheels. Yet this same cynical hardliner Maisie paid a barrowboy an entire month's salary on the promise of three hitherto undiscovered manuscripts by Ben Jonson, Shakespeare's pal. She didn't know the vendor, hadn't seen the manuscripts, knew nothing about Ben Jonson, had never clapped eyes on the barrowboy before, couldn't tell parchment from pawpaw. See? Greed, like murder, will out. Never mind those famous sayings about fame being the spur; greed's the biggest mover on earth. It's horrible.

I've seen the coolest individuals fall for a non-existent cache of non-Sheraton furniture in a non-existent garden shed. I've seen clergymen fall for fake Dead Sea Scrolls. I've known widows in an investment club lose everything, including reputations, when buying a non-existent Caribbean island. And seen a Munich millionaire go to prison for frantically buying the six-acre greensward of a non-existent Oxford college. Don't think you can't fall for the same con more than once. The widows' investment group I mentioned did it again two years later, buying imaginary salmon-fishing rights to a mythical river.

The rush of emotional memories gave me a headache. I'd have killed for a cup of tea. I told Sorbo, but he's bad at hints.

'Brick? Clocks, Lovejoy.'

Well, I groaned out loud.

'Everybody on earth fakes clocks, Sorbo. Boy scouts find rare Early English movements in steeple belfries. It's like furniture. Everybody's got a rotten old clock that won't go, so greed naturally enters.' Hence the honest old public pretends that some hacky Woolworth alarm clock is a priceless Cartier discovered in Grandpa's attic. It's as natural as breathing. My respect for Colette's instincts plunged.

'She was actually taken in by an antique clock scam?'

'To the hilt, Lovejoy. That was how Arthur died, see. It was his canal.'

Canal? Sorbo drained the Rodney flask with a roustabout's

glug, then withdrew a new bottle of Graham's vintage port from a cupboard, decanted it carefully into the fake flask.

He spoke with love. 'Port takes time, Lovejoy.' Then switched to hate. 'If I could kill Dieter Gluck and get away with it, I'd do it.' I listened, dry as a bone, the port maturing before my eyes in the glow. 'Everybody could see it except Colette.'

'Did nobody say?'

He swung on me. I'd never seen him angry before. It shook me. 'You think I didn't? And where were her sodding friends, Lovejoy? You quick-prick hick. How often did you phone, visit, drop a postcard? She had others, fine. They were all vanishers, just like you.'

Insults have to be swallowed. I've found that. 'How'd he do it?' Trout had more or less said the same, Dieter Gluck kills people. 'And what canal?'

'Arthur's position seemed enviable, to Gluck. Nobility, lineage, land, plus a wife who played at being the grand Chelsea antiques dealer. A plum for the picking! Gluck had no money of his own, so he wheedled in. Became a partner by foregoing.'

You can do this in the antiques trade. Foregoing always makes me a bit uneasy. If you want to become a partner in a small antique dealer's shop, you go through three phases. First, you work there for nothing, make yourself indispensible. The owners get to depend on your wit, help, luck even. Then you sadly but tactfully hint that you've got an excellent offer from a rival. This may not be true, but so? Avarice spurs you on. Phase Two comes along. The owner says, 'Hey, don't go. How about I give you a salary?' You say, 'Ta, pal. I really don't want to go because I've been so-o-o happy working with you. How about I stay, take no payment, but take the salary in equity?' That is, you become a junior partner, however fractionally small the increments. Phase Three, you're the cuckoo. You ditch the owner.

You're in. You've made it, name on the notepaper. Foregoing.

'His expertise was automata, clockworks, all those?'

'Has a good knowledge, give him that.' Sorbo hated admitting this. He took a long pull at the port, set it down, eyes watering. The fumes wafted across.

'Genuine?' I'm always scared some enemy's going to turn out a divvy like me.

'He pulled off one or two successes. Astrolabes, navigationals, spheres, microscopes. I got the feeling it was all breading, but who can prove that?'

'Breading' is what anglers do. They chuck bread balls onto a river so the fish will congregate. It means putting an enticing antique into somebody's path. This way, they're inveigled into making offers for other items you've got. Many dealers bread at a loss, to increase a buyer's trust.

'And Colette thought—'

'The sun shone out of the bloke?' Sorbo completed for me. 'Yes. Then he put the gold brick in. It needed a guarantee, see?'

It was like a bad dream. I was aghast. 'Didn't Arthur say no?'

'You know – knew – Arthur, Lovejoy. He went along, put up the shop and his manor as guarantee when Colette said.'

'And didn't think to ask me?' I almost shouted it.

He said nothing. Then, 'You never answer letters, Lovejoy. Your phone's always on the blink, or you're in trouble somewhere. I told Arthur to send for you. He just smiled and said, "First catch your hare, Sorbo." Like Mrs Beeton's recipe.'

'It wasn't Mrs Beeton. It was Mrs Hannah Glasse.' Dr John Hill's pen-name was Mrs Hannah Glasse – he being embarrassed, you see, at writing the brilliant *Cook's Oracle* cookery book. Born in 1716, he first wrote that most famed phrase *Take your hare when it is cased* . . . Which became scatched, then catch. Arthur knew this. He often talked in local dialect, and 'scatch' is an old East Anglian word meaning to skin. In fact, we'd once had a mock argument about the authorship of this very saying. My eyes watered. I wondered if it was a message, from Arthur to an absent friend. Me, say. Because Arthur had been well and truly skinned.

'Arthur had a canal, Lovejoy. He wanted to link it with the sea estuary. Always on about it.' Sorbo showed guilt at having been bored stiff by Arthur.

'Like the Ribble, wasn't it?'

Sorbo sniffed, maudlin. 'Make a new lock gate from Saffron Fields canal into the estuary, you'd be able to sail a longboat barge from the North Sea up the heart of the country to the Lake District.'

'These schemes are always resurfacing, now that leisure is big money.'

'I think Colette just wanted to give Arthur the money to build his canal's sea gate. Repay Arthur for all the lovers she'd had over the years.'

He swigged, belched. I sat in the gloaming, sick at heart.

'Know what, Lovejoy? I think it's women. Take your average bloke. He sees a luscious bird, old or young, fancies her.'

Sorbo was blaming me for it all. He was right. If I'd stood by Arthur, this wouldn't have happened.

Sorbo went on, 'The bloke either makes love to the bird if he's lucky, or fails. Either way, he lives with it. But women are different. A woman gets the bit between her teeth about a man, something weird happens. She throws everything to the winds. Morality, money, propriety, common sense. Goes crazy.'

I rose and took the Rodney flask from his hand. Unbelievably light, from its synthetic composition. Sorbo had invented quite a fake. I bent to stare into his eyes.

'Sorbo. Gluck's scheme was to rob who of what?'

'Them, Lovejoy. The Clockmakers' Company.'

It couldn't be done. People had tried, and nobody had done it yet. I'd even thought of it myself – not really in true life, but when you're just drifting off to sleep and pleasant thoughts entice. I pulled myself together.

'It would need multo gelt, Lovejoy. Colette made Arthur put up the Chelsea business and the manor, guarantee Gluck a loan.'

'Some loan,' I said bitterly. 'A fortune.'

'Had to be big, see, because Gluck reckoned he'd found a new – I mean antique – Harrison wooder.'

I swayed away and sat. I still held Sorbo's Rodney and took a long draught, choked a bit. The Harrison wooder would do for a gold brick all right.

'Why didn't Gluck go through with it, once he'd got the money?'

Sorbo retrieved the flask with an air of injury, took a swig to show who was boss round here.

'He found something about the manor. Cheeky bastard went to inspect it, like it was his. Spoke to Arthur. Arthur always did have a weak ticker. Died in hospital that evening. Heart attack.'

'Where was Trout in all this?'

'That little bugger? Gluck gave him the push for lowering the tone of the place. When Arthur passed away

Gluck brought in this Bern goon instead of me. Bern's supposed to be an antiques restorer. I got dundied without a bean.' Dundied, made redundant. 'I make do now with—'

'Aye, aye,' I said testily. I didn't want a list of Sorbo's odd jobs. 'You go to Arthur's funeral?'

'No. I was plastered for a fortnight. Anyway, it was out in some forest.'

Where some lad had sung a song for Arthur. There'd been four at the burial in the glade. And somebody had watched me when I'd visited there.

'Arthur died exactly when everything he owned passed legally to Gluck. Convenient, eh?'

'Colette was stunned. Gluck threw her out. All London was talking about it. She can't give antiques up, Lovejoy. Like you, like me, like everybody else with the bug. So she's a scrubber.'

For a long time I sat watching the shadows leap across the workbench, stretch and vanish among his instruments. I cleared my throat.

'Sorbo. We outnumber Gluck.'

'I'm not deaf.'

He took up a small wood-shaper chisel and started to hone it on an oilstone. Seeing other fakers use an instrument always narks me, no matter how skilled they are. We forgers always reckon we can do everything better than anybody else. Robbery, even.

'There's Trout, Tinker, me, you, and my apprentice Lydia. There's only two of him. Anybody else?'

'To do what?'

Words don't come easy. I didn't want to say kill exactly, because killing's wrong. And punish sounds like school, hands out and this hurts me more than it'll hurt you, the executioner's usual lies.

'To restore the balance,' I said eventually.

He said, 'Sounds fair. What do we do?'

I said, 'We do Gluck's robbery for him. Or a better one.'

'Robberies that good can't be done, Lovejoy.'

'Then,' I said evenly, 'somebody'll get caught, won't they?'

That night I kipped in Waterloo Station, light of heart, thinking what a wonderful place London was. Dick Whittington had found that, and he'd made Lord Mayor, boss of the City of London itself, of all the ancient prerogatives and immense wealth. London truly is a magical place, for somebody with ambition.

Breakfast in the station buffet cost me the earth. London's a lousy rotten dump.

15

THE GUN SHOOT. I managed to reach Caprice by telephonic sorcery and demanded why I wasn't being wined and dined aroynd aboyt the coynty, dwaahling. She swore inelegantly at having had to make her own toast this cruel dawn.

'I've got you in tomorrow's shoot, Lovejoy,' she told me between bursts of invective. She went to a posh finishing school, so can swear like a longshoreman. 'Clovis will kit you out. Don't you dare be freaking late or I'll see you never breathe East Anglian air again. Clovis is mad on punctuality. Eight o'clock for pre-shoot breakfast. The awards night's a full fig affair, remember.'

The rest of her prattle didn't matter, relating as it did to celebrities, Who Would Be On Our Table, and last night's terrible deeds backstage. I'd no intention of going to her crummy do. Dieter Gluck had found some murder-worthy link among London's street markets, antiques, and the dark brooding countryside of East Anglia. I was tracking him.

On to Portobello Road, every hunter's favourite.

*

The Portobello runs so close and parallel to its next street that you wonder why they bothered to make two. Kensington Park Road, the B415, does a decent job of zooming from Notting Hill Gate, where there's a Tube, nearly to Ladbroke Grove, where there's another Tube if you're worn out. You can't possibly get exhausted, because the length of Portobello Road is bliss, aka antiques. Some are rum, and the folk are rummer still.

Westbourne Park Road completes the T. What with three Tube stations, one at every extremity, and the buses plying through, it's a wonder that you meet people who've never been there. I looked at the grandly named Westway – the weary old A40 trying to pretend it's a real motorway. The place was all on the go. Incidentally, be prepared for a plod of several hours. Stalls extend all the way to the flyover, usurping practically every nook to Golborne Road and beyond. By the time this ink's dry the market might well have spread to Birmingham (joke) or vanished (j).

It wasn't easy deciding who to chat up first. I chose Deeloriss – her spelling; she started out Dolores. She did prison time once for stalking a Dieppe dealer who'd sold her a fake 1795 cabinet. She got arrested at Dover for stabbing him. Deeloriss would understand hatred, if anybody would.

The market's usually thronged at weekends. Once, it was only Saturdays, under the Westway flyover. Now, though, there's so much money screaming for an antique to protect its cold soul from nasty old inflation that antiques stretch through the week.

Deeloriss looks so charitable, not at all like a knifer. Wears only black and white, with hair to match. I've even seen her with her cheeks done in chequerboard harlequin squares, putting the fear of God in me. Today she was demure, regretfully shaking her head winsomely at a foreign robed gent. I saw her wrap something. He paid, pressed her hand meaningfully, and went.

'Wotcher, Deel. Good girl, pull it off?'

'Wotcher, Lovejoy.' She gazed after the man laconically. 'I'd have had to pull more than a deal off with some of these customers. It's getting more like a slave auction every day.'

'How's Pierre?' Pierre was her Dieppe knifee, so to speak. They married when she got out of clink and he got out of hospital.

'Swine took off with some Scotch bitch.' She smiled beatifically at customers who paused, interested in her corner cupboards. They moved on. Her smile vanished.

'What happened to the fake cabinet, Deel?' I ahemed, casual. 'It was pretty well made, I heard.'

'You made it, you bastard,' she said. I gulped, backed away a step. 'Those feet were swept out lovely. You must have used tons of heartwood.'

'Er, aye, love.' The so-called French foot, on furniture made in the fifteen years astride 1800, is bonny to carve. It's best faked with the outward swoop brought straight from the bottom corner of the cabinet. Okay, so housewives won't thank you when they keep tripping up over each elegant projection, but is that too big a price for loveliness? Until now, I'd assumed Deeloriss hadn't known it was one of my creations. 'I'll buy it back, eh?'

'The swine took it with him.' She patted a passing child on the head. Its parents smiled, I smiled, Deeloriss smiled. We were nauseating.

'Pity.' I wanted something to defraud Gluck with. 'Seen Colette?'

'Poor mare.'

Deeloriss lit a cigarette in an Edwardian amber-and-ivory fagholder. It's a recurring thought of mine that women might – only might, note – feel a little frisson of delight when some calamity overtakes a lady friend. Deel seemed less than heartbroken at Colette's misfortune.

'I thought I glimpsed her in Bermondsey. It was only some bag lady.'

'Don't tart about, Lovejoy. You know what's happened.'

'Sorry.' I pretended to be shamefaced, her shrewdness catching me out. 'I just don't know who to ask.'

She flicked ash with a woman's sharp grace. 'Serves the snooty bitch right. Stuck-up mare, her and her ancient title. Well, she got her come-uppance with that Gluck. Out on her ear, not two coppers to rub together.'

'Why is she still his doormat?'

That made her smile. 'When a woman goes overboard for a man, Lovejoy, she's got to keep on. To walk away admits that everybody else was right and she wrong.'

'It mystifies me.' I fiddled with a steel-soled panel plane. Just a carpenter's bench tool made of gunmetal. They are worth a new car, these Norris 50 series implements, especially when you see a variant style – a differently sited screw adjustment or suchlike. Two blokes at Needham Market made the prices soar, sharing toolmakers' history with collectors everywhere. Deeloriss took it back, put it on her stand.

'You can't afford it, Lovejoy.'

'Women often say that they've been stupid. It's their thing.'

'You might have something there, Lovejoy. Most women would have given up after all this time. Maybe it's her Arthur, and she's grief-hugging?'

'Deel, love.' I hesitated. 'Heard of any decent scams?'

She eyed me. 'Astronomy forgeries have hit the barrows lately. Ever since that new Ophiuchus zodiac came in. Somebody out your way worked a scam before the news broke, don't know how. He used two elderly ladies. Going?'

'Er, ta, Deel, got to be off. Ta-ra.'

She called something after me, smiling, but I didn't pause. The new zodiac scam had been mine. The Ophiuchus constellation hadn't then smashed the headlines, giving everybody who watches their star signs a fright if they're born between 30 November and 17 December. My getting there first had been pure luck. If luck was a talent, I needed it now.

Hello Bates was still near the Chepstow corner. He hailed me.

'Shout "Hello Bates", Lovejoy!'

It's his greeting and farewell. Consequently nobody ever forgets Hello Bates. I hate what Hello does – strips wooden furniture, cabinets, Davenport chests, by immersing the furniture in sodium hydroxide solution then hosing it down. Vandalism technology.

'Hello Bates!' We both shouted it like a password, people all about grinning and shaking their heads. He beckoned me over to his booth for a coffee. He had several decent pieces of Victorian furniture in – pole screens, sewing workboxes, ink standishes.

'Heard you're looking for a decent scam, Lovejoy.' I wasn't surprised. Words have fleet wings on the Portobello. 'Everything's paintings lately. Them Russians—'

'No, Batesy.' I'd recently been involved in war loot in Guernsey.

'That Munch picture *The Scream*?' he suggested. 'Crammy's done a couple, very decent. He'll be in today, Talbot Road.'

'Paintings are getting the screws on.' It was true. Old Masters received more attention than the national debt. 'That American two hundred million dollar job at the Isabella Stuart Gallery in Boston set everything alight.'

We considered the world's unfairness, sipping his horrible liquid. He makes it with coffee essence from a bottle. The things I do for friends.

'That Munch, though, shows it can still be done,' Hello persuaded earnestly. 'All Norway came unglued. Gluck would fall for it like.'

'Here, nark it, Batesy.' I was really irritated. Did the universe know of my hopes for Gluck?

He was off into reverie. 'Brilliant robbery, that *Scream*. Ninety seconds. Wire cutters, a ladder, window open, off in a motor, beautiful.'

Bravely I finished my coffee. The street was filling with gazers. Time I too went wandering.

'No, but ta. Too many ifs.'

Hello looked downcast. 'I'll help if you're stuck, Lovejoy. Here,' he called after, as I started towards the Portobello Silver Galleries. 'Gaylord Fauntleroy's been asking after you. Try him. Say "Hello Bates", Lovejoy!'

'Hello Bates,' I called back, feeling a nerk.

Daft as a brush he might be, yet Hello had managed one amazing thing. With no knowledge of antiques worth a light, monumental laziness, nothing more than a porcelain bath and a hosepipe, Hello not only made a living but had me and hundreds of others shouting his name. A lesson in there somewhere.

Gaylord Fauntleroy? At least it was somebody asking for me instead of me simply blundering. I ploughed on among the arcades. I deliberately avoided mention of Dieter Gluck, just chatted, drifted, listening, listening. All the time my mind was shrieking how to do Gluck down. Surely it wasn't much to ask? Two more dealers said Gaylord wanted me. I'm good at ignoring genuine offers of help, useless at providing any.

Getting nowhere, I turned left after Denbigh Terrace, leaving the corner pub behind me. And there in all its shabby glory was Gaylord Fauntleroy's gaudy caravan, him beside it arguing with a traffic warden.

Gaylord isn't as exotic as he sounds. Okay, he is highly mannered, and given to shrill denunciations when there's an audience. He loves malicious gossip. But I know he funds a hospice ward in the Midlands. He takes his ancient Auntie Vi everywhere with him, hence the trailer, when he could have dumped her. If we were all so exotic the world wouldn't be in such a mess.

'It's my calves, officer!' Gaylord was screaming, doubled with pain. 'They're agony! I missed my mint tea yesterday!'

People all about were grinning, enjoying Gaylord's show.

'Yes, sir,' the warden intoned. 'Please move your vehicle.'

'How *can* I?' Gaylord appealing to the heavens. He wears the robes of an Orthodox priest, biretta as well, with trailing capacious sleeves. His pink sandals have Aladdin toes like you see in pantomimes. He carries a diamante-studded wand that plays tunes and lights up, and dances to demonstrate any antique that he thinks worthy of such tribute. He has a degree in fine art from the Courtauld, teaches somewhere. It must be quite a course. He is one of these blokes who look normal-sized, until you realise that he's simply huge. Like the Woolwich Rotunda building.

'Lovejoy! He's here, officer! My mother's doctor! In the nick of time!'

'Eh?' I recoiled from the traffic warden's glare.

'Is that right, sir?'

I hate it when they take out their notebooks. They remind me of magistrates. Dressed as I was in my usual threadbare jacket, frayed shirt, trousers that had seen better days, years, I couldn't pass as anybody's physician.

'Er, she thinks I'm her brain surgeon,' I said, smiling. I thought quickly. Social workers are scruffy. 'I'm her social worker. What's the trouble?'

'Not allowed to park here, even if he does have a barmy old coot inside.'

'I'll see to it, officer. They'll be gone in five minutes.'

He pocketed his book and stalked off. I glared at Gaylord. He did a pirouette of balletic joy. People all about were catcalling at his antics. So this was my offer of help? I needed action and vengeance – no delete that. I'm honestly not one for vendettas.

'Come in, Lovejoy! Wait for me, oh people!' He opened the caravan door and waved goodbye to the world.

These trailer things amaze me. From the outside they look made for luggage. Inside, they expand to the horizon, rooms in every direction. This held Auntie Vi, still with her eye patch, still smoking a clay pipe, rocking by a radio. She wears a shawl, clogs, black garb.

'Lovejoy, you reprobate! About time!'

'Still pretending you're straight out of *Silas Marner*, Vi?' I believe she's got the vision of an owl, part of her act. I coughed. 'Put that pipe out for God's sake. I can't see through this blinking fug. I'm still coughing from Puntasia's crud.'

She beamed. 'You know, Gaylord, I like this beast. Have a glass.'

'More than I got from Hello Bates, or from Deeloriss.' Or any other sympathetic dealer I'd talked with so far. What good's sympathy?

'They offered you ideas for a good scam, though?' Her one eye judged me candidly. 'For Dieter Gluck?'

I said bitterly, 'Next time we're at war, I'll recruit the antiques trade as spies. We'd win in a week.'

'Don't be cross, Lovejoy. They're your friends.'

'Then why didn't they let me know when Arthur got done?'

'They thought you'd know.' She belched noisily. I leant away from the rum fumes. 'Being Colette's shagger.'

'I'm here now. Much good I'm doing.'

'Don't feel sorry for yourself, you prat. It's Arthur who's got murdered.'

'I'm racking my brains, Vi.' I was aware Gaylord was standing in silence. 'I've had hints about gold brick cons, none very convincing. I can't think of anything. I don't know this Dieter bloke. I've got my apprentice lass Lydia sussing him out. And Trout and Tinker. Sorbo's willing, so that's five. I'm hoping they'll come up with something.'

'You're thick, Lovejoy. What've you considered?'

'Everything from robbing the Prado to selling Gluck the Copenhagen Mermaid. They've all been done. Selling Tower Bridge, the Mona Lisa, the Holy Grail, Rembrandts, you name it.'

'He doesn't know, Auntie,' Gaylord said, so quietly I almost didn't hear.

'Hush, Gaylord. Go on, Lovejoy.'

'I've even thought of rigging some of the scams I've already done. That Guernsey thing. That Scotch clan auction, the Welsh valleys with those poor mental cases, Roman gold, East Anglian witchcraft. Even that new Impressionist painter I created in Hong Kong. This Gluck has me stumped.'

'Try Chinese antiques, Lovejoy. They're your best bet.'

'Only good forger of Chinese antiques is Wrinkle, and he's gone to earth. It's the cricket season, and Wrinkle lives for the game.'

'You went and got yourself arrested. Inspector Saintly, wa'n't it?'

Thank you, Radio Antiques. 'Aye. Got off with a warning. And that Bern scares me witless. I contacted Colette, but he booted me.'

'You're right, Gaylord. He hasn't a clue.' Auntie Vi looked at me. I got narked.

'I'm off. Play your queer games without me. Ta-ra.'

I'd actually risen when she said, 'You visited Arthur's grave. Did you see the lad?'

Which stopped me. Some lad sang at the interment, that vicar said. I hadn't stared at the figure in the foliage. It could as easily have been a motionless youth as an adult. I hadn't felt threatened, just spooked.

'Who is he?'

'Their son. His name's Mortimer.'

They hadn't a son. 'Colette's and Arthur's?'

She replied drily, 'We presume so, Lovejoy. Do you know different?'

'No, no.' I repeated this in the interests of veracity. 'Where is he?'

'Haunting the markets, but in a different way from Colette. You never see him, but you couldn't miss Colette. Sight, smell.'

'Son?' I said. 'As in reproducing?'

'My godson, you see,' Auntie Vi shocked me by saying. 'I stood for him. Gaylord's his godfather.' Her eye glared defiance and accusation. 'We're not much, Lovejoy, but we're all the team Mortimer has.'

'Named after some flintlock gunmaker, Lovejoy,'

Gaylord said. 'The name was Colette's idea. Never said who the father was, though.'

Henry Walklate Mortimer was one of the truly great gunsmiths of olden days. He ranks with Nock, Manton, Wogden, Wilkinson, Durs Egg. I know their names as well as my own. I felt my eyes water, Vi's horrible pipe.

'Wish you'd dock that frigging tobacco, Vi. It's corroding my lungs.'

'Tell him, Auntie,' Gaylord said.

'There's one bait Dieter Gluck can't resist, Lovejoy.'

'What is it?' I looked, one to the other.

Auntie Vi puffed smoke like a blanket signal.

'He's a snob,' she said. 'A complete and utter snob.'

There came a knock on the door. A voice I knew outside said that if Lovejoy was in there he should come out, please, to be arrested. I opened the door, and walked to the waiting police motor with Mr Saintly. Never there when you want one, and always there when you don't, the plod.

16

AN INTERESTED CROWD gathered outside. To ironic cheers, I ducked shamefaced into Saintly's motor while everybody laughed and pointed, hey, look, our good old police arresting a crook, serves him right.

'Look, guv,' I started in a Richter Four whine, 'I didn't—'

'That will do, Lovejoy.'

He sat beside me, fingering the card I'd written my message to Arthur on. A serf ploddite drove us along the No. 15 bus route until he could park in an illegal space.

'Divvy, that's what you are, Lovejoy. Hence this scrawl. I only just put two and two together.' He gestured me to shut up in case I wanted to exercise my right to freedom of speech. 'That's my favourite London bus, Lovejoy, the old Number Fifteen. East Ham, Piccadilly Circus, Ladbroke Grove.'

'It's—' I started.

The driver turned, looked, so I shut up. Freedom of speech is for overlords.

Saintly went on, 'Plod having favourite bus routes, eh?' The way he spoke was reflective. I didn't like this. Like seeing them smile, you just know something's wrong. 'I like the old Seventy-eight. Shoreditch, Bermondsey market,

Dulwich. You see a lot from a London bus. And the One Five Nine = odd those yellow numbers, don't you think?' He paused, letting me chance a verb. I stayed silent. 'Oxford Circus to Streatham Hill.'

Did he know I'd called on Sorbo?

'Last night you caused a disturbance in a Soho caff. Why?'

'By accident I met an old friend. I stood her a cuppa. Some passing bloke misunderstood. I scarpered.'

'Not quite, Lovejoy.' So far he'd only stared out of the window. 'It was Dame Colette Goldhorn, widow of Arthur, lately owner of Lovely Colette Antiques, and a manorial estate in East Anglia. Both properties are now owned by Mr Gluck.'

'She's still a friend.'

Now he did look at me. 'You're visiting a lot of old friends, Lovejoy. Your path keeps crossing Gluck's.'

'So what, Mr Saintly? I'm in antiques, and Mr Gluck's an antiques dealer. I'm employed to find some tom – jewellery, gems. I didn't want to come to the Smoke. I got sent.'

'Why the recruiting drive?' I didn't answer. 'You're collecting enough old pals to start a war, Lovejoy.'

'Me?' I acted bitter, not difficult in these circumstances. 'You've done your homework, Mr Saintly. You'll know that I'm the bloke whose bread always hits the floor marmalade side down. Whose grapefruit always spits in my eye, whose girl spots me admiring another woman's legs. I know not to go on crusades.'

'Oh, I do know you're a prat, Lovejoy,' he said reasonably. The serf in the driving seat snickered. 'My question is, are you a dangerous prat?'

I'd had enough, but you never dare say so. 'At Gaylord's

caravan you told me to come out and be arrested. They're wrong words, aren't they? I'm not actually nicked.'

'I don't want you troubling eminent Chelsea businessmen. Understand?'

'Yes, sir.' A grovel never does harm.

'And your old friend Arthur Goldhorn simply misjudged his dose of digoxin. Nothing sinister. It's what sick folk do. Understand?'

'Yes, Mr Saintly.'

That was it. As I left he raised a hand.

'Is it true, this divvy thing? You *feel* genuine antiques?'

'Aye. And it gives me a headache.'

He considered this. 'It'd be worth a headache. Does it work for people too? You see through fraudsters?'

'No. I get people wrong.'

He almost smiled. 'Let me know how your search goes, eh?'

'Search?' I froze on the door, scared. 'What search?'

'For the gems, Lovejoy. What d'you think I meant?'

A bit ago I said there were too many ifs knocking about. The truth is that in life there's never enough. I emerged into the press of people heading into the Belly, trying not to look red in the face from embarrassment at having alighted from a plod motor.

Snob. So Gluck who killed Arthur, was a snob. Did that help? Auntie Vi and Gaylord reckoned so.

Well, sometimes. Look at The Great Castellani.

Excitement began to throb in me. Just a little, but starting up. I went and sat in Maria's Caff over tea and a wadge wondering if I'd found the answer. It had come to me when Saintly had been yapping. Something he said

gave me a sudden vision. He'd said *see through*. One diffi-
culty in seeing through to an antique's dazzling soul is
patina. In fact some dealers claim that patina is everything.
Trying to look bored, yet sensing the thrill a con trick
brings, I sat, noshed, and wondered about appearances.
What else is snobbery but appearance?

My mind scoured its memory pits, and I came up with
the answer.

Long ago – we're in mid-Victorian days – the Ancient
World was all the rage. Bring home Etruscan, Greek, Egyp-
tian, Babylonian, and you were admired. Gentlemen had
cabinets crammed higgledy-piggledy with antiquities they
collected on the Grand Tour. Trophy time. To prove you
were educated to the correct degree of snobbery you *had*
to display ancient scarabs and funereal artefacts from Meso-
potamia. If you couldn't afford to go on the Grand Tour,
you saved up at home then quietly bought a cabinet stuffed
with a dealer's miscellany. It was the reliquary chasse but
more personal. These collections were mere aggregations
bought without thought. They occasionally come to auctions nowadays. When they do, dealers fall on them because
the items are usually untouched. They've got a 'late provenance'. This means that since those intaglio rings were
purchased in Damascus one hundred and fifty years back
they've just lain in Great-grandpa's bureau.

Which, put bluntly, was snobbery.

This isn't to say that travelling gentry didn't pay through
the nose for those antiquities. They often paid too much.
And everything in these collector's cabinets isn't always
genuine, because they're often gruesome fakes of the most
transparent silliness. Some are so clumsy you have to laugh,
or weep.

And some are so genuine they melt your heart.

I don't even go to see these cabinets when they surface. I can't. I think they're a bit spooky, like entering a temple then realizing you're in a mausoleum. It's the difference between life and pretended life. I can understand a bloke collecting penknives, fossils, sparking plugs for heaven's sake. But somebody who sets out simply to *accumulate* is just a gannet. No points for that. Snobbery is as snobbery does.

It wasn't only society folk on the Grand Tour, though. Snobbery struck museums, famous galleries, eminent societies, even nations. And where snobbery goes, can shame be far behind?

Enter the British Museum, and The Great Castellani.

Now, this prestigious museum is one of the great places on earth. I'm a fan. It's also honest – well, narrow that down, maybe it edges near to honesty. It proves this by putting on displays of its mistakes. Antique dealers don't advertise our clangers from the rooftops. We certainly don't go racing after some lady calling out that the mid-eighteenth century kneehole desk, 'made in London's Long Acre', that we've just sold her is actually a fake we made last weekend from a Utility, World War II vintage wardrobe. (This sort of fake is common, because horrible Utility furniture was made from the right thickness of wood, and antedates chipboard.)

All of us, blokes and birds alike, don't advertise past sins. We keep quiet about our holiday in Folkestone, don't we?

One of the BM's mistakes was multiple. It involved a superb nineteenth-century jeweller in Rome, called Alessandro Castellani. Now, good old Alessandro's firm was highly regarded. It employed only eminent craftsmen. He sold his quality jewellery and 'restored' antiques to international buyers. Much of the allure of those days centred on patina. Look it up. A patina was once a flattish dish used in the Eucharist, but the word also means a film or incrustation forming on old bronze, usually green 'and', adds the OED drily, 'esteemed as an ornament'.

Take any ancient bronze statuette or bowl. Let's suppose it's genuine Etruscan, just the right trophy for your living room, to impress neighbours, make friends jealous. Its surface colour, texture, *appearance* (remember appearance) is a conspicuous sea green. Okay, it feels slightly granular, looks a little matt in oblique light on account of its great age. And after all, didn't the Roman and Ancient Greek bronzes always have that delectable leaf green or even green-black colour?

No, not really. Paintings that have survived from those times show Ancient World statuary. I'm always rocked back onto my heels by the immediacy of the faces, the astounding impact of the colours, the clothes, the brightness of the eyes. Look closely. The statues are painted flesh colour! Or, if they're made of bronze, they're *painted* bronze! They're not black, not green. Collectors over the past two centuries only *believed* they were. So they went about hunting the opposite of what was right.

In other words, snobbery made them seek, and pay through the nose for, antiques that were the opposite of genuine. The real Ancient World wanted its statues lifelike, the more flesh-coloured and red-nippled the better. And so what, if the ancient artists had to use a little russet copper to pink up the statue's lips? Living women use cosmetics, everybody dyes their favourite shirts and skirts. Nobody today wants a dead statue, a moribund painting, stuporose art. And they didn't Back Then, either.

Enter the forger, anybody who could do a hand's turn with a crucible of wood ash and a few impure chemicals.

There's a saying about patina, among antique dealer illiterati, that 'green is great, black is bosh'. Don't trust this motto. It stems from the great collectors of the early 1800s, who believed that ancient bronzes of pretty goddesses, incense burners and the like, were originally black. So when they bought genuine antique bronzes with greenish patina, they thought, oops, wrong colour. By then, of course, emerging industries could offer collectors a range of chemicals. So you can find marvellously convincing ancient bronzes unaccountably black, when they ought to be lovely matt green. The Chinese have made replicates, new 'fakes', over the past aeons, mimicking patina as a kind of testimony to ancestral creativity. Like, a bronze bowl made in the Ming (say Good Queen Bess's time) period and decorated with a phoney patina is highly valuable even though it's a clear copy of an artefact buried in the Shang period one thousand years BC.

It's customary nowadays to blame Pliny's remark about patination by bitumen for the notorious black-should-be-green fallacy, but I say leave Pliny alone. We can't go on whining that every mistake we make is somebody else's fault, though that's the modern fashion. Some sins – can this be true? – are of our own making, and we deserve the blame. Mea, in fact, culpa.

There's chemicals you can buy. Suppose you pick up a modern statuette. Maybe you've even seen it cast in some holiday pottery, foundry, or even in some 'resin-and-rubber', as they're known, moulding shop where tourist trinkets are created. You rather like the bronze appearance of the pretty dancing girl, say. You buy it for pennies. On the way home, you realize how very similar the little figurine is to that statuette Uncle George once had, so cruelly stolen by your nasty cousin from Sunderland. How nice, you think, if this little cheapo had the same patina!

Any antiques workshop will do it for you. Cost? The price of a cup of coffee. Time? Come back tomorrow, and collect. (On the Ponte Vecchio in Florence, people give you any patina you like *while you drink* the coffee.) Everything made in antique days develops a patina with time, from flints to ironwork, coins to statues, exposed stonework, glass even. And every patina is different. Chlorides, carbonates, sulphides and sulphates, all change metals. My own trick was currently deep in an East Anglian fen. I'd made a series of hammered silver coins of Harold II vintage. They're easily done, if you have the correct die. About ten weeks before, I'd buried three score of these little hammered silver pennies in the slimy fens. A spell of wet weather, a dismal wintertide, and I'd dig them up by spring. The patina – darkish sulphurous black, smooth and shiny once cleaned – would do the selling for me to other dealers, maybe Chris Ollerenshaw in Wormingford. I'd not need to advertise. Grub money for a few weeks, with luck. Where was I?

With Alessandro Castellani, in nineteenth-century Rome, while great institutions bought his 'antiquities'.

Look at Sotheby's, Christie's, Philips, Bonham, Agnews, the rest. Reputation is justifiable snobbery. We go with the flow of common approval when in fact there's no sense in it. Buyers the world over love to say to friends, 'Ah, I know they're expensive, but dealers allow me a special price.' Or, 'This restaurant always keeps me a table.' Daft, isn't it. Snobbery costs. It's as if we love being ripped off, because it proves we can afford to get done.

The problem is, it's inextricably mixed with trust.

Signore Castellani, eminent, thoroughly proper, sold antiques. The greater the museums buying his items, the more he was exalted. The costlier, the higher soared Castellani's fame. There was however one cloud on the horizon. His workshops also produced new items of jewellery 'in the style archeological', as he freely advertised. A few dark suspicions must have lurked unspoken, because his craftsmen slogged to 'restore' the assumed original appearances of certain antiques.

A small step to fakery.

Over two thousand items of ancient jewellery were imported from Castellani's in 1872. Modern laboratory tests prove that his beaten gold filigree is actually made from modern drawn wire. The trace-metal analyses don't hold up. His stuff is what dealers call 'tiler fakery' – that is, a bit of so-say genuine antique here, a bit there, joined by forger's hands. Genuine antique beads or miniature figurines mounted as a modern gold necklace is one of Castellani's typical jokes. They were still coming eighty years later, ending only in the 1930s, when skilled rivals entered the market.

I don't blame the fakers. They were poor, working for peanuts. British dealers being paramount in Georgian days, several of them set up on the spot. Thomas Jenkins was the faker's maestro. This hero even employed English artists to assist local talent. He had a factory making cameos, amber jewellery, rings, intaglios, actually in – that's *in* – Rome's Colosseum. His blokes did no more than sit round whittling, carving, supplying Jenkins with gems, ambers, cameos, whatever. Some of his pals kept notes, and produced laughable tales – like Joe Nollekens the sculptor, who used to help out by assembling the bits of statues dug up in the vicinity. Jenkins paid off Nollekens with dollops of fakes 'to say nothing', he records with blithe honesty for posterity to read. The very best forgers in Rome were Pistrucci and Nathaniel Marchant. I'd give a lot to hold some of Marchant's engraved gems. See the problem? Brilliant artisans, wondrous jewellers, using the same skills and gemstones as the Ancient World. Can you call their creations fakes, forgeries, Sexton Blakes, duplicates, replicas?

Some antique bronzes Castellani stripped of their genuine patina, and 'restored' them, with more fashionable patinas which museums would more readily buy. It is easily chipped off, and the genuine antique beneath seen clearly.

Great opportunities there. For the murderous Dieter Gluck.

Time was getting on. I had to meet my team. I finished my cold tea.

This canal business – where and what? And Colette. Does a woman hang about because she's addicted to a scene? Because that's what she told me. She was a street-market lover, just like me, she'd said.

Now, I don't know much about women. Being a bloke I go about saying I do, but that's only me pretending I'm Beau Nash or whoever. I do know one thing, though. It's this: A bloke will slog away at something just because it's that something. He'll slave away building a dream because it's his dream – build a tower, change a coastline. A woman won't. She's too practical. Sooner or later she'll think, good heavens, here am I hauling logs to build a path across this swamp, when I'll never even see its completion. And she'll think, stuff it. She'll leave.

Unless it's for a Somebody. She'll carry on with might

and main *for somebody else*. She'll go hungry, be humiliated, shamed before the herd, suffer indignity year on year. It's noble. You may only see an old scrubber woman's degradation as you drive past in your Rolls, but get to know her and she's putting her grandson through medical school or guarding her dead man's memory. Nowadays we're not supposed to be sentimental. We've left that behind in Charlie Chaplin films. But it's still about, if you look.

Or if you happen to know somebody like Colette. Who must therefore be protecting somebody dear to her. Who else but her son Mortimer? Presumably he was the lone singer at his dad's funeral in the forest by the vineyard.

Admittedly only half a tale, but there were glimmerings. I'd get Lydia to piece it together, while I thought of patina and what conceivably might lie beneath. For the first time I felt real hope. For me it's usually not a good omen, but despair makes ghosts, so hope's better.

17

OPPOSITE THE EARL of Lonsdale tavern there was this sign, WOMEN something. It made me think of Colette, and the son she was protecting by becoming Gluck's slag. I couldn't work it out, because motive is rubbish. Maybe I was tired, but the five letters kept rearranging themselves. Strange, the words you can make from that one word, women. Own. New. We. Nemo. I even got a weird sentence: Now women own me, owe no new woe. Woe? The daft game set me nodding off.

Trout was the first to enter. 'Tinker's about, Lovejoy. Just saw him.'

'Them padpas, Trout?' Every time we met he got smaller. I got him some bar grub. He looked famished.

'Your pal Sturffie *was* the one who sold them, handed them to Chev for delivery. Chev's the courier man, from Aldgate East. He's still in Edinburgh.'

Bad news. Sturffie might have supplied honest padpa gems, and this Chev could have swapped them. Or Sturffie'd gone bad.

Tinker came a few yards behind his thunderous cough, clearing spaces through the late afternoon drinkers. I'd had the foresight to have three pints on the table waiting with some pasties.

He engulfed two pints, then said hello.

'Floggell's the pits, Lovejoy,' he gravelled out. 'I asked him to help. He chucked me out.'

'Floggell?' I couldn't believe it. 'He's a pal.'

'Not now, Lovejoy. He said don't come back.'

We considered this grim news. To ask an antiques burglar to burgle antiques is like asking fish to swim. Old Masters from an undeserving college, priceless Chinese celadon glaze ware from a museum, Hepplewhite furniture in somebody's home, antiques burglars will always agree. If the job's too big, they simply recruit.

'Why?' Trout asked. I was proud of him. Good question.

'Because it's you, Lovejoy. Anybody else, he'd say yes.'

Me? What had I done, except nothing? I'd come to London, seen one or two friends. And now I'm shunned by old pals who ought to be leaping at the jobs I was bringing. It didn't make sense.

A gorgeous shadow showed in the doorway. For a second I thought it was Lydia, but this was too tall.

'How did you get on, Lovejoy?' Trout asked.

The shadow stilled, listening. This in broad daylight, dealers in and out having an ale, a truly average scene.

'Wait till Lydia gets back—'

'Er,' I interrupted loudly, 'aye, let's do that. I only spoke to Sorbo. Happened on him by chance, but he only grumbled. You know him.'

The best I could do. I went to the bar, and caught the girl's reflection. It was Sir Ponsonby's elegant lass Moiya December. Last seen in Dieter Gluck's monster Bentley. She gave a wave and left. It wasn't odd, nothing that couldn't be explained by chance. I mean, antiques abounding, and she was an antiques gofer. Was it her fault if she overheard some idle pub talk? Her wave hadn't been directed at me. I made a stumble, which let me glance about. A stout balding man, pipe smoker, looked away in good time. He held a bowler comfortably on his knees, your routine pint-and-baccy Londoner.

After a while I went to scour for Lydia, and found her in the Hovis bakery beyond the Earl of Lonsdale. I rescued her. We all reunited in the beer garden. She'd had a whale of a time, and just adored Dieter Gluck.

'Lovely Colette Antiques is wonderful!' she trilled. 'I had a marvellous time! Herr Gluck is an absolute linguist! His manservant Bern was somewhat taciturn but—'

'What did you discover, love?' I asked. Trout gave me that look.

'Dieter was so kind! He showed me his sales book. And provided me with a list of his interests! He has a share in a restaurant. Simply smashing!'

'Smashing,' I agreed gravely. From Herr Gluck to Dieter in one.

'Lovejoy,' Trout said in his throaty bass. 'I don't believe this.'

Tinker gave Lydia a tomato juice. The world paused while she made absolutely definitely certain it was salt-free.

'Love, what questions did Gluck ask you?'

'None!' She simpered a little. 'I had to insist, or he'd have known absolutely nothing about me! I explained I was interested in his background for my newspaper.'

We breathed collective relief. 'You told him you're a reporter?'

'Of course!' She laughed merrily. 'Do the three of you assume I am totally devoid of equivocation? I said I was from the St Edmundsbury *Tatler and Gazette*!' She sobered.

'Having previously ascertained that there is no such journal, or it would have been highly improper.'

'Of course.' I felt us all relax.

She laughed. 'Certainly! My subterfuge had an almost miraculous effect. We had a lovely meal at the Gluck Orpheo, his establishment.'

'And he learned nothing about you, Lydia?' I was uneasy. Pint-and-baccy had moved closer, to the next bench.

'No.'

She was so proud. I didn't have the heart to question her further, just took Gluck's list from her and stuffed it into my pocket.

'Right, then,' I said quietly, drawing them in close like spies at a bomb plot. Really pathetic, especially as I was probably imagining things about the stout bloke. 'Here's what we do. Lydia, take on Holloway University. Suss out their paintings, get me off the hook. This is my lawyer.' I gave her Shar's address. 'Trout, you'd best steer clear of Gluck from now on. You and Tinker go back to East Anglia. Suss out Dosh Callaghan. From what dealers here say, he couldn't possibly have been taken in like he says. Nobody's that dim.'

'What will you be doing, Lovejoy?' Lydia never trusts me.

'I'm going shooting. Everybody meet up the day after tomorrow in Camden Passage antiques markets. You know it. The Angel, Islington. Don't go to King's Cross. It's hell of a walk up Pentonville Road.'

'I like Camden Passage,' Tinker said. 'They pull a good pint at The York.'

So much for culture. I concluded, 'We must find a youth called Goldhorn. Colette's son.'

'Mortimer?' Trout said. 'I can find him in an hour.'

For a little bloke, he certainly stopped conversations. 'Eh?'

Trout grinned. Gnomes have good grins. 'I like the lad. He talks to birds and dogs in their own lingo.'

'Birds, or birds?' I was startled. Was Mortimer barmy, and that was Colette's dreadful secret?

'Not women, you randy git,' Trout said patiently. 'Birds that fly. And hares. And bats, owls, foxes.' We all waited while Trout rummaged in his mind for more quaintness. He found a bit. 'He whistles at fish.'

'Oh, good.' I'd had enough. 'Lydia, please get me Ordnance Survey maps, massive scale and one inchers, of Saffron Fields. The map shop's in Long Acre, Leicester Square end.' I beckoned them closer. 'Do we let Sorbo join us?'

'Yes,' Trout said. 'Gluck ripped him off badly. He'd done Arthur a score of intaglios in white Baltic amber for pendants. Some of the amber belonged to Sorbo's mum. When Sorbo asked Gluck for payment, that Bern duffed him up then windowed them as his own work.'

Tinker almost exploded. 'He what? That's a 'angin' offence.'

I shoved a brimming glass his way to keep the silence, but Tinker was right. Fakers who are true craftsmen, like Sorbo, have pride. To have their forgeries passed off as by another faker is criminal.

'Right, Sorbo's in. He'll do us a good job, when we find out what to do. Anybody know any titled folk, anyone upper crust, carriage trade? Gluck's Achilles heel is he's a supersnob.'

'Oh, that can't be true, Lovejoy!' Lydia exclaimed. 'He was charming!'

Trout said from deep in his miniature chest, 'He's made a fan.'

Lydia coloured. 'Stop it, all of you! You're making a great deal of fuss about nothing! Your opinions are wholly misconstrued. You've only to meet Dieter.'

'I suppose you're right, Lydia,' I said evenly, giving Trout the bent eye to shut up. It was clearly time to sling Lydia. Her credit cards were useful, but she was a liability. We wanted loyal soldiery, not a dreamy-eyed fifth column. High time Lydia vanished into the ivory towers of academe. 'Maybe we're being just melodramatic.'

'And poor Arthur did die of natural causes,' she reminded us.

'Leave Sorbo to me. Ta, everybody.'

The stout bloke drained his pint, folded his newspaper. My tone must have pinged Lydia's antennae because she frowned.

'With whom are you going hunting, Lovejoy? Not that wretched Caprice Rhodes?'

'No, love. Her husband Clovis. And I hope to murder not one living thing.'

Some hopes. I didn't know it then, but I was heading for a really bad day. We parted amiably, Lydia still suspicious. I left her paying Trout and Tinker their expenses, and hit the road. With luck, my cottage wouldn't have been repossessed by the building society. I had enough for the fare.

All the way home I wondered if really this wasn't a task for Doomsday Walberswick and his enticing missus. But you can have too many cooks for one broth, or so they say. Tally ho to the county set.

18

J ACKO GAVE ME a lift in his bone-shaking coal lorry. He sings opera, badly, like all opera singers except two.

'Join in, Lovejoy!' he kept urging. 'Don't you like music?'

'Yes.'

That set him off laughing so much we nearly hit a tree. I've a lot of time for Jacko, though he's got a nerve asking me for payment every time I con him into taking me somewhere. Travelling in the gale of his cabin, shattered by the million-decibel rattle, poisoned by engine fumes, I deserved danger money, yet he charges me penny a mile. This morning he treated the world to *Deserto in terra*. Everybody thinks they've got the best voice in the world. They're wrong. It's really me.

East Anglia's supposed to be lovely in the dawn. I think it's eerie. Ghostly trees assume scary shapes. The occasional shire horse stands there watching. Dense mists slide along rivers. Unexpected bridges lurk near deserted railway cuttings. You need nerve. Jacko was born here, and thinks this is normal. I wasn't, so know there's an alternative to countryside known as civilization. It lives in towns.

Jacko slammed us to a halt so sudden I nearly shot over

the bonnet. I couldn't see a damned thing. He ended his aria with a flourish, flat.

'We're here, Lovejoy. Dykers Heath.'

The mist closed in. I thought I saw a vague thicking that might have been a gateway. Darker blotches could have been an ornamental hedge, or not. Dykers Heath's the name of Caprice and Clovis's estate. I'd been there once, on a balmy summery day.

'You sure, Jacko?' Suddenly I didn't like this. Why was I here? To suss out the county set's gossip about Arthur's death. 'Look. Maybe I'd better—' I screeched as a hand reached in and clutched my arm.

Jacko fell about, rolled in the aisles. 'That'll be a tenner, Lovejoy.'

'I'll owe you, Jacko. Ta-ra.'

There stood this lad, maybe fourteen, thin, fairish hair turning teenage mousey. His blue-eyed features looked familiar. He wore a thick jacket, the sort you see horsey folk don for the dank outdoors. He had the nerve to help me down. Angrily I shook him off. He'd look a grown man in some wood. I ignored Jacko's imprecations for money.

We started between the gates. He wore cut-down wellingtons, moved with that countryfied sloth that shifts ground quickly underfoot.

'It's this way.'

When you're lost, miles into the lalang like now, you have to believe these rural clowns. Except he was no clown. He imparted instant confidence. Immediately the mist's sinister shadows became simple trees and without menace. The earth beneath turned into honest gravel, no grim ditches. Hooded deformed ghouls turned into bushes, quite pleasant really if you like that sort of thing. I couldn't help glancing at the lad. He hadn't said his name.

'I'm Lovejoy, er . . .?'

'I know. Mr Rhodes said to kit you up.'

'You're one of the beaters, then?'

He nodded, or maybe he didn't. These folk who live beyond village boundaries are strange. They assume you'll know the answer, so say nothing. If you guess wrong, the more fool you. And they talk in dialect, hard to follow.

A car's headlights showed off to the right, its engine purring to silence. Doors slammed. Women's voices raised in that posh country-house scream. I heard a man call welcome. The clans were gathering.

Not long since, some sociologists – nothing better to do – dug into the nation's pastimes. They 'discovered' the most amazing fact. It's this: folk sometimes go fishing, bird watching, studying nature. This 'research survey' – their term – cost thousands, every groat of which could have been spent on antiques or leprosy. I suppose we were even now being studied by sociologists concealed in the foliage as I glimpsed Clovis's imposing dwelling.

'No. This way.'

Round the back? The Queen Anne frontage emerged from the mists. A butler, no less, and two maids scurried as guests arrived. Shooting brakes, estate cars, Bentleys and Rolls-Royces, one sulking Jaguar, showed the visitors' worth. Me and the lad went round the side of the house, in at a small door and up stairs to a gun room. Arrays of double-barrelled shotguns, with several rifles, were chained in racks behind reinforced glass. No antique flintlocks, worse luck, love of my life. A whiskery old countryman was checking the guns.

'Lovejoy, Mr Hartson.'

'Right, Mort. Morning, sir.'

Mort for Mortimer, my brilliant mind snapped up. I saw

him in the light. Familiar, indeed. Probably Arthur I was seeing, or hints of Colette.

'Morning,' I said. 'Look. I don't know what—'

'In the ante-room, sir, please.'

Next door was a changing place. I got thick brogues, tartanish stockings, plus fours, a deerstalker hat, shooting jacket, cape. I looked like a duckegg trying to be Sherlock Holmes. Mr Hartson promised me a Westley Richards double-barrelled shotgun. I could war against innocent birds.

'Mort's your bearer, sir. Mr Rhodes is expecting you at breakfast.'

'Ta.'

A right prune in this clobber, I entered the long hall. Twenty guests were already noshing. A chorus of names rose in introduction. I grinned with embarrassment. Nobody joked about my attire, thank God. I shuffled down the hall.

Most were young middle-agers. Several women were clobbered up for the day's cruelty, but two or three others were fashionably attired, obviously ready for a sloggingly hard gossip over coffee and cream cakes. I don't know about you, but these Sloanies always seem to have bandsaw voices. They look dazzling, clothes that cost a fortune an inch, yet their endless 'Okayee, yah?' is really dispiriting. Like their protruberant teeth. They don't pronounce the letter M because their lips never meet.

'Hellayo,' said one gorgeous Sloane Ranger in a black sheath dress. She was whaling into hot kidneys, bacon, liver, fried black pudding, eggs, and a stack of fried bread. Despite this nosh, she looked on a hunger strike. Some females can do it. Most groan at the sight of an irresistible chip, and biscuits are death. ''Orning. Fleury La Ney.'

'Morning,' I greeted everybody, Ms to the fore, teeth defiantly behind my lips. 'Lovejoy.'

'Oy saaah!' she exclaimed. 'Quayte a nane, hot?'

She hooted with laughter. I smiled weakly and got grub from the sideboard. When Clovis Rhodes and Caprice bought Dykers Heath mansion they scoured everywhere for reproduction furniture. Crazy. For the same money they could have furnished the place with Victorian, maybe late Georgian, furniture. Our plates for instance were a massively complete set of modern antiquey Japanese porcelain. I'd warned Caprice off this, because for *less* than the cost of this new junk they could have bought genuine second-hand Royal Doulton, maybe even Derby, in mint condition. I honestly don't understand. Caprice hadn't long been married when I met her. I can hear her yet. 'No!' She'd put her hands over her ears when I'd tried to tell her. 'I don't want other women's cast-offs!' She'll change when she learns sense, but by then it'll be too late. The price of fine old porcelain will have gone through the roof and she'll complain about the scandalous prices. Might as well talk to the wall.

'Morning, Lovejoy.' Astonishingly it was Doc Lancaster, our village doc. He was having dry toast, a scrape of marmalade, and weak tea with skimmed milk. He's a maniac, wants to set me jogging on some punishment machine in his surgery, the loon. 'You, in killing mode!'

Chuckle chuckle round the repro table. I tried to hide my loaded plate from Doc Lancaster's accusing gaze. Was I expected to starve? Just because I'd got a bit of decent grub the lunatic gives me his stare of pure wheat germ. Truculently I fed myself, told him I was here to make up numbers.

'Trouble is, Lovejoy,' Doc said affably, 'there's not a single flintlock!'

Then the wash of explanations, Lovejoy's an antique dealer, etc. I let them talk. Inevitably the divvy question came up.

'Lovejoy can tell antiques a mile off,' Doc told everybody. 'I've seen him do it. I had an early set of surgical instruments . . .'

Doc started demonstrating the antique Chamberlen obstetric forceps. A set now costs a king's ransom. Heaven knows why, when the hated Chamberlen family of doctors – Huguenot refugee doctors, lived in Essex, avarice personified – were reviled for keeping their precious forceps secret. I switched off as Doc explained the gruesome details. His audience was fascinated. The wicked ancient rhyme went through my head about Dr Hugh Chamberlen:

> To give you his character truly complete
> He's doctor, projector, man-midwife, and cheat.

'What a strange little rhyme!' a lady said. Fortyish, bonny, tweed suit, managing to look normal. She spoke without the Sloanie's shout, and there was an M in there. Her lips met!

'Eh? Sorry. Didn't realize I'd spoken aloud.'

'Was he really a cheat?' she asked, interested.

'Folk thought he should have remembered his oath, instead of cashing in.'

'Is it true, this divvy thing? Gloria Dee, Ashwood Pentney.'

'Hello. Aye. It gives me a headache.'

'How fascinating. Do you accept orders?' She saw my

anxious frown, and smiled. 'I mean do you do it professionally? Could you test some antiques of mine, for instance?'

She meant for hire. Posh society avoids mentioning lucre, it being filthy rotten stuff and beneath one.

'Afraid so.'

'Watch him, Gloria,' Doc Lancaster called amiably. 'If he doesn't like you he'll let you down. He's known for it.'

Mrs Dee smiled. 'Like so many!'

'I'm not that bad!' I exclaimed, heated. Conversation became humorous as Clovis entered, everybody getting excited at the coming shoot, saying how many they'd bagged the previous week, and was old Jarvis still gamekeeper at the Breakspeares' estate. I felt depressed. It was all so jolly hockeysticks. Clovis came over, said hello, good of me to come. Dunno what tale Caprice had fed him.

'I shall invite you,' Gloria Dee said. 'Would you mind?'

'No, fine.' I wondered if I could get away with wiping my plate with some bread. That's the only decent way to end a meal, but in East Anglia you're not supposed to. (Why not, when it's good manners in France?)

'I suppose you must get fed up, people asking you to value things. Please don't mind saying no.'

For the first time I really looked at her. Decent, I suppose the word is. Her gaze was level. I don't know exactly what a level gaze means, because a gaze that isn't level is in real trouble. 'Got them with you?'

She shook her head. 'Far too big to carry, Lovejoy. You'll have to come. Expenses, of course,' she added quietly as people noisily moved off.

'Very well.'

'One thing,' she said, rising with me. 'Guests bet on the shoot. I'd be disinclined to give anyone the nod. It's rather taken as binding, you see. Bets start at a thousand guineas.'

God Almighty. What was I doing here?

Her eyes searched mine. 'I do hope you're not offended at my mentioning it, Lovejoy? Sometimes people feel obliged to pretend they're high fliers when . . .'

'I'm not?' I got her off the hook.

She smiled. 'I can't afford to gamble either, you see.'

We trudged out in clusters. Sherry, madeira, and port were offered in beautiful but phonily new silver stirrup cups. Everybody started saying toodle-pip and suchlike. Odd, but here it sounded quite normal. Genuine, possibly? I'd have sounded ridiculous saying anything like that. A stompy old colonel kept on, 'What? What?' to me. I just grinned back, which pleased him. I quite liked the man, but didn't like the modern double-barrelled shotguns he handled like toothpicks.

Gloria Dee came with us in the estate cars. I noticed she brought an artist's palette box. I tried to get into the same Range Rover but was shunted into the last. We drove off as the mist dwindled and the world appeared in all its murderous glory.

There's a bloke and his missus I know who buy and sell antiques solely to save up money to kill ducks on the Norfolk Broads. He's Jepp and she's Zina. They have a house full of trophies, and talk endlessly about duckocide, this one shot at a seventy-three angle in a ninety-knot wind, all that. I don't visit, unless I'm delivering some antique. They're desperate to show me yet another photograph of themselves proudly holding up another dead creature. Deep down they suspect that I hate them, so taunt-torture me with their accounts. 'Our triumph wall, Lovejoy!' Zina says. I ask you. To kill an unarmed bird, for Christ's sake, a triumph? Zina's offered me more than a glimpse of her trophy wall, but I couldn't in a million years. I'd keep seeing those poor reproachful slaughtered birds just as we . . . No, no. I'd like to tell her straight out, but can't. I think I'm basically weak.

Here, I was to admire the trophies in course of creation, so to speak. Mort, Mr Hartson and other countrymen were waiting along a small valley. Mort attached himself to me. He carried two double-barrelled shotguns, under-and-overs. I said nothing. He whistled a gentle trill. A black dog appeared from nowhere, wagging along its entire length, grinning up.

'Jasper's your retriever for the day,' Mort said.

'What do I have to do?'

'I load. You fire when the birds come.'

'Do we have to hide? Or be camouflaged?'

He brightened at my ignorance. 'Not today. The beaters start soon. Please don't shoot low. Keep the gun high. Avoid the hunters.' A hint of dryness there? Cocky little sod.

We stood in a line along the shoulder of the vale. Each shooter had a dog. They seemed to know far more than me what was happening. To my immediate left was a tallish man wearing more or less the same gear as me. Beyond him stood a loudmouth, telling how many he'd bagged at the Southworth's place in Dorset. I saw the look Mort gave him. Good. A few more glances like that, I'd be able to assess these people's usefulness for me.

'Hey, Lovejoy,' the colonel called. 'Don't know how much of this you've done, but under-and-overs are more difficult. Don't mind my saying, hey?'

'Not at all, sir,' I called as Mort avoided my eyes. 'The hard way!'

'Harf harf,' the old gent laughed. 'You young uns, what?'

While we were waiting I asked Mort, quiet, who every-body was. He started telling me. I listened to his inflexion, not the words. I wasn't so thick that I'd missed the coinci-dence – Mort, the one I wanted to talk to, appearing at the only shoot I'd ever joined, same day, time, place, and being made my bearer. It couldn't be coincidence. Trout's influ-ence? Anyhow, I'd deliberately asked Caprice to slot me in because Clovis's land almost adjoins Saffron Fields, the old Carting's Vineyard just over the river.

'That one over there's a big land buyer. Has boats, him and his cronies.'

'Cronies? Who?'

'Sir Jesson Tethroe.' The name was familiar. 'The MP.'

Dots joined swiftly in my head. The Hon. J. Tethroe, MP, whose seat was unsafe, next election. Who'd been partly disgraced, after that affair with some Spanish lass, lost Cabinet promotion on account of it. He definitely was one of the people I'd need. Titled snobbery counts double.

'Lives in Westminster and Weymouth. Rich. Shrewd.'

'Even better,' I'd said before I could stop myself. 'I mean, even better that he's, er, made a go of life.'

Mort ran down the list. I noticed Gloria Dee setting up her easel and watercolours. A Midlands engineer contractor called Talleyton had fetched his own gunbearer. And a timber merchant from the coast. And a lady called Mrs Patterson they called Maeve, expert shooter.

'They're coming,' Mort said, with anguish. He'd heard the signals.

The first gunshot startled me. I felt grieved. The birds flew so heavily, having to work at it, monstrous energy for so little speed. God must have been all thumbs the day he made ducks. I shot last. The recoil almost knocked me over, slamming into my shoulder. I missed by a mile.

The roar steadied, kept up as the birds came in rushes, darting to avoid the beaters thrashing the bracken. I thought, 'Keep hidden, you daft sods, and you'll be safe.' Terrified creatures never do the right thing. I'd learned that from me.

Before long I realized I was following Mort's signals. He'd give a wave of his hand down by his side. 'Right, high,' I'd mutter, pulling the trigger. The birds coming at me would angle slightly, making it over the line of us shooters to safety beyond. Mort'd pat his leg rapidly, and I'd translate, 'Quick, left,' blasting merrily away into the void, and another bird would make it. I missed successfully, every time.

They'd put muffs on me so I could only hear the distant thump of the gun as it cracked my shoulder. Once, taking the reloaded gun from Mort, I saw the dog, Jasper. It was gaping at me with utter disbelief, obviously thinking, God, expert shooters everywhere and I draw this nerk. I gave it a wink. It turned aside in disgust, watching its mates jauntily bringing back dead birds, tails wagging. You can't win. Save a duck, you get ballocked by a hound.

The slaughter ended. I was worn out, my shoulder creaking. I handed the gun to Mort. He took it without a word, started stowing things in satchels.

'Good day's work, eh?' I tried not to sound appalled. Jasper sneered.

'Thank you, Lovejoy,' Mort said quietly.

'Sorry, old chap,' Colonel Humbert bawled in sympathy. 'Did warn you, what? Under-and-overs! Direction!'

'Should have listened to you, sir.'

He chuckled. I looked for the estate cars. None.

'It's lunch, Lovejoy,' Mort said. 'You go again, across the heath.'

'Right!' I said heartily, concealing my groan. 'Looking forward to it!'

The nosh they provided was superb, hampers of exotic food. I spoke with Mrs Dee, having checked that Mr Dee wasn't here.

'Don't worry. I shan't study your paintings.' Artists hate ramblers peering over their shoulder.

She laughed. 'You paint too, Lovejoy.' And answered my unspoken question, 'Sir Jesson told me. He's a collector.'

'You meant warned.' Was she a special friend of the scandal-riddled parliamentarian?

'Yes, warned.' She was amused.

'You're not using acrylics?' I asked in mock horror, looking at the peeling cerulean blue on her fingers.

'As a matter of fact I am.'

'Then the deal's off, love.' I returned to the trenches, her laughter following.

I won't go into details about that day of carnage. I finally reeled away sickened. I didn't harm a single thing, thanks to Mort. He had a series of cunning hoots and shrill keenings that somehow diverted birds from their flight paths away from the shooters. Even so, our scattered lead shot will pollute the earth for the next frigging millennium. God help us, we're a rotten lot.

Teatime. I changed back, getting a mouthful of astonishment at my fashion style from Fleury La Ney. I liked her, though. She wore a ton of makeup, thick mascara, rouge, dense eye-liner, plastered lipstick, blusher inches thick, so she was class even for a Sloanie. I noticed Gloria Dee sitting with Sir Jesson Tethroe. They looked a pair – item, do they say now? I caught her glance when Sir Jesson asked about me. Fine. They'd see me soon enough. They didn't know it yet but they were on my team.

I spoke a bit with Clovis and Maeve Patterson. She was lively, fifties, stridey, endlessly on about horses. I sensed a looming invitation to come riding, and quickly told her I was allergic. She had fishing rights along the river almost all the way to the estuary. I thought, hey, any canals? I spoke sadly of some bloke I used to know nearby called Arthur Goldhorn. It turned out she'd known him.

'Poor man,' she said. 'Born loser, Arthur. He tried riding point-to-point at Marks Tey, fell off. That cow Colette's gone to the dogs. Lost everything except the title, over some loony investment in London.'

'Haven't they a son?' I asked, thinking, title?

'A token yokel, hardly literate, lives wild. Does odd jobs. Shouldn't be allowed, I say. You'd think the social services'd do something, instead of bugger all.'

It's always a shock to hear a lady swear, but I agreed on principle.

'Heart attack,' my other cultivar, Talleyton, cut in. 'Arthur get any further with that canal thing, Maeve?'

'No. He invented that magnet. I couldn't see what the canal hold-up was. Mind you,' Maeve added, lowering her voice so we drew in close not to miss a whiff of scandal, 'Colette went mental over some local antique dealer. Queer fish with an odd name. I always think the woman should control sex, don't you?'

My throat thickened. How long had it been since me and Colette made smiles? Years. I put in quickly, 'What canal thing?'

'Goldhorn owned Saffron Fields. Has an extinct canal. The inland length is all right, but it's a mess further down. Arthur had the idea of linking it with the estuary. It would join the North Sea to the Lake District.'

'Good idea,' I said, smiling, still working out how long

it had been since I'd known Colette. But the canal story seemed reliable enough.

Before leaving, I thanked Clovis for his hospitality. He said he was glad I'd enjoyed it. 'You were popular, Lovejoy,' he said, accompanying me to the hall. 'I noticed Gloria Dee and Sir Jesson giving you their cards. And Maeve and Bert Talleyton. So you're interested in canal engineering! It's his speciality. He does the Leicester Loop, you know. Pity you shot a zero. I'll tell Caprice you bagged a dozen, shall I?'

'Clovis,' I said with feeling, 'you're a gent.'

Outside I walked off, ready to start thumbing a lift. Mort suddenly fell in with me, coming from nowhere. The watery sun was slanting across the huge ornamental gates. I didn't know what to say, kept looking at the lad.

'This way.' He led me down a gully. No time at all, we were among trees, then undergrowth. I finally halted, tired. The dog Jasper was with us.

'Look, Mort,' I said lamely. 'I'd better get home.'

'We're here.'

A ramshackle hut was somehow there. You could stand within yards and not notice it. I heard a brook's gurgle nearby. He pulled branches aside. I recalled Maeve's remark about Colette's boy who lived wild. Yet Mr Hartson the head gamekeeper trusted Mort completely, left him alone with all those priceless guns. I stepped in after him.

'I collected these for you,' Mort said, shy.

'For me?' I was stunned.

'I knew you'd come.'

Garden implements, maybe a score, and all different. It sounds stupid, but nothing's more elegant than Edwin Budding's lawn mower. The world's first, patented in 1830. Looked at from the side, it has a lovely Hogarthish curve. His pal John Ferrabee manufactured them, in Stroud.

Budding actually invented the idea from watching machines cut cloth in a textile mill. Check that it has that delectable curve, its five blades arranged as a sort of empty cylinder, with a strange toothed roller to adjust cutting height, and you've found a fortune. It's worth a look in your old garden shed, I promise. By the following year, 1831, Budding's lawn mowers were being used in Regent's Park – one man pulling, one pushing, doing the work of 'six men with scythes and brooms', Loudon the great gardener wrote.

Snobbery persisted, though. Traditionalists grumbled that all 'effective' grass cutting must be done 'by the scythe'.

'You haven't raided any gardening museums, have you?' I croaked.

He shook his head. 'Mr Hartson lets me have old implements the nearby estates throw out.'

'Does he now.' I sat on a stool, weak. On rough shelves stood arrays of watering pots and cans. Every single one was a genuine antique. 'Watering pots' were from 1706 on. Somehow, Mort had acquired examples of all the important variants. He had a bulbous Dutch mid-eighteenth-century thing, fifteen inches tall, black-painted copper with a vast rose on its spout and a hooped top handle. Shining bright was a Victorian teapot can, its copper polished to a gleam, with a dainty drooping spout and no rose, hardly a hand's span tall. Desirable enough to make my mouth water was an English clay watering pot, seventeenth-century, jug-shaped and hardly a foot tall, with a fixed half-cover and a stubby spout ending in a flattish rose. I'd only ever seen one of these before in my whole life, even in East Anglia. I gaped at the lad.

'You're rich,' I told him. 'How did you know what to save?'

Mr Hartson stepped into the hut. 'He says they tell him.'

I jumped. 'I wish you'd stop bloody creeping about,' I said, narked. 'You lot scare me to frigging death.' I waited. 'They *tell* him?'

'Like speaking.' The gamekeeper shrugged. 'He feels odd. Sometimes he has to sit down.'

Quickly I stood up. 'Well, between you, you've amassed a fortune. The great gardener J. C. Loudon advocated all of these.' I pointed. 'That one is Money's "inverted" watering can. Date 1830, give or take a day. Loudon was a strict old codger, especially about watering seedlings. Said water should never fall with "more than its own weight". Very stern on what he called "carelessness on the part of the operator" washing soil from seedlings. Have you got one of Loudon's French thumbers? The flow's controlled by your thumb on a hole. It had been invented in England a decade earlier, but . . .' I petered out. 'What?'

'Mortimer needs your help, Lovejoy,' Mr Hartson said.

'To sell this lot? It's serious money.' So the lad had the divvy gift, same as me. Two rare birds in one shed. What are the chances of that?

'Not these, Lovejoy,' the old gamekeeper said. 'We believe Saffron Fields is in the wrong hands, and rightly should be returned to Mortimer.'

'Aye,' sez me, thick as a plank. 'But rightly doesn't work.' I looked at Mortimer's fantastic array. 'I mean, if I wanted a pricey collection of gardening implements, I'd get two serfs and steal the greatest assembly in the world, Queen Victoria's children's handmades at Osborne House on the Isle of Wight, all tools labelled and no security to shake a stick at. See what I mean? Rights are only what you can hang on to.'

'Wrong, Lovejoy,' Mr Hartson said directly to me with those gamekeeper's eyes. 'Rights must be preserved.'

And then the most astonishing thing happened.

'That will do,' Mortimer said quietly.

That was it. No more. Yet Mr Hartson, head gamekeeper and Mortimer's boss, with wellnigh absolute power over several large estates and scores of underlings, simply nodded and said, 'I'll be getting on, then. I bid you good day, Lovejoy.' And left. *That will do*, from a sprog young enough to be . . . My thoughts ran out of steam.

Minutes later, me and Mort stood by the roadside. Evening was falling.

'How long will it take?' I asked after a bit.

'The bird numbers? They'll be up this time next year. To die again.'

What to say to his quiet voice, these haunting words? He gave a little click and Jasper materialized at his side.

'Don't *do* that,' I said, narked. 'Can't you shout his bloody name like ordinary people?'

He almost smiled, didn't make it. 'You live in a cottage,' he said. 'I walk past it. Can I visit?'

'Aye. Any time.' I cleared my throat. 'Er, knock first, eh? Only, sometimes a lady might stay.'

He held out his hand. A robin immediately flew on it, sticking like they do. Mort had a tiny white thing in his fingers. The robin took it, eyed me with a cock-of-the-walk sneer, and flirted away.

'They eat cheese instead of grubs,' I said, narked.

'They need living things,' he said. 'Cheese alone won't do. This bus is Mount Bures.'

This bus? I looked about. Nothing. We stood by the gate, spoke for a bit. I asked if he'd been in the wood the day I visited Arthur's grave. He nodded. I didn't mention Colette, but asked about Arthur's canal plans. He told me. Then a bus really did chug into sight.

'You kept the title? Lord of the Manor, Saffron Fields?'

He nodded. 'Primogeniture. Dad kept it back when he signed the guarantees.'

'See you soon, then, Mort. Come any time.'

'Thanks again for missing the birds. Write to me care of Mr Hartson.'

Did you shake hands with somebody you ought to have known all his life? I dithered, finally didn't, caught the bus. I watched him until the bus rocked round the bend.

That was the good bit of the day, slaughtering all that wildlife and encountering Mort. Now read on.

19

FOR THE LIFE of me I couldn't remember
what Sorbo had told me about his deal-
ings with Gluck. Was it how Sorbo had
been done out of his mother's ambers and intaglios, that
had set me off thinking about Thomas Jenkins and the
Great Castellani? Something about Sorbo not being paid
for 'the half he'd delivered, slaved for nigh on a year'.

Tired as I was, shoulder hurting from not killing birds,
I got the connecting train from Sudbury. I was worried
about Sorbo. Something I should have said, done, thought
of, rankled. So I fled the darkening countryside and hours
later I arrived in London's bright lights, caught the 133 bus.
I was sweating, nauseous, not hungry. Bad signs.

The trouble with London is it can look stuporous yet be in
a ferment. Tranquil surface, seething below. Streatham Hill
in the lamp hours is streets with trees, closed shops, a few
restaurants still at it, the train station kiosk just closing. I
hurried. Sorbo doesn't believe in phones.

As I puffed up the quiet avenue, I tried to talk myself
out of fear. I get into these horrors, telling myself I should
have done this or that. Usually it's silly imagination. My

Gran used to tell me, 'Always have clean on underneath, in case you get run over.' As if it would prevent accidents, placate some God of the Unclean. Imagination is dafter than motive.

The house looked the same in the gloaming. I halted, wheezing. Steps, a faint light through the vestibule. I almost fell over the dustbin, knocked. Silence.

And felt for the bell. I tried the handle, shouted 'Sorbo!' through the letterbox flap. More silence. I could see the light in his room.

'I'll try the back, Sorbo!' I shouted, then stumbled my way round the side. A group of people went laughing up the road. I was unseen, the tall London plane trees dappling the street lighting.

These houses were built for manufacturers drawn into late Victorian London. They always seem taller than they need be. It's because they have cellars, a basement where housemaids lived. I proved this by falling down the cellar steps and hurting my good shoulder. Lovejoy, cat burglar to the gentry.

The cellar door was barred. Wearily I climbed up into the indefinable garden, couldn't see a damned thing. Brambles caught my face. I hunched against them, felt along the house wall. Duck down, you can see silhouettes against sky glow. I made the back steps. That door was also locked. Maddening to see the faint light inside. I did my knock, shouted who I was. Nil.

It's then that my anxiety began to fade. I'm weak as water. I sat on the steps and talked myself out of worrying. I'd dashed to London to make sure Sorbo was safe, enrol him into my anti-Gluck platoon, and found the house quiet. Sorbo was probably boozing in some local pub. I'd wasted all that anxiety. Why wasn't he on the phone like everybody else except me? Sorbo'd thoughtlessly got me frantic for nothing.

Nothing for it, but to resume where I'd left off, visit the carder man. A carder is a kind of private clerk who keeps records of antiques sales, thefts, transactions, rumours, anything and everything to do with antiques. For instance, you'd go to the carder man to buy from him details of major mother-of-pearl Edwardian brooches recently sold, stolen, in museums, plus the addresses and charges of the best fakers and forgers of mother-of-pearl antiques. You pay for his 'card' on the subject, hence the name. Nowadays it's computers, but he's still called a carder man.

Sighing, I rose. Maybe with luck I could get Saunty to put me up. It was getting late. I felt my way down the steps, and fell over something bulky. I went headlong. I swore, scuffed my hand on the ground, damned near broke a bone. Just what I needed. Getting upright, I touched it, this obstacle. I put my hand on a face.

For a second I actually felt about. Stubble, a nose, an eyeball half covered. I withdrew, the penny still not dropping. Then I screamed, didn't scream, stifled my noise, recoiled falling over some chance thing, a brick maybe, hands to my face in horror gasping and going 'Oooh, oooh,' and holding my hands away in the black night because they'd actually felt somebody's dead face and it was horror and my hands were sticky.

I ran. It didn't have the decency to rain so I could get clean. I dashed blindly out, making a hell of a clatter as I ran slap into the dustbin and brought myself down, slamming my cheek bone against the wall, reeling towards the avenue. I heard my throat moaning but couldn't stop. I was violently sick near Sorbo's front wall. It saved me. I had the sense to stay huddled down shivering and retching while a crowd of late-nighters walked by yelling football threats to another group across the road. A trannie blared pop music from a passing car. A bus trundled past twisting shadows. I wanted to throw my hands away.

Sorbo. I wished I'd got Lydia. She'd have a flashlight and know what to do. She'd go back and inspect the corpse, make sure. Typical of her, selfish cow, never in the right place. What if it wasn't dead, though? I should be helping it, stopping arteries, doing that respiration stuff I didn't know how to do. Maybe it wasn't even human? Could it have been only a dead dog? A *sleeping* dog? But dogs instantly bounce awake at the prospect of my company. Except Jasper, who knew a wimp when he saw one.

It'd been a human face. My pathetic mind whimpered, still hoping, do dogs have stubble? I should have sprinted for help, but didn't move. The road went quiet. I crouched, a worm in sheep's clothing. Gradually I became cold. My teeth chattered.

After midnight, when any chance of helping Sorbo had surely gone, I rose, peered for last revellers or snogging car couples, and walked stiffly out. I did a really pathetic thing. I dialled 999 from the phone box near the corner, said to send an ambulance to a man who'd fallen down the steps of his house. Frightened, in the booth's light I saw why my hands were sticky. I cleaned them with spit and newspaper I got from a litter bin.

The 133 bus took me to Liverpool Street. I made the last train out of London into dank East Anglia, where only birds got exterminated. And innocents, like Arthur.

For all Dosh's promise of money, I was strapped. Next morning, I decided to call on Icky, and got a lift from the station. He's one of the few antiques merchants who really knows the business. He lives with this songstress who's one day going to take over the Royal Opera House with her rendition of Tosca, Lucia de Lammermoor, et endless cetera, and win fame and fortune. She's bonny, winsome, sells plants in the Garden Centre, but has a voice like a foghorn. Two furlongs off, I knew they were home. Eleanora was clearly audible across the shires, trilling up and down scales.

'Wotcher, Icky.'

He was really pleased to see me. 'Lovejoy! Just brewed up.'

Icky's workshop is a little caravan parked in his garden. Mounds of paperwork, a computer, eight phones, wires everywhere. Just finding Icky was a miracle of detection, because Eleanora brings discards from the plant shop. Her artistic soul forbids throwing living herbage out. Consequently the back garden's like a rain forest. It was how I met her, actually, buying a Tan Faah plant for a lady. We'd got talking, then it was, 'Oh, my gentleman's in antiques! You must come round!' and so on.

'I won't say it, Icky.'

'Thank goodness, Lovejoy.'

Everybody who hacks their way through Eleanora's greenery jokes, 'Doctor Livingstone, I presume?' It gets on Icky's nerves. He lives on tenterhooks anyway, because of his con. Every – that's every single – antique dealer has a pet con trick, so watch out.

'Where are you this week, Icky?'

'Westmoreland.' He grinned his wicked grin. 'Called Cumbria now.'

'Got many takers?' I watched admiringly.

'Fourteen, so far.'

He scribbled on, opening envelopes, spiking cheques, entering credit card numbers. In the world of antiques, easiest is best.

Icky advertises in posh magazines: 'Antiques Course! Starting soon!! Correspond or attend!! Apply now!! Antique experts give *Personal Tuition*!!' He varies the lies, of course, and his address is anywhere in the kingdom. Internet and computer advertising's made his thievery that much simpler. His only risk is dropping some obvious clanger, like using the same phoney address twice. Naturally, his courses never take place.

I winced as Eleanora gave the universe a particularly horrendous arpeggio. He smiled in sympathy.

'Sorry, Lovejoy. She'll be across any sec to sell you tickets for next week's concert.'

Best hurry, then. 'Listen, Icky. You ever been involved with Dosh Callaghan?' He shook his head. 'Arthur Goldhorn? Colette? Bermondsey? Portobello Road? Camden Passage?' No, no, no.

'My job's private and confidential, Lovejoy.' He spoke with pride.

'I can see that, Icky. Dieter Gluck?'

'No. He got Saffron Fields, didn't he? Big antiques man. My only brush with anyone from that area was some young lad applying to do my antiques course.' Icky waxed indignant. 'Cheeky young sod asked for credit. He was connected with the Goldhorns. Arthur went spare. I got blistered. No, Lovejoy. I steer clear of the trade.'

'Seeing your courses never happen, Icky, that's fair.'

My remark narked him. 'Listen here, Lovejoy. Where else can ordinary people get an insider's view of the antiques trade? I'm their only source. Think of it like that.'

The song of the trickster has always been the same:

What marvels I offer! Like all con artists, Icky believed his own myth. Everything Icky runs is fantasy – except for the money you applicants pay in.

'I'm honest, Lovejoy,' he complained, getting out a bottle of madeira with two paper cups. 'If folk demand why the course hasn't happened and want their money back, I always send it by return of post – less a ten per cent booking fee.'

'How many do?' I was interested in spite of myself.

'Half,' he said, grinning. 'The others forget, wonder what's gone on. By then my phoney address has moved to another parish. Sometimes,' he spoke with admiration, 'I wonder if I'm legit.'

'Tell me what scams are around, Icky. I need one.'

He grimaced at his stale madeira. 'Get a carder man for that. I'd try Saunty. You know him?'

'Aye,' I said, reluctant. Saunty, our best carder man, cohabits with a bird Yamta in a perennial state of frolicsome nudity. I didn't have time for an orgy.

'Don't settle for second best, Lovejoy,' Icky said piously, straight out of his adverts. 'Give him my regards.'

'Cheers, Icky. Ta for the hooch.' I left most of the drink.

Eleanora caught me by leaping out of her shrubbery as I made my way through the jungle. She's buxom when you get close. Her arms are the floppy sort, wobbling under her armpits.

'Lovejoy! Daraleeng!' She affects a pseudo accent, to show she's a true artiste. 'Coyme! I sink yust por yoh!'

'Er, ta, El. I'm in a hurry.'

She linked my arm. 'You like my drrress, no?'

It seemed all metal, centurion-style slabs of tin, her bodice a cylinder of shiny bronze. Her helmet was some Britannia thing.

'Very pretty, El. Is it for your songs?'

'You'll come, Lovejoy?' She warbled a snatch of falsetto gunge. I nodded, to support the arts. 'Icky told you about Arthur's boy wanting to be apprenticed?'

That stopped me. Apprenticed? Icky'd only said a course. 'Er, no.'

'I stopped it straight away! On your behalf.' She beat her breast meaningfully, bending metal. ' "Desist!" I cry. "Lovejoy is Colette's lovver!" I tell heem. "Lovejoy kill people!"' She stabbed herself with a pretend knife and crooned some scatty song to die with.

This was a bit much. The plod also jump to conclusions, like that Saintly.

'Then Arthur die. Colette loses all.' She came to for an instant, gave me a mischievous glance. 'She lost you too, hey, Lovejoy?' We were at the house now. She clasped me. 'Mek me sweet music, Lovejoy. I did you a favour.'

She plonked her mouth on mine. It was a struggle, but I wriggled free seconds short of asphyxiation. I got away by promising to see her at the concert, hoping nobody had seen me snogging goodbye to a tin lady. It had to be Saunty the carder man, then. But one thing niggled. Why didn't Icky tell me he'd almost taken Arthur's lad on as an apprentice? Something wrong somewhere, but what can you do?

20

GO ALMOST DUE east from St Edmundsbury, and you hit a hamlet. It's famous for Doldrum and Mercy. Separate reasons, nothing to do with sailing ships or qualities of. The former is famed among the silent folk of East Anglia for dangerous motor cars, the latter for a brothel. Until Doldrum and Mercy hove in, the tiny hamlet was typical. Absent vicar, congregation down to nine, fences overgrown, post office closed, school desperate. A hamlet on its last legs.

Then, shazam, or whatever the comics say. Enter Doldrum, master of the dud second-hand motor. He was closely followed by Mercy. In three weeks it was boom city. The genteel old hamlet finally jerked to life and entered the Jet Age.

Suddenly its one street rumbled to the sound of car merchants' wagons. They brought derelict crash vehicles, winched them into an old barnyard Doldrum had hired for a peppercorn, and departed with 'restored' vehicles pristine as the day they'd rolled down the ramps of august car makers. It was, of course, the notorious 'cut-and-shut'. Highly illegal, but done everywhere. You get a handful of wrecked cars, any night. Hire some welding equipment, a farmyard, and you become a 'classic car restorer'.

Stalwart mechanics slice the ruined vehicle. When you've enough unruined bits, weld them together jigsaw fashion. A quick respray, and you sell the car as a 'secondhand bargain'. Naturally, you don't let on that it's simply crashed fragments pieced together. You also don't state that its chassis is twisted, the doors unsafe, the engine number ground off, the tyres unbalanced, the steering kaput, the floor as porous as a tea strainer. The registration's also duff, taken from an honest lookalike model totalled at some accident black spot.

Doldrum throve.

For this tiny rural hamlet, the sequence was inevitable. Its two pubs revitalized. The grocery shop recovered. Retailers returned, hired baffled village girls. Crumbling dwellings were snapped up. Doddering parish councillors thrilled to dreams of maybe building a village hall – an ambition temporarily shelved in AD 1371 but hanging on, hanging on. Weekend folk stopped for lunch, and saw how truly rural the quaint hamlet was. They bought derelict cottages, restored them. A building merchant started a satellite shop – nails, paint, wallpaper, ladders. The post office reopened. Heavenly choirs sang as commerce raised its head. Quaintdom flourishes, where money ebbs and flows.

Ebbing and flowing better than anybody in East Anglia was Mercy. She heard of this thriving hamlet, and brought her brothel.

Don't laugh. And especially please don't scorn the like of Mercy Faldrop. She's part of civilization's rich pattern. When ancient armies rested after hacking through the hinterland, along came Mercy's kind to help the rude and licentious soldiery do the resting bit. And where miners dug gold, or fur-trappers trapped, where cathedrals soared and tired masons momentarily laid aside their tools reaching for ale to slake their terrible thirsts, who was it served the foaming jugs? It was Mercy and her ilk. And when, parched throats quenched, the artisans and trail-blazers stretched out to rest, what more natural than that Mercy should help them stretch that little bit more?

So, one day up drove Mercy, demure and fetching. Her grand Rolls Bentley made the place gawp. Her pretty cousins – Mercy has lots of pretty cousins – followed. Still meek and shy, Mercy purchased the Old Rectory outright in a cash transaction that set the hamlet's dusty old solicitor tutting. The dwelling was opulently restored. Its many visitors often stayed all night because the hamlet's so far from anywhere and you get tired after a long drive, isn't that so? Visitors need feeding, so the hamlet's bakery burgeoned. Cars need fuel, so the garage reopened. Wealth brought light into the dark countryside. Passing artists saw the light was good, and stayed to start weekend courses. The bus service resumed.

And it came to pass in the little hamlet that life's merry pageant carouselled on and heaven smiled on the righteous and meek lasses like Mercy really do inherit the earth.

East Anglia has many complex nooks. This had all the right ingredients. Mercy first.

The Old Rectory is at the end of a longish drive, among tall trees full of the noisiest birds in East Anglia. Several splendid motors were parked in the walled car park. As I walked round, Mercy emerged onto the verandah to take coffee at a white iron table. I'd sold her the wrought-iron garden furniture and the Victorian statuary. She looked a picture, flowered hat, long flounced pink dress, lace shawl. I'd sold her that, too.

'You look gorgeous, Mercy.'

'How do you do, Lovejoy? Another cup for the gentleman, Abagail.'

The middle-aged servant bobbed and withdrew. I looked around. Vines, trellises, lichen-covered walls, a fountain playing, water tumbling gently into a pool where koi carp lazed. It was straight from some Edwardian film set. Mercy the Gainsborough lady. I sat, obedient to her gesture. The cup came. The serf poured, bobbed, vanished.

'You are thirty-nine days late, Lovejoy.'

Mercy offered me ratafia. I selected one – take more, you get blistered when Mercy's in a mood.

'Er, sorry, love. Something, er, happened.'

She raised her eyebrows. With admiration, I watched them move. She's eminently watchable, is Mercy. She is – no jest – twenty-two years old and a millionairess. A catch for any gay (original English meaning, please) bachelor who fancies his chances. Perhaps not, though. The one bloke who, earnest young lad, proposed marriage got coldly told her hourly price for sexual cavorting. He retired, as they politely say at cricket when the fast bowler's shattered your skull and you've been dragged off the field senseless. (He married a Wolverhampton gym mistress, has three kiddies.)

'A gentleman would have a decent excuse, Lovejoy.'

'I know,' I admitted humbly. 'I'm pathetic.'

Well, she burst out laughing, fell out of her poise. I watched gravely. What had I said? They once did a survey in some northern university, and discovered that women are attracted to men who (a) amuse, and (b) are interested in them. Sex follows where the magnets point, as it were.

'You're a bleed'n tonic, Lovejoy, frigging straight up. Nearly wet me knickers.'

She came to, cleared her throat, blotted her eyes.

'Er, what was I supposed to've come for, Mercy?' What was I doing thirty-nine days ago, for God's sake? Even when I was a little lad I couldn't remember what I'd been doing the day before, let alone yonks agone.

'Paintings, you stupid prat,' said this paragon of loveliness.

Had this visit come to mind from thinking of the Holloway University's Old Masters? I vaguely remembered. She'd sent one of her lasses with a hand-written missive asking for 'thurty reely old pikchures'. Mercy's not literary. Doesn't need to be, seeing she gets everything she wants anyway. I can't quite make her out. She reads George Eliot, Mrs Gaskell, Dickens, Thackeray. I think she acts her fantasies, more ways than smidgen.

'Were I not a lady of kindly disposition,' said this beauty, back in mode, 'I might harbour the suspicion that you mislaid my request.'

'That's so, love. Sorry. Will forgeries do?'

You can speak so with friends.

'Duplicity has never been formative to my character,' Mercy reprimanded sweetly.

She raised a lace-gloved hand – I'd bought that for her too (the lace gloves, not the hand) – and the villein creaked forth with a genuine William IV parasol, to shade Mercy's features. The watery sun was hardly burning with tropical intensity, but she looked even prettier. I'm sure that thought didn't enter her head.

'However,' she continued, 'realizing, as compassion obliges, the compelling stringencies besetting those who follow more mercantilic vocations than others of my acquaintance, Lovejoy, I am prepared to show condescension towards what you might provide. Bespoke or copied, I shall not enquire as to origin.'

You have to respect class. I listened with admiration. And Mercy was sheer unadulterated class. Well, maybe a little adulterated, but I still liked her. You don't see better on telly.

'Ta, Mercy.' She meant that forgeries or stolen would do.

'Now, Lovejoy. What, might I be given to understand, is the purpose of your visit?'

I took a sip of coffee. God, it was naff, really terrible. Yet she buys from posh London shops, has panniers of pricey victuals delivered by yak drovers each rustic dawn. I'd have liked some instant, but there you go. Mercy never ruins a performance except by accident.

'A friend died. I'm stuck to help his teenage son.'

'Ah.'

She lowered her parasol, brought a fan from a reticule, preparing the decks for action. Hastily I shook my head.

'No, love. Nothing to do with introducing him to sex. It's just he's in a plight. Murder's on the cards. He's been kept safe so far by kindly locals, lives more or less wild.'

'Such contumely!'

'He's keeping out of the way of some people. I need to know what folk come here. Anything that might help.'

She was pleased. 'To my establishment? One characteristic constantly delights a lady's heart, Lovejoy. It is emotion.' Her eyes closed in rapture. 'Hate, anger, passion, love, desire.' She swallowed, fanned herself, sipped to calm down.

'Well, something's got to be done, Mercy.' Even to me I sounded lame.

'I shall assist, Lovejoy. And you shall deliver me a dozen other works of art. Payment,' she said, eyes over the rim of her cup, 'to be arranged.'

'Right. About these folk, then.'

'Might I enquire if they include the . . .' she moaned a little ' . . . the slayer?'

'Possibly,' I said. 'But possibly means possibly not.'

'Will you kill them, Lovejoy?' She was breathing hard now, breasts rising and falling, lace handkerchief dabbing her throat. 'You've been involved in such occurrences. I realize that I have never actually been present at such a reprehensible event. It almost precipitates one's inner sentiments into a strange ineluctible craving to witness the perpetration of such a catastrophic calamity.'

What the hell did she mean? I went all noble. 'I shall simply bring them to justice, if it's any of these.'

She took the list I passed her, her eyes holding mine.

'Pull the other leg, Lovejoy,' she said coarsely. 'It's got fucking bells on.'

I'd listed everybody I could think of, from New Caledonian Market on. I'd even included me, to show the extent of my desperation, but kept Mortimer's name off. I arranged to phone her for news. I wanted to leave with some cavalier quip, but what can you say to a vision of purity? I said so-long, and left her on her terrace, sipping from her Royal Doulton, reading my list and moaning softly.

How different men and women are. My visit to Doldrum's scrapyard took a millisec by comparison.

Maybe forty or fifty diced vehicles were crammed into the farmyard. I found him under some motor. Doldrum's been in the same overalls ever since I met him. Fortyish, chunky, decisive, he only ever hires from Cockneys because, he says, they are thick as thieves anyway. You daren't laugh.

'Doldrum? It's me, Lovejoy.'

'Wotcher, mate.' He rolled out on some skateboardy thing, grinning. He leaves his teeth in a jamjar in his shed. Don't ask me. 'Heh's yer fahver?'

'Fine, ta, Doldrum. You?'

'Slogging my guts aht. Wanner motor?'

'No, ta. Any news of local blokes selling posh motors?'

He inflated his lungs, bawled a few names, yelled, 'Get lorsst, will yer?'

Three or four oil-soiled blokes emerged from vehicles and wandered into a wooden shed, shutting the door. Doldrum stood, lit a fag by striking a match on a drum of petrol, flicking the match anywhere. I winced, but we made it. He blew smoke.

'Local? When?'

'Eastern Hundreds. Lately.'

He gazed about, smoked a bit. You've to let blokes like Doldrum think. I knew him from coming across an old motor car in the corner of a neighbouring farmer's field. It turned out to be an Invicta, 4.5 litre S-Type, the ugliest racing tourer you ever did see. I'd dissuaded the farmer's lady from taking it to the auctions, and instead got Doldrum to do a half-and-half with her. Half the proceeds of restoration go to the restorer, half to the owner. He sold it to a crook, but it did Doldrum – and the lady, who still sees Doldrum on the sly – a power of monetary good. I knew I'd get a straight answer.

He eventually started mentioning names. Mostly blokes, some women. He mixed folk up with cars indiscriminately. E-Type this, S-Type that, numbers and letters, descriptions of sales, the fate of this motor, that axle. He must have been going maybe quarter of an hour before he said a name I recognized.

'Goldhorn?'

'He's croaked. Five motors, two near mint, nuffin on the clock.'

'Who came, Doldrum? Where?'

'Foreign bloke called Gluck brung Goldhorn's motors. Wonnied cash up front,' he grumbled. 'He'd already sold them to a mate down Catford.'

'When?'

'Said he were running a posh antiques gaff down Chelsea Reach. Showed me Goldhorn's registrations. I made the lads see him orff. Pushy burke, thought I were born yesterday. It wer wivvin a monff or two.'

'He sold them, then?'

'Fortune.' Doldrum gets really glum thinking of deals done without him. 'That it, Lovejoy?'

As I said so-long he said after me, 'Hear of anybody wrappin' their motor, Lovejoy, let me know.'

'Promise,' I said. 'Tarra.'

See how uncomplicated talking with a bloke is? Now I knew Gluck was so desperate for money that he'd tried to sell Arthur Goldhorn's pristine old motor cars to two separate car dealers. Hell of a risk. Gluck was on even thinner ice than I'd assumed. And even more desperate for gelt.

21

D AWN RAIN CAME swirling up the
estuary on North Sea wind. The
instant I'd tottered home I washed,
naked as a grape, at my garden well. I still felt polluted.
Odd, seeing that not long before I'd been narked because
Sorbo wouldn't give me a drop of his hooch. I used rain to
do it again, scrubbing like a maniac with soap homemade
from ashes and candle fat.

You mustn't miss breakfast, most important meal of the
day. Porridge made like Gran used to, with water alone,
fills you longer. Then a biscuit the mice hadn't found,
greedy little sods. I went into my cellar hidey hole, moving
the divan and lifting the flagstone on its ring. I used a
candle, electricity not making it, and descended into bliss.
I too keep records. A carder man like Saunty sells to
whoever will buy. I would visit him and his merry lass later.

They're in boxes, no real order. Scraps torn from magazines,
photos nicked from dentists' waiting rooms, cyclostyled
run-offs stapled in remote Norfolk sheds, it's all here. I
crouched to go through what I had, realized with fright

that I'd assumed the same hunched position in Sorbo's front garden, so sat instead on the ladder step.

Some people can assimilate without effort. I'm like that, but can't for the life of me classify the stuff. It's haphazard osmosis. I'm no gardener, for example, but I'm in the happy position of being able to inform the world that a perfectly nourished tomato plant can attain a height of twenty feet, six whole metres. Further, those unable to sleep for wondering who was our very first car fatality can now nod off – it was poor Bridget Driscoll, a London lady in her forties, who in 1896 was watching a strange new horseless contrivance at Crystal Palace. See? No rhyme or reason.

But I did the best I could, with my head spinning and Sorbo everywhere. Despite lingering horror, I amazed myself. As I read, I calmed. With this many weird happenings, surely there was one way to hook a killer and then do what? I shelved the answer – do I mean the question? – and rummaged deeper.

Some scams leap like kids in class: *me, teacher, me!* The primo scam these days is always caches of antiques and Old Masters looted in wartime. I'd thought of this, but binned it as corny. I mean, walk down London's famed Duke Street, look up, and you'll be gazing at a window that conceals one such, the Menzel Mystery. Ten a penny but fascinating for a' that.

Adolphe Menzel isn't really ancient or famed. It's been maybe a century since his passing. Worth considering, though, when a stranger drops in to sell half a dozen Menzel sketches, which is what truly happened. Imagine a dealer's horror when he later opens a rare book – and sees them illustrated among stolen sketches. This honest – no kidding – dealer zoomed them back to grateful old Dresden, which said, Ta muchly, but does anybody know who has *the remaining 1,550*, please? I pondered this contender, because that huge number includes Durer, Cranach, Altdorfer *et al*.

The mystery doesn't end there. The Soviets in 1945 hoovered antiques up – they returned over a million to Berlin in the fifties – and at least that many are still on the lamm. In round numbers, a million – except Dr Johnson says, 'Round numbers are almost always fake.' See the temptation? If Gluck the Greedy were offered a load of valuable paintings, sketches, whatever, I was sure he'd bite, even though they'd been looted from some Bavarian castle. It's the eternal question: If your Grampa left you a priceless sketch that he'd picked up in wartime, would *you* pop it in the post to somebody who claimed it was theirs? I don't wish to offend, but I suspect that maybe you might tell them to get lost and hug it to your bosom.

Continental museums sob that, okay, the German Statute of Limitations expires at thirty years, so you couldn't go to prison. I still think that maybe you'd cry, It's mine, all mine! and let international relations go hang. Why shouldn't you? There's no reliable international law. Common European Market laws likewise stay silent. They know greed.

'No.' I spoke to myself. I was freezing. Cellars are cold. 'It's been done.'

I wanted an original scam that would hook Snob Gluck. He'd killed Arthur for a grand estate plus an antiques firm, missing out on the ancient lordship title because of the existence of young Mortimer, whom he'd presumably not known about. And killed Sorbo over the intaglios I'd heard of. Gluck was desperately short of money. And murderously evil, but not dim. With the right scam, I'd protect Mort, and rescue Colette from her bag-lady hell.

An hour or so later, still surging on, I heard someone moving about in my cottage. I always pull the flagstone to when I'm down there, on account of debt collectors or rival dealers after money. Wisely I kept the candle burning – nothing's so pungent as a smoking candle wick – and stilled until they'd gone. It might have been Dosh, wanting answers at last. It might have been police. The cottage door lock never works, and anybody can wander in.

When my candle had guttered to a one-eyed glow, I gave up and cautiously crept into daylight. The place was empty, the door pulled to. There was a note:

> Dear Lovejoy,
>   The canal where you fell. Teatime.
>   Sincerely,
>   Mort.

That made me think about time. I hurried down the lane to Eleanor's house – I babysit for her Henry sometimes – and borrowed her bicycle. I set off to the carder man's house. I'd kill him if he wasn't in.

Ever since I realized that Eve's apple wasn't the whole story, sex has worried me. Not my own, you understand. I mean people's, like Saunty's. His activities would baffle the Archbishop of Canterbury.

He's a simple-looking bloke, listens to new orchestral music all day long. Once, he was deputy mayor somewhere. It's a famous local tale, how he was in an important council meeting, when to his own astonishment he heard himself go, 'Ladies and gentlemen, I wish to announce that politics is crap.' And upped and offed. His wife divorced him, his shamed children marched out. He was left destitute but happy. A psychiatric nurse assigned to correct that wayward politician, please, arrived, and promptly moved in. They 'behave abominably', say our local newspapers. Outraged people are forever ringing the police because Saunty and his nurse are yet again copulating in the garden. The nurse, Yamta, tells magistrates that she and Saunty are a 'living sculptile'. I don't know what it means either. One wry magistrate asked coldly, 'Do you imply, madam, that this sculptile is for sale?' and fined her a hundred zlotniks. Rotten sports, magistrates. What harm do they do, sculpting away? Heaven's sakes, it's Saunty's own garden. And villagers who don't want to be outraged can walk down a different lane, but don't. Saunty's lane is a well-travelled thorough-fare. Everybody passes by, to be outraged some more.

Which is why I began ringing the bicycle bell two fur-longs off. They were in the garden laughing at yet another court summons. I pulled my trouser turn-ups from my socks, and walked in trying to look like everything was normal. They were naked, having coffee and sloe sherry Yamta brews. Purple drinks always look Wicked Queen to me, but I accepted. I felt really odd sitting there fully clothed.

'Aren't you cold?' I asked, curious. It's my experience that women always feel a draught. Boil them alive, they'd still say shut that door it's freezing.

'You always ask that.' Yamta smacked me playfully. She's thirty-eight, bulbous with straggly hair. By comparison Saunty's like a stick insect, James Joyce minus the specs. She sobered. 'We heard, Lovejoy.'

'Who from?' I wasn't taking any chances.

'Gaylord faxed me,' Saunty said. He looked dreamy. I noticed he was smoking a churchwarden. Yamta grows certain prohibited flora, to enhance spontaneous merriment.

It's their other scandal, but not on a par with frolics. 'Gluck's got to be stopped, Lovejoy.'

'Shall we get down to it, then?' Yamta said.

'Er . . .' I'm never sure what she means. Orgy's never far.

We went in. Saunty takes an hour to set up, computer, paper, tomes built up like a redoubt with him in the centre. Saunty can't think naked, so they both get dressed. I use this term loosely. It's only dressing gowns and slippers. Yamta put on some atonal orchestral music, quite pleasant with the proper side of your brain.

'Terms are ten per cent of the gross, Lovejoy,' Yamta said, 'payable a fortnight after the scam goes down. Even if you don't use Saunty's scheme.'

'Right.' I'd have agreed to anything. This is a standard carder man's fee, not cheap.

She brewed tea. We got chairs. By the time he began Saunty looked like a spud in a kiln, with stacks ringed about him. We had to peer over a parapet of documents. The last hour, Battle of Rorke's Drift.

'You want to restrict the scam to anything in particular, Lovejoy?'

'Anything, as long as it works.'

Yamta looked at me, spotting my desperation I suppose, and started flopping about lifting folders while Saunty clicked his PC.

'Mars meteorite fragments any good?' he suggested. 'Ever since they found primitive carbonate deposits in those polar ice-cap SNC chunks, even small fragments have shot up in value ten thousand times. No? I've blokes who only sell guaranteed Martian nitrogen isotopic signatures, with geochemical spectroscopic certificates. Proven pieces of Planet Mars.'

'No, ta. Everybody's doing it.' All museums were busy

cashing in while scientists excitedly worked out extraterrestrial DNA.

Files moved. The screen blinked, scrolled.

'Mermaids, Lovejoy?' he offered. 'Good scam, that would be.'

'Have to be in Zennor in Cornwall, though.'

We have an ancient law: all mermaids caught in UK's territorial waters – or on land, if your luck's really in – belong to our Sovereign. Like swans on the Thames, and sturgeons. Only one mermaid actually doesn't. Every Evensong in Zennor's ancient church, she flops in from the sea and sits in the rearmost pew. She does this in penance for the village lad she enticed away one Sunday. Never seen again, poor lad. Angry villagers carved her figure into the pew. Don't pinch her place, incidentally, or you're for it. There her fishy spirit lingers, safe from being snaffled as royal prerogative decrees. You can see her there any Sunday. The one that got away, so to speak. Gluck was no romantic.

'No, ta. It'd be another DNA job.'

'Or an ancient carving? Pillock's still in business, does mostly limewood carvings for Zurich, but he'd be keen to help. Or antique parrots?'

'That Aussie thing? Painted some birds' feathers?'

Saunty chuckled. 'Common green Aussie parrots, they were. He dyed them with cinnamon shampoo, sold them off as rare Indian Ringnecks for seven thousand quid a pair instead of the cost of a meal. Any good?'

'No, ta.'

'Them little Chinese monkeys?'

'What's this interest in biology, Saunty?' I was narked. Yamta's dressing gown had proved too warm. Busy among the files, she'd cast it off. So I had to suffer, thoughtless cow.

'The Chinese Ink Monkey was extinct,' Saunty rambled joyously on. 'Scholars trained them to fetch manuscripts and mix ink. They were rediscovered couple of years ago. Priceless, an extinct species that made it back! Any good?'

'No, ta.'

'For a really big con,' Saunty said after a while, 'how about another Sheppard's?'

I hesitated. 'It's an idea, Saunty.'

It was the world's biggest recorded robbery ever. Astonishingly, it was a simple daylight mugging in, of all places, King William Street, in fair London town. Incredible to relate, a Sheppard's messenger strolled unguarded carrying nearly three hundred million pounds sterling, Treasury bearer bonds to be precise. A bloke with a knife threatened the messenger, who saw sense. Gone, quick as it takes to tell. Now, the City of London hardly ever has daylight muggings. The CID, Interpol, and FBI came into it, some Texan wheeler dealer died in Houston, people hid in Cyprus. It got really ugly.

'Of course,' Saunty continued blithely, 'they should have sent them straight to Indonesia, held them there for a twelve-month. Instead,' he said with scorn, 'they floated them in dribs and drabs – Cyprus, Miami, Glasgow. Nerks.'

'Didn't they try Liechtenstein?' Yamta wafted erotically by. 'I've always wanted to go there.'

'Just too stunned when they got away with it. Operation Starling, the plod called it.'

'No, ta. Antiques, please.'

'How about Manhattan Island, Lovejoy?'

'No, ta. Too many people called Edwards.'

Yet it wasn't a bad suggestion. It's founded in fact, which every good con trick should really be. In a gold bricker, at least the gold brick is genuine. Back in the eighteenth century Robert Edwards, a Welsh buccaneer from Ponty-pridd, was rewarded for bravely fighting wicked Spaniards. His present was seventy-seven acres, nice plot of land worth almost one hundred English pounds. It's now known as Lower Manhattan, and – be prepared – its value has risen somewhat! To trillions. Needless to say, where unclaimed wealth goes, can scams be far behind?

Not neglected, though. The trouble is it's claimed by the world and his wife, for who here doesn't have an Edwards in the family tree? Some eleven thousand have been claiming away for two hundred years. The tease is: prove you're Robert's direct descendant, and Lower Manhattan's yours. There's even an association of Robert's heirs, hard at it in Six Mile Run, Pennsylvania. Flourishing scams hover everywhere, advising would-be claimants to have a go. 'Use our cast-iron guaranteed genealogy services!!!' and all that.

'It's going to be a TV Revelation Documentary next year,' Yamta said.

'Forget it, Saunty,' I said. Just my luck to have a film crew interview Gluck just as I got to the sting.

'A public school find? Or a seminary jaunt?' Saunty was unperturbed. He loves this kind of thing, a chance to delve in his con tricks, testing himself.

'School? Like what?' I thought of Holloway and Shar.

'Isn't this music a racket?' Yamta asked fondly, toting and hauling files. Saunty whistled along with atonal violas.

'Wimborne!' he exclaimed. 'I'm longing for somebody to try it. This school had a copy of an ancient Assyrian bas-relief. The boys used to play darts near it, little buggers. Turned out it was genuine frieze, King Ashurnasirpal II of Nimrud. Christie's I think got a record twelve mill US for it. You like, Lovejoy? Easy peasy. Tell Gluck you've found another, ha-ha. The school was once the stately home of the patron who financed the excavations at Nimrud. No?'

'Not bad,' I said. Close, and getting closer.

'Calcata? The Holy Foreskin? It's still missing.'

'I like this one,' Yamta said wistfully. 'Tea, Lovejoy?'

It came up on Saunty's screen. 'Christ's foreskin used to be in St John Lateran until Rome got sacked. It finished up in a casket in Calcata. Dozy little hill town north of Rome. I can give you directions. The reliquary was gorgeous. The parish priest kept it in a shoebox under his bed. Any good?'

'What happened to the reliquary?'

'Its gems drifted.' He chuckled. 'The Vatican forbade Catholics from talking about it, 1900 onwards, under pain of excommunication. I've details of fourteen other foreskins in Europe. The bit of Christ that didn't ascend to heaven, see?'

'Anything similar? Not Thomas à Becket, though.' I was still thinking reliquaries.

'Christ's manger any good, from Bethlehem? It's in the Santa María Maggiore, in Rome. It's not been used in con tricks lately.'

Pagans also have miracles, I told myself, as convincing as those of orthodox religions.

'No, ta.' Closer still, though.

Yamta set the tea tray down. I had to look away. Naked women are callous. No thought of the effects they're creating.

'Famous writer's lost manuscript?'

I guessed he meant Kipling's unknown play *Upstairs*, written late 1913 or so, that surfaced lately. I grimaced.

'Here's what you're looking for, Lovejoy. The Louvre!'

'Not another Louvre fraud.' They're a yawn, but I kept my I'm-still-interested smile so as not to offend.

'It's got museum curators sobbing into their ale, scared they'll never be able to buy again.' He wheezed in merriment, his poppy tobacco doing its narcotic stuff. 'It was them two women, and that lawyer.'

My ears pricked. Whatever anybody says, women are always more interesting. They can turn dislike into hate, hatred into vendettas, faster than wink.

'That rich French heiress, her collection of Old Masters. The nurse seems to've done a deal with lawyers, who did a deal with some Parisian curator of Guess Where, to buy *The Gentleman of Seville*. Spaniard called Murillo – ugly bastard, he was – did it. The French curator got done for receiving stolen goods. You like, Lovejoy?'

Saunty provides a sort of weird after-sales service – photographs, copies of court records, photos of the perpetrators, police names. He's good value.

'Nice one,' I said cautiously.

Saunty was pleased. 'I'd give it a go, for Gluck, Lovejoy. See, the heiress had a sensible sister – they didn't speak, hate each other. Her bulb lit. She sued for the paintings. I've photo transparencies if you want.'

'What's the curators' grouse?'

He snorted (I mean with scorn). 'It made the greedy bastards suddenly scared to buy anything. They want priceless antiques for a bent farthing, bring tourists, see? They're hand in glove with lawyers, and lawyers are crooked. Add curators and law, you've got a thieves' mucky midden.'

'Not bad. Museums are a gift.' I thought museums.

'What about those old motors?' Yamta put in.

'Lovejoy hates engines.' Saunty laughed, digging files. A heap fell over. Yamta knelt to retrieve them. 'But that George Thingy in Surrey's the wizard. No?'

'It's got to be confidential.'

Saunty fell about laughing. Yamta laughed, quivering so much I had to think of Blackpool.

'Nark it,' I said, indignant. 'I want confidential, not another Piltdown.'

The Piltdown Scam is fabled in song and story, when *Eoanthropus dawsoni*, the infamous Dawn Man of Sussex, was excavated near Lewes in 1912. It's such an obvious scam I wonder they don't teach it in school. There are scores of books written about whodunit. Myself, I blame Smith Woodward of the British Museum. Saunty sobered.

'Never thought I'd hear you use a word like confidential, Lovejoy, especially when you're going to sink a rodent like Gluck. Know what confidential means nowadays? It means Scottish Water customers' "confidential" details turning up as wrappings on fireworks made in Ceylon. It means secret SAS manuals sold at a boot fair. It means MI5 security documents on a council rubbish tip. And medical patients' laboratory test details found in dustbins. I can list two thousand breaches of confidentiality, Lovejoy. Want it?'

'No.' I struggled to think. 'It's got to be posh. He's a snob.'

Instant delight. Yamta crowed, hurtled into the stacks.

'Why didn't you say so, Lovejoy? We're home and dry!'

'We are?' I was too tired, scared for Mort.

'Snob means royalty, or rescue. Prestige, see?'

No, I didn't. He sat back.

'Listen, Lovejoy. There was a bloke in the fen country. Declared himself King of Upware, his village, nineteenth century. Renamed his pub Five Miles From Anywhere No Hurry. Barmy. Guess what? People flocked.'

'That's not for me. I want fake, not flake.'

'Some bloke fifty years back declared his village independent, offered it for sale to the USA, Soviet Russia. No takers. He finally "donated" it to the Queen, ending the reign of King Len. I've scores of others.'

Saunty scented success. 'Lord This, Earl That, Baron von God-knows-what. It's the oldest con in the world. It's only pretending. And it's legal to invent – and use – a title. Anybody can do it.'

'They can?' I was startled.

Yamta was loving this. 'Want to be the Marquis of London, Lovejoy? Just say you are! You can't get arrested. Want your girlfriend to be the Princess of Whitehall? Just have her visiting cards printed, and presto!'

'What if somebody checks up?'

'You're in the clear. But don't use it to commit a fraud, Lovejoy.'

A long pause. 'Ah,' I said.

Saunty grinned at my expression. 'Ah, indeed! We there?'

'Well done, everybody,' Yamta said. 'I knew you'd do it. Now a little break, I think.'

I escaped an orgy by promising to return when I'd more time. I carried with me a folder compiled by Saunty. The question was how much to tell Mort. I got a lucky lift on a Long Melford furniture lorry, and reached the canal where I'd once fallen in. Teatime in Suffolk's four o'clock. I couldn't help pretending that I'd cycled all the way, so fit that I hardly raised a sweat. Pathetic.

22

STANDING IN THE woodland, where the big river didn't quite reach the sea estuary, I reflected that everybody does the unexpected. A man marries the wrong bird. A girl takes the wrong subject at college. You order the wrong meal. Women especially don't do what I expect – which only means I'm thick, I suppose. I turned to the offshore wind. I love air. It makes me remember how wrong you can be about people.

There was this woman, Leanne. Leanne was the most meticulous bird on earth. Ever. It took me two years to become her friend. I'll be honest. I wanted an antique pasglas she had. This is an unusual cylindrical beaker Rhineland pubs kept for jovial conviviality when drinking groups gathered. You get occasional ones with enamel designs on that sell for a fortune. This valuable drinking vessel has a kind of groove, sometimes a thread, that shows where old Heinrich is allowed to drink to. Share and share, you durstn't gulp beyond your mark. Well, Leanne had an enamelled pasglas with an external notched spiral decoration on it, marked with the insignia of some Bavarian shooting club. Its value was a row of serious noughts. I met her while helping our parson to mend his gate. I ran her home in my

Austin Ruby. She invited me in. I saw the pasglas, asked to buy it. She refused, so I fell in love with her and started wheedling.

Not, I can admit, casually. If Leanne said coffee at ten, she meant literally ten of the clock. Arrive at nine-fifty or ten past, your knock remained unanswered. And only coffee, no hanky panky. As months passed, she slowly unbent, so to speak. The trouble was, I actually began to like her. In antiques, fondness is bad news. Keep your eyes on the prize. In fact, when I finally reaped the pasglas, we were making regular smiles behind her drawn chintz. So there was Leanne in her cottage, pleasant, plump, and pliant, when the sky fell in.

She won the lottery.

Instant multi-millionairess. Only person I'd ever heard of who did it. The world veered on its axis.

Leanne instantly bought a yacht, to sit idle in her minuscule garden. It never sailed. Day Two, she bought an ostrich farm in Devonshire, never went to see it. That first weekend she shopped like a maniac, ran London's prestigious stores ragged. We made love in her bedroom among seventy-one new hats. Oxford Street sent two huge pantechnicon trucks full of new shoes. She bought three stone fountains for conservatories she didn't have, bought motor cars she couldn't drive. As for clothes, they arrived in roomfuls.

This, note, was my meticulous Leanne, who once sternly asked me to leave for dropping my teaspoon. And the same Leanne who wrote to the Home Secretary whenever the post girl came later than six-forty a.m. 'Standards, Lovejoy,' she'd say primly, 'must not fall.' She even said it in bed.

Three months, she'd spent up. I tried to stem the spending tide, and failed. Penniless, Leanne sat in her tiny thatched cottage among her purchases, on her face a look of utter rapture. A remote cousin hurtled in to dispose of the loot. Leanne smiled on, replete. By autumn she was back to her pernicketty self, scolding village shopkeepers for dusty shelves. I still see her, by precise arrangement. She embroiders samplers for me, two hundred stitches each afternoon. I sell them every Lady Day. My point is, I'd have staked my all on Leanne investing every groat of her lottery windfall, and following the Stock Exchange indices on the TV noon bulletin with graphs pinned on her parlour wall. I could imagine other winners going instant fruitbowl, but Leanne? Never.

See what I mean? I get things wrong.

'Hello, Lovejoy.'

I leapt with a squawk. 'You scared me stiff.' I calmed sweatily. 'Hello, Mort.'

He looked crestfallen. We stood looking over the fields to the sea. I didn't know quite what to say. Well, you don't.

'This is where I got your dad wrong,' I said, starting where my thoughts had left off. 'It was the only time Arthur ever shouted at me. I'd only cursed, said it was a horrible place.'

'You fell in the mud.'

'I didn't see you. Were you there too?'

Wind ruffled his hair. 'I hide. I like being among trees. I like here, not just because Dad guarded it so. Because.' Mort pointed.

I peered along his arm. Nothing. 'What?'

'The oxlip. See it? *Primula elatior*.' He meant a little flower. 'It's not the false oxlip, which is only a cowslip-primrose hybrid. The true oxlip is East Anglian, grows in ancient woodland.'

'Does it really!' I cleared my throat, edgy. The lad wanted

to tell me about frigging daffodils, fine. But why meet miles from anywhere on a windy shore?

'The oxlip is rare in hedges,' was his next winner.

'Goodness gracious.' Whatever next?

'It spreads about one stride a year, into modern woodlands that are less than four hundred years old.'

I thought, here I am wanting ways to kill – no, I mean restrain – the homicidal Gluck, and I get the biography of a frond?

'The small-leaved lime's my favourite.' I looked at the floor's greenery. 'No, Lovejoy,' he said patiently. 'Mesolithic wildwood trees. They mark ancient woodland. Also rare in hedges.'

'Rare in hedges!' I repeated, impressed. I was frantic to say something to the lad. This was his special treat, hungering for somebody on his side, telling me this junk. 'Rare like the, er . . .' Jesus, what was it, primrose?

'Oxlip.' I almost fainted with relief. 'There *is* the occasional hedgerow of solid small-leaved lime trees. Shelley in Suffolk has one. But it's only the remaining edge of an ancient Mesolithic woodland.'

'Well, it would be,' I exclaimed, trying like mad. Is this how women feel, anxious to say the right thing when some bloke's wittering about carburettors and Gregorian chant harmonics?

'And it's where Grampa is,' he ended.

That shut me up. Grampa? Uneasy, I looked about. We were some distance from the vineyard where Arthur was buried. No headstones among these trees.

Behind us the wooded slope shielded the bend of the river. It was soporific, as all countryside. Cows, a couple of anglers, fields beyond the trees. Facing, the downward slope to the gleaming muddy shore and the North Sea. To the far right, a low headland, houses, a small factory thing with a chimney stub. Left, more trees. This was where Arthur dreamed of cutting his canal, until something had stopped him. Maybe Grampa's grave? I brightened. A link at last? In the distance there was one huge solid tree. I glanced a question.

'Yes, that's Dad's mulberry. King James wanted everybody to grow them, bring the silk industry. Wrong mulberry, of course.'

Silly old King James, then. They say he was a pillock. 'Er, your grandfather?'

'Yes.' He didn't point. 'He's in the sand.'

I wanted to ask why the hell did Arthur bury his dad in the sands of the seashore, but couldn't. There's all sorts of barmy protocol for asking if you want sugar or biscuits, but we've none for essentials.

'Grampa's in his aeroplane.' Mort looked so sad. 'It got shot. He managed to keep it flying, and reached home.'

A small lugger jibed, reaching for the headland. I watched it. In the distance, a low tanker smudged the horizon. I worked out chronology, wartime, dogfights, fighters on old newsreels.

Mort was speaking. 'The old canal locks are a league up-river. Here's the narrowest gap from the river to the estuary.'

So if anybody wanted to link the canal – read the entire inland waterways – with the river and the sea, they'd have to cut through the woodland where we were standing. As if he scanned my mind he added, 'Only two furlongs, Lovejoy.'

Of old woodland and field, blocking the commercial goldmine. I cleared my throat, said nothing.

'Me, Lovejoy. Dad sold it to me, the manor's river rights and navigation rights. Of this little stretch.' He smiled the sort of smile you could easily mistake for a smile, if you weren't careful. 'For a farthing.'

My mind went: but Arthur didn't need to sell it to his son, surely? Ancient manorial rights pass father to son, with the lordship title, plus the rights to hold village markets and ancient leet courts, the lot.

'He assigned me the title, and this bit of land, before he signed the guarantees Mother wanted to give to somebody. Dad made me buy the lordship, the title, and this narrow stretch. It's called dryland. Strictly, anybody wanting even to walk a dog here ought to pay me a copper or two.'

So Arthur kept this ancient piece in Mort's possession, even though everything else – the manor of Saffron Fields, the estate, the Chelsea antiques firm – went to guarantee Gluck's escapades.

It was hard, but I finally spoke. 'Arthur *made* you *buy* it?'

'Yes.' Mort crouched, peered at some grassy thing to avoid talking directly. 'I'd never seen a farthing. Dad laughed. It has a robin on it. I had to hand it to him in the lawyer's office. I felt silly.'

Well, you would. Nobody's as embarrassed as a teenager. And nobody as embarrassing as an insistent dad.

'This is where your grandad . . .?'

'Crashed, yes. Dad knew exactly. He invented a magnet to trawl the waters at low tide. He was so surprised when it worked. The aeroplane's just there where the sea marsh begins. Nobody else knows, you see.'

My feet felt suddenly as if they were interlopers. Sometimes you want to hover. The flier must have limped his wounded plane homeward, felt relief seeing the coast appear, maybe smoke fuming from his engine, the pistons coughing, losing power, sinking, the gleaming sea marsh edging nearer as the waves rushed up and—

'Are you all right?' Mort was helping me up. 'There's a tea shop down the hard.'

'Course I'm all right, you silly bugger – er, fine, ta. I slipped.'

We walked along the shore, me sneaking looks at the coast. I told Mort the village tea shop would be closed, and it was. Mort knocked on the back door. The lady opened and served us tea and cakes as a matter of course. Mort didn't pay, I noticed. I pondered this.

Glenda was a pleasant lass, had two children watching school television. They shouted hopeful hellos, but Glenda wouldn't let them escape their lesson. Her husband, a coast-guard, was digging in the garden. His uniform hung behind the kitchen door. She said Mortimer, never Mort, and served him first.

Well, I'd found my link. I'd have realized what it was yonks ago if I'd been thinking straight. Arthur had deliber-ately excluded the small stretch of land from the guarantee Colette had forced him to give Gluck. It denied Gluck a vast commercial opportunity. And it protected the spot where the lone wartime flier had crashed and sunk into the shore marshes. To Arthur, the spot where his dad's plane lay was sacred. No wonder he'd wanted himself to lie beneath the mulberry tree. It was in view of his own father's resting place.

It was also the one place Arthur had lost his temper with me. You don't let somebody curse like a trooper near your brave dad's grave.

'Are you all right, Lovejoy?' Glenda asked. When I said I was fine, ta, she asked Mort, 'Is Lovejoy to stay here the night, Mortimer? He looks decidedly peaky.' She didn't ask me. The children shouted yes, yes.

'No, thank you, Mrs Elgar,' Mort said. The pair instantly

quietened. 'Please get Alan to drive him and his bike home.'
He wasn't asking, just saying that's what had to be. Glenda
smiled, glad everything was in its proper place.

'Alan'll be pleased to, Mortimer. Say when.'

Alan drove me home, chatting of tides, ships, lifeboats,
nothing of importance. I shouted ta from my gate as he
drove away, and stood for a long while as dusk drank the
day. Now I had the link, what to do with it? I went to
the Treble Tile for supper, had a think about snobbery,
money, antiques, and how the three might possibly be made
into one long unbreakable noose for somebody. Did I mean
chain? Handcuff? Noose was surely wrong.

23

LUCKILY, LISA WAS in the Treble Tile. She's the best newspaper reporter in the business, she says. She's bonny, slim, has a flat down St Leonard's parish by the town's docks. I like her.

'Don't worry, swine.' She plonked herself down. 'I've got my own sodding drink.'

'I would have offered!' I said indignantly. Lisa curses with aplomb. Actually, I'll omit her invective, if that's all right. Her degree was sociology, so she thinks swearing is propriety.

'You want something.' She eyed me narrowly, couldn't keep it up and heaved a sigh. I like women who heave sighs. 'Things are so effing quiet. I need a scoop.'

'Don't you just report Nessie again?'

'Don't muck about, Lovejoy.' But it's true. Since monks reported Nessie in the Middle Ages there's been over five thousand original new sightings of the Loch Ness Monster, which is only three hundred fewer separate paparazzi scoop reports of Queen Liz Two's pregnancies. There's still money to be made in it. I mean, the big-game hunter Montague Weatherall coined it in the 1930s by finding Nessie's foot-print – it was only a stuffed hippo's print. And Mussolini, no less, made mileage by broadcasting that his Italian war-planes had bombed Nessie to oblivion on a daring raid. Me? I think Nessie's only various eels, otters, or a whacking Baltic sturgeon having forgotten which way to migrate. Our joke is, Nessie can't be hard to find. She basks on the surface twice a day – ten minutes before you arrive, and ten minutes after you've gone home.

'I'll have a scoop for you, Lisa.' She's given up angrily spelling me her name. It's Liza, Leesa, Lisa, or any near combination. 'If you'll help.'

'Soon?' she squealed. Heads turned. She whispered, 'Soon?'

'Almost soon.' I noshed a bit until people stopped listening. 'Tell me about Saffron Fields. Arthur Goldhorn who died.'

'Dieter Gluck got the estate,' she hissed instantly. 'He's hunting loans.'

Thank you, God. 'The scoop's yours, Lize. I'm talking tabloids.'

She moaned, sounding in orgasm. Now heads really did swivel. 'You're fucking beautiful, Lovejoy,' she said huskily. My fork halted. I honestly think reporters are deranged. Lust, for a mere headline? Talking to Lize is like defining north – where you're standing is vital.

'I need more, though. Tell all about friend Dieter.'

'It's yours, darling.' Darling, when so soon a swine?

By now folk nearby were craning at obtuse angles, ears flapping in the pub smog. The tavern of a thousand ears. I finished my grub. 'Let's move.'

We went to sit in the bay window.

'Some folk crave prestige, Lovejoy.' She swore for a few breaths at other people's impertinence. 'Want to be county set. They slog forty years for a tin gong. Or bribe to be photographed with the Monarch's ninth footman.' She cursed equality.

'Please concentrate, love. Dieter Gluck.'

She eyed me, curious. 'He nicked Colette from you, didn't he?'

'He's leery.' I'd brought Saunty's file along, in case.

'Okay.' Her features screwed up, Lize the intrepid news hound cerebrating. 'Gluck badly needs funds. He's onto a development scheme.'

'Short of gelt when he owns the Chelsea antiques shop and Saffron Fields?'

Lize raised her eyes in exasperation.

'The mansion house is a protected stately home. The estate is a listed conservation area. Gluck came a real cropper. The instant he took possession, he spent on credit like a drunk thinking he'd snaffled a fortune. Everybody laughed. He assumed the manorial lands could be sold for development. The authorities slammed him like a ton of bricks. You know Arthur and Colette. Nice folks, but kept poor by inherited obligations. That's why they went into antiques, trying to make a fortune.'

Good news. I rejoiced, but had the sense to look glum. 'Couldn't Gluck raise gelt on the antiques business?'

Scorn showed. 'Don't act, Lovejoy. Gluck knows less about antiques than me, even. Ever seen his catalogues? His antiques either aren't his, or they're fakes. The bank manager turned the loan down. Can you believe it? Gluck even tried to sell the Lord of the Manor title – until he realized it was Arthur's son, Mortimer's.'

So Gluck was shrewd, until greed and snobbery made him stupid. Better.

'What's his development scheme?' I already knew, the waterway.

'Container terminal, gateway to Europe, all that.' She brought out a small bag. It slung a million bells into me. I reeled, reached out for it, but she held it with a knowing smile. 'Every coastal village longs to be a European marina linked to the inland waterways.'

A dozen schemes had been floated, only to fade for lack of money. Gluck was into a serious game. I shuddered from the vibes of her bag.

'Please, Lize.'

Lize handed it over. It almost glowed. With trembling hands I undid the purse string, brought out a small blue disc of glass. I shook with excitement.

'Twenty!' I croaked. Ten blue, ten colourless. 'Roman gaming counters.'

There had been a number of local Roman finds, and I mean orthodox archaeological discoveries. One was at Gosbeck's Farm, where they'd unearthed a latrunculus game, almost complete with ten counters a side, but no board.

'Got anything with it?'

'Only four little metal L things, very rusted. My boy-friend Mat has a metal detector.'

She coloured slightly. So Mat was illicit. Bad news for me, though. I'd never get these gaming counters off her now without a king's ransom. When all else fails, try honesty.

'Highly valuable, Lize. It's the Roman game of "soldiers", a sort of draughts. I think latrunculus means a highwayman. Those metal angles are the board's corners. Tell Mat to suss the whole area. Nobody's ever found a complete Roman counters game.' I looked, weighing my chances with her. 'Lucky Mat. I'm jealous.'

She reddened more. 'Don't start, Lovejoy.'

Worth a try. Love sometimes works, and passion has

been known to make friends and influence people. 'Here. Your Mat really into detectors?'

'He's an electrical engineer.' She sounded resigned. 'Talk of it night and day if I'd let him. Are these bits worth reporting in the newspaper?'

'Do a special article, love. Be photographed with them. Ask Carr at St Edmundsbury, tell him I sent you. He'll give you the history.'

'Thanks, Lovejoy.'

With a pang I returned her Roman counters, stealing them honestly far from my mind.

'Does Mat want a treasure-hunting job? Only take one night. Tell him,' I said carefully, 'it'll be a cert.'

At last I'd got my team together, and replaced Sorbo, *requiescat in pace*. Time I got to Camden Passage, met the troops and got on with it. I knew enough – I thought. I was sure of my next move. I said so-long, swore undying devotion, and fled.

On the train I dozed, woke blearily in London, caught the Northern Line from Moorgate to the Angel, Islington, where all antiques, they say, pass. Stand near the old green clock of J. Smith & Sons, still saying the metal firm can be found at 42-54, St John's Square, London EC1. In a year you'll see every antique in the world, stolen or legit. It's not true, but what is? It's the gateway to the great – I *mean* great – antiques market of Camden Passage.

Pleased at the proximity of antiques in The Mall (ugly building; so what?) and the York Antiques Arcade, I felt optimistic. I had the crucial ingredient – Dieter Gluck's desperate need for money, and his snobbery. Lize had confirmed it. Her boyfriend Mat, lucky swine, was the electronic seek-and-bleep treasure hunter I could get to help Mort with the sunken aircraft in the estuary's sand marshes. My full team would avenge Sorbo and Arthur. Victory was in sight!

Making an outing of it, I had a lovely time wandering the shops, noshing a bit, sussing out antiques. It's the best free day in London, doesn't cost a groat. There are difficulties. One is Camden Passage itself. Take Islington High Street and Upper Street. Which do you think is the more important? Answer: Upper Street. Because the grandly named Islington High Street starts off as a splendidly wide thoroughfare, then astonishingly gives up, dives into a miserable little ginnel you wouldn't even glance down. But Upper Street, which sounds like a leftover from some manky Lower Street, is wide, busy, and important. That's where Camden Passage is. It looks alley thin, but is the centre of the universe.

Upper Street's called that because it was more elevated than nearby Lower Street. I like it. (Incidentally, never mind what history says – Good Queen Bess really *did* visit Sir Walter Raleigh there in his Upper Street house across the road. Mind you, she also nipped round the corner to spend candle hours with the Earl of Leicester. I never did like him, untrustworthy sod.)

'Lovely!' I exclaimed at the scent and throb, mobs of agog hunters.

'Ain't it just, Lovejoy!' Sorbo said.

'Honest to God, Sorb,' I said, bliss in my soul. 'This place . . .'

My mind went, Sorbo? *Dead* Sorbo? I saw Trout between the dense traffic, and Lydia, smiling in anticipation. I heard Tinker's cough resounding mightily near the Camden Head pub.

I went dizzy. 'You're frigging dead, wack.' I'd put my hand on his dead face in the dark. His eye had been beaten into a bloody mess.

He stood there just as I remembered him in life. His eyes widened. 'Here, Lovejoy. You didn't think . . .? Catch him, mate!'

A passing bus inspector got me under the arms. I swayed about for a year or so, came to in the corner nosh bar with Sorbo telling an outraged Lydia how I'd keeled over when all he'd done was say hello. She was all for whisking me to Guy's Hospital for brain surgery. ('Everybody's conduct is disgraceful,' etc.) I settled for a quiet stroll up past St Mary's church and the fire station to the Hope and Anchor pub facing the long thin gardens near Canonbury Lane. I wanted tea, a wad, and explanation.

In that perfect tavern's interior Lydia looked like fresh from Westminster Steps, her loyal skiff doubtless waiting on the Thames. Dealers were lusting away. She, of course, was oblivious.

'What'd I do?' Sorbo was giving indignantly. The caff was crowded. 'Lovejoy said be here, so I come.'

Tinker swigged his bottled nourishment, lying to Lydia that he badly needed fluid, being a diabetic under doctor's orders.

'Lovejoy thought you'd been croaked, silly bleeder,' he grumbled.

'Me? It was Bern. It's in the frigging papers.'

They all looked accusingly at me. Dauntless leader of the pack, I'd discovered a body and not read all about it.

'Listen, everyone.' Lydia rapped the pub's grotty table. 'I must remonstrate. This atrocious language must stop. We each have certain essential information. Sorbo's is that he is not yet deceased.' Her luscious mouth set in a firm line. Nearby West Country dealers groaned. She turned to Sorbo. 'We are delighted to welcome you back to, ah . . .' We waited. 'To us,' she ended lamely.

The dead face in the tabloid was Bern's, Gluck's oppo. So who'd killed him? I couldn't help looking at Sorbo. He didn't usually wander this far from Streatham Hill. *Had* I told him to come? I couldn't remember.

'I was to investigate the paintings sold by Holloway University.' She placed her gloved hands on her lap. 'Gainsborough, Turner, and Constable. They are already successfully sold, via London auction houses.' She beamed. 'Isn't that wonderful? So much money for the poor struggling students!'

'Idle bleeders,' Tinker growled. 'Drunken moronic sods.'

'Mr Dill!' Lydia scolded. 'I shan't tell you again.'

'And Shar the lawyer?'

Lydia held a brief antagonistic silence. 'I was pleased. She acts for Dieter.' Meaning she wasn't pleased at all. 'Dieter tried to buy a Gainsborough from Holloway on credit. They declined.'

Shar acted for Dieter Gluck? Trout caught my eye, his glance saying: Lydia's a liability, so get rid. I wished he'd stop signalling that.

'Shar is very concerned about you, Lovejoy. The magistrates—'

I quickly stifled that. 'Ta, love. Tinker?'

'Dosh Callaghan wants to know whyn't you got whoever stiffed him over the padpas yet. Funny, he didn't seem concerned, Lovejoy. Are they worth much?'

The stout bowler-hatted gent had arrived, and was chatting up the serving lady. He had all my bad habits, glancing into wall mirrors, speculating. Once is chance. Twice is coincidence. Third time, it's a plot. How often had he been nearby unnoticed?

'Dosh dursn't be scorned. The lads'd crucify him.'

'Then why did he order so few?' Trout persisted. 'Five small gems aren't worth much.'

'Five? Was that all?' Trout was right. If you're going to bother, you want a hefty shipment to make profit. I'd been slow.

'If I were you, Lovejoy, I'd see Sturffie. He must have asked that same question when Dosh placed the order, right?' Trout was sympathetic. 'I know Sturffie's your pal, Lovejoy, but you gotter tackle him.'

'Trout,' I said earnestly. 'If ever I want a Tarzan-O-Gram, I'll see you're hired.'

'Ta, Lovejoy,' he said modestly. 'I do a good job. I'm also a Snake-O-Gram. I got a cobra suit.'

'Some other time,' I said faintly. Snakes make me queasy. 'So we go for it, okay? Gluck's the mark. Snobbery and greed are the prod. The question is, what antique's the carrot?' I'd already made my mind up.

Sorbo said. 'We'll need fair money, and a couple of pretty birds.' He eyed Lydia. 'Got a sister, love?'

'Lydia's out,' I told him, thinking of Gloria Dee's antiques. 'I'll get the money. Let's hear it, Sorbo.'

The stout man was arguing with the bar lady while lighting his pipe. I wasn't taken in. He was here because we were.

'And keep your voice down,' I added. We bent to listen.

24

THEY TOLD ME at the manse that Mrs Dee was out painting. It meant a trudge of a mile before I found her at her easel by a river's oxbow bend.

You never know with artists. They mostly hate gawpers, especially those who say, 'Hey, you've got the clouds wrong.' So I stood there like a spare tool. In countryside, everything's hunting. A heron standing on one foot, a kestrel flicking the sky, a crow on a branch, all itch to slaughter. An angler downstream proving that fishing is a good doze ruined.

'Thank you,' she said eventually. 'Others can't resist talking.'

'Okay.' I felt awkward. She seemed at home amid country carnage.

'You're dying to tell me what I'm doing wrong, Lovejoy.' Her smile was mischievous. I didn't move to help her pack up. Artists are funny about that, too.

'No.' Though I was, of course. Why the hell did she use a sable No. 12 brush, her washes so thick on 120 Whatman paper? 'Don't blame people, Mrs Dee. The eye can distinguish six million different hues. Bound to be argument.'

She smiled, folding the easel, drying the paint wells with

tissues. No litter from this lady. Clicked her box. Ready, steady.

'Did they say when's teatime?' she asked. I took the wooden box, leaving her to tote her priceless works of art.

'No. They never invite me in, at strange houses.'

I was glad her hair was long. The Other Woman always has longer hair than The Betrayed Wife. Odd but true. A moral in there? Let your hair grow long, you'll not only keep your own bloke but snaffle some other woman's?

'I heard they do. Invite you in, I mean.' She seemed to find me funny.

Had she sussed me out? I didn't like that. Today I wanted everybody to be gullible. Especially Mrs Gloria Dee, who had antiques. I needed money to do Dieter Gluck. You can't con a crooked dealer without being at least a bit rich. Those two admirable Italians proved that, with their now fabled 'Walt Disney Scam'.

They ordered four million dollars' worth of jewels in Place Vendôme. Cleverly, they hinted at illicit arms deals, knavish underworld connections, and in France's posh Hotel Intercontinental showed the jeweller two cases bulging with German banknotes. 'Assure us of privacy,' was their line, 'and we'll pay over the odds.' What salesman could resist? The jewels and money were swapped, the Italian conmen vanished. The money proved to be marked 'Banknote Walt Disney', with Mickey Mouse logos. This cheeky scam proved the universal law that greed rules us all. And Gluck.

We came in sight of the manse where her village began and countryside, thank God, ended. She hesitated.

'The question is, Lovejoy, whose side are you on?' Her blue eyes held me.

I didn't know what to say. 'In what?'

'In poor Mortimer versus Dieter Gluck.'

Women are often ahead of me when I think I'm miles up front. 'Dieter who?'

She smiled, nodded as if to herself. 'That's sensible. You don't really know me, do you?' We entered the short drive. 'I might be an enemy, after all. Do come in. My husband will soon be home.'

That almost stopped me. I'd assumed that she and Sir Jesson Tethroe, Member of Parliament, were sort of, well, frankly lovers. The housekeeper who'd first responded to my knock took Mrs Dee's clobber and we went through into a homely parlour overlooking a neat garden. Manse indeed. Christian books everywhere. I should have guessed. Mr Dee was a minister.

We sat to tea and crumpets. No antiques, though. I listened to my chest. Not a thing. I must have looked accusing. She placed herself opposite with that in situ casualness women have. I ate quickly. Survival is timed speed. No antiques meant I ought to be going.

'Look, missus.' I gestured at her home. Quite posh. Nothing like Clovis's grand manor, but well furnished, good Axminster carpets. 'I came to see antiques. Er . . .?' I wanted to ask if they were at Tethroe's, but married women's love is thin ice.

'Yes, Lovejoy. I would like you to assess their authenticity. If they're forgeries, please say. If not, do a valuation.'

This value thing's a problem. Any antiques dealer can guess what an antique will bring. Look at TV programmes, those 'Road Shows' which, the presenters piously preach, 'are not about money; they're about learning'. Watch for five minutes, you soon see whether they're about money or not. Out here in real life, dealers will charge you for 'valuation'. Their fee's a percentage. Please remember that *not one guess is worth a single groat*. If some dealer says he charges a 'valuation fee', tell him you'll charge him exactly the same fee for a look at your antique, and stalk off. It's a blinking nerve.

'Thank you, Lovejoy. I didn't think dealers were so honest.'

'Eh?' I must have been thinking aloud. Better watch that.

'Robert seems late. Shall we take a look?'

She rose with that one-move smoothness men can't do. I angled up, a bag of spanners, and followed through the french windows to a small conservatory. No jungles here. The lawn was stencilled, bushes in line, grass swept, trees clinging to their leaves for dear life like nervous visitors scared of spilling crumbs.

It's a queer thing, this divvying. I suddenly felt truly clammy and shivery, like sudden flu. The conservatory curtains, sap green, were drawn.

'I keep it locked, Lovejoy.' She wore a replica chatelaine, and used a key. We entered the conservatory's encapsulated dusk. I halted. She was speaking. I knew that because her mouth was moving, but I didn't hear.

Above the very centre, from reinforced struts, hung a chandelier. Now, everybody knows a chandelier. Some are valuable. But, porcelain? A few lustres hung from the limbs to reflect light. I stood looking up, my chest bonging, sweat stinging my eyes. I felt it drip off my chin.

'Sit, for heaven's sake. Don't you just hate it?'

She had her hand under my elbow and helped me to a chair. I reached it on the slant before my knees went.

'I'm fine,' I snarled. 'Leave me alone, silly cow. I'm okay.'

'Stay still. Is it the antiques?'

'Shut your row.'

'I didn't know you would be like this.' She was all anxious. 'I thought it was just a matter of taking a look.'

Porcelain is a world of history. From *porca*, Latin for sow, since it suggested pigskin. The stuff itself's quite simple – mix the right sort of clay with a fusible fedspathic rock, shape it, bake it in a kiln. The Chinese began it in the eighth century, and perfected it with their usual brilliance during our Middle Ages. China's original clay is the plasticky kaolin. The rock was called 'petuntse' by the French missionaries. This 'true' porcelain was the genuine stuff. It came first to Germany's Meissen, then Vienna about 1720-ish. Nearly fifty years later, the great names of France and England got going, and porcelain was king. We English copied the Chinese porcelain, from the 1740s on, by mixing 'frit' – glassy bits fused with lime or plain chalk. This made a 'soft' porcelain. There were other 'soft' porcelains – Bow and Chelsea and Liverpool – made with calcined bone chucked in. Soft-paste porcelains I always think are merely beginners' tries. Real porcelain is the hard Chinese type, white, translucent, and lovely. One annoying fad is to speak with bated breath of 'bone china', brought out by Josiah Spode in 1794, but it's only hard porcelain formula with added bones. Purists regard it with contempt as an in-between.

This chandelier was true hard porcelain of the Vienna factory. This manufactory's products are among the most highly prized and priced. Even at a distance, I could see the coloured onion-shaped churches and steepled roofs of houses depicted on the chandelier limbs. I must have moaned, because she cried, 'I'll get some water!' I restrained her.

Rarest of all in those days was the porcelain room. It sounds enough to make you ill, yet it was once all the rage. Great houses and palaces had rooms where furnishings, tables, and even walls, were porcelain. To me it's over the top, but who am I, when wealth defines luxury? The Vienna factory was created by du Paquier in 1719. It had ups and downs, going broke then thriving only to dive again. Empress Maria Theresa herself even had a go in 1744, but it tottered to a close in 1864. This financial swingbacking always provides one of the antique trade's ingredients for desirability – rarity.

'Got a table? Chair with porcelain inset?' I asked, hoarse. This was what I needed, to hunt Gluck.

'No,' she said simply. 'Only half a dozen mugs with black figures painted on.' She brought out a couple from under a sheet. 'Aren't they just horrible? Fat men sitting on barrels playing bagpipes?'

So I keeled over. One of us had to.

'Who is he?' this minister was saying, peering at me. Last rites, was it?

'Lovejoy,' I grunted, hauling myself upright.

'He fell when I showed him those pot things.'

I didn't say, but should have done, that her 'pot things' would buy half her village.

'Hot sweet tea, he needs,' the housekeeper said. She was a nice old dear with the self-righteousness all women have when somebody's ailing. 'People don't eat right any more. It's not good enough.'

She poured tea into me until I was waterlogged. Then provided biscuits, cakes, buttered scones, jam. I began to recover.

'I'm Robert,' said the bloke. 'You saw Arthur's pottery?'

'Yes.' My mind called a halt to honesty. 'Er, is it for sale?'

Arthur? The most sought-after porcelain is 'schwarzlot'.

Collectors go mad for it. They're not all bobby-dazzlers, just mugs or other items decorated with rustic scenes depicting travellers at an inn, pipers playing for a drink. Importantly, it's not at all flashy, just monochrome, black. Sometimes du Paquier's men touched up the figures' hands or cheeks with a dab of red, maybe with a little gilding for light relief. These still qualify as schwarzlot items, so don't go chucking any away (joke). One such mug will buy you a brand new car. A full schwarzlot drinking set will buy you a new house, plus a motor, plus a round-the-world cruise with a bawbee left over. Rare, they're out there waiting to be spotted.

'No, we can't sell them. They belong to a friend's son. Arthur's died, but gave them to us in trust for the boy. Only—' Here Robert paused, looked anxiously at his wife.

'Only what?' I was starting to piece things together. Mortimer, Arthur Goldhorn. But how come Arthur knew he was at risk? And why hadn't Colette taken any such steps? It was almost as if . . . I caught Gloria weighing me up, and stopped thinking. Women see through me.

'Only, lately we've had two people call.' He made a determined face when Gloria exclaimed. 'No, dearest. We must tell him. Arthur mentioned Lovejoy. I distinctly remember the awful name. He said that Lovejoy would call sooner or later and help us. Now,' he intoned nobly, 'is the time.'

My head was splitting. 'Any chance of some more tea, love?' I asked the housekeeper. 'And an aspirin?'

She scurried. I dithered upright. They walked me about a bit until I got breathing organized, then we sat like decent folk while I told them what they'd got. If the antiques were Arthur's – read Mortimer's – I had to answer Gloria's question by my actions, and prove whose side I was on.

My own question came on its own. 'Look. If money could make Mortimer safe, would you borrow on those antiques?' And the most marvellous thing happened. Gloria smiled.

25

THINKING OF OLD Masters and skull-duggery, as I was, you can't help thinking of one of the kindest, brightest blokes who ever was. Odd, but true.

Once upon a time it was 1819. A baby was born, eleventh of March, near where I was sprung. Slogging in Liverpool from his thirteenth year, little Henry Tate soared to financial fame through honest endeavour, in spite of being Unitarian Chapel. Soon he had several retail shops, and settled down to procreating babs with his missus Jane. Deep inside Henry a dream lurked. It was nothing less than sugar. It became Henry's battle cry. Feed workers clean wholesome sugar!

Victorians like Henry Tate thought on a scale nobody's ever quite matched since. The Cecil Rhodes of saccharides, he invented the sugar cube, no stopping him. Sprinkling his sons around his factories – Jane doing her stuff – Henry Tate pondered Life. Reading, he finally decided, was another of Life's essentials, and Art was another. He developed another slogan. Give folk free access to Books and show them Art!

He started giving public libraries. Then he got some land on Millbank, by the Thames. There, he stashed his art collection for people to visit and lift their spirits. So passed the wise Sir Henry Tate, leaving us the happiest, pleasantest of art galleries. Be careful, though. London never calls its bits by the correct name. Ask a taxi driver to take you to the 'National Gallery of British Art' he'll say, 'Eh?' You've to say, 'Tate, please.' Beats me.

Terms for con tricks, though, are etched in granite.

It was at the Tate that the peculiar con trick known as the Nicholson arose. It's very cunning. It's out to get you.

Great art galleries have archives. These are references, notes kept by old curators, artists' comments, auction receipts, letters. You want to authenticate an O'Conor painting of 1902? You delve in the archives, make a firm attribution the rest of us can trust. Eventual purchasers of O'Conor's paintings will then know when they're being offered a pig in a poke. Okay?

Well, *nearly* okay. As long as visiting scholars and art experts behave themselves, all alone down in your gallery's dungeons. By custom, from courtesy, you send copies of your own researches, catalogues, theses, publications, because fair's fair. The next generation of researchers will want accurate references. Decent people, art experts.

Yet – didn't I say? – fraud, like murder, will out. And crooks will in.

Enter the Nicholson, the 'Nick Trick' in dealer parlance.

It's called after Ben Nicholson, an honest modern painter. There's a vogue for his art. See one, buy it. Before you fumble in your pockets for pennies, though, think a mo. Why not authenticate this delectable painting? Go and search the archives, where, lo and behold, you find details of the colours he liked and letters telling how he painted it! Maybe even notes about it from some lady friend! You're convinced. The painting the dealer offered you is genuine!

But what if those references, old auction records, detailed notes in the archives *themselves are fake*? Then you've been had. You'll go smiling brightly, and buy a forgery. It's terrible. Why? Because you have no come-back. Your savings are down the chute. You'll have bought a daub not worth the price of the canvas. In short, you're broke.

The Nicholson con trick, then, is simple. You fake a painting 'in the style of' some artist. You gain access to a gallery's archives, pretending to research the artist's life and works. While you're down there, you slip into the archives details of some historical auction that *never in fact took place*, and include a description of your faked painting. Then only do you emerge, smiling brightly, and sell your fake. It's now '*archive-authentic*'! The archives which you've cunningly altered are there for all to see. Poor Ben Nicholson's name? Well, his were the paintings that brought the trick to fame. And the Tate's name is forever linked to this con. Scotland Yard's men are plodding about the vaults of our esteemed galleries even as you read. They'll get nowhere, take my word.

It came into being a few years before the new millennium. Strangely, the works were all easily fakable, from du Buffet to Sutherland, Nicholson, Giacometti. And in the V. & A. as well as the Tate, I suppose on the principle that you never change a winning con. So the Nick Trick rides with us into the sunset, 'proving' forgeries and fakes to be infallibly genuine. It's a disgusting con, begun at the gallery established by the most decent bloke who ever trod land. Aren't we rotten? I decided that London's oldest gallery deserved a look. Where was the harm?

*

I decided against taking Lydia to the Dulwich Picture Gallery.

There's no doubt, women hold life's core. Blokes don't. I don't mean understanding, so much as power. Give an example: Edna was bonny, with that magic colouring that holds your gaze even when you don't know why the heck you're staring. Shapely blondes with blue eyes have it. Middle-aged women with quiet faces and greying hair have it. And Edna – blue-rinsed, grey-eyed, bow-mouthed Edna – had it. She caused me problems, though, did Edna, because she was a chef who cooked by astrology. This astrologist moved in with me, installing ovens, fridges, shelves. She had the water and electricity turned back on.

Blodge, our local greengrocer, was deliriously happy at the sudden rash of deliveries. I couldn't move for bags of spuds and cauliflowers. If I stood up my head vanished among a forest of dangling herbs and onions. It was okay, though, because she was a skilled cook and a rapacious lover. Paradise? For a short spell, yes. I'd nothing against a chef checking for planets and comets before basting her carrots. Edna though was *ruled* by heavenly bodies.

For two days we ravished and dined, loved and noshed. The third evening I found no grub ready, so smilingly reached for her. Pale, she shoved me away. The cottage was still, kitchen cold. The planets had struck.

'It's Raphael's astronomical ephemeris, Lovejoy,' she said. 'I've made a terrible mistake. Just look at the Complete Aspectarian.' Edna never went anywhere without a folder containing charts.

'Eh? Does it matter?'

'We mustn't eat until the Planet Saturn's off the cusp, Lovejoy.' I can't remember the details – it might have been

Planet Cusp for all I knew. The gist, however, was that starvation was our menu all day.

And the next day.

By then, though, I'd fled, surviving by eating the Treble Tile down to its last butty. For three days I never went home. When finally I tiptoed into the garden, my cottage was bare. Edna had gone, taking her last twig of parsley.

See my point? Women have this terrific omnipotence. Women rule. Edna said 'Starve,' so I did, at least for an hour, until I was at death's dark door. It's their reasons that puzzle me. Starving in a good cause is fine, but because stars move about more on some nights than on others? I ask you.

The only original toll still going in London's tangled spread is in Dulwich's College Road. The guide books say that your motor is allowed past for five pence. Don't believe a word. By the time this gets printed it's like to cost you an arm. A lorry costs you a leg, which is important if you're casually dropping by to steal the Dulwich Picture Gallery's entire contents. It happens, incidentally, to be our kingdom's oldest picture gallery. History books tell you that it's all owned by 'Alleyn's College of God's Gift'. Means some school.

Edward Alleyn was an actor who made a fortune from bear baiting, dog fights, 'sports' like bull baiting in James I's time. He made even more by owning Paris Garden in Southwark – the same noble mansion house where the fated Jane Seymour, of Henry VIII fame, lived before. In 1613 Alleyn started building a school, with chapel and lodgings. Poor lads were to be taught there. It worked. The Fellows nobly pawned the college silver for the (losing) royalist side in the Great Civil War. Cromwell's Roundheads later gave tit for tat, melted the college's organ pipes into bullets. I walked past the college, round the pond, and into College Road.

With theft in mind.

Of course, you can deceive without actually storming a single rampart. Like, a famous Aboriginal artist lately painted highly sought primitive masterpieces – until a white highborn Australian lady was shown to be the creator. Good for her, I say, and no harm done, for who's to say she wasn't somehow influenced – maybe even darkly taken over – by some Aboriginal spirit? Sorry if this seems blasphemous, but how can we know?

Then again you *can* storm ramparts, like the man with the shotgun in the famous Lefevre Gallery theft in London's posh West End. He calmly walked in, took Picasso's portrait of the delectable Dora Maar, Picasso's mistress, and zoomed off, politely paying the taxi's fare in Battersea. Timing is everything in robbery.

From across the road I stared at the Dulwich Picture Gallery. It's so beautiful that tears wet my eyes. That it is crammed with wondrous Old Masters makes it more evocative. The building is ground floor only, set back one hundred paces from leafy College Road, across the bonniest lawn in the land. A wooden fence becomes a brick wall by the gateway. It feels homely, the only art gallery on earth that makes you want to move next door and live there forever. Okay, its Old Masters aren't well lit. And arrangement? Well, a generous two out of ten. But the genuine quality slams you before you're even in the gate. They haven't yet got round to doing a full catalogue, incidentally. And you want crumpets for tea, you weary visitor? Then hie ye out, where a route march will take you to Dulwich

Village's tea houses, and may you make it before hypogly-caemia lays you low.

For me, Dulwich Picture Gallery – lovely, lovely – is forever the portrait of Rembrandt's son *Titus*. I drew breath and went in past the counter of slides, postcards, what not.

Edward Alleyn bequeathed his collection when he popped his clogs in 1626. Since then, others have chipped in. Of course, there was some dicey goings-on about the time of Waterloo, when Sir Francis Bourgeois crated in nearly four hundred masterpieces. Some of them were assembled by a fabled art dealer called Desenfans, suppos-edly for Warsaw. Praise be, they ended up in Dulwich. To still greater rejoicing, Mrs Desenfans picked up the tab for the new gallery. What you now see is the *restored* restored gallery, seeing it got bombed in 1944. It's the best day's worth in London. Go there, and you'll see.

So I went in. The joke among dealers is, its security hasn't been improved since they took down the barrage balloons and Ack-Ack gun emplacements, which means it shouldn't be too hard to burgle. There's the usual stories, endlessly told among antique dealers, about how best to lift the lovely Van Dyck, how the security near their Poussin compares with that of their Gainsborough. Myself, I'd say their Murillo and Rubens are most vulnerable – unless they shift them on reading this – but I'm not worth listening to. Disturbingly, the famous gallery only pretended to be English cosy, villagey dozy. There was nasty evidence of thirty-six security appliances, including the new UV sensiti-sors. It was unassailable, impregnable. But useful if I wanted it as a decoy.

Ignoring the stout bowler-hatted gent, who was there before me, I spent a marvellous afternoon, feeling the great artists' vibes. I was almost sick twice but went out for a breath in the nick of time. I judged windows, asked the stewards about the lighting, studiously paced the floors when I was alone. Lovejoy's Law of Theft: Patience is the vice of the artist and the virtue of the thief. I was so patient that warm afternoon. By the time I caught the train I felt replete, like you do after making smiles with a lass you truly deeply love. That's antiques for you.

To teach the trailing bloke a lesson I strolled through lovely Dulwich Village. Teatime, I caught the train at North Dulwich. I bought a ninepenny notebook and started sketching nonsensical doodles, busily counting on my fingers like planning some secret robbery. My follower hesitated. Finally, he sat in the same compartment in a sulk, probably having left his car in Dulwich. I wasn't sure who he worked for, but it hardly mattered now. Gluck? Maybe. Saintly? Possible. Whoever it was, he didn't stand an earthly.

26

THE NEAREST I ever got to monogamy, I was nineteen, barely out of the egg. Joanne (M.A., Oxoniensis) proposed. In Latin, so I had to ask what she said. Laughingly, she told me she'd already fixed things with the vicar in Broxham. It was on a bridge over a lonely river, where a fisherman was angling and massacring. Joanne told me the scene was idyllic. I agreed, because I already knew it was a woman's world.

'We'll live in that cottage,' she said mistily. She indicated remote fields.

'Er, I hate countryside,' I said, uneasy.

'I love it, Lovejoy. And,' she pointed out, 'I am wealthy. You are destitute.'

'Er, what about my antiques?' I'd actually got none. You know what I mean.

'Give them up, darling.' She was so rational. It was only my future after all. 'I'm the better judge.'

And she did have an M.A. in fine art, while I was a serf. Fair's fair.

The angler below the bridge had periodically been yanking out wriggling fish. Each time I turned away.

Suddenly Joanne screeched with laughter, clapped her hands. I looked.

The man was struggling, emitting a noise like 'Argh-argh-argh!' on and on, frantically capering about like someone demented. For a second I couldn't see why. Then I glimpsed something horrible, slimy, wrapped around his forearm. Desperately, he was endeavouring to unravel the evil beast. It seemed yards long. A snake! No, something else.

Finally he cut savagely at it with a fletching knife. It fell off onto the river bank. He kicked it into the water and sheepishly grinned up at us.

'Sorry.' He tried to pass his alarm off with aplomb. 'Bloody eels.'

Joanne fell about. 'Wasn't that hilarious?' She dabbed her eyes. 'Honestly! Townies! An absolute hoot!'

Guess how long we lasted. One thing I did learn from the encounter was that if you want to know anything about countryside, you've to safari out and ask some yokel. Waterways meant eels. And eels meant Clatter. You 'clatter' for eels in East Anglia, hence his nickname.

He was on the river bank near the Saffron Fields lock gate.

'Stop still, Lovejooy,' he shouted. It was odd. He was facing the other way so couldn't have seen me.

Clatter's a rotund bloke in corduroys, bald as a badger, wheezes like a train, smokes a filthy pipe. He had six buckets on the bank. How he does it beats me, lying down in dank grass holding out that horrible twenty-foot long pole.

'What's on the end, Clatter?' I asked despite myself. His pole dangled a curious rope thing.

He laughed. 'What you arsk fower, booy, if ya don't wanter know?' He came to. 'It's a clat. You clat for eels with worms, Lovejoy. First, a teaspoon of mustard water down every earthworm cast in the moornin', yer gets up a load of earthworms. Thread a yard of worms on a four-foot length of wool with a needle. That's yer clat, see?'

God, lovely countryside. I almost retched.

'Make a figure-of-eight of yer wool, hang it like I'm doing into the water on yer pole. The eels bite. Their teeth tangle in the wool, see?'

Suddenly he yanked his pole up onto the bank. Three eels dropped there. I looked away while he collared them. I heard them splashing in his bucket.

'You'll never make a country booy, Lovejooy.' He lit his pipe. I didn't look at his hands. 'Must be mortal bad to bring you here while I'm clattin', son.'

I gestured to the river, the country. 'Arthur Goldhorn's place.'

You don't have to say much. He got the point. I moved upwind. His pipe stank. I hoped it was only tobacco in there.

'Arthur were a fool, booy. Give that woif of his anything she wannied. Colette'd never no time for her lad Mortimer. Arthur had, even though Mortimer weren't his. Arthur tried to hang on to Saffron Fields fer the booy's sake.'

'He lost everything to Dieter Gluck.'

'That Colette and her French name. Anything in trousers – though you knew that, eh, booy?'

No need for barbs. I gave him my bent eye. He shrugged and looked away.

'This river, Clatter. Can it be linked to the old canal?'

'Ar. That were the old plan, until the railways come. Only take one cut, mebbe couple or three locks through the closed field.'

'Closed field?' I'd never heard the term. The landscape looked depressingly open to me.

He smiled. 'A closed field's where you grow forbidden, Lovejoy. I only know this one in the whole kingdom. Behind you.'

'One field's the same as any other, Clatter.'

'Growed poppy there these eight generations, Lovejoy. Arthur were signature for it, see?'

That made me walk back up the bank and take a long look.

'This land grew poppies?' I already knew people liked flowers.

'Special folk did the harvest, loik. In olden days. The Ministry took away permission when Arthur died. Aborted the crop by spraying. Didn' arf stink.'

Now, *Papaver somniferum* is famed. Opium is its principal yield, cause of our country's notoriously unjust Opium Wars with China. I'd heard fanciful rumours of four official acres in Suffolk where morphine base was got from an opium crop.

'Who owns the closed field?'

'The only bit of Saffron Fields Manor that thief didn't manage to get.' Clatter spat into the sluggish river. 'Arthur gived it to the booy separate afoor he died. By then, that Colette had gone orff with the foreigner.'

'Ta, Clatter.'

Inland, beyond the closed field, I could see a line of trees along the old canal. Seaward, the river bent into its estuary where the dead airman lay in his plane beneath the sands. So two rich reasons existed for Gluck to snaffle this unprepossessing chunk. One, he could make a fortune from developing the waterways leisure industry. Two, he would own one of the few approved opium fields in the whole country. Except that Gluck hadn't thought it out: he'd killed Arthur – driving a man to his death is the same as murder, to me – and grabbed everything he could. Unfortunately for him, the Lord of the Manor title and these priceless few acres had already been ceded to Mortimer for a farthing. Stupidly Gluck had slain the goose and not got the golden egg. Arthur had seen, guessed, suspected Gluck's intentions. I grieved. Why hadn't he come to me?

I knew the answer. Arthur knew about me and Colette. I was just as phoney as Gluck, taking advantage of Arthur's benign nature, cuckolding my friend. I'm not even pathetic. I'm worse.

'All roit, booy?' Clatter said sympathetically. 'It weren't yor fault, son.'

Thank you, friend. 'I'll manage now, Clatter.'

Grief's always too late. I set off back, leaving the lonely river to Clatter and his eels. My old Gran said once, 'A funeral's only ham butties and a slow walk, luv. Pretending that your grief is for a loved one, when it's only self-pity.' My trouble is, I think too late.

My eyes filled. I stumbled over the stile onto the road where I hoped to get a lift to the railway station. Talking time was over, and fighting time was come, as Don John of Austria said at Lepanto. But he'd had a fleet of war galleys, and I had only a few suppositions about a dead airman.

27

THAT DAY, EVERYTHING happened, double bad. I finally remembered to phone Mercy Faldrop in her booming hamlet. She came on after a succession of kulaks had told me that The Lady (sic) would be pleased to speak.

'Lady Mercy? Lovejoy. Got anything?'

'Your listed folk don't come here, Lovejoy. Except for that engineer man Talleyton. He brings two surveyors, buys them supper and a girl each.'

My heart sank. 'Not Sir Jesson Tethroe?' I went through my list.

'No, Lovejoy. Sorry.'

Typical. Just when I wanted a dishonest MP. Now I'd have to use Gloria Dee to somehow bring him in.

'I barred that Gluck.'

'Eh?' Gluck at Mercy's after all?

'Rotten bastard, he were. Drew blood on a couple-three of my girls, into S and M. Finishing school, him. I put the word out.'

'Dieter Gluck? You sure?' Finishing school is brothel-speak for sadism to the point of killing. Needless to say, madams don't let such a bloke over the threshold.

'Leave it aht, Lovejoy.' Meaning don't be stupid. 'He goes down Soho now. I don't handle his sort.'

'Anything else about him?'

'Rumour is he did for a working girl, Continent somewhere.'

'Keep trying, Mercy. You're a lady.'

She purred. 'Thank you, kind sir. If ever the gentleman wishes to partake of ultimate personal solace, please rest assured . . .' etc, etc.

Nothing from Doldrum. No news from Lydia, no messages from Mars. Tinker, Trout, Sorbo had gone silent. I felt really narked. I was slogging my heart out, and all my team had gone walkabout. So much for loyalty.

What had Gaylord Fauntleroy's old auntie said? Something about Chinese antiques being my best bet.

A street busker called Cleat – careful how you say her name – near Tower Hill always has news. Cleat's an electric chain dancer, draws tourist crowds near the Tower of London. Two bronzed stalwarts fasten her in chains, to exotic drum music. During her writhing prance, bulbs all over her flash on and off. The cliffhanger: she's to leap free of her chains before the record ends, or a great carboy of water suspended above her will uncork and drench her. Electrified as she is with bulbs and wires, she will then frazzle and die and, the stalwarts bellow threateningly, 'The Glamorous Cleat will be no more!'

When I arrived she'd just escaped, taken the collection, and was sitting having a fag with her blokes. I like Cleat. She has a cousin who can yodel.

'They were asking after you, Lovejoy,' she told me. 'You didn't turn up.'

Somebody else now? I sighed. Was I simply a walking crime?

'Billia and Dang. He's hiding in the churchyard. And Gaylord's up the Lane.'

I'd quite forgotten them. Billia had told me she needed help when I'd met her at Bermondsey. Some boxing hoods wanted Dang to throw, win, duck, or vice versa, and he'd got confused. What was Billia's tale? Dang had to repay the match fixers' lost debt. I should have met them at the Nell of Old Drury, seven o'clock once upon a time. I eyed the huge dangling carboy over her dancing pitch, couldn't help asking.

'Is that real, love?' Only, the thought of it and electrocuting her was really unpleasant.

She split her sides. Her stalwarts roared. I reddened, said so-long, and walked off, the only duckegg in London. I put my best foot under me. Londoners don't walk much. Tourists are the same, struggle might and main for taxis, when their destination's barely a furlong. I walked up the Minories, made it round St Botolph's church where the buses go mad, and was in Petticoat Lane in minutes.

Note, however, that Petticoat Lane isn't properly that. But if you tell your taxi driver Middlesex Street he'll say, 'D'you mean Petticoat Lane?' London's full of these hitches. Like, Dalston Waste is famous, but isn't labelled in the maps. I got lost once, delivering a vanload of forged Wedgwood jasper cameos. Like a fool I searched the A–Z Guide, got nowhere until I asked a bright little pickpocket in Whitechapel. 'Maps,' he'd said with all the dignity of his ten years, 'is alluz wrong, mate.'

Petticoat Lane, then. At the Aldgate end, clothes barrows and jellied eel stalls crush together, awnings so dense there seems no way through. Struggle north up the narrow thoroughfare, yet more groaning barrows, with shops looking eager to step off the pavement. It's an exciting turmoil. Cutler Street Silver Market's now a grand emporium, a mini-Crystal Palace stuck out near Aldgate East station. It used to be a small dogleg going nowhere near Houndsditch, but that's evolution. Street markets start off superb grot, then go posh.

Gaylord couldn't park his caravan in this press, so I shoved my way towards St Mary Axe. There it stood among a handful of dealers. Gaylord was waxing eloquent about some dross he was trying to auction. You can tell when nobody's going to buy. I went closer. The item was a tantalus, a grand brass-and-mahogany carrying device used by butlers for several glass decanters. I reached and touched one. Slightly rough, but not a single chime.

'I'll have that, mister,' I said. 'How much?'

'More than you can afford, sir.' Gaylord's quick on the uptake. 'You don't realize its value.'

The dealers looked from me to Gaylord's antique, wondering. I heard a bloke whisper my name, saw him out of the corner of my eye make a slight chopping gesture to his mate, suggesting they'd split the cost and profits equally.

'Is it from the *Duoro*?' I demanded.

The ill-starred Royal Mail steamship *Duoro* is famous for colliding with a Spanish liner and sinking off Cape Finisterre in 1882, taking with it some seventeen souls and a fortune in diamonds and gold. The date's important for glassware. In 1890 posh decanters were rough to the feel, being wheel-engraved. The acid-polishing process only properly took off about 1890. Try it yourself. Touch a modern acid-polished decanter, it's smooth as silk. (There are fakes, so watch it.) But rough engraving means pre-1890; smooth means later. Antiques that can be dated by some reliable technique are, as dealers say, 'landmarked' and are easier to sell.

A bloke organized an ocean dive in the 1990s, and in true romantic treasure-hunting fashion pulled off a brilliant salvage. I get bitter telling this, because it wasn't me. Spink's did the final auction, a mere twenty-eight thousand gold coins, plus artefacts and gems, bringing millions. I was not involved.

'This tantalus is unique, sir.' Gaylord pursed his lips. 'Maybe I've underestimated its value.'

'Thousand two hundred?' I said. I hadn't a groat.

'Let's have a gander, Gaylord.' One dealer stepped up.

'Excuse me, mate,' I said, narked. 'I've already offered. I can claim it. Mark ovvat.' Which is our slang way of saying 'market overt'. It's supposed to have been repealed a couple of years back, this ancient law. Trouble is, street dealers never change. If street law was once thus, it is now and so ever shall be. Buy an antique in uncovered daylight in open market, it's yours for always. Never mind whether it was nicked, stolen, or got by thuggery. A sale is a sale is a sale. That was the old law, and still is among us market lovers.

'It wasn't sold,' the dealer said quickly. He appealed to the crowd. 'Was it, Ven? Was it, Sol? Two thousand five hunnert.'

'Don't get nasty, gentlemen.' Gaylord acted unhappy, and handed his fake over for a bundle of bunce.

The crowd dispersed. Gaylord went in, closed the door. I wandered off. Ten minutes later, I nigged round the far side of his caravan and slipped in. Auntie Vi had the kettle on.

'Thank you, Lovejoy. You're sweet. Are you better?'

'Not been poorly.'

Gaylord, in an even glitzier caftan, smiled. 'Grief shines

from you like black light, Lovejoy. Don't feel bad about Arthur and Colette.'

'Shut your teeth, Gaylord,' I snarled. 'They weren't my responsibility.'

'You're like Grimaldi, Lovejoy,' Auntie Vi said, puffing her foul pipe.

'Eh?'

'It happened in Victorian times. Man went to his doctor. Couldn't stop crying from sorrow. His doctor couldn't find a thing wrong, told him to go and see the famous comic clown Grimaldi, toast of Victorian London, have a good laugh. The man said, "But I *am* Grimaldi." See, Lovejoy?'

No, I didn't see. 'You said something about duping Dieter Gluck.'

'Do the old double shift,' Auntie Vi said, rocking in her chair. 'We used it for years, until computers come in. Gaylord agrees, don't you, dear? Think Chinese.'

Chinese meant Wrinkle, as I've said.

'I've been thinking of an art gallery. Biggest profit. I'm going to visit Terence O'Shaughnessy.' Tel O'Shaughnessy is a crook at the best of times. I said this.

'Aren't we all, Lovejoy?'

'But we're the good ones.'

'Dismas and Gestas, on Calvary, were both antique dealers, son. It's a fact.' She continued, 'They still got crucified with Christ. The steal of approval!'

She cackled, rocked. Homilies make me sick. I got up to leave but Gaylord shoved me down and poured me some liqueur he brews from oranges.

'Saunty sent these folders over.'

Eagerly I grabbed them from him, riffled through. There were basically four ideas, all of them terrific, almost foolproof. The question was, would any of them do? I wanted the manor back for Mortimer, and Arthur's lands including his mulberry tree.

'You need a tame Yank, Lovejoy. Gluck'll bite like a pike in a pool.'

'Where'll I get a Yank?' I said bitterly. 'He'd have to be able to act. And be trustworthy. Maybe I simply ought to pay some Leeds tankers two grand to top Gluck. Then Mortimer's friends could club together for lawyers to sort the manor out for the lad.'

After all, Gluck had the plod on his side. I'd already been warned off by Saintly. I said tarra, swigged the hooch and made to leave.

'Good luck,' they both called.

I stepped into rain-soaked London. Outside, the crowd was diminishing. I heard Gaylord say something after me but took no notice. Where now? Well, Billia and Dang hadn't done me any harm. I dithered, but finally started west. Cleat had said 'the churchyard'. In London this means St Paul's until specified as somewhere else.

For some reason I felt odd, looked about but saw nobody I knew. I can't stand those horrible new cobbly underfoots along London Wall, so instead walked along Leadenhall and Cornhill, emerging near the Mansion House. Normally I'd have gone nearer the River Thames – it's only a step – so I could pass the Monument, but today didn't feel like it. Everything's nostalgia in London. The fact you weren't alive when things happened centuries agone doesn't matter. Feelings get your bones. I resisted the little antiques painting shop near Bread Street and went straight ahead towards Ludgate Hill.

More temptation, because only a little way west you walk into Dr Johnson's very own house, and can sit in his very own triangular chair. Some tourists were still about, the traffic dense as ever. Even in drizzle folk were sitting on the cathedral steps. I looked. No sign of Dang – though there wouldn't be, would there, if he was hiding. I went round the great building, thinking of the young Dr Christopher Wren, who turned his hand to architecture because his new idea called blood transfusion was too cranky – oh, sorry, I mentioned that some time since. I wondered whether to go in.

Ghosts, though. They're here in London. They're also there, and among hurrying crowds. They stand looking at you across the road. I honestly believe that our old places somehow invoke them, call them back. Yet nearby folk were playing a kind of netball. Office people were ambling, noshing butties, drinking tins of fizz. The trouble is, we know the ghosts. Here in St Paul's churchyard she's the notorious She Wolf. Actually not canine but definitely lupine and female to degree. It was the Londoners' nickname for Queen Isabella, French spouse of our Edward II. She was a leading sinner. So bad, indeed, that her Gallic team made sure that she was buried in a grey habit nicked from the Christchurch Greyfriars. A careful lot, their idea was to trick heaven's Recording Angel, whose tired eyes, accustomed only to black or white, would fail to spot the grey. Naughty Isabella hoped to slip into paradise, sins and all. Bad luck, though, for the vigilant Angel wasn't tricked and hauled her out. In a temper, he angrily sentenced her to wander for all eternity, grieving and doomed, in St Paul's churchyard and serve her right. Your average Londoner pooh-poohs it. But the grey figure certainly scares the hell out of postmen at the nearby GPO. The way to avoid her, incidentally, is *not to look*. Dart anxious glances hither and yon while visiting St Paul's, you'll see her sure as eggs. She still lusts after men, you see, and takes a stare as an invitation, with dire consequences I won't go into if you don't mind. Women she hates, and takes a female's look as a challenge, with double-dire results.

'Lovejoy,' Dieter Gluck said. I yelped out of my reverie. He looked the business, neat, height of fashion, cool, handsome.

'Mr Gluck,' I said. No ghost, he.

'Don't whine, Lovejoy. Time to speak?'

'I'm meeting a friend,' I said. It's hard to be polite when you're working out how to knock that person off. I've often found that.

'Here?' He looked about, quite amused. A cool swine, give him that. 'Handful of tramps, busloads of visitors, a mob of office clerks? No, Lovejoy. You're planning deceit. I can smell it. And,' he said reasonably, 'I've learned a great deal. You are a thief, a scoundrel who lives off women, and a forger.'

'Here, nark it.' I could have clocked him one, except so far I'd not had much luck. He looked calm, like he had a servile bruiser handy.

'Don't take offence, Lovejoy. I'm one also. I have a proposition.'

'You got me done over, arrested, and clobbered by your tame ape.' I still ached from my beating in Soho.

'Do not speak ill of the dead, please,' said this killer. 'Consecrated ground. It's time we joined forces, Lovejoy.' He lit a cigarette from a silver case. 'What is this famous scam of yours?' He smiled. 'So secret, so uniquely aimed at my destruction?'

From the corner of my eye I saw Billia start towards me, Dang with her. They were coming down the broad expanse of steps. I passed my hand in front of my forehead to signal them away. Dang hesitated, thank God. I turned.

'Who said I've got a scam brewing?'

He said, pleasant, 'All London's street markets. Now, how much will it cost? What's the profit? And what odds on success?'

I keep a special headache for times like these. It screeched into my temple and exploded, ruining my vision and thought processes. Kindly, Dieter Gluck took me by the elbow and walked me down to the London Hospital Tavern on Ludgate Hill. It stands almost midway between Blackfriars Bridge – where the Vatican these days murders its troublesome bankers and hangs their bodies from the girders over the Thames – and the Old Bailey, where the Vatican's hired assassins are never tried.

This particular murderer sat opposite me in the tap room and brought me a drink. Smiling pleasantly, he toasted me.

'To partnership,' he said.

28

For a time, I sat on the facade facing the buses chugging towards the Bank, motors, office girls darting between deaths shrieking, folk smiling, a bobby telling them off. To my right, tourists noshed their pizza slices, swigging from cans and littering culture. I had an overdue think.

Sit still a minute, London descends like dew, steeping the soul in feelings you didn't know you had. Things flow in your brain. Like a fool I actually turned to look, but there was no smoke in the sky.

It happened here, the Great Fire that began in Pudding Lane. The street's still there, a spit downstream of London Bridge. I'd just walked past. From the Monument, you can look down into its narrow thoroughfare. History books don't tell you of the stark terror. It takes a coward like me, scared from an encounter with Dieter Gluck, to feel fright. And to see there in front of me the people whose spirits still scream and run. I honestly believe that horror more than any other human emotion lurks all about us, in stones, in the air, in the ground that once bubbled and buckled from the heat. In the Great Fire bells melted, Ludgate Hill to my right running with molten metal as buildings heat-cracked into rubble.

'You all right, mate?' a passing window cleaner asked. He had squeegees sticking out of his overalls.

'Aye, ta, mate,' I managed to say. 'Bit dizzy for a sec.'

That terrible Sunday, second of August in 1666, the real outbreak occurred. A daft preacher – is there any other? – afterwards proved what caused it. 'It couldn't have been caused by London's blasphemy,' he boomed, 'or the Great Fire would have begun in Billingsgate.' Nor lewdness and roistering, for then it would have started in Drury Lane. Nor lying and untruth (nice touch, this) or God would have torched the law courts of Westminster Hall. No, gluttony did it – for didn't the Great Fire start in *Pudding* Lane, and finally end at *Pie* Corner? Oddly, hardly anybody died. The old *London Gazette*'s death count was exactly nil. Even the stern Bills of Mortality notched only six. God must have had a weak throwing arm that week. Divine calamities usually rock the averages.

Our behaviour, back then, was like now. We did what we do. Greed, as I keep saying, like murder, will out. Samuel Pepys tells it in all its grue. The only difference is that the avarice of rich politicians was just that bit more obvious. Alderman Starling, of incredible wealth, gave a measly penny to the thirty labourers who saved his priceless possessions from the flames. Sir Richard Brown was just as stingy, when workmen rescued his chest stuffed with enough money to buy several streets.

Pandemonium reigned as the Great Fire engulfed the city. In all human crucibles, rumour rules. Invasions, political plots, the whole kaleidoscope of mayhem, unloosed panic-stricken mobs. Blackened thousands staggered to Moor Fields and Tower Hill. As the conflagration leapt about with sparks on the wind, the black smoke shadowed riders as far away as Oxford. The phrases are all the same.

You can't get away from the image of Old St Paul's standing like some huge warship upon a flaming ocean as the terrible sun set.

Sound advice went begging, and greed rose to make matters hell of a sight worse. The best plan came from 'some stout seamen' who, knowing fire, early on wanted to blow up a few streets and save the entire city. London's wealthy plutocrats refused. So it was that Sunday vanished in an inferno. Then Monday, the fire enveloping dozens of churches and their parishes. 'Avaricious men, aldermen, would not permit,' mourned Evelyn, 'because their own houses must have been of the first . . .' It's these memories that plague me. Would I have been any better? No.

Finally, catastrophe shoved selfishness out of the picture. The seamen's pleas were finally accepted. Charles II rowed up in his royal barge and ended all arguments, himself seeing to the demolition of houses rimming the Tower's moats. Meanwhile, London's goldsmiths did themselves a power of good by rushing their goods into the Tower. They didn't lift another finger, of course. Booksellers crammed their combustible stacks of books into St Faith's, which happened to be underneath Old St Paul's, so adding fuel to the bonfire. The world blazed, even the air seeming cleft asunder.

History doesn't tell much. It never does. Only in odd corners do stories make sense. A schoolboy called Will Taswell painstakingly wrote his horrendous account that very Thursday. He'd trudged east among huge mounds of burning ruins. 'I endeavoured to reach St Paul's,' he quilled into his notebook. 'The ground so hot as almost to scorch my shoes.' The very air was afire. Faint, he had to rest in Fleet Street. Struggling on, the lad reached about where I'd run into Gluck. He saw the melted bells of the cathedral, molten rivulets running down Ludgate. Plodding through the furnace, he saw the fire engines burning, the firemen leaping to escape erratic outbreaks. Childlike, young Taswell picked up a cooling piece of bell metal to take home to show his friends, and gasping for breath made his way home. Of them all, who would I be? The King, struggling to force scatterbrain politicians to act? Or one of the riff-raff, dragging my belongings north among the refugees streaming along the City Road? Certainly not one of the brave jolly jack tars straddling roofs in the flames with their kegs of gunpowder. Maybe one of the rich aldermen, disdainfully pressing farthings into the hands of stalwarts who saved an ill-gotten fortune?

'You, Lovejoy?' Billia said. 'You'd be the little lad scribbling it down.'

How long had she been there? I asked, 'How long've you been there?'

'Since folk started looking at you talking to yourself.'

The window cleaner was sitting further along. He looked pretty muscular for a window cleaner. He gave me a worried nod. Dang?

'Wotcher, Lovejoy,' Dang said.

'We kept out of your way while Gluck was batting your ear, Lovejoy. Safer.' Billia looks all appetite.

'You know him?' I was surprised.

'He's one of the betting syndicate that's after my bloke. He's got backers. They've tried everything from cornering antiques to fixing boxing.'

Desperater and desperater.

'He's sussed me, Billia,' I admitted. 'Just told me he knew my darkest plans in detail.'

'Hell fire, Lovejoy. He's probably watching us now.'

'Hang on, love.' This was important. If Billia and Dang

were running scared from Gluck, then this odd couple might well be my best allies. What proof had I that Sorbo and Trout were honest? When suspicion begins, you're alone. Paranoia becomes forward planning. I could trust Lydia, Tinker too. Gluck might well be taping us. 'See you where we said before, okay?'

'In the—?'

'That's it, love,' I said quickly. 'Don't be late.'

Billia's eyes darted about. She flagged a taxi. I offed on Shank's pony, following little William Taswell's route of centuries before. Fleet Street, passing the little court leading to Dr Johnson's house. The Strand, right into Aldwych, breathing the air like nectar. My old stamping ground, Drury Lane. Thence into Covent Garden, where Pepys had dallied with loose lasses, where Boswell took his sinful pleasure and afterwards had to wash his hot willy in the Serpentine.

Gluck had exuded charm in the pub. You have to hand it to killers. They put a smile on your face as they pull the rug from under and slide you to perdition.

'We must deal, Lovejoy,' he'd said. I was frankly scared. He took my folder, leafed through it. 'Choice of four, I see.'

'The Louvre is best of them,' I said. One thing, at the first sign of opposition, I chuck the towel in.

'The Louvre's Jew loot? And the Musée d'Orsay?' he said, approving. 'Hasn't it been done?'

'Stolen wartime loot always has, Mr Gluck. That's the point.'

'Thomas Harrington's clocks.' He frowned at that, read

carefully, shook his head. 'I'm clock mad, but Greenwich has too many guards, Lovejoy.'

'Tourists are protective colour, Mr Gluck.'

He smiled. 'Seriously, Lovejoy. Which were you going for?'

'The Rotherham porcelain museum.' I filled in when his silence prompted me. 'It's priceless. And the area's politically dicey, so the government would rejoice when I saved it from being robbed. And you'd take the bait, hoping for a knighthood.'

That gave him a laugh, tanned features setting off his superb white incisors. How come some people have everything?

'You read me accurately, Lovejoy.' He grew wistful. 'Being a foreigner, my dream is of nobility.'

'Why?' I was curious. 'Most honours are sham. Invent one for yourself. Nobody cares.'

His eyes gleamed. 'I came from foreign slums, Lovejoy. This would be my accolade.' He eyed me. 'I'd not touched the drink. 'Reluctant, are we? Is it because you shagged – is that your slang word – Colette?' He leant forward. I was suddenly relieved. He had terrible breath, at last a drawback. 'Did you hope for her estate yourself? To take over from that buffoon of a husband?'

He suddenly emitted an inane cackle that set heads turning all about the taproom.

'I like this fourth effort best, Lovejoy. The shipment thing. Of what?'

I did my most convincing shrug. 'Any indigenous antiques. Good ones. Dulwich Picture Gallery's the one I have in mind.'

'Dulwich?' His eyes narrowed suspiciously, the way I wish I could do. 'Isn't it impregnable now?'

'Not really,' I lied. 'Plus it has a trump card. The Ace.' I smiled, with humility and cowardice in there. 'It can't afford insurance.'

He gaped. '*Can't . . .?*'

'So many priceless Old Masters. Get it, Mr Gluck? A thief—'

'Could dictate his own terms!' I'd never seen such fervour. He couldn't keep still.

'To the Minister for Arts, National Heritage. Think of the nation's gratitude when somebody returned them to a grateful country!'

Well, I swear he almost choked. 'Lovejoy, that's beautiful! I'd be the white knight! Adored! Worshipped!' He shook my hand against my will. Uneasily I imagined rumours getting back to friends. 'Then do it, Lovejoy. I am your partner. Tell me when it's set up, not before.' He rose, elegant, in charge.

'Hang on,' I bleated. 'What's the deal?'

'You pull the robbery. Then you offer them to me. I buy them back, saving the nation's honour. Of course, no money will change hands, because I have none. But I will pretend I paid a fortune to the robbers.'

I croaked, 'What robbers? Who? What about me?'

'You do the best you can to escape the consequences, Lovejoy.' He smiled as Sir Ponsonby and his luscious Moiya came to join him. She looked even more glorious. Sir P. had the grace to look embarrassed. 'Highly placed politicians will recommend me! It's foolproof, and it's not yet even taken place!'

He left, laughing. Moiya December swung every cell of her anatomy, drawing eyes. Sir P. mouthed a faint regret to me, and stumbled in their wake. They embarked in a waiting

Rolls. So much for leading righteousness's charge against evil. I was now my enemy's serf.

The four best scams – that I'd paid to have planned out for me – were now known to Gluck. He would win. I'd lose, and Mortimer would go down with me.

Smouldering, I knew that I'd been careless. I needed a last-minute plan Gluck couldn't even guess at.

29

LONDON HAS EVERYTHING. That doesn't mean it's yours for the taking. But it's there, it's there.

Terence O'Shaughnessy's claim to being Irish is that he once drank a pint of their black stout. In Germany. Nonetheless, he talks a good nationality, as they say. His workshop's off Drury Lane, a stone's throw from a myriad theatres. I found the building, went over the wall, saw a light in his basement. He's janitor of this night school – creative writing, leaping in leotards to music, self-identity through inner plasms.

'Tel?' I went into his one room with care, remembering when I'd barged in on Wrinkle and what he'd been up to. Tel didn't even look round. He has this giant St Bernard dog, slavering and droopy, called Plato. 'Wotcher, Plato.'

'Top o' the morning, Lovejoy.'

Oirish brogue still. Once, he'd been a big-spending Yemeni oil baron, but came unstuck when the police pointed out that he wasn't anything of the kind. He's the only bloke I know really born in a suitcase. His grandma delivered him. I've met her, heard the story a hundred times. The telly was on, racing at Newmarket.

'Don't give me your County Galway, Tel.'

O'Shaughnessy's room is always a shambles. Old clothes strewn everywhere, plastic bin bags, newspapers, half-eaten grub, soiled plates there since I'd seen him a year since. He wore a singlet, braces dangling, the same smeared slippers, belly protruberant, stained trousers. He'd improved. Usually he's a mess.

'Can't offer yer any ale, Lovejoy. I'm thirsty meself.'

He had a row of brown ale tins ready for action. A heap of empties had accumulated nearby in a kind of metallic snowfall. As he spoke he lobbed a new empty. It landed on the pile, which slid a bit. He popped a replacement with a sigh of repletion.

'It's okay, Tel.' Plato came and drenched me with saliva. I patted his head, but distantly. Stroke him once or twice, you get enough hairs to knit another dog.

Terence O'Shaughnessy is a knowledgeable bloke. Living as he does in London's Drury Lane heartland, he makes money selling information indiscriminately. This was my reason.

'Can I ask, Tel, or are you busy?'

He phones bookmakers with last-minute losers. Plato snuffled, demanding another pat. I responded, finished up covered with hair.

'Ten minutes before the off, Lovejoy. What is it?'

'Dulwich Picture Gallery,' I said without preamble.

His several bellies quivered delight. He opened a tin of ale for Plato, who lapped it down. His tongue's like a sponge mat.

'Self-service theft, that place used to be, Lovejoy.' Tel guffawed. 'Any day of the week. Not now, though.'

'Sell me the security, Tel, and potholes?'

'Sure. Cost you half a long, Lovejoy. Half a grand to the blokes.'

Translation: fifty zlotniks to Tel, five hundred to the security sussers. These are ruffians who don't actually ruff. They just know who'll be on duty, if the electronics surveillance people have flu, where you should arrange a van to break down, a robber's essentials. Potholes are flaws in standing security procedures. Some naughty security firms actually incorporate flaws, to be sold to would-be crooks on request. It's modern double-think.

'That's blinking dear, Tel,' I groused.

'Art theft's gone up. Dulwich's been done too frigging often. They learned the hard way. Now, the place only *looks* easy. If I was you, I'd try somewhere else.' He gave a booming laugh, sweaty mounds shaking. 'They can't afford the insurance. Said so on telly, last time somebody lifted their recycled Rembrandt.'

True. I was relieved Tel knew about it. Dealers joke that their Rembrandt was stolen so often in the old days it went in and out like a fiddler's elbow. I wanted him to be sure to remember this conversation.

'What'll you charge to keep shtum, Tel?' I asked, trying to look threatening. I can't do it, but try. 'I don't want all London coming to watch, if I try to nick Dulwich's Old Masters.'

'Another.' Meaning fifty zlotniks more.

We haggled. I stroked Plato. Like Mortimer's dog Jasper, it knew I wasn't up to much, so watched the horses line up on TV. I agreed Tel's fees. Interestingly, they weren't all that exorbitant, proving that Tel knew Dulwich was the hardest place on earth to burgle. I knew that anyway. As long as he told the world that Lovejoy was going to give it a go, it would be money well spent. He would give me details of Dulwich Picture Gallery's security arrangements with supposed potholes.

I said so-long to Plato. Leaving, I hoped whoever Dieter Gluck had trailing me could take a decent photo, and that my stalker was good enough.

Two phone calls later, I started my plan.

Luckily, the day turned out brilliant. It was like a St Thomas's summer down at Henley when I got there. I told the steward on the gate I was a guest of Sir Jesson Tethroe, MP, and Mrs Gloria Dee. With disdain, I was given a blazer and an anonymous tie, and made to wait.

I honestly wonder if women have some inbuilt radar that tells them how our weather will be. She looked dazzling in green taffeta, hair filling out with sun, complexion marvellous. Sir Jesson harrrumphed, eyed me, gave my attire a reluctant nod. He mellowed when Mrs Dee greeted me kindly.

'Call me Jesson, Lovejoy,' he said, like awarding me a discount.

He wrung my hand, clearly chairman of the board. I stared with admiration. He wore a boater, very Henley-on-Thames, and a smart blazer that talked down to scruffy me. If I were him, though, I'd have got a new tie. It had faded to a vague grey. People all around nodded or fawned, according to station. Waiters hung in hopes. Alluring ladies smiled at Sir Jesson.

We were on a kind of tatty wooden jetty. I suppose class is as class does. I caught Gloria Dee's amused smile.

'Henley is superb, Lovejoy, is it not?' she said. I got the irony.

'Best place on earth,' Sir Jesson bellowed. 'The royals,' he intoned, stooping to confide in a stentorian boom, 'don't come here much. Obsessed with horses. Ascot people common as dung, what? And Wimbledon's for ball-fiddlin' poofters, beggin' ya pardon, what?'

'Er,' I said, lost.

'Standards, Lovejoy!' he thundered, ordering drinks with nothing more than a finger twiddle. Waiters sprinted. 'Princess Grace of Monte Carlo – y'know her? Second Division crown, o'course, not top notch. Her pa got excluded from Henley, what?'

'Why, Jesson?' Gloria Dee asked, sweet with innocence. She'd obviously heard the tale a thousand times.

'General Rules, Rule One brackets e,' he foghorned across the Thames. 'Manual labourer. Blighter was a common bricklayer, some place called Philadelphia. Actually wanted to scull at Henley. Can ya believe it?'

'Good heavens,' I said politely. The waiter deposited the drinks, glared at my clothing.

Gentlemen milled and strolled in white flannels, coloured socks. Ladies called loudly for 'Pimm's, daaahling!' and complained about the shampahs. Striped blazers – you never see so many buttons as on Henley cuffs – and heavy-duty grins, flowered hats and swirly dresses.

'Leander,' Gloria whispered as Jesson rose to greet a gaudy mob. Salmon pink seemed to be their colour. I'd never heard such brash laughter. 'Very up, Leander.'

For a second we were on our own. Sir Jesson was saying, 'Like wagering for Dartmouth, what?' and folk were chortling. It was another world.

'Ta for letting me come, love,' I said quietly. 'Would you do a robbery?'

She leant away, to look better, her smile draining.

'I'll accept the danger and suffer the consequences. It could save a young lad's life. And rescue somebody else.'

'A robbery?' she asked faintly. 'You mean steal?'

'No, love. Theft is mild, like pickpocketing. Robbery is violent.'

Fingering her pearls, she repeated the word, her gaze off the scale. 'Violent as in . . .?'

'As in damage, love. I need you, Gloria.' For a second I waited. 'I'll try to keep you out of any problems.'

A gust of haw-haws made all speech impossible before she could respond.

'You're vital, Gloria. Without you, a lad'll probably die at the hands of a proven murderer.'

'Why am I essential?' She knew I meant Mortimer. 'My antiques?'

I inclined my head indicating Jesson Tethroe and his adherents.

'They're in reserve. You know high society.' I had a hard time getting the rest out. 'And I like you.'

Sir Jesson returned, plonked himself down. 'Problem,' he said grimly. 'Some bounder's woman came with a dress above her knees, what? Trouble is, now ladies are actually allowed to *row*!'

I gasped. 'Honestly?' I'd landed in some time warp.

'Good God, man, we'll be having commercial sponsors giving us money next!' He became apoplectic at the thought. 'Folk who want scruffy standards should go to scruffy places – like Wimbledon, or the Derby.'

'Lovejoy has a scheme he wants to discuss, Jesson.'

His eyes narrowed, he swilled his drink. I hadn't touched my glass.

'I'm afraid it concerns money, Jesson,' I confessed, reluctant. 'Rather sordid, I'm afraid. Commercial. Nothing to do with rowing, sculls, Henley.'

'Above board, though, is it?'

'Hundred per cent,' I said, avoiding Gloria's eye. 'It's just that the commercial side is somewhat traditionalist. They only wish to do business with gentry.' I shrugged. 'My firm isn't well connected. If only we had a gentleman in high public esteem.'

The rest can go unspoken, if that's all right. An ingrate's lot is not a happy one. I toadied, hinted, all for the very best motives of decency and patriotism. Forty minutes later, he agreed.

As I said goodbye, I arranged to meet Gloria next day and start the game. Sir Jesson we left by the river talking to pals.

'Buy him a new tie if we succeed,' I joked.

'Lovejoy.' She was laughing inside. I could tell. 'The mark of distinction here is an old tie with its blue faded to grey. Eton.'

'Just joking,' I lied lamely.

She looked worried. 'Will it be as horrid as you said, Lovejoy?'

'Worse, luv.' I bussed her and left.

They caught me at the gate and made me give the blazer and tie back. No class, some people. To arms.

30

THE WAR BEGAN, like all wars, with a series of blunders. First I went to Shar's office to sign a few papers, keep Law from interrupting. Shar was definitely cool, made sharp comments about Lydia. I pretended Lydia and me were just bad friends.

'You realize what these mean, Lovejoy?' she preached, no smiles.

'I've to behave, and leave Holloway University alone.'

'Also?'

'Pay you your exorbitant fees?'

She had the grace to redden. 'And avoid trouble *forever*. That means steer clear of forgery, murder, and—'

'Wild, wild women?' Easier said than done.

Gluck's shop was being redecorated, painters outside dolling it up. Not entirely destitute, then. He was inside talking to the lovely Moiya, now permanently on his team. She gave me a cool appraising look and melted away.

'Mr Gluck?' I was humble.

'What the hell are you doing here?' He frogmarched me to the door and thrust me into the street.

'I want you to visit Dulwich Picture Gallery, Mr Gluck. We've to make arrangements—'

'I said contact me on my mobile, dumbhead.'

The door slammed, leaving me on the pavement. The decorating men laughed on their ladders.

'Worth a try, mate,' one called. 'That bird's a blinder.'

Meaning Moiya. Trout joined me heading for the Tube. The ticket barriers always remind me of sheep-dips.

'Get it?' I asked, anxious.

He carried a camcorder. 'Yes. You look rotten on film, Lovejoy. I posted the tape to Lydia's address like she said.'

'We'll start now, then. Where are we?'

'Tinker's at the Camden Passage pub. Sorbo's waiting in Portobello antique market. Here's their mobile phone numbers.'

'Well done, Trout.' I hesitated, worried. 'Here, mate. Who's the one of us most likely to be duff?' I meant traitor, but couldn't get it out.

'Lydia,' he appalled me by saying. 'Sorry, Lovejoy. Seeing you're crazy about her.' We got shoved apart by commuters, found each other again. 'She'll have a ton of good reasons to shop you, Lovejoy. Morality, sympathy, suchlike crap.' He shook his head at the folly of beautiful women.

'Tinker?' I asked. 'Sorbo?' Then, after a bit, 'You?'

His gaze was level. 'Lovejoy, I can see why Tinker says you're a prat. What do you want me to do?'

'Go to the Dulwich. Get permission, and film every nook and cranny. We'll need every picture.'

'Here, Lovejoy,' he called as I got a ticket and started through. 'Any idea when we start getting paid?'

'Pay?' I gave back. 'With free morality and sympathy?'

I heard his croaky laughter, and I was off on my ultimate deception. A miniature bloke carrying a camcorder round the fashionable Dulwich Picture Gallery would be a decoy if anything would. Now for the real scam, which I would do on my own. Then if my team got in trouble with the police it'd be their hard luck, and I'd get away scotage free. I felt a surge of optimism.

Which only proved how stupid I really am.

London's ghosts I've already told you about. Even at noon, you get some strange feelings. I'm not one of these spiritual people, omens and ectoplasm everywhere. Nor do I find portents in freak face-in-the-cloud photographs. I mean, this week's seen the opening of our kingdom's very first shop devoted to fairies (original meaning, please). I honestly wish it well. Rock on, sprites everywhere. And I'll applaud vigorously to keep Tinkerbell's little red glow burning bright. But don't ask me to stalk clanking figures on fogbound moors, or explore yon dank castle in the candle hours, please. Wander down Haunted Hollow of a midnight, you're on your own. I'll hold your coat and stay in my cottage, ta very much.

No, I'm not spookish. I'm no mystic. People say I must be, since I feel the vibes of genuine antiques. They're wrong. It's totally different. I mean, a *craftsman* made that wondrous Davenport desk, not a ghost. I once said this to Lydia when we were arguing about it – she reads horoscopes. She only said, 'But that eighteenth-century craftsman *is* a ghost now. Don't you see, Lovejoy?' I called her a stupid cow, and stalked off. She laughed, like she'd won.

Despite my disbelief, I stood there on the pavement outside Wrinkle's workshop with its corrugated roof and locked doors somehow *knowing* he'd done a bunk. Maybe it was the lack of chimes from his three genuine antique pieces of furniture, telling me? Except I can't feel them at a distance. I've got to be within chime-shot.

I went round the back, climbed to where I'd seen Honor waggle her fingers at me as I'd gaped at her and Wrinkle making smiles, and broke in by clubbing the begrimed glass pane with my elbow. It hurt like hell. I unlocked the window, and nearly broke my frigging ankle tumbling down, missing the bench and almost braining myself on a stool. I puffed upright, switched on the light. Nothing but wood shavings, neatly swept mounds of sawdust ready for bagging up in plastic containers. We use heartwood remnants for infillings and other deceptions. I mean forgers do.

From sheer fury, I almost wept. The swine had done a moonlight, probably funded by the cheque-toting Honor. Did he suspect I'd be furious because Honor's cheque had bounced, and I'd come to throttle him for the money he still owed me? Or, evil thought, had Gluck somehow got wind of my treble-bluff and somehow got to Wrinkle?

Blokes with lifelong dreams – Wrinkle's an example – are a pest. For secrecy they are unmatched. They have more hidey-holes than a hedge dunnock. They're also loners. The antiques trade hasn't much time for them, because whatever it is they're up to it's too long a haul. Dealers want money now, if not yesterday. If the money's vaguely promised for next Kissing Friday, they'll laugh in your face. This is the real problem with 'longers', as Wrinkle's merry band of long-haul forgers are termed. If, say, a bloke is making a complete collection of Royal Doulton figures, he'll never come within a light year of completion in his own lifetime. It can't be done. And if another is faking every known painting by Gainsborough he'll run out of old canvas so there's a hitch. And so on. Antique dealers always pass them by. Occasionally you'll hear the lads in some pub having a laugh at Old Jake in Carlisle who's making, faking, forgeries of every Parian ware piece ever recorded. Old Jake's real, incidentally. I'm not making him up. He's still nowhere near finishing his epic slog. Pondering, I swung my feet over the edge of Wrinkle's workbench, on which he and Honor had cruelly reached ecstasy without a single thought for my welfare.

Parian ware is an unglazed porcelainy stuff you make figurines and statues from. It's faintly translucent – think of greased fish-and-chip paper. Its matt surface has a satiny feel. You can't mistake it, once seen. Much hallway statuary is Parian, in fact. It came in when Copeland in Stoke-on-Trent brought it about in 1846. Soon it was made by everybody. So you'll find even genuine Wedgwood, and Minton, Parian pieces. The most pricey, though, are American Parians made in Bennington, USA, because they're rarer. Was it worth phoning Jake in Carlisle?

Desultorily I hunted clues. It would take weeks to find Wrinkle. Think of London as a collection of villages, where gossip is common knowledge among the villagers but inaccessible to outsiders. I picked up bits of wood, shavings, scanned the browning notices tacked to the wall. Nil. I'd actually started to climb out when something struck me. One scrap was a little card, with dates of cricket fixtures. It was labelled 'MCC'. One fixture was today's date. And I remembered that Wrinkle was a cricket addict.

We'd once argued about Len Hutton's captaincy in Test matches. I'd accidentally said Hutton was duff. Wrinkle went ballistic. I'd never seen such apoplexy. Me, I couldn't have cared less. He'd seen every Aussie match at the Oval and Lord's since Adam dressed. And the Australians were playing today! I climbed out, dropped nonchalantly to the pavement near an old dear pushing a pram load of faggots, and dashed to find Lydia. Two hours later, I was spruced up in borrowed plumage, entering the hallowed vicinity of Lord's cricket ground with Lydia, trying not to lie.

Cricket is beyond mere explanation because it's unknowable. I was never any good, being a leg-break bowler until I went sane. As a game, cricket's got every known drawback. For a start, one Test – international – match takes five *days*. No kidding. Start in the morning, play until darkness rescues the world. Injuries abound. The ball hurts like hell. Exhaustion eventually sets in among spectators and players alike. My own attraction for the game, of course, is its antiques, because antiques cricketana (I'm honestly not making the name up) is priceless. Proof? Rummage in your attic.

An elderly lady neighbour had an old husband she loved. Okay? He fell ill, needed constant nursing. She was broke. Their children were estranged, for family reasons beyond understanding. The DHSS social services thought up this solution: 'Sell your house, missus. Then, being destitute and homeless, you can buy the nursing care your hubby needs.' Enter Lovejoy. Raquel told me about them, a DHSS lass I was seeing. I booted her out, which she richly deserved, and visited the old dear in the nick of time. I looked at her furniture, trying to save her selling up.

Thrill of thrills, I found a painting of some geezers playing cricket. Dated 1787. Elegant ladies in the foreground, players batting and fielding, it was mindbendingly dull. The old lady heard my yelp of glee and, pleased, made tea, the better to show me her grandad's cricket memoirs. The old geezer had played at the Marylebone Cricket Club in his youth. Bless him, he'd kept detailed diaries. It was a gold mine. In case you don't know, the MCC to cricket is the world centre. I came away with two more paintings, one of the first Eton and Harrow cricket match. Not important, you say? Not unless you admire Lord Byron, a club-footed titch bravely playing in 1805. (His side, Harrow, lost.)

The most valuable painting was of a game in Dorset Square, the first really important cricket ground of plain *Mister* Thomas Lord. (Don't for heaven's sake get him wrong, or cricketers from Rawalpindi to Lahore, from Durban to Sydney, will drum you out of the Brownies.) Yorkshire Tom Lord set up in Dorset Square in 1787. Go there today, its houses on the north side are unchanged, give or take varnish. I rejoiced, and sold the paintings for enough to keep the old lady and her ailing hubby in clover. See? Cricketana is in. Old cricket balls, bats, boots even, caps – don't throw them away. Get me to sell them. You'll make a mint, if genuine that is. Noble me, I took no commission, and didn't steal a single thing of the old dear's. But I did forge each painting, for sordid gain. I think they were better than the originals. I really do believe that I have a lovely nature.

'What's the score, mate?' I asked a newspaper lad on the corner opposite the main entrance. He pulled a face, the Aussies were winning.

Lord's has Father Time, complete with scythe, stuck up there. Another quirk is a line of Sir Henry Newbolt's poem 'Vitaï Lampada' on a wall, corner of St John's Wood Road. I stood, heard the applause and groans of the crowd within. Test matches you can't get into. No hope of buying a ticket and wandering the stands. Wrinkle must be a member, so he'd be in posh. I could phone an urgent message with some heart-plucking story, but I didn't know what name he was using. Antique dealers often use pseudonyms, like crooks. I've heard.

Wrinkle was dedicated. He'd watch until close of play. I settled. The poem was maddening. I'd learned the wretched thing at school, couldn't remember a blinking line.

Two hours later, me as desiccated as a prune, the crowd surged out, scrambled for buses and dashed for the Tube. No Wrinkle. The mob dwindled, left me like a lemon. Surely I couldn't be wrong? By then I was almost in a dream, saying over to myself that bit from 'Vitaï Lampada', 'Play up, play up, and play the game!' It should have been Kipling's poem 'If', because there's more cheating in cricket than—

'The emphasis in "If" ought to be on the initial syllable.' Honor slipped her arm through mine. 'Otherwise, the closing line can't stress on the final "And". Criticism from a Yank okay?'

'Fine.' I was so relieved. 'Is Wrinkle still inside?'

'Due out after drinks.' She smiled. I liked her. 'What's your deal, Lovejoy? I don't fish for tiddlers.'

'It's huge. And a matter of life and death.'

She shivered deliciously. 'Wrinkle's told me all about you. I was sorry about last time. Shall we go?'

She had a massive sports motor, the shape of a sucked toffee. I had to practically lie down to get in. As Wrinkle came into view, she spoke with intensity.

'For years I've hunted for somebody like Wrinkle, Lovejoy. I won't sell him cheap. Capeesh?'

'I really like Americans, Honor.' I smiled as I said it. When a Yank comes in at the door, doubt dives out of the window. They crave certainty. 'When do we meet?'

'An hour after I've worn him out,' she said tersely, then

switched moods as Wrinkle opened the door. 'Darling! Look who's found us!'

He got in, stared morosely back at Lord's cricket ground. 'Where's all the spin bowlers gone, Lovejoy? I blame the bloody schools.'

The whole journey he grumbled. I daresay I would have agreed with every word, except I fell asleep before we'd gone a yard. I dreamt of killing somebody.

31

WOULD YOU CREDIT it, but Wrinkle's new workshop was only round the corner from where he'd been before in Spitalfields. The window was filled with old radios, gramophones, a jukebox.

'Cunning enough, Lovejoy?' Honor blithely led the way. 'Where do you hide a tree? In a forest. I knew you'd never find us.'

'Except for cricket, I wouldn't have.'

'You got lucky,' she snapped. 'I never thought to check his notices.'

The place was astonishing. I counted at least a dozen jukeboxes, their old 78 black records stacked within, and ancient TV sets of every size and hue with tiny bulbous screens. It was a great collection, if you like that sort of thing.

A sharp-suited bloke stepped straight out of the sixties from behind an array of this junk. He wore a wide-shouldered suit, drainpipe trousers, a thin tash like an old Movietone announcer, trilby at a spivvy angle.

'Who's this, honey?' He was actually flicking a US dollar.

'Lovejoy. An antique dealer.' I thought, so much scorn,

so little time? 'Friend of Wrinkle's. Watch he doesn't pinch anything.' She glared at me. 'Hymie's my brother, Lovejoy.'

'Indeed,' I said politely. Who was kidding, and about what? 'How do, Hymie.' You can tell, can't you, if there's something between a man and a woman. And if they're siblings. Or, as in this case, not. I shook hands like an American.

'You're dressed like a gangster,' I told him, striving for a Class A ingrate. 'You look smart!'

He preened. Any prat who dressed 1920s must crave admiration even from a scruff.

'Thanks,' he said modestly. 'I go for decor. Like the place? I've only been here a month.'

'Hymie!' Honor burst out, furious. 'I've warned you! Lovejoy's a hood.'

'Nark it,' I grumbled. 'I'm just Wrinkle's pal.' I gazed round open-mouthed. 'Are these all yours, Hymie? Congratulations!' I wandered, acting like I couldn't bring myself to touch. I know next to nothing about old electricals. Dealers call them Vintage Communications and Tellyana. They're made-up words, but add to the mad prices.

'It's not bad.' Hymie was delighted.

'Not *bad*?' I surged on. 'It's the holy of holies! My God! Isn't that a Rockola?' Lucky it was labelled.

'It sure is!'

Hymie started showing me round while Honor tried to get him to shut up. Wrinkle morosely went through into the back. I heard a door slam, and a distant hum begin as he switched on his power lighting. Lighting is almost everything when faking. I knew the feeling. Restore your spirits by delving into forgery.

'Hymie, you've a fortune here!' I was bored stiff.

This is the trouble. Antiques now being so costly, folk

move into 'antiques of the future'. Vintage Communications, mere bygones, leads the way. The trouble is they're so bulky. You can only get two Hi-Fi Wurlitzer Stereo jukeboxes in the average living-room and still breathe. Also, some people – include me, please – wouldn't want them at any price. On the *other* other hand, though, they're soaring in value. Get a hand-cranked gramophone for a few pence, varnish the wood, give the turntable a quick wipe, you can sell it for a good week's wage. The best vintage gramophone shop is at Mildenhall, in Suffolk, beloved of American buyers. Jukeboxes? Well, Hymie here had a good supply, but he'd got real competition in Berkhamstead. Me? I was hard put to keep awake. Crud isn't real antiques.

'Ever go to the National Vintage Communications Fair, Hymie?' I asked with reverence.

'Sure do, Lovejoy!' He almost fainted from the thrill, another living person having heard of it.

'I'd love to go myself,' I said, wistful. 'Except, you need to go with somebody who knows the difference between a BAL-AMI and an Ecko Portable TV, what, 1958?'

'Three years out, Lovejoy,' he chuckled. 'Nearly right! I'm restoring a genuine Philips 834 radio!'

'Not . . .?' I gasped, nearly yawning. I could hear Wrinkle hauling something across the workshop floor. An extractor fan began its whirr.

'Indeedy!' Hymie cried. 'Historic 1933 vintage!'

'You clever swine,' I said, with envy. Nobody can resist admiration plus envy. Even the Emperor Nero was desperate for underlings to admire his inept warblings. So desperate, indeed, that when Nero fell from his chariot early in the race they actually declared him victor.

'Come with me, Lovejoy,' Hymie said airily. 'In a couple of months we're going to do a mighty big spend.'

'Hymie.' Honor's quiet word felled Hymie's pride like an axe. He paled, gave me a look of sorrow, and vanished into his office.

'What?' I was indignant. 'This stuff is rare. They're tomorrow's antiques!'

Honor drew me to the window, her hand a clasp of iron. We stood there. Traffic moved past. People looked in, drifting by. It was some beats before she spoke.

'Lovejoy. Learn something vital.' She gazed at me, small and venomous. I felt a scary twinge. This lady was attractive, but on a crusade. 'I've scoured Europe for a treasure like Wrinkle. Don't think your goodness-gracious act with Hymie will do you any good. Wrinkle's collection is mine. So is Wrinkle. Understand that.'

Stoically, I didn't shiver. 'Fine by me, Honor. It's just that I'm broke. Wrinkle owes me. His collection. If I got somebody interested, would you pay me commission?'

'On a sale?' She almost laughed. 'You've a nerve, Lovejoy.'

'Look, love. What if somebody paid up, and you *didn't deliver*?'

She breathed, 'You mean, sell the collection twice?' A smile began, widened.

'First, to a mark I want to hurt. Then you can sell it again after I'd gone.'

Her smile dazzled as understanding lit from within. 'Lovejoy, that's beautiful! We sell Wrinkle's collection to some idiot, then default?'

'It would only leave me legally liable,' I said modestly. 'Not you.'

'Leaving me with Wrinkle's valuable collection!' She was thrilled. 'I get the profit, you take the risk?'

'That's it.'

'Glorious, Lovejoy.' She would have come closer, except we were in the window. 'It's a deal. Do you have to show them to the mark first?'

'One or two pieces at least, to hook them.'

'I want forty per cent commission, Lovejoy.'

'Ten,' I gave back.

We settled on 30 per cent, which was criminal extortion. I was narked, even though I'd no intention of going through with it, because even a duckegg like me has pride. What worried me was that Honor talked as if Wrinkle got nothing. He'd somehow slipped out of the reckoning.

'Where is Hymie in all this?' I asked.

'He does what I tell him,' she said, laughing at me.

I went red. 'About the money Wrinkle owes me. Can't your brother Hymie lend it? I'll need a bit to bring the mark.'

'Okay. I'll fix it with Hymie. He's the only one with keys.' Her gaze held me, threat in there. 'No tricks, Lovejoy, right?'

Which was how we left things. Me to bring my mark – aka Dieter Gluck, though I wasn't going to tell her his name – to see Wrinkle's glorious work on the sly, and Honor to make sure Wrinkle didn't hear about it.

'Don't let me down, Honor,' I begged.

'Likewise,' Honor said, no smiles this time.

I swallowed and left through Wrinkle's workshop. It was a galaxy, him already hard at it. His wonderful fakes were around the walls. His three genuine originals stood on a dias, under one brilliant redwood canopy. It looked like red eyne wood, that dealers call soymida. I was desperate to feel the wood, because red eyne rubs oily to the finger, dull yet smooth. Its pale streaks give it away. Tough as nails, and insects give up.

'Nice workshop, Wrinkle,' I praised, on my way.

He just grunted, labouring. He was doing a rotary cut veneer from a piece of red eyne. It looked lovely, though it's hellish difficult because of its knots. Furniture made from it costs the earth. Beauty, like vengeance, doesn't come easy.

I left through the yard, noticing two Chubb locks, standard deadbolts, the fingered interlocks, the electronic alarms. I had a cup of coffee at a corner caff, wondering who I could get. I'd only got tonight to burgle the place. Not long.

Tinker was the man. Hardly the quietest crook on earth, but I wanted reliability. Billia and Dang could help me, because nobody knew them much in the antiques trade. Worth a go?

32

WAITING FOR TINKER in the Nell of Old Drury, I thought how odd life can be. It's people's attitudes.

I loved this lady, once. Every time we met behind the auction sheds in Stowmarket for a snog, though, I had the uneasy feeling we were being watched. Her bloke was notorious for jealousy, which scared me, but she only laughed. Risk, she kept saying, adds spice. This is my point: The only time I felt safe with Marsha was in Stratford-on-Avon one weekend, and it was exactly then that her aggressive fiancé turned up. I escaped by the skin of my teeth. Going to meet Billia and Dang, I *felt* secure because the stout bowler-hatted geezer wasn't around any more. Was I wrong?

Tinker entered, coughing his way through the throng of complaining actors. He was merry as a sparrow, instantly into the two pints I had ready.

'Wotcher, Tinker. Look sharp. We're meeting Billia in Covent Garden.'

'Why not here, Lovejoy?' he grumbled. 'Daft plodding through London when we're already boozing.'

Pubs and taverns to Tinker are like stepping-stones across life's stormy waters. It was only five minutes' walk to

Covent Garden, a distance he saw as the Hellespont. He slurped up. We started out, but not before I loudly asked him what Dang had done wrong. Several people must have overheard.

Tinker was still explaining as we headed up Russell Street. 'Dang dived in the fourth round. The backers'd told him the third. No brains, see.'

'What's the threat, then?' I was glad Dang was thick as a plank. My plan needed two dupes. Dang could be one.

'He's got four days, to pay back the bets they lost on him.' He told me how much. It set me spluttering. 'Or Dang'll get blammed. The fight was a championship eliminator.'

'Who are they, Tinker?' Dang would accidentally die in some hit-and-run accident.

'Cockneys.' Tinker slowed hopefully outside a pub. Cockneys? I needed Sturffie. But was he already in the enemy camp?

Billia and Dang were sitting on the benches in Covent Garden watching a juggler. A nearby carousel whirled gaudily. The Transport Museum was flourishing, crowds surging. It's one of my favourite places.

'Hello, Lovejoy.' Billia budged up, gave me room.

She sounded really down. Dang sat massively there, a vacuous grin on his face. He gasped when the juggler's wooden balls vanished one by one then magically reappeared.

'Wotcher, love.' The crowd applauded. A girl entered the space to catch skittles. Tinker stood by, forlorn, without ale. 'I'm going to do a lift in Dulwich. I'll need Dang. No,' I said hastily as her eyes widened in alarm. 'No scrapping. Just carrying stuff. I've done all the donkeywork. It's tonight.'

'Will you be there?' She shushed me as some colourful Americans came to enjoy the show.

'Yes,' I whispered. Honest to God, we were like joke Russian spies in a West End farce. 'The money's good. It'll pay off Dang's gamblers.'

'How soon?' she asked. Dang gaped as the juggler balanced a huge beachball.

'Pay day immediately after. Coin of the realm, love.'

Dang clapped, huge hands flapping. I tried not to think of a circus sea lion. Not for the first time, I wondered about the attraction between this gormless hulk and the dainty lass seated by me. Could it be solely bedwork? Or was it something deeper, the need of a pretty bird to protect an inept monster who couldn't even count? Enough. I'd sown the seed. In Covent Garden, we were secret as a broadcast. No need to be more explicit. I slipped Tinker a note, told him I'd join him later in the Eagle, the pub of 'Pop goes the weasel' fame.

'Take Dang, Tinker. I'll go over the details with Billia.'

'Right, Lovejoy. Come on, mate.'

Dang left, looking back. The juggler bowed to applause, was replaced by a robot dancer. His pretty girl went round with her hat for nobbins. The crowd instantly thinned, stingy as all crowds at free street shows.

'Now, love,' I said quietly. 'Here's what. Ten o'clock tonight you and Dang walk down College Road, Dulwich. The art gallery's well signposted.'

And so on. I made her repeat the plan over and over. Count the windows, sketch the exits. Look for burglar alarms. She asked pertinent questions until she started to get on my nerves and I had to speak sharply. I mean, it isn't as though you can trust a woman, is it? Ten minutes, I chucked some coins into the robot dancer's cap, and told

Billia to tell Tinker I'd changed my mind and gone instead to find Sturffie in Bermondsey. I made her repeat that, too. If she and Dang didn't get arrested tonight it wouldn't be for want of trying. No harm in making sure when you want friends to get something really wrong.

I like plenty of people. I've already said how my Gran warned me against pretty women – 'A rag, a bone, and a hank of hair'. Well, aye, but take Billia. Truly bonny, for all her daftness about Dang. And you couldn't beat Lydia (no pun) because despite her primness she was everything a bloke could crave. I've only to walk her into the Antiques Arcade for the lads to set up a communal groan that really narks Giselle who runs the coffee stall. Likeability works with blokes, too, but different. Like, Tinker's a mate. He'd go to gaol for me (he has) and I for him (I haven't; pressure of time). And I've already said how I owe Sturffie, who saved me from a mangling. You just have to like folk.

Sturffie I eventually found sorting through some stuff outside the antiques place, top of Bond Street. His van's distinctive when it's his. At other times, Sturffie changes its signs, logos, and colour so often you're never sure. Without a word I climbed into the van and started helping. He seemed pleased to see me.

'Lovejoy! Tell me if any of this is genuine.'

'It's all dross, except one piece. On your own?'

A policeman put his head in and told Sturffie he'd got ten minutes to move on.

'Right, mate. Ta.' Sturffie stared at his wares. 'Which is it?'

'That.' An ordinary chair, looking like some suburbanite's

idea of an imitation throne. I couldn't help smiling. Like meeting an old friend unexpectedly.

'You sure?' He stepped over to it, curious. 'Isn't it chipboard? It's still got the bar code on it. I only took this off the dealer's hands to make up a price.'

'It's so square it has to be wrong, Sturffie. Look at it.'

Some DIY enthusiast had tried to make a wooden upright armchair. The back had three panels, the middle one slender, knobbly and darkly overpainted. The two lateral panels were modern chipboard. The seat was all wood, too, but its dark triangular centre had been squared off by the addition of chipboard edges. I looked below. The original back stretcher had been sawn off and replaced by a modern broom handle. The whole chair had then been varnished nearly black. It was an execution. The antiques trade is a vale of tears littered with murder. Is it any wonder I hate people?

'You all right, Lovejoy? Sit yerself, mate.'

I slumped on a chest optimistically marked 'Early Georgian'. I felt the familiar strangeness.

'It is chipboard, Sturffie, but built onto a caqueteuse.'

When I try to talk a French word, it comes out a mockery. Unintentional. We all do it. Like most dealers, I can only say cack-tooze, rhyme with hack-booze.

'I thought cacktoozes were Scotch, Lovejoy.'

No wonder Sturffie was mystified. He'd bought a chipboard modern 'filler', as dealers call worthless pieces bought for the sake of bodying out their wares, and seen me, the only true divvy he'd ever known, go queer over it. In the sixteenth century, Scotland started copying French styles of chair. The caqueteuse is called from a French word meaning, they say, to chatter. Triangular seat, narrow panelled back, widening arms, it's made for ladies to sit and gossip. Somebody had tried to improve a truly antique chair, pre-dating the Armada, by nailing pieces of chipboard onto it. It was just lucky the maniac hadn't had enough carpentry skill to improve it to extinction. I shivered at the thought, my teeth rattling like dead bones.

'Here, Lovejoy. Come and have a cuppa.'

He fastened the van. We got in and drove out and along Piccadilly, round Trafalgar Square and managed to stop in Charing Cross Road. Sturffie put a note saying *Urgent Medical Deliveries* in his window, and we walked to St Martin-in-the-Fields, the one place we'd not be snooped on. We got some nosh in their crypt caff, the one that has art exhibitions done by talented prisoners.

'How much?' Sturffie asked. 'Thousand? Two?'

'Sell it as it is,' I said, wincing at the thought of Sturffie getting out an electric sander to start a crazy restoration. 'The Society of Antiquaries has one chair, but English, 1585. Don't trade it for less than a house.' He gaped. I nodded, let him pay for the grub. Why do they always have African students serving in these places nowadays? 'Do me a favour, Sturffie?'

'You want commission?' he asked, shrewd.

'No, mate. I want a door opened, and alarms switched off.'

'Christ, Lovejoy,' he said, frowning. 'That's impossible.' His face broke in a cracking grin. 'My joke. Who're we robbing?'

'Nobody,' I said. 'Open a door for me some time tonight, just so I can walk round for ten minutes.'

He was even more mystified. 'Easiest fortune I've ever made! You're a real pal, Lovejoy.' For a second he looked crestfallen. 'Listen, mate. I've something to tell you.'

'What, Sturffie?' I asked, innocently, knowing.

'It's about some gemstones. Padpas. You come asking in Bermondsey.'

'Aye. Dosh Callaghan's paying me to—'

'It were me, mate.' He looked so sad I felt sorry for him. I didn't interrupt. Confession's good for the soul. 'Dosh Callaghan got me to swap some padpas – you know them odd-coloured sapphires? – for cheap tsavorites.'

Acting time. I did a theatrical gape, almost choked myself on goulash. 'It was you, Sturffie?'

'Dosh simply wanted a reason to send you to the Smoke, Lovejoy. He insisted on that Moiya tart pretending she was Sir Ponsonby's bird. I heard them laughing about it in the pub.'

'Why, Sturffie?' I'd have been a star if I'd gone on the stage. I'm really good.

'Dunno. They had a brief along, some tart with long hair.'

'Really?' I said, acting baffled. 'Ta, Sturffie. I don't feel so bad now I know.'

'You're okay about it, Lovejoy?' he asked, worried. 'I don't know why Dosh wanted you sniffing round the London street markets, though.'

'Forget it. Life's just one big mystery. Look, Sturffie, about tonight. Will it be you, or some mate?'

'Me,' he said, indignant. 'Unless it's something special?'

Remembering what I could, I described Hymie's security.

'It'll only take me twenty minutes, Lovejoy. Is it far?'

'No. Ten o'clock tonight okay?' Pub time is vital, this being when alibis grow on trees.

After that, we started general talk over deals done and not done, the antique lore that makes life worth living. The one worry still nagging away was whether Dieter Gluck knew Sturffie. I calmed, laughing at Sturffie's tales.

An hour later I waved him off, having given him a gillion warnings about his caqueteuse chair, what to say, how to offer it for sale. Then I phoned Dieter Gluck on his mobile.

'It's tonight,' I said without preamble. 'I'll show you the stuff. You'll need an antiques expert with you.'

'Where? I'll drive there. In my saloon.'

'Be by your mobile phone at nine. It's London local.'

I rang off without waiting. He'd be there.

33

NOBODY WANTS WORRY. Even if there's no such things as spectres, memories create them where none existed. Since I'd never been sure where imagination begins and memory ends, I'm always half in, half out, of incipient fright.

Tonight I unnerved myself for nothing. I mean, Spitalfields on an average London night is hardly a spooky nook. I waited on edge, wondering what I'd missed. Gluck on his way, fine. Hymie I'd phoned earlier, told him of three Japanese radio and gramophone buyers, eager to collect Columbia Grafanola machines and early Edison Amerolas, waiting, money in hand, in one of four Kensington hotels. I'd looked these names up in the public library, Charing Cross Road. 'They'll be there between nine and ten tonight,' I told him. 'Take a credit-card witness.' Whatever *that* was. I wanted to make sure Honor was with him. Breathless, Hymie asked me to spell the names. I rang off. Spell Japanese names? People nark me. Tell a penny lie, they want linguistics.

I'd told Gluck to be at Aldgate in a taxi. Had I forgotten anything? No.

Yet I was jumpy. Like I'd reminisced before, this area was Jack the Ripper's haunt. A thousand enthusiasts have written definitive volumes on the killer who'd called himself 'Saucy Jack'. Books prove this or that, everybody a suspect. Sometimes it seems there's nobody left in Old London who hasn't been accused of being him. Only I know the really real solution: Jack the Ripper was a mortician worker at The London Hospital, down the road from here. Somebody touched my shoulder. I screeched and leapt a mile.

'Christ!' I was bathed in sweat, feeling like a rag.

'What's up?' Sturffie stared at me in the gloaming. 'Gawd, Lovejoy, you're in a frigging state. You should see a doctor.'

'I'm fine, Sturffie. Just thinking.'

Theft by breaking and entering is one of the only two enterprises you should do in silence. I simply walked to the rear of Hymie's premises and gave Sturffie the nod. A hall light showed in the workshop corridor, a giveaway. Who stays in with only a hall light on? Nobody.

'My van's round the corner, Lovejoy.' He gave me the keys. 'It's cleaned and empty. No windows.' He meant no clues.

In less than ten minutes, he had the alarms sussed and the locks fiddled. I told him ta, to come back in an hour to set it all to rights again. He shrugged and left. I went inside, checked for the absence of Jack the Ripper, closed the back door and drove Sturffie's van through Commercial Street to Aldgate. I made absolutely certain that I didn't think of Martha Turner, dreadfully murdered and mangled by J the R – thirty slashes – as I drove past the site of George Yard Buildings. Nor did I gulp as I doglegged past Mitre Square (Catherine Beddowes, one of Saucy Jack's bloodiest, on a terrible Sunday).

It went like clockwork. I saw Gluck and two – *two?* – others in a saloon car waiting by the great glass emporium of the Cutler Street Silver building. I parked close, flashed my beam. Gluck and a portly gent stepped out with Moiya December, setting some lads heading down Whitechapel whistling. She looked glorious in the night lamps.

'In the back, gents,' I said. 'Not you, miss. Sorry.'

Gluck tried it on, but I wasn't having him seeing where we were going. I insisted. They boarded, nervously sitting on the van floor. I locked the rear doors, and waited to see Moiya go back to the posh saloon and sit glowering. I drove off, twisting down unnecessary detours for quite twenty minutes. Accidentally I found myself in Hanbury Street (Annie Chapman, whom J the R bizarrely laid out with brass rings and copper coins) and accelerated so quickly that Gluck and his stout gent shouted in anger. Lovejoy stayed cool, I'm pleased to report. I revved into Hymie's narrow yard, checked the gate was closed, and let them out.

Gluck was furious. 'Is that your best driving?'

'Is this behaviour essential?' the gent asked.

No names, no pack drill, they say. I'd already had a good look. No street names were visible from here. Okay, they'd find Hymie's place in a couple of days if they really tried, and could then talk to Hymie and Honor all they wished. Wrinkle too. By then I'd be over the hills and far away.

'Any ferreting, all deals are off, okay? Inside.'

They went in. I wouldn't let them switch on the lights. Sturffie had thoughtfully dowsed the hall lamp. I shone a pencil torch ahead. Nothing like compulsory darkness to enforce dependence.

'Those three pieces,' I told them. 'You can lift the sheets.'

Wrinkle screened his genuine pieces from the work area, but there was no disguising the blissfilled aromas and sights of the dust, shavings. Wrinkle was a craftsman of superb tidiness, much neater than I am. All his pieces were either crated or covered.

The pudgy bloke was a real pro. His sharp intake of breath told me all. He knew Chinese antique furniture, touched the wood with reverence, glanced at Gluck as if to ask him how on earth such superb genuine pieces had got here. I wouldn't let him invert any.

'Crawl under if you have to. Don't lift.'

I wouldn't give an inch on this. Antiques is always a seller's market. Please don't tell me it isn't, that your friend Elsie's had terrible trouble trying to sell her reproduction mascot from her dad's old motor car. I did say 'antiques', so tough luck on Elsie and all modern junk. If Elsie's antique turned out to be, say, a Continental silver christening set – tiny knife, fork, spoon, feeding spoon, three little cups and a silver and ivory rattle, William IV vintage – then she'd have dealers clamouring at her garden gate and worshipping her hair, etc., because dealers will do anything for genuine antiques. They'll even – I've heard – offer the going market price.

'Can I ask for provenance?' the gent wheezed, straightening.

'No,' I said bluntly. 'If you want provenance for these, you're useless.'

He almost smiled. He had a goatee beard, waxed moustache grey as a brock badger. Like he was trying to seem Edwardian. I thought, Sotheby's, moonlighting? Or did gentry still only come from Christie's?

'Any others?'

'Out,' I replied.

I did the journey in reverse, the boxed-in pair of them clinging on. I did my best among the streets, but still unnerved myself by blundering about the site of Buck's

Row in Whitechapel (Mary Ann Nicholls, J the R's second prostitute victim, dead on the cobbles after trolling in Limehouse). Mercifully the lovely Moiya was still alive and sulking in her grand saloon. I let the two men out. Gluck was furious. He tried to see the van's registration. I let him try. It was covered in mud, Sturffie's attention to detail.

Whether Gluck told the old expert who I was didn't matter. Tinker would have my alibi chiselled in granite. I waved them off. Ten minutes later, I gave Sturffie back his van, waited until he'd set Wrinkle's alarms to rights, and let him drop me off in the Strand. Finding a phone these days is an ordeal, but I got one after hunting Charing Cross for a century, and rang Gluck.

'On or off?' I asked him, knowing the answer.

'On,' he said. 'Details of the other event?'

'Going like a dream,' I lied. He meant the Dulwich robbery. 'It'll be in the papers day after tomorrow. About payment.'

'Any default,' he said, 'you know who'll suffer. Any trick will mean permanent exit for both of them, followed by somebody else. That is three.'

'I know. Payment?'

He chuckled. 'I like your directness. Tomorrow noon, when dining with influence.'

'Deal,' I said, and rang off.

So if I didn't deliver the Dulwich Picture Gallery's masterpieces for Dieter Gluck to rescue for the nation, and if I failed to provide him with a selection of genuine antique Chinese furniture pieces so he could make a fortune, then Mortimer, Colette, and me would go to the wall. I went, whistling, wondering if Tinker had got hold of Lydia yet.

34

I DON'T KNOW if people these days are familiar with doss houses. Different from days of yore, of course. The old phrase 'I'm so tired I could sleep on a clothesline' started there. You tied a rope between walls, draped your arms on the line, and slept like that because the floor was crammed with too many other lucky derelicts. Now, you pay a tithe for a 'semi-special' nook of partitioned sanctuary, and get breakfast for a pittance, then it's out into London's bright day. I mean raining.

Optimism's not my strong suit. I'm good at getting by, but frankly I'm scared of aggro. Like, Gluck had won Colette's antiques firm, Saffron Fields, the land, canal. And he was a killer. If I knew all that, so must the police. Proof was a different matter. And a contract's a contract. Colette and Arthur had signed almost everything over to Gluck, nothing anybody could do.

But Gluck needed that one bit of land to dig the link canal. Which meant he needed money. Mortimer stood in the way. Give Gluck those two fields, plus Mortimer's lordship title, Gluck would be taipan, big in the land.

I explained this to Gloria Dee at the Royal Academy in

Piccadilly. No sense in holding back the cruel details. We sat on a bench.

'You, frightened?' She seemed astonished.

'Scared stiff.' I reminded her that Gluck's bloke Bern had been bludgeoned to death.

'But the police said the poor man simply fell, or surprised a robber.'

'Oh, aye. You know what to do?'

A crocodile of children came under the arch, chattering away. How come teachers look so cool? I'm frantic just babysitting Henry – my other job – and he can hardly crawl.

'You've told me what I'm to say, Lovejoy.' She didn't look scared, but then women have no need to be. 'Sir Jesson and I meet Mr Gluck. Public-spirited, Mr Gluck will tell Jesson that a major theft will soon happen, from an unnamed but important public art gallery.'

'Good. And?'

'And that Gluck has ways of rescuing the stolen art works for the nation.'

'That's when you ask your all-important question, love.' I watched her lovely mouth move as she got ready. Politicians like Sir Jesson have everything – wealth, sinecures, and lovely women like Mrs Dee.

'I ask Mr Gluck, "Why don't you simply tell the police?" And he replies—'

'That the robbers will then know he's an informer. They will exact retribution.' I was proud of the phrase, having rehearsed Gluck through it on the phone. Gloria sounded better. I couldn't help asking. 'You and Sir Jesson. Are you . . .?'

Her eyes widened. 'Lovejoy, I'm a married woman!'

Two ladies entering the Academy heard and turned to stare.

'You mean, er, you and he aren't—?'

'It's time this conversation ended, Lovejoy,' she said primly, gathering her handbag.

'Can I help you about art?' I asked desperately. Hardly Romeo wooing, but the best I could think of. 'Teach you how to forge an Old Master?' I threw in my last lie. 'No obligation.'

Her eyes were a lovely blue, steady as a hunter's. 'Why, Lovejoy?'

'It's all I have to offer.'

'Why would you want to help me?'

No answer to that, because women already know. She was smiling as we parted, she to Fortnum & Mason's posh restaurant, me to wait out the performance. From across the road I saw the lanky form of Sir Jesson arrive in his Rolls. The stage was set. I couldn't work out what felt wrong.

When you feel lost, antiques are the antidote. I went to Alfie's, a famed antiques place, and wandered among the stalls. I overheard dealers arguing about Chelsea porcelain. They were on about Triangle Period pieces – the Chelsea mark was a simple triangle cut into the soft paste. Shine a strong light through the piece, you see tiny translucent spots we call 'pinholes', though they're not holes at all. Try it right now on any oldish porcelain you have in the house. You might get lucky.

Nervy as I was, I had to smile. One dealer was trying to tell the other it was a definite proof of 1745 to 1749 Chelsea. I hung about, listening. They were wrong, because modern fakers mix shredded glass into modern clay. Adjust the temperature, you can get a pretty good imitation. And you don't have to be an expert potter, because the first Chelsea wares which Nicholas Sprimont started when he sailed in from Flanders were really rotten efforts, dead clumsy. For four years, 1749 on, the mark was a raised anchor. The translucent pinholes became translucent patches, the famous 'Chelsea moons'. You can easily fake these—

'Coffee, Lovejoy?' Saintly said. 'Having a good day?'

'No. It's gruesome. Ta.' We sat at a table. When the plod offer you something, watch out. He actually forked out for biscuits, so he'd want blood.

'Who is your current lady these days? I haven't seen your apprentice lately – Lydia, is it?'

'Got none, and yes to Lydia.' I wished I'd walked out.

'Hear about that little bloke, did you?'

My hand didn't manage to lift the mug. 'What little bloke?'

'Trout, they call him.' He made great play of wanting more sugar. Cops are all overweight. 'Got himself arrested. Flew at Mr Gluck in a rage. Noticed any mental instability in Trout, have you?'

It was so innocent it was creepy. The ghost feeling came back.

'No. He's Tinker's pal, if you've got the right one.'

Saintly chuckled. 'Not many antique-dealing dwarf Tarzan-O-Grams around, Lovejoy.'

'Tinker there, was he?' I asked, casual.

'Tried to pull him off, but the little bloke was berserk. Mr Gluck stated Trout tried to stab him. Luckily Mr Gluck's cousin was in town, a bruiser. Trout rather suffered, I'm afraid.'

I swallowed. I'd warned Trout to steer clear of Gluck, stupid little sod. I didn't need this, with Gloria and Sir Jesson's set-up nosh taking place with Gluck across the road in Fortnum's, and my head spinning. Maybe Shar could spring him from clink? 'Where've you taken him?'

'Hospital, naturally.' He flashed a watch. 'They're operating.'

'Tinker too?' I croaked. No wonder Saintly had paid for coffee.

'St Thomas's Hospital,' Saintly called after me. 'You know it? On the Thames. There's a bus—'

Saintly and his bloody buses. One day somebody'd shove him under one. Now I wish I'd not thought that evil thought. Thinking's always trouble.

Hospitals scare me. It's a different world. Everybody except me seems to know where they're going. Everybody else also looks twice as fit. Doctors always glare like they're working out what illnesses I have. Nurses weigh me up, like what tubes do they have to pass and into what orifice. Not only that, I've only to walk down any hospital corridor to start to feel my right leg dragging, a rare lethal fever, double vision. And all the time those accusing stares from passing housemen, stethoscopes at the ready to diagnose my multiple fatal ailments. So I tend to shuffle along avoiding eye contact, hoping somebody will give me directions without amputating some vital bit. Hospitals are the pits.

Tinker was in a surgical ward. I found him by homing in on his cough. I halted, aghast. One plastered leg was raised at an absurd angle up into a maze of pulleys. He was bandaged, forehead and one eye. An arm was plastered. He looked like he'd rolled under a war.

'Wotcher, Lovejoy,' he said. Thank God he was conscious.

'Gluck did it?'

'And a bruiser called Kenelley. Last night.'

'Why were you in Chelsea, Tinker?' I couldn't really get mad.

His one eye grew reproachful. 'We wus doing nuffink. I wouldn't have gone down Chelsea if you'd said not to. You know that.'

'Sorry, Tinker. I'm out of kilter.' I looked about the ward. God, it looked a killing field. 'Anything you want?'

'Fags. A bleedin' drink. Bloody nurses are stingy cows.'

The ward sister came clacking along. 'I heard that, Mr Dill. The surgeon says nothing by mouth for two more hours. And I'll thank you to keep a civil tongue in your head . . .' et caring cetera.

'I'll send Lydia in.' I had to go. I was behind time. 'Saintly told me Trout went for Gluck with a knife.'

'It's balls, Lovejoy. They set out to do us over. I know the difference, wack. Here, why's Trout in a different ward?'

The sister must have had hearing like a bat.

'Your friend is still in theatre,' she said briskly. 'I'll let you know as soon as we get news.' She avoided my eyes, clipped off along the polished floor.

'I'll be back. Cheers, mate.'

'Tarra, son. Care, now. And watch the lad, eh?'

After this warning, I didn't need telling. It was Gluck's reminder, after I'd treated him with disdain last night in front of his girl and his expert with the goatee beard. Gluck would have to win now, whatever happened. But so would I.

35

T HE THAMES LOOKED unchanged. I couldn't stop my hands trembling. I've no illusions. We're a rotten species, do anything for gain. Like blam Tinker, a harmless old soak, just to threaten me. And hire some bruiser to wellnigh kill a titch like Trout.

The reason? I'd shown Gluck and his expert the true value of the antiques. Okay, they belonged to Wrinkle. Gluck didn't yet know that. But he wasn't thick. If I could stroll into a tatty workshop, show him genuine Chinese furniture worth a fortune, I could just as easily nick them. Gluck's warning spoke louder than words. The 'third person' Gluck threatened was Mortimer, or Lydia, or me. So one of us would have to be risked. As long as it wasn't me. I slipped down off the wall, still feeling sick, and walked to the South Bank. Ugliest theatres on earth.

Eat before a scrap, is the Royal Navy's dictum. The Duke of Wellington's advice was to pee whenever you could. I did both. Time to scrap.

'How did it go?' I asked Billia at the National Gallery, Trafalgar Square. I was astonished to see her. Why hadn't

Dulwich's perfect security systems arrested her? Now I'd have to go through with the charade.

'It went well, Lovejoy.' She handed me a sheaf of notes. 'You got one name wrong. It was by Pinxit.'

A headache came on. 'Gent in a brown velvet frock coat, brilliant white satin undercoat?'

'That's it.'

'You ignorant cow. Thomas Hudson wrote Pinxit after his signature. It means *painted* it. Latin.'

'Oh. You missed a Reynolds, Lovejoy. In the foyer. Margaret Morris.'

'That's a modern copy.' Now my headache was crippling me lopsided. 'The eyes are out of line, different sizes, like from two different women. Reynolds didn't make those mistakes. What's this?'

'You said do sketches of the exits and alarms.'

'Oh, aye. Great.' I'd forgotten. I scanned them looking as furtive as possible. 'Well done.' And they were remarkably good, a professional job. 'You could go into the suss business, love.'

'Thank you, Lovejoy.' She asked about money.

'Eh?' To buy off Dang's betting syndicate. 'Tomorrow morning,' I said with deep honesty. 'I mean that most sincerely.'

Her eyes filled. 'Thank you, sweetheart.' We were into emotion. 'I promise, Lovejoy, I'll do anything for you, when Dang's out of this scrape. And I do mean anything.'

My throat constricted. All me paid attention.

'The robbery's tonight. You and Dang walk up to the main entrance of Dulwich Picture Gallery.' I found it on the sketch, beautifully to scale. 'Just like it's still daylight. Dress like two workmen, overalls and that.' As long as they were conspicuous.

She was doubtful. 'Have we to hide?'

'No.' I invented my way through a folder. The words came out. 'That would be a giveaway. Carry a bag of tools. Wear overalls with an electricity logo. Midnight.'

'Midnight.' Carefully she repeated the details. 'From which direction do we approach, Lovejoy?'

'From the pond.'

'That side's awfully well lit, Lovejoy.'

'That's allowed for,' I told her. Her painstaking attention to detail was getting me narked. There wasn't going to be any Dulwich robbery, for heaven's sake. 'Once you're in the shadows, my insiders will lower the paintings to you.'

'There are no shadows round the building, Lovejoy.'

I sighed. She was a bloody nuisance.

'There will be,' I said knowingly. 'At midnight.'

'Who are the insiders? And how do we get the paintings away?'

Had she no imagination, for God's sake? As for helpers, I'd just made them up.

'Two false police vans will come to the front of the building,' I invented impatiently. It was the best I could think up on the spur. 'Okay? Load up and drive off.'

'Where to, Lovejoy?'

Jesus, but I was worn out. Coldly I stared her down until she coloured and started to apologize.

'Who's lost sleep to help you?' I demanded. 'Who's spent a fortune phoning, er, Amsterdam, just to pay off those Cockney fight-fixers?' I waxed indignant, thinking what a martyr I was and what ungrateful bastards friends were.

'I'm so sorry, Lovejoy. I didn't mean—'

'It's all right,' I said, broken, a real sob in my voice. 'All I need is honesty.'

She promised. I said fine, and went to find a friend.

Judith Falconer's the world's most desirable radio reporter. Her station doesn't rival the BBC, being a decaying mansion outside London. I've hungered for her some years, with no luck. Every time I've drawn breath to suggest she takes me on holiday to Monet's Giverny and ravages my poor defenceless body she just makes casual conversation. She was waiting as arranged facing Eros, gorgeous as usual. We did the usual coffee fencing then got down to it.

'Want a scoop, outside broadcast? Judith, you can be the saviour of the nation.' Okay, so I'd promised Lisa. But was she here? No.

Judith was unfazed. 'Do you know how much an outside broadcast costs?'

'A titchy dictaphone will do. The only thing is, you don't air it until next morning.'

Her lovely brown eyes held me. 'What do you get out of this, Lovejoy?'

'Nothing,' I said, no acting needed. 'But if you'd come to Giverny with me, no obligation, I'd be glad.' She said nothing.

Being scooped by TV is the radio reporter's greatest fear. Her eyes sparkled.

'Can I trust you, Lovejoy?'

The world was low on trust today, I said. She smiled, said okay. Nothing about Giverny, selfish cow. See what I mean? Help others, you get nothing back.

We parted amicably. I walked round the Tate until the vibrations from the paintings made me feel queasy. I phoned Saintly, told him about the forthcoming robbery tonight at an unnamed art gallery.

'I'll phone you about ten o'clock tonight,' I said blithely. 'By then, I'll have sussed out who's doing it and where.'

'Is this on the level, Lovejoy?'

'Straight up,' I said. 'If nothing happens, you can arrest me. Incidentally, don't make too much noise or they might get away. And don't arrest a reporter called Judith who'll be describing events from the bushes.'

Lovely feeling, being honest to the police. I'd never done it before. I felt holy. In spite of my new-found piety I didn't call into St Paul's for a quick prayer as I went past. No sense in risking the She Wolf's ghost at this late stage. I rang St Thomas's Hospital. Tinker was stable. They wouldn't give me any news about Trout. I insisted I was his brother, but they were adamant. It betokened bad.

The trains were running on time. I made it to East Anglia, got a lift from an old lady who'd just come from the dentist. She gave me a cheery monologue on the most reliable adhesive for dental plates, should I ever reach false teeth. I said ta. She told me she collected antique hat pins. Don't laugh. You can buy handfuls for a farthing at any boot fair – today, that is. Tomorrow, nobody knows. If I'd spare change, I'd buy up every old hat pin in sight. For less than an afternoon's wages you could have a massive display – ivory, Edwardian silver, Victorian, early plastics (soaring, unbelievably rare), unique porcelain-headed hat pins made in craft potteries. We'd just got talking when she dropped me off at Best River Outcomes, Ltd. I was sorry to see her go. 'Come to tea, Saturday, Lovejoy,' she offered roguishly. 'I'll have my new teeth in.'

'It's a date, Tranquillity.' I waved her off. Her collection sounded worth something. She'd described several original Art Deco pins.

Alone, I surveyed the canal. After London the stillness was unnerving. The boatyard was soporific, the water motionless. It looked painted by a stoned artist. Three longboats lay canted on the bank, to voyage no more. Others rotted in the yard pool, one down at the stern. A moorhen chugged out of a half-submerged window. Only one longboat looked worthy. No wonder developers like Talleyton and Gluck had itchy fingers. It was an investor's dream – a pittance now, for a fortune tomorrow.

A half-hearted hammer struck metal. 'Wotcher, Kettle,' I called.

'That you?' a voice quavered.

'Can you be more specific?'

'Hello, Lovejoy.' The old bargee emerged with his little grandson Jack.

'Can I take my pick of these longboats?'

He hid his astonishment. 'Jack, show Lovejoy the engine.'

'This way, Lovejoy.'

Little Jack took my hand as if I were senile. He's six. At the non-sinking boat he held up his arms. I lifted him aboard, clambered after. Old Kettle sat on a bollard and lit his pipe while Jack showed me starter, forward, reverse. I heard him out and said ta.

'I want to go to Saffron Fields, Kettle. Tonight.'

He spat, tamped his pipe and wiped the stubber on his trouser leg. 'Not allowed night journeys on a canal, Lovejoy.'

'But I'm a crook,' I said, narked.

'The canal's blocked up,' Jack said. 'It tried to reach the sea but doesn't.'

I looked at him. 'Don't be a nosey little sod, you.'

'Lovejoy swore, Grampa.'

'There's three locks, Chelmer style,' Kettle said. He used to make barge ware from sheet tin. I helped him to paint his jugs, kettles, tin vases, in the old style. We sold well to tourists, but he lost heart as his longboats failed. 'The last lock's our terminus.' He spat, eyed me. 'It's two fields from the sea estuary.'

'Why're you telling me this?' I asked, indignant. 'Think I'm going to smuggle a barge load out of the country, onto some blacked-out ship like they used to do in olden days?'

'Course not, Lovejoy,' Kettle said evenly.

Four o'clock in the afternoon I went back to my cottage to nosh on bread and fried tomatoes, have a sleep. It would be a long night.

36

ABOUT SEVEN I rang Gluck from the phone box by the chapel. It seemed impossible that he wouldn't hear my blood rushing in my ears.

'The news of a gallery theft breaks soon. The eastern promise is set up.'

'Where and when?'

'Dawn. All one shipment.' I made myself sound shakier than I was. 'I can get the lot to your manor. You'll get a legit bill of sale.'

'Wait.' He spoke to somebody, muffled. I didn't catch a word. 'Legit?'

'Above board. I deliver the antiques. You're allowed thirty days to pay.'

'It sounds good.' Yet he sounded wary. I thought, Dear God, must I lead everybody by the nose? Any dealer'd jump at it. I could see I'd have to make difficulties, to make him bite harder. I looked outside. The light was fading.

'There's a problem, Gluck. The eastern promise just arrived offshore.'

'Offshore where?'

Hooked him. 'Can't you guess? It'll all soon be on your land. But there's a risk.'

'I don't like risks.' His speech became guttural. He *hated* risks.

What the hell did I say now? There *was* no risk. With Billia and Dang under arrest soon, Judith the broadcaster observantly recording every detail in Dulwich's dark ditches, with Wrinkle and Honor fornicating among Jack the Ripper's ghosts in Spitalfields, every menace was safely neutralized. There wasn't even a risk for me, an all-time first. My brilliant planning had finally triumphed.

'The risk is I might need to get a van from somewhere.'

'Silence.' He actually said that, like a schoolmaster. 'It will be dark. You will have the excess items covered. No rain.'

Okay, I was to see it didn't rain. 'Right, Mr Gluck. When you have all the antiques, you will leave the lad and the rest of us alone?' He said of course. 'Where do we meet?'

'The end lock, in three hours.' He sniggered. 'I shall be strolling on my canal path, looking for trespassers.'

Don't sniggers sound unpleasant? I was wet with sweat. I went to get the longboat from Kettle.

'Going far, captain?'

'Avast me hearties.' Normally I'd ignore repartee because I'm no good at it, but as I clambered aboard I had a crazy impulse to ask the old man to come too.

'You all right, son?' He passed me the heavy iron key. 'Don't lose it.'

The engine started first time. The best thing about these old canal longboats is they stay put. Until you engage gear there's no motion, because a canal isn't a river. No current, no parking problems. You want to stop, just glide to the bank and switch off. Best holiday in the world, a canal longboat. Every mile there's steps up to some tavern for your dinner. And canals pierce our towns and cities. Go up canal stairs, you're astonishingly in the middle of, say, Birmingham, Manchester, with glittery shops.

Hell, but a canal's quiet in the country. And black. Apart from the muted thump of the engine, nothing. Fields invisible, trees looking at you thinking who's this interloper. It's like night unmasks countryside's hidden menace. I had a torch, shone it all about. Nobody. Something splashed ahead. I hate night splashes. I hate daytime splashes too. In fact, I'd go so far as to say that all splashes are bad news.

Longboats on canals, some old law, are restricted to four miles an hour, the walking speed of a barge horse, so all engines are governed. Two miles from the boatyard, I passed a pub and chugged under a disused bridge. I knew the bridge. Only cows use it, crossing between pastures.

By then I'd remembered how to steer. The tiller's just a stick. Move it slowly. Remember that the barge weighs tons and has no brakes.

I came to the first lockgate, cut the engine. A canal lock's a place for lovers. Maybe that's why night travel's against the law?

'Night travel's against the law,' somebody told me a yard away.

I screeched in fright, almost dropped the huge lock key.

'You stupid sod!' I shouted. 'Scared me witless!'

There was an angler on the bank. It wasn't Clatter. I shone my light. He was encased in oilskins. Rod, folding stool, wicker baskets, keep net, and a small green tent. Maniac, at this hour.

'Night barges spoil fishing,' he groused.

No lovers, only mad anglers. I ignored him.

A canal lock is basically a box of water, doors at each

end. This box was empty. Open the uphill door, it fills and you can sail into the box. Close the uphill and undo the lower door, and out you sail. Into more empty darkness.

In five minutes I was missing the bad-tempered loon angler. A car went along a distant road, bouncing jauntily behind its cone of light. Lovers off, I thought bitterly, to heavy breathing among the bulrushes, selfish sods.

The second lock came and went. I began to glimpse seashore lights through trees and heard the long moan of a distant ship. Under another bridge. Nobody. Then the straight overgrown stretch, so long my torchlight wouldn't reach to the end. Trees closed in, the waterway becoming silted. Logs, branches, scraped my longboat's tin hull. Twice I felt the longboat tug on the canal bed. I was near the canal's sealed extremity.

No more lights now, just the skyglow from a town miles up the coast. A faint yellow sheen reflected on a cloud as the Hook of Holland ferry headed inshore. But space and time are a coast's deceivers. What looks like a mile can be a few paces or a league, and a short friendly path can be an endless quagmire. Give me streets every time.

The keel grounded. I reversed the engine, managed to slowly back away. Ahead, my beam revealed only tangled foliage with maybe a hint of a solid structure somewhere within. I'd reached the last lock, where ancient builders had finally lost to the railways.

No need to moor the longboat. I struggled ashore into a mass of brambles, branches nearly poking my eyes out. No footpath. I just had to flounder. The lock wasn't even completed, its seaward gate bricked up, like everyone had wearily thought oh what the hell. Beyond, a small copse and the dark closed fields between the canal and the estuary. The tide was in. I could hear it. I stood on the mound watching a river cruiser's lights about a mile away. I could hear music, screams of laughter. It turned south, following the coast, lights and noise receding. Lucky folk.

Three hours, was it, since I'd spoken to Gluck? I let the torch lead the way directly to the sea. I was there in no time. I know an old poacher who counts his steps, reckons he never gets lost.

The hard was rimmed with sea. The tide now covered the mud flats, a few boats bobbing in the bay. One or two wore lights, thank God, but nobody was about. The cottages further along looked in bed, with a couple of lamps as reminders.

No cars. No sign of Gluck. Had there been some mistake, me misjudging the time? Maybe I ought to have listened to the traffic news for congestion on the London road. One niggle: I'd rung Gluck on his mobile phone. Maybe he was already in East Anglia. I looked about, saw nobody. I walked slowly along the foreshore by the line of hawthorns. And back.

About here, was it? I stood looking at the waves. Strange to think the sea covered that lonely dead pilot in his plane under the mudflats only a few strides away. I shone my light, just making sure no ghostly figure was rising from the waters. I noticed that a pram, a small rowboat, and a nearby river coracle were no longer moving. The tide must be on the ebb. A cutter too was listing idly, ready to flop over like a dog for a kip until the next tide.

'Lovejoy.'

'Hello, Gluck.' He must have approached from the bushes. Where was his car? And his bruiser? I wanted him here mob-handed, all in one bag.

'Where are my antiques?'

He ought not to sound so amused, holding in a laugh.

When people do that it's always at my expense. He should be worried sick, sensing treachery. I suddenly felt alone, but had to go along with it and say my prepared line.

'I've got them, Gluck. Where you'll never find them.' My plan was simple – tell him that Wrinkle's collection was stashed in our town's crummy Antiques Arcade. Anybody tried to rob it, the lads would descend like the Keystone Kops.

'Really, Lovejoy?' He clicked a cigarette lighter, lit a fag, inhaled, still suppressing chuckles. He had something in his other hand. It glinted in my beam. Gunmetal blue. He palmed it, smiling. 'Only a two-two, but hollow-drilled nose rounds. Well? Where are they?'

When I said nothing, he tutted. 'You wouldn't betray me, would you? The arrangement is you provide me with the oriental antiques you showed me. I write a promissory note to pay for them.' He looked about, really enjoying playing his part. 'Yet you have no antiques.'

'You've checked the longboat?' I knew he would have. Was that angler his new bruiser, Kenelley, the one who'd done Trout and Tinker?

'Of course. It is empty. We watched you arrive, Lovejoy.'

We is plural. I didn't like the thought of being followed in the gloaming.

'I've already hidden the antiques, Gluck.'

'Dear me.' He wasn't at all distressed. 'What's your price?'

Stick to your plan you can't go wrong. I kept telling myself that.

'Tomorrow, you sign over the manor house and Saffron Fields to Mortimer, Colette's son. In exchange you get the antiques.'

'And Dulwich? I'm counting on that.'

'It's all in hand. Agreed?'

He finally laughed. It was like a dam bursting. He rolled in the aisles, fell about. I watched, astonished. He cackled, guffawed, blotted his eyes, bellowed.

'No, Lovejoy,' he said, choking.

What was wrong? 'No what?'

'No deal. No deception. You *have* no antiques.'

Yet some of Wrinkle's were genuine, and Wrinkle's fakes would deceive any dealer. A fortune by any other name, for heaven's sake.

'I admit some of the pieces are—'

'Tell him,' Gluck gasped, wheezing.

A woman stepped from the tree-lined darkness. I thought, eh?

'You're a fool, Lovejoy.' Honor was calm as a pond. 'I told you I'd combed the world for a real opportunity. Dieter jumped at me.' She gave an ugly giggle. 'I mean my deal – among other things.'

'You're in with Gluck,' I said dully. 'What does Wrinkle think?'

'He's not going to think any more, Lovejoy.' No regret in her querulous voice. 'He was so fucking boring.'

Wrinkle, past tense? Which meant my thinking days were also already over. Gluck sobered, took my torch.

'Come, Lovejoy.' The outrage was that he sounded kindly, a sadistic teacher's benevolence. 'It won't hurt. We'll do it properly. No hard feelings?'

Honor nagged, 'We should have brought the auto down the side road. Those shitty fields.'

I quaked. 'Look, Dieter,' I said, my voice trembling. 'I've some antiques worth a mint, if only—'

'No, Lovejoy,' he said with regret. 'No more ifs.'

We left the shore. I gave a desperate glance at the

receding tide, the sluggish boats, the tilting dinghies. No ghost rose from the sea to rescue me, Mortimer's only helper. Gluck gestured me to turn round. I felt something cold click on my wrists. Handcuffs?

'Walk on,' he purred. They say that to horses.

37

WE CUT OVER ploughed ground. Like a fool I lost my bearings from lurching to my knees. Every time I stumbled Gluck did his laugh. I realized he was quite mad. He'd slipped a rope under the handcuffs, thought it was a huge joke to yank me sideways, bring me down every few yards.

Away from the sea the night grew darker, the shushing of the waves quieter. I could only hear my laboured breathing, Gluck's lunatic cackling, and Honor's perennial grumbling about the chill. I hadn't a notion where we were going. A car in the distance, some selfish sod off to the boozer.

We came on the canal all of a sudden. No path, no lock gate. Just a cold breath on my face, as you feel near waterways. Yet what could Gluck do to me? Saintly knew that Gluck and I were enemies. If anything befell me, Gluck would catch it. And he couldn't have an alibi. I began to hope.

'Onto the bank, Lovejoy.'

Was there a farm cottage near the second bridge? That's where we seemed to be. Honor came behind me. She had the frigging nerve to clutch my arm and pull herself up. Gluck shone the light at my longboat, still and silent. Somebody must have moved it, right? Hope surged. Who? Could it be Sorbo, my one remaining trusty pal? If so, how come Dieter Gluck knew it would be waiting at this exact spot? The instant the light clicked out, I glimpsed a coracle among the floating weeds, maybe ten paces off. For a frantic second I had visions of making a heroic bound for freedom, swimming underwater, hiding among the bulrushes.

'Escape, Lovejoy?' Gluck gloated. 'I think not.' His gun clicked. Why *do* they do that? 'Dive in if you like. I'd shoot you when you surfaced. Nobody would hear. Get him aboard, Honor.'

Honor went across the gangplank first. I followed, wobbling perilously.

'About time,' Hymie's voice said from the cabin. 'Hello, Lovejoy.'

'Hello, Hymie,' I said, pathetically still hoping.

'Let's do it and get the fuck ahta here,' Hymie said. 'This country's the pits for cold and damp.'

Hope can't be trusted. 'Kill me, Hymie?' I quavered, scared stiff. 'You think that will be the end of it? Kill me, you'll be in clover? Dream on.'

'That's enough, Lovejoy.'

Gluck must have clubbed me, for I felt a shudder, went onto my knees. I tried to keep talking. A small door tapped its brass bolt on my temple, joining the fun.

'You're no more Honor's brother than I am, Hymie,' I said to the deck. Torchlight flickered more madness before my eyes. 'Are you Gluck's supposed cousin, the bruiser Tinker called Kenelley? Gluck and Honor will let you kill me, then they'll top you. They'll make it look like we fought each other. Can't you see the frigging obvious?'

A movement behind told me Gluck was readying another

swing. I hunched, took a stunning blow to the side of my jaw. A torch shone, blinding me.

'Fewer shares see, Hymie?' I mumbled into the light coming from below.

Hymie stood in the longboat's main well, between two bunks. The cabin had shelves, a little shower, an oven, stove, a fridge. These irrelevant facts my idiotic brain noted down, for use in the Great Beyond.

'What's he saying, Honor?' Hymie asked.

'You're next, Honor,' I added, brain functioning at last. 'Where d'you think the lovely young Moiya December is? She's busy laying down an alibi for Dieter, her boyfriend.'

Honor kicked my side savagely. 'Do it, Dieter. Or give me the fucking gun.'

The light stilled. A roar almost took my head off. I saw a hole appear in Hymie's left eye. Something moist sounded, like a hideous gulp. He tried to speak, quite as if starting to explain something terribly complicated. He even raised his hand, the one with the flashlight so it shone up, making a gruesome All Hallows E'en mask of his face. He rocked back. The light dowsed. I heard nothing, all sounds gone.

A gnat shrilled near me in Honor's voice, 'Do Lovejoy, then let's get the fuck out.'

'Why?' I croaked, sounding like a bassoon. 'I can be useful. I'll say, sign anything. My friends—'

Honor shrieked at that. Gluck's mad laughter shook the boat.

'Who particularly, Lovejoy? Name any ten. Name one!'

I struggled to think. Gaylord? Dosh Callaghan, who'd sent me on this wildgoose chase? Sorbo? Like the rest of East Anglia, like London, they were all abed or swilling the last pints down their undeserving gullets while I suffered.

Bitterly I cursed the coast, its miserable selfish swinish inhabitants—

'Don't do that.' The quiet words took me by surprise. It seemed to come from the canal bridge, maybe twenty paces off. 'You're all under arrest.'

Saintly? I almost cried with relief, strove to stand. I cried, 'Yes, I surrender! I—'

'Do it, for fuck's sake!' Honor shouted. 'It's not the police! They can't do a fucking thing!'

Gluck shoved me to one side with a yell. His gun thumped the night, its momentary glare blinding me. I fell into the longboat cabin, the steps scraping my chin. Two more shots made me cower. A barmy image had me kicking the starter into action, steaming away from this fusilade, but I stayed true, curled under the bulwark, whimpering promises, begging for mercy. I'd no idea how long it went on, who fired, how many shots. I felt crazed. Somebody tumbled nearby and seemed to be trying to croak a message. There came a heavy slithery splash, took a long time about it.

Then nothing. I was scared to open my eyes. Who'd won?

'Lovejoy?'

Familiar? Familiar had meant lethal tonight. I opened my eyes. A dead face was inches away. I screeched, tried to kick the horrible blooded mess from me.

'It's all right, Lovejoy.' *Mortimer?* 'You're safe.'

I was still blubbering and puking. Mr Hartson hauled me upright.

'Pull yourself together, man,' he said with disgust. 'You're not hurt, for God's sake. I had to do it. They shot at Mortimer.'

'Sorry.' My hands came free. I tried to be firm, stout of heart. 'I, ah, hope I distracted them enough for you.'

'Survey the canal, please, Mr Hartson,' Mortimer said. 'Take Jasper.'

Mr Hartson nodded and simply seemed to evaporate. Two flashlights lay on the deck. Mortimer held another. He was calm, decisive. Who the hell did he take after? I wondered, narked. Certainly not me. But it had been me being murdered, and I'm not at my best then. Honor wasn't to be seen. Hymie and Gluck were dead on board, the latter curled impossibly by the stern. I tried not to look. I remembered that horrid long slow splash. Honor?

'What do we do, Mort?' I asked humbly.

'Check the shots have produced no response.' He surveyed the boat. 'You go to the hard. Wait there until dawn. Ask everybody who arrives or passes in the morning if they've seen anybody asking for you answering to Mr Gluck's description. They'll say no.'

I was lost. 'What if they say yes?'

His weary sigh sounded just like mine when I'm dealing with an idiot.

'They shall say no, Lovejoy.' Born in the north, I've never got the hang of *shall* and *will*, so took him on trust. 'Return to where you left this longboat, at the canal's end. By then, police and hullabaloo will be occurring. You act astonished, say you'd arranged to meet Gluck last night.'

Mr Hartson materialized. I wish he'd got a bloody bell round his neck.

'Nothing, Mortimer,' he said.

'You were the angler!' I said, the penny dropping.

'Angler?' they both said together.

'Must have imagined it.' By then I'd have believed anything and anyone. Even me. 'Look,' I said, chastened. 'Thank you. If it hadn't been—'

'Go now, Lovejoy,' Mr Hartson said. 'Take your torch. Proceed by way of the canal. Goodnight.'

'Er, goodnight,' I said formally. Like leaving a tavern instead of a bloodbath.

Jasper scornfully watched me disembark. I could tell he still thought me pathetic. I patted him. One thing, though. I've always believed in country folk. True friends, always there when you need a helping hand. I've always loved and admired every single one. Countryside, too.

38

NOON NEXT DAY Kettle made a mono-syllabic statement to the police. I made mine, over and over the same thing. I denied seeing anybody. I told them that I'd stood on the lonely seashore, waiting for Gluck. He never arrived.

'Why there, Lovejoy?' the police kept asking.

'No idea.'

'Why the longboat? Why sail down a disused canal?'

'Because the customer said so.' I did a routine shrug. 'I've done deals in dafter places than the seaside. And used loonier vehicles than a barge.'

'We know that, Lovejoy,' a newish CID bloke called Wendlesham said politely. 'You have a rum history. But three corpses seems excessive. Especially as they're all known to you.' A shotgun was found in the canal by police divers. I'd been shown it. I'd shrugged. It was some Belgian import. I knew it would be untraceable.

For a tenth time I went over my encounters with Wrinkle. My meeting Honor I described as a polite hand-shake, not a burglar's eye view of her naked seduction of Wrinkle on his workbench. I'd not seen them, I told Wendlesham piously, since I bumped into Wrinkle at Lord's, and visited his workshop at Hymie's in Spitalfields.

Wendlesham woke up at that. The plod love sports. 'Didn't know you followed cricket, Lovejoy. Who was playing?'

Whoops. 'Er, the West Indies, I think.' Silence. Wrong? His eyebrows met in a frown. 'India?' I offered hopefully. Who the hell had Wrinkle been so gloomy about? 'Australia?'

'You dozed off, I expect,' he said.

'I was after some cricket memorabilia,' I invented, wildly trying to remember the names of some ancient cricketers. A schooldays poem surfaced. 'Er, Hornby and Barlow were batting, I think.'

Strangely, they didn't press me on the point. A few extra repetitions, they let me go. I left, a prickly feeling between my shoulders. I couldn't believe it when I got on the train and not a plod in sight. What the hell had happened to Wrinkle?

The New Caledonian Market was coming off the boil when I finally got there. I caught sight of myself in a dressing glass, first antique wholesaler's on the right, and said 'God Almighty!' I looked a wreck.

'Cheap, too!' The dealer was canting to Lydia, but mistook my exclamation for admiration. Canting means to extol, prior to a sale. He mistook Lydia for gormless, which she's not, and an innocent, which she is.

'No, love.'

I stayed Lydia's hand. She was writing a cheque. Not a single vibe. The small porcelain-framed mirror 'dressing glass' was made to hang on a wall above a plain dressing table. Find a genuine one, it will buy you a three-year holiday cruise, with cash to spend at every port of call. No kidding.

'Look, Lovejoy!' She pointed. 'It says *Royal Furbil Pottery, AD 1722.*'

She'd been crying, so I was kind. 'No, love. "Royal" as a precursor only came in about 1850.'

''Ere, what's your game?' The dealer belligerently pushed between us. 'I'm trying to earn a living—'

I'd had enough. 'Want me to date the rest of your stock, mate?' I offered. 'Announce fake or genuine to every buyer in Bermondsey?'

'Smart-arse.' He watched us leave. After a moment he called, 'You're Lovejoy, are yer?' Then he grinned, unpleasant. 'Good luck.'

'What is it, love? Not more bad news, surely to God.'

People were already drifting away. All antiques markets start and end early, though they're tending towards normal shop hours as years pass. I'd be lucky to find the people I wanted. There were things to settle.

Bravely Lydia stifled her sob. 'There's been a terrible accident. Have you heard?' I said no. She continued, 'Tinker told me, but I have no details. That nice policeman was leaving the hospital.'

She meant Mr Saintly. 'How are they?'

'Tinker is recovering. Poor Trout.' She took advantage of the diminishing throng to blot her eyes. 'He will be lame, Lovejoy. Still, he has survived. Not like poor Dieter.' Which made me glance at her. Sobs for mad murderer Gluck, dry eyes for a dwarf savagely mangled into additional deformity?

I said it just to make sure. 'What terrible news.'

'And that horrid old bag hag has reclaimed Dieter's

antique shop in Chelsea *and* Saffron Fields. Is it fair, Lovejoy? Dieter was such a gentleman!'

'It's okay,' I said, content now I knew who the tears really were for. Trout was right. Some things I had to leave Lydia out of. 'Look, love. You know Edwina Holleran? Small, bonny, deals in silver? You met her in her dad's silver place where—'

'She showed you her skills?' Lydia completed sweetly. 'In a dark corner of the workshop? Yes, I do remember, Lovejoy.'

'*Every* silver furnace is in a dark corner,' I said, narked. 'When you anneal silver you have to judge its heat by naked eye. You can only do it in darkness, see?' I grew vehement. Women always blame me. 'I wasn't doing anything. She was showing me how to turn, spin and work over.'

Her sorrow evaporated in new annoyance. 'And you were so *thrilled*, spinning and turning! How could I possibly forget dear Edwina!'

'Stop it. You make her sound like a bloody spider. She'll be in Camden Passage tonight. Tell her the deal's on, okay?'

'Very well, Lovejoy.'

We separated by the church. Everything still felt wrong.

The market was folding. I'm always sad, seeing the trestles stacked under tarpaulins, hearing the barrows rattle away on the stones. It's civilization ending. Even the last vans revving up make me sorrowful. Dealers were making final come-on deals, the sort that sound a brilliant bargain and never are. From a throng of thousands, maybe a couple of hundred listless refugee customers were left. Tip: these woebegone remnants who can't bear to leave are hopeless. Lovejoy's Law: Never be the first or last to buy, but sell any time.

Not all was dross today, though, as the shadows

lengthened. Mimi Welkinshaw was still trying to flog one last bargain – a pair of flatback brown-and-white pottery dogs for Victorian mantelpieces. They're ten-a-penny antiques, meaning a week's wage nowadays and ugly as sin. Every bloke with a backyard big enough turned out these King Charles's spaniels in the Black Country, no telling exactly who. A little cluster of expectant dealers goggled at Mimi's last performance. Next to her van Palace Alice was folding her awning. Beyond, Gaylord Fauntleroy loaded gunge into his motor while his one-eyed Auntie Vi sat smoking her foul pipe on their trailer steps. I could hear Hello Bates doing his familiar shout, getting only the occasional 'Sod off, Batesy.' Sir Ponsonby was popping a champagne cork, Moiya December holding the glasses. She was back on station, seeing that times – and available personnel – had changed.

'What went wrong, Lovejoy?' some lass said, strolling past.

'Eh?' I halted. It was Billia.

She stopped, furtive. A barrow dealer boxing up his fake kakeimon vases hopefully started a harangue. I drew her on.

'I thought I wasn't supposed to know you, Lovejoy!' she said.

I was at least as thunderstruck as she was. Why wasn't she in gaol? Okay, so I didn't need the phoney robbery at Dulwich Picture Gallery any longer, Gluck being dead. But at least my plans should be working somewhere, however phoney. She was only a red herring, for God's sake. Even plans I'd assumed tightly knitted were unravelling.

'Why,' I began, then halted. I could hardly expect an answer to why aren't you arrested with your bloke Dang, when I'd betrayed her dud burglary attempt to the police. 'Why did you say that, Billia?'

We drew in the shadow of trestle stacks for further incoherence.

'Me and Dang did everything you said, Lovejoy. Nobody came.'

'Great.' I thought quickly. 'It's been postponed to tonight. I'll be doing it with you.'

She looked full of doubt, untrusting cow. I'd sweated my socks off for this woman, risked my life among maniacs, and she hadn't the loyalty to catch the Dulwich bus? People are rotten. 'Honest, Lovejoy?'

'Of *course* honest,' I said, narked.

'And you'll have the money to get Dang off?'

'Hand on my heart, Billia.' A bonny lass, but what a blinking pest. I got rid of her by pretending I was being beckoned by an important illegal importer. 'He's a pal of that Caravaggio conspiracy geezer,' I lied quickly. 'Sotheby's and all that. Don't be late tonight, love.'

And escaped into the dwindling market. Nothing sadder than a folding street market or a fading day. I know one forger, English watercolours, who can only work at teatime in autumn as the light dwindles. I've never yet seen him smile. It must be his soul. This attractive woman stopped me, said hello.

'Is that you?' I asked. Is there a dafter question? Nobody can say no, can they?

'Colette, Lovejoy.' Her smile was radiant. She was dressed to kill. Hair done, teeth a-dazzle, clothes guinea-an-inch. 'You approve?'

Bags under her eyes, though. A facial and new earrings can't hide heartbreak. Yet hadn't her Mortimer been saved from death? And herself from poverty? And, small point, by me? That's a woman for you.

'Beautiful, love.' She'd probably dressed up for me. It was her sign that we were going to resume where we'd left off. I warmed to her. 'You look good enough to eat. Congrats.'

'Yes.' Bravely she forced a smile. 'When we signed everything over to Dieter there was a legal who-goes-last clause.' Her lovely lip trembled. 'I now realize that Dieter, poor lamb, intended to make sure he alone was left. He was driven to it, of course. He'd been awfully deprived as a child.'

'Him and Honor,' I said, cruelly, but wanting to know.

'That bitch is well dead,' Colette said with venom. 'Dieter was easily led. Handsome men with ambition, falling into the hands of some evil old crone like her,' et unbelievable cetera.

A rag, a bone, and a hank of hair? Maybe – plus a fearsome power of self-delusion.

'Moiya December's consoling herself, I see.'

The pretty lass was sprawled on the bonnet of Sir Ponsonby's motor, eating cherries in what can only be called an erotic manner while the world held its breath.

'She's another whore,' Colette said.

'Look, love. Sign Saffron Fields over to Mortimer before the day's out,' I begged. 'I'd hate for things to go askew at this stage.'

'It's already done,' she said. 'Through Arthur's old lawyer.'

Relief swept over me. 'Deo gratias. Love, you seen Sorbo?'

'He was here,' she said. A ripple of laughs made me look. Mimi had sold her gruesome dogs. She was taking the money, walking across for a last word with Auntie Vi. 'Keep in touch, Lovejoy.'

Not for me after all. Forlorn hope. Colette was already moving on. I mean, Dieter Gluck was a crazed killer, yet he'd had Lydia, Colette, Honor, Moiya all panting after him. Is life fair? I wandered to the three remaining stalls still on the go, when Sorbo touched my arm. He still wore his ancient frock coat, was fat as a duck.

'Lovejoy? He wants you. In Fauntleroy's trailer.'

'Who, Sorbo?' It could only be one of two.

'Saintly. Sorry, Lovejoy.'

Sorry is the traitor word. I went in, lamb to the slaughter, through Auntie Vi's carcinogenic cloud. Sorbo stood back. I passed Fauntleroy, his attire gaudier than ever. First time I'd ever seen him looking pale. He was watching me on the pavement. Saintly's driver waved Auntie Vi and Fauntleroy away. Fine time to discover the truth, I thought bitterly. Always stupid until it's too late.

39

SAINTLY LOOKED PARTICULARLY dapper today. Some folk are smarmy. I tend to envy them because it looks cool.

'What, sir?' I said.

'Door, please.'

I shut it. He was sipping sherry from a fair-sized glass square-foot goblet. Some duckegg had clumsily engraved a two-budded English rose on it. This was the Jacobite emblem, the two buds being the Old and Young Pretenders. The goblet was modern pressed glass, yet an innocent buyer might believe some dealer's persuasive patter and buy the pathetic fake. Fauntleroy routinely sold such monstrosities.

'Remain standing, Lovejoy.'

As if with great reluctance he sighed, put his dud glass down.

'What am I here for?' Suddenly I couldn't do speech properly. Yet surely I was safe, the Bermondsey market still wrapping up out there? Except you can have one too many maniacs.

'To realize the truth, Lovejoy.' He bent forward, stared into me. 'Jesus, you already have! I'd never have believed it!' Satisfied, he nodded in self-congratulation.

'You are Gluck's principal backer, Mr Saintly.'

Best I could do. I didn't want to say the rest, in case it hurried him into doing something I'd regret. Yet I was still safe, in Bermondsey's daylight. All he could do was arrest me, right?

Saintly agreed, 'I did contribute money, plus influence.'

'I don't see why.'

'That's because you're a member of the fucking ignorant public.' It was a sudden snarl. He rose, strode at me, clouted me sideways. 'I'm paid a pittance, Lovejoy. To take responsibility for filth like you. What do I get for it? A paltry pension and a tinfoil gong. I had a decent thing going. Dieter and me go back years. It was me brought him in. Then you came along, you absurd bastard.'

My mouth was bleeding. I righted myself, more trembly than I should have been. Odd, because I'd been knocked silly before and felt better than this.

'As far as I'm concerned you can get on with it,' I said shakily. 'Please let me go.'

'And you "won't say anything", is that it?'

'Honest. I'll help you to do the Dulwich job. Gluck's dead.'

'I can't understand why Wendlesham let you go, Lovejoy.' He seemed reflective, an academic discussing haiku poetics. 'Clearly, it was you who somehow killed Dieter.'

'I never touched him or his two pals.'

'*Three* pals,' he jeered. 'Don't forget Bern.'

'Was that Sorbo's doing?' It just came out in astonishment.

'Me and Gluck shared the honours. Sorbo's a nonentity, just does as he's told. Can you imagine? A bruiser like Bern getting fond of an ageing trollop like Colette? He tried reasoning with Dieter and me, after I'd ordered him to dust you over the night you traced Colette to St Anne's churchyard.' Saintly fetched out Sorbo's Nock weapon.

Simultaneously, I saw the empty maroon bag. It had held Sorbo's antique Nock double-barrelled flintlock. I should have realized the beautiful antique was what made me feel odd. Sorbo's presence outside should have tipped me off. The bag was squashed flat beneath Saintly's drinking glass. Which meant the spherical lead bullets and powder flask had come into use.

Look at one of these exquisite weapons in the Tower of London's Armories – lately shifted to Leeds – and you can't help thinking, how pretty! No wonder Gluck had been hooked on Regency flintlocks. Brown, with a subdued matt shine, six-inch barrels set side by side, the loveliest engravings ever done. A miracle of engineering. Never mind that Samuel Nock must have been insanely jealous of his famed uncle, the great Henry Nock. He did all right for himself in Regent Street, becoming Gunmaker-in-Ordinary to all the monarchs. I found myself smiling, extending a trembling hand. I moved carefully. Both flints were fully cocked. One touch on the triggers and—

'No, Lovejoy.' Saintly watched me, so pleased. 'I've never seen you do it before – your divvy trick. Just look at you. Shaking like a leaf, sweat trickling off you. No wonder Dieter said you were essential.'

'What happens now?' I asked, wiping my clammy face with a sleeve.

'I sail into the Mediterranean with Moiya, for as long as she serves me as I wish. Sir Ponsonby and Sorbo do Wrinkle's place over when things cool down.'

'Things?' I asked hoarsely. 'What things?'

'The one thing left.' He smiled. 'You. I'm afraid this terminates your contract with, well, everybody. I've already dictated Sorbo's statement. He actually has it in his pocket, to hand to me after we enact this charade.'

'You rotten sod.'

'He will testify that he's just sold you this flintlock. You've made no secret of your desire for it these past years. My tale is, you came in here and threatened me with it. We struggled. It went off. You perished.'

'Please don't,' I cried out, backing away, hands outstretched. 'I'll do anything—'

And the world suddenly spoke. I really do mean the whole world thundered, like the voice of God.

'Mr Saintly,' a voice boomed. The trailer resonated. 'This is the police. Put down your weapon and come out.'

Crockery rattled. It was like an earth tremor. Saintly looked stunned.

'Who, Lovejoy?' he asked quietly. 'You're wired, aren't you?'

'Eh? Me? No!' I yelled. 'I don't know what fucking wired means! Honest to God! I only ever do as I'm told for God's sake—'

'Lovejoy's ignorant, Mr Saintly,' the heavens thundered. I felt the vibes of every syllable. 'Step out. Lay your weapon aside.'

'It's you, Lovejoy,' Saintly said, extending the flintlock. The twin muzzles looked Chunnel-sized.

'No!' I shouted. 'Please! I know nowt—'

He pressed the triggers. I saw his fingers whiten. Both flints slammed forward onto their steels. Sparks flew.

Nothing.

Nothing. I tottered to the door, opened it onto a still world. Individuals were standing frozen all about the market, listening, watching. It was Eisenstein's *Nevsky*. Sir Ponsonby stood among uniformed policemen with Moiya.

Sorbo was handcuffed near a police car. Sturffie was there, silent among a cluster of others, including Palace Alice, Gaylord and Auntie Vi.

And Lydia, with the portly gent I'd seen before, who'd followed us everywhere. No bowler hat this time, just country tweeds and plus-fours. I wondered how often he'd changed his guises while he trailed me around. He had a small microphone. When he spoke it made me jump.

'It's over, Mr Saintly. Show yourself.'

I went down the steps and walked away through the silent market. I'd felt shame before, but not like this.

40

DAWNS COME OVER our estuaries, rather than simply up out of the east. They steal in over the bluish samphire sea marsh as if direction hardly matters. They could start from any point of the compass, west, north, anywhere. I'd been watching the team place buoys and markers since four o'clock. Tides decide hours.

Mortimer had gone with me. Not because I'm scared of the dark or anything, honest, only because I might not have known the way. Mr Hartson silently joined us about fiveish. Bert and Ake, amateur enthusiasts, were using a fantastic metal gadget to locate the crashed aircraft. Mat, Lisa's illicit boyfriend, had joined them. He'd helped to rig Arthur's massive underwater magnet on its drag ropes. It worked a treat. Nice blokes, I thought, shame about their hobby. There's horror in our seashores. Like the bodies of Rapparee Cove near Ilfracombe, where all sixty slaves drowned in the *London* in 1796, which sank with all hands. The blokes were dressed like goggle-eyed black frogs.

'It's marvellous!' Bert called. 'Fifth marker in an hour!'

'Great, Bert,' I said. I was merely glad it was Bert who kept rising to the surface and not some gruesome apparition.

'Dad knew it would work,' Mortimer confided.

'Great, Mort.'

'Arthur was a true craftsman,' Mr Hartson added.

A little oblique criticism in there? I didn't glance at him. I got the idea it was goodbye time, leave Mortimer to resume his ownership of Saffron Fields, title, mulberry tree and all, and get the hell back to dusty antiques.

Three other amateur divers arrived as daylight took hold. Mercifully two of their birds motored up with tea and buttered crumpets in some magic hot box, to save civilization. By mid-morning the marker team had pegs and ropes placed over half the mudflat. A crowd of knowalls assembled to express assorted ignorance. Ake, Mat, and Bert flopped over to report. They addressed Mortimer, not me.

'It looks real, Mortimer,' Ake said, swigging from his woman's flask. Mat and Bert looked at Ake. They were deciding who should say it.

'We'd best notify the Air Ministry,' Bert said. 'Mortimer, my cousin helped them trawl up an American Mustang off Clacton. They have a little museum. The old Martello tower, Point Clear.'

Bert stalled to silence. Ake took it up. 'They found a German Junkers Eighty-eight the RAF shot down, too.'

'This looks like a Spitfire, Mortimer.' Bert gestured to the sea's expanse. 'Guessing roughly, it looks like your dad was right.'

'Thank you, Bert.'

It was odd, seeing them all address this lad as if he were boss.

Ake grinned, clearing the air. 'Want to join, Lovejoy? Our club's diving the Goodwin Sands soon.'

'Ta, Bert, but I'm busy.' Old mariners still call it the Goodwin Graveyard, where hundreds of ships have sunk to doom in the drear black waters.

Bert guffawed. 'You'm white, booy.'

'That will do,' Mortimer said quietly. 'Lovejoy's been poorly.'

'Sorry, Mortimer,' the diver said quickly, the women tutting indignantly.

'Morning, everyone,' Colette said brightly. 'Everything going well?'

'Yes, m'm.' Bert was thrilled to be back on muddy technicalities. 'Found the aircraft for sure. Half a dozen tides, we'll start lifting. Spread about, o'course, because of its trajectory—'

'Great.' I moved away.

Colette looked like a million quid, decades younger now, dressed to kill. I saw Dang standing nearby. He grinned, nodded. Dang? No sign of Billia. I went to nosh the last ergs from the women's basket. They told me to take no notice of That Bert and his silly remarks, and not to go diving in the North Sea if I didn't want. I said ta.

'Lovejoy?' Colette came and the women tactfully faded. 'I think it's better if we don't take up again.'

'Great,' I said.

'Dang and I got talking after Bermondsey. He's never really been happy with Billia. And the poor lamb's in trouble with some East End gamblers. Only an older woman like me can extricate him. You do understand, Lovejoy?'

'Great.' Lots of poor lambs about.

'Naturally, I'd assumed you and me could make a go of it. But Dang's such a sweetie.'

'Great,' I said.

She patted my arm. 'I knew you'd understand. Do call in. Did I tell you I'm going to concentrate on Rockingham porcelain?'

She bussed me in a waft of costly perfume, waved to

everyone, gave Mortimer a quick peck, and clipped off on Dang's arm. No need to worry about Dang's debts with any Cockney fight-fixers. He'd found his niche, no pun intended.

'You'll be at your cottage, Lovejoy?' Mortimer asked.

'Maybe I'll call at the vineyard.' I didn't want to admit I was broke, now had nowhere else to go for grub, female solace, a groat to start my next enterprise.

'Er, well, actually . . .' He petered out.

Mr Hartson tactfully helped. 'Dottie Kelvedon is getting married, Lovejoy. But I'm sure you'll be invited.'

'Great.'

Wendlesham came walking over the fields with two people from the direction of the old canal. I turned aside. He came right up to me.

'Morning, Lovejoy. Digging up more antiques, eh?'

'No. Mortimer's ancestor crashed his fighter here.'

'You know Mr Herald, I think.'

It was Bowler Hat, today in a mac and every inch a plod. I went red from shame. I'd broadcast my cowardice to the whole of Bermondsey, something else I'd never live down. He was the one who'd arranged it. A pal.

'Didn't recognize you without a microphone.'

'Don't take umbrage, Lovejoy,' Mr Herald said pleasantly. 'We couldn't have told you the barrels weren't loaded, or Saintly would have tumbled.'

And I'd not have been terrified into begging for my life for all London to laugh at, ta very much.

'Look on the bright side,' Wendlesham went on. Happy ploddites are poison. 'Your activities go into your record as cooperation with the police, to protect young Mortimer there, not as planned preliminaries to murder, burglary, extortion, and grievous bodily harm.'

'How?' I was truly morose. So far I hadn't even glanced at Lydia. She was the other person with them. 'I never told you what I was doing.'

'You haven't forgotten, Lovejoy?' Lydia put in quickly. 'Didn't you suggest that I tell my Uncle Thomas your plans just in case?' That made me look from Herald to Lydia. Uncle? But that meant she'd had plod in her family tree all this while and I hadn't known.

Wendlesham smiled. 'Your apprentice made a full and frank statement beforehand, Lovejoy. On your instructions, I was led to believe.'

'Wrinkle.' I cleared my throat, scared to ask. 'He was—'

'Billia is helping him to sort out his furniture factory,' Wendlesham said calmly, as Bert and his team flopped out onto the mud among their coloured markers. 'Wonder those blokes don't catch their death of cold. Marvellous, such enthusiasm. I suppose this foreshore'll be a designated War Graves Commission place.'

'No,' Mortimer said. He'd been listening. 'I shall order an interment on Saffron Fields by the giant mulberry.'

'Very good, sir,' the policemen said politely together. Wendlesham went on, 'We shall have to obtain permission to exhume Mr Goldhorn. Further tests, in the light of what's transpired about Gluck, and what Saintly admitted at police interview. There's a question of digitalis.'

'Very well,' said Mort. 'Please keep me informed.'

'Very good, sir. Oh, Sir Jesson Tethroe has decided to advance your pal Wrinkle's collection as a special contribution to Anglo-Chinese relations.' Wendlesham made a sarcastic quotation of it. 'There's already mention of an honour coming Wrinkle's way. And Billia sends her love, Lovejoy.'

'Great.'

'Politicians for you.' Mr Herald grimaced.

I could just see Billia, all dolled up, at Henley Regatta, Lord's, Handel's *Messiah* in St Paul's at Easter.

Mortimer said, 'Lovejoy, I shall need teaching about antiques, please. For a fee, of course. Distinguishing genuine from fake is easy. They simply feel different. But *then* what do you do?'

Indeed, I thought. That's the bit I always make a mess of. Where had he inherited the divvy gene?

'I'll teach you for nowt, Mort. Ta-ra, Mr Hartson.'

'Which ends it, Lovejoy,' Mr Herald said. 'Except you're due in court. Holloway University versus you. Need a lift?'

'Ta,' I said. I didn't look at Lydia. The plod don't offer. They command.

The old duffers on the bench looked moribund. Court's a funny sort of place. I've been in better bus shelters. Mr Herald sat there among a dozen lowlifes, me to the fore. I swear he was reading a folded tabloid, our eagle-eyed vigilant constabulary.

Shar, beautiful and serenely indifferent to justice, sprang to my defence by making out a fair case for having me hanged at Tyburn. The magistracy agreed, fined me a fortune. I had a few coins.

'I'm sorry. I'm broke,' I told them.

Shar rose, a picture of misery. Glaring at me, she told them the fine had been met. I was dismissed with dire warnings not to be innocent again, or else. Outside in the corridor I collared her.

'Thanks, love.' I tried to embrace her. 'I mean that most sincerely.'

She stared, hatred in every erg. 'You don't think I paid

your fine? You miserable worm! You're not worth Dieter's little finger!' There was more, invective being the hallmark of the lawyer–client relationship.

'Look, love. Any chance of a sub? Only, I'm—'

With a sweet smile she handed me an envelope. Aren't people marvellous? I said a husky ta as I opened it, and brought out no money, but a bill that stunned my last threadbare neurones. I screwed it up and deposited it in a litter bin.

In despair I rang Lisa, fearless reporter, with my begging whine, and was instantly told that she'd murder me if ever she saw me again, for one Judith Falconer had broadcast every detail over the Home Counties that morning. Then Yamta and Saunty who, fornicating breathlessly, gasped that they'd ring me back. I rang Hello Bates, Deeloriss, Palace Alice, Puntasia, Gaylord, Sturffie. They all laughed about my blubbering cowardice when facing no possible harm.

As a last try I rang Dosh Callaghan.

'Dosh? Lovejoy. Y'know, the padpa job?'

'What job? I never hired you. You're a criminal. Get lost.' Click. Burr.

On the way to the Tube, a Martian on a bike thundered alongside and rocked to stillness.

'Lovejoy? Tel O'Shaughnessy sends this. Your suss for nicking that Dulwich place's Old Masters.'

A thick envelope, full of circuit diagrams, typed pages, photographs. I said ta and watched him roar off. Lucky Tel hadn't sent it to me in court. As it was, I saw some people in a bus queue staring curiously at me. I smiled weakly.

'Film script,' I said, and got to Dulwich an hour before closing.

There's no doubt about buildings. They're not lifeless. They breathe, form opinions of us just as we do of them.

Architects don't know this, which is why modern buildings look like a heap of slabs. Not Dulwich Picture Gallery, though I'm biased. To me, a mansion containing a Rembrandt becomes heaven.

Within seconds of entering the long gallery I'd reeled to a seat, sat there with my head between my knees.

'Are you unwell, sir?' a pair of security boots asked. I dripped sweat onto the shiny toecaps.

'It's all right,' a pair of neat brogues replied. 'I know this gentleman.'

A woman artist had been copying a Turner – frigging nerve – as I'd ambled in. Oddly, her voice was familiar.

She sat with me. 'Take deep breaths, Lovejoy.'

'Ta, love. I'll be all right in a minute.'

She left her easel and paints, and took me outside into the watery sun. We perched on the steps.

'Lovejoy,' she said eventually, 'you're rather a problem, aren't you?'

'It's the others, Gloria. Not me.' I had a think. 'Ta for paying my fine.'

She smiled. Her scent was turpentine. 'You know why I came here? I got to thinking about thieves, who'd steal from such a superb ancient gallery as this. Unscrupulous dealers and such.'

'Why aren't you with Sir Jesson?' I asked.

'You thought wrongly. I finished his portrait.'

A uniformed bobby brought over O'Shaughnessy's massive manila envelope.

'Here, missus. He dropped this.'

'Thank you, constable.' She gave him a sweet smile.

I went pale. Luckily it wasn't labelled *Burglar's Suss of Dulwich Gallery's Security*, Tel's only concession to secrecy.

Gloria Dee touched the envelope. 'Is that—?'

'Dunno, love.' I went guarded. 'Not read it yet.' A detailed aerial photo of the gallery roof slid out. I hastily retrieved it. 'It's okay. The security here's cast iron. It can't be robbed. I only commissioned it for show.'

For a while we sat watching visitors departing, each with our thoughts. A minibus came, collected a group of little children. Security folk began shepherding people out. Closing time.

'Lovejoy,' Gloria said at last. 'Are you well enough to travel?'

'Fine. Ta for asking.'

'Only, I'm driving to East Anglia. I could quite easily give you a lift.'

'I've just been released from court, love. You might lob me out miles from anywhere. I'm in no fit state.'

'I can see that. It will do us no harm at least to glance at the fascinating details you have there. I mean, just for an example to other art galleries. Will you wait for me?'

'Aye. Ta.'

She went inside for her easel and paints. Which left one green bottle thinking on the wall. She'd never make a forger in a million years. I mean, she mixed Permanent Rose and Windsor Blue. Can you believe some people? Yet she was solvent, bonny, interested in antiques. And seemed keen. And hadn't she been just that little bit intrigued by my burglar's envelope? It spelled potential.

Not only that, Gloria Dee might just be willing to pause at a night caff on the eastern trunk road and buy me a nosh. She was a kindly soul. She might be compassionate enough to provide me with more than a fry-up.

'Ready, Lovejoy?' she called from the car at the kerb. Her smile decided me. I'd been lost in thought. 'Don't forget your envelope.'

'Coming.' Red-faced, I went back for it.

'The quicker we get started,' she said, 'the better it will be for both of us, don't you think?'

To my relief her expression was completely innocent. She hadn't intended any hidden meaning. I'd had rather too much of duplicitous women lately. This was the sort I wanted: friendly, willing, and innocent. A rag, a bone, and a hank of hair maybe, but if the sum conveys paradise, so what?

'Right,' I agreed. Anyway, if Gloria proved too difficult, I could always escape to Caprice and her grotty Theatre Awards Night.

I'll never know how Gloria didn't see Lydia's frantic signals to us from across the road. We just kept going.